As was his habit Luke took his time.

He savored the chocolate Kiss Mari had handed him, wringing every last bit of pleasure from the sweet. Slowly Luke licked his lips. "That's mighty fine, ma'am. Mighty fine. However…"

She arched a curious brow as he continued, "I'm not the one selling Kisses. As good as your chocolate Kisses are, I think you should try mine before you claim yours are superior."

"You make chocolates, sir?"

"I'm talkin' kisses. Are you confident enough to compare?"

Luke reached for her sample plate and snagged a Kiss. Mari's mouth opened, and he fed her the chocolate, his thumb brushing slowly across her lower lip. Luke stared deeply into her eyes as she sucked on the candy. It felt as if they were the only two people in the room.

When her tongue slipped from her mouth to rim her lips, he knew a surge of pure lust that transformed the moment from light flirtation to something much more intense. "Delicious?" he asked. "The best you've ever had?"

Licking her lips once more, Mari nodded.

"Then I think it's time to expand your sample base, don't you?" He trailed his fingers across her downy cheek, then gently cupped her chin. Leaning forward, he lowered his mouth to hers….

GERALYN DAWSON

Her Bodyguard

HQN™

ISBN 0-373-77043-X

HER BODYGUARD

www.HQNBooks.com

Printed in U.S.A.

For Mary Dickerson

I'll always treasure your friendship.
Here's wishing you great happiness in your new home,
and say fervent thanks for e-mail and airline passes.

PROLOGUE

Fort Worth, Texas 1888

MARI MCBRIDE HADN'T visited a whorehouse after dark in years, but as she passed the gilded front door of Rachel Warden's Social Emporium, she was tempted to stop in and say hello. Rachel and her girls had always been particularly kind to Mari and her two sisters before their father, Trace McBride, went respectable and moved his family out of the infamous section of town known as Hell's Half Acre. The madam had insisted that the McBride girls were always welcome to visit. Of course, ten o'clock on a Saturday night probably wasn't the best time for three virginal young women to go socializing at a brothel.

Yet Mari had the feeling that she and her two sisters might be safer fighting off lusty cowboys at Rachel Warden's Social Emporium than where they were headed.

"We shouldn't be here," she said to her sisters as they walked along the lantern-lit boardwalk, the tinny music of a poorly tuned piano swirling around them. "This was an exceptionally bad idea."

Her older sister Emma tore her attention away from an upstairs window across the street, where a half-naked couple stood locked in an embrace. "Don't be a spoilsport, Mari."

"That's right," her younger sister Kat chimed in, wrinkling her nose as they passed a saloon door and the scent of stale bodies and old beer wafted over them. "Next week this time, Emma will be a respectable married woman. This is our last chance to be true McBride Menaces."

"Hallelujah," Mari muttered as she lifted her skirts and stepped carefully over a missing board on the boardwalk. At twenty, eighteen and sixteen, respectively, the McBride Menaces were plenty old enough to retire from the business of mischief making. Mari had plans for herself, for her future, that her reputation negatively affected. Banks were slow to loan any woman money to establish a business, and there wasn't a banker in all of north Texas who'd sit down to talk business with a McBride Menace. Never mind that Mari had learned at the knees of one of the most successful female entrepreneurs in the state— her beloved stepmother, Jenny. If Mari ever wanted to achieve her dream, she'd need to put her menacing ways behind her and establish a respectable reputation.

"Actually," Kat continued, "visiting a fortune-teller isn't even all that terrible a thing to do. If not for the fact that we're alone in the Acre after dark on a Saturday night, it wouldn't even be worthy of the Menaces."

As they walked by the open doorway of the Palace Saloon, a gunshot rang out inside. All three girls glanced into the saloon to see an obviously inebriated cowboy taking aim at a billiard ball. "Pistol pool," Emma said on a sigh. "I always hated when they started playing that at Papa's place."

"Papa didn't mind," Mari recalled. He'd earned good money from adding a surcharge to the bill of cowboys who shot even worse with their six-shooters than they did with their pool cues.

"Remember that time a couple of men from the Double R shot up three pool tables in one night?"

Emma nodded. "Papa bought us each a new doll the next day."

The girls shared a smile. Back in the days when Trace ran the End of the Line Saloon, money was tight for the McBride family. Gifts presented at a time other than Christmas or a birthday made an impression upon them all.

They continued up Houston Street ignoring catcalls, declining invitations, and veering around three separate brawls between men who tumbled through the swinging doors of saloons and rolled into the dusty street trading punches and spitting insults. With every step closer to their destination, Mari's trepidation built. Something about this escapade tonight felt bad in her bones.

She couldn't pinpoint exactly what the problem was. She wasn't worried about what the fortune-teller might tell them. Despite having a family history full of legends like the Bad Luck Wedding Dress and the Bad Luck Wedding Cake, along with a fond memory of a childhood pet christened Spike the Fortune-Teller Fish, Mari didn't believe in such nonsense. Crystal balls and tarot cards were nothing more than a charlatan's props. Her sisters might set store in what Madame Valentina had to say, but Mari knew better.

At least, that's what she tried to tell herself.

"She's full of nonsense, you know," Mari said, her tone defiant as she reacted to the unease seeping through her. "Madame Valentina read tea leaves at the Literary Society's spring social and predicted that Pauline Johnston would marry Bobbie Ellison by the end of the year. Two days later, Pauline eloped with Jimmy Talbot."

"Oh, stop it," Emma said, giving her sister's shoulder a light backhanded slap. "I know Madame Valentina is probably a fake, but this adventure is all in good fun."

"We're in Hell's Half Acre on a Saturday night!" Mari protested.

Emma's eyes gleamed. "Yes, and we all brought our guns, didn't we? We're safe enough."

"Emma!"

"Kat is right, Mari. We needed one last McBride Menace escapade. *I* needed it. As much as I can't wait to become Mrs. Casey Tate, it's difficult for me to think that I'm leaving the McBride name behind. You must admit, there are times when it's fun to be infamous."

"Perhaps on rare occasions," Mari agreed. "Very rare."

Kat sighed. "You worry me, Mari. You've become such a stick-in-the-mud ever since Wendell Hapsburg told Johnny Walton that he wouldn't ask you to the Harvest Dance because you're too wild."

"Pardon me?" Mari halted abruptly. "I am not a stick-in-the-mud, and my behavior has nothing at all to do with that smug Wendell Hapsburg." *Liar.* Angry with herself, she added starch to her voice when she continued, "Katrina, have you forgotten that *I* am the one who sneaked into Uncle Tye's house and hid all his shoes in the attic just two weeks ago?"

Kat tilted her head, reconsidering. "That was a good prank, and he did have it coming after his remark about our fondness for dancing slippers. All right, I take back the stick-in-the-mud remark."

"Thank you. Also, allow me to point out that caution isn't necessarily something to disparage. Drunken cowboys can be vicious animals."

"You're right, Mari." Kat eyed the middle-aged man weaving his way down the middle of the street with new respect. "However, you have to admit that the thought of what Madame Valentine has to tell us is exciting." Kat pulled a folded sheet of paper from her skirt pocket and quoted, "'I will share with you news of the man you are destined to marry.'"

Mari sighed at her sister's naïveté.

Eyes shining with excitement, Kat added, "I hope she tells me he's tall and blond and blue-eyed."

Emma's mouth twitched with a grin. "More likely she'll tell you he won't pick up his dirty socks."

Kat laughed and Mari's mouth twisted in a wry smile as they continued on their way. The abandoned sock argument was an ongoing issue between their father and stepmother. Not a week went by that Jenny didn't snap at Trace for leaving his socks somewhere other than where they belonged. He always apologized, then proceeded to melt her pique with kisses. The girls had long suspected he left his socks on the floor on purpose.

Reaching the intersection of Rusk and First streets, the girls skirted a large group of men making bets on the eventual victor of the fistfight taking place in the center of the street. From the frequency of whacks and grunts and thuds, Mari predicted that within minutes, a doctor would be required to provide treatment to the two battling cowboys.

"Look," Kat said, pointing toward a wooden plaque attached to the side of a building. "There's the sign."

The small, painted wooden sign read Madame Valentina, Seer Extraordinare. An arrow pointed the way down a deeply shadowed alley. "Wonderful." Mari halted abruptly. "A dark alley in Hell's Half Acre. This is an exceptionally poor idea."

For the first time, Emma appeared less that certain of their course of action. Addressing Kat, she said, "Maybe Mari's right. Maybe we should come back another time. In daylight."

"Listen to you two old hens clucking away. Don't be sissies. We've come this far. If you simply must leave, then go. I'm not about to display a yellow stripe now." Then Kat took off down the alley, leaving her sisters little choice but to follow.

Halfway down the narrow passage, an old tin stable lantern hung from a nail pounded into the wooden wall and illuminated a doorway draped in strings of glass beads. Kat pushed aside the beads and ducked her head inside. "Hello? Is anyone there?"

Standing right behind Kat and beside Emma, Mari's sense of foreboding returned in force. "No one is here. Let's go. We can come back another time."

From directly behind Mari, an ethereal voice said, "Welcome, Misses McBride. I have been waiting for you. "

Mari all but jumped out of her stockings.

The woman was tall and lithe and…perfect. Thick, honey-blond hair spilled like a waterfall down her back. Eyes the color of bluebonnets in springtime gleamed with warmth, and rose-red lips curved in a welcoming smile. Her cheekbones were high and defined, her nose thin and straight. She wore a flowing gown of ice-blue silk and a long gold chain around her neck from which dangled a clear crystal the size of a robin's egg.

"You're not Madame Valentina," Kat said.

"I am Roslin of Strathardle. The gypsy fortune-teller has graciously offered me her hospitality for the evening."

"Strathardle?" Kat repeated, testing the unfamiliar

word on her tongue. To Mari, she said softly, "I think that's down near San Antonio."

"Strathardle is in Scotland," the woman replied, amusement sparkling in her eyes.

"You know our names," Emma observed. "Have we met?"

"Not directly, no."

Mari waited for her to elaborate, but instead, the woman reached out and cupped Emma's cheek. Staring deeply into her eyes, she said, "You have a nurturing soul."

Kat's mouth rounded and she breathed, "Oh…that's right. She does. Ma'am, can you tell us about the men we'll marry, like Madame Valentina?"

Roslin's smile widened. "Come inside, my adventurous one."

She swept past them through the beads, and Kat fell right in behind the woman. Following her younger sister, Mari ducked her head toward Emma and murmured, "Said the spider to the fly."

Candles and oil lamps lit the small, square room, and the scent of jasmine hung in the air. Shelves filled with books, and candles and uniquely decorated boxes lined three of the four walls. Plush pillows lay scattered around the wooden floor. At the center of the room sat a round table draped in a midnight-blue cloth surrounded by three stools and a graceful thronelike chair. At the center of the table sat the expected crystal ball.

"You have come to me for knowledge." Roslin gestured for them to take seats on the stools set around the table.

"Yes," Kat said, her gaze going dreamy. "I would like to know about the ma—"

"We'd like to know who you are," Mari interrupted,

shooting her younger sister a quelling look. "And how you know about us."

"I am a seer." An enigmatic smile played about the woman's face. "While all in Fort Worth know of the McBride Menaces, I have, shall we say, a special knowledge. We are connected. In times past, my...family...knew yours."

Emma leaned forward. "You're from the Carolinas?"

"Mmm...further back. In keeping with tradition, on the eve of the first marriage in a new generation, I offer you my talents."

Mari folded her arms. "What talents?"

The lady's eyes twinkled at Mari, before she turned to Emma. "You wish for knowledge?"

"Her wedding," Kat piped up. "I convinced her to come to find out about her wedding. It's next week and we want everything to be perfect, only our family has a bit of a history regarding bad luck and weddings."

Emma cleared her throat. "My fiancé and I are very much in love, and I have no doubt at all about the marriage, but the wedding itself is making both of us a little nervous."

"Wool socks," a pragmatic Mari said. "That's what both you and Casey need. Wool socks warm cold feet quite nicely."

"We're not having cold feet," Emma insisted. "It's not that."

"I think it's the boys, our brothers," Kat told the seer. "I think they're planning some shenanigans and Emma can sense it and that's why she's feeling jumpy about the wedding. So, if you could give us a hint about what the Monsters might be up to?"

Despite the fact that Mari didn't believe this woman

possessed supernatural abilities, she nevertheless leaned forward to listen closely to the woman's response. Billy, Tommy and Bobby McBride caused more trouble in one month than their sisters had in an entire year at their ages.

"You misunderstand." Roslin motioned for the McBrides to take seats on the stools, then shifted three large pillar candles from the shelf to the center of the table. "You'll witness no parlor tricks from me. I suggest if you wish to learn what your brothers have planned, you eavesdrop beneath their tree house on an afternoon after school."

Taking a seat to Emma's right, Mari shot her a significant look. That was her suggestion exactly. Though how did this woman know about the tree house? Had she been spying on the McBrides? Was that what Mari's intuition had picked up on?

The seer continued, "I can, however, explain your inheritance to you."

"Our inheritance?" Mari's sisters asked simultaneously.

Roslin lit the candles, then took a seat in her queen's chair. As the melting wax released a scent of sandalwood, she closed her eyes and made three wide circles above the flickering flames. She murmured words in a language that sounded to Mari like the Gaelic heard during visits with their Scottish cousins, the Rosses.

It was as if a light went on in Mari's brain. "Are you related to the Rosses of Rowanclere? They've come for the wedding. Are you with them?"

The seer gave Mari an approving smile. "Not exactly, no. I have sent young Melanie a letter. I hope to visit with her quite soon. In the meantime, shall we proceed?"

"Yes, please," Kat said.

No, let's not. Mari's pulse began to race. *Let's go home. Now. Before it's too late.*

"Emmaline Suzanne, your right hand, please?"

Emma glanced at Mari, then extended her hand across the table. "Hmm..." The seer studied Emma's palm. Pursing her lips, she traced the lines on Emma's hand with her index finger.

"What is it?" Kat asked, staring at her sister's hand, excitement painting a rose stain on her creamy complexion.

"Patience would be a helpmate to you, Katrina," said Roslin. "Your hand, please."

Kat plopped her right hand on the table, palm up. The seer bent over it intently, then went completely still. "Maribeth? I'll see yours."

Mari hesitated. Her teeth tugged at her bottom lip and her palm literally itched. She did not want to do this. "No thank you."

The candle flames flared and outside, the wind began to howl.

"You better show her, Mari," Kat said.

"I'd rather not."

"Your sisters need you, child," the Scotswoman said quietly. "You literally hold their happiness in the palm of your hand."

Kat reached over, grabbed Mari's hand and shoved it across the table for Roslin to see. "I'll work on my impatience, Mari," Kat said, "but you need to do something about your stubbornness."

"I'm not—" Mari's sputtering protest died the moment Roslin took Mari's hand in hers. A warm, gentle peace flowed into her body, totally banishing the tension that had dwelled within her since the moment her sisters proposed this trip to Hell's Half Acre.

Having studied Mari's palm, the seer released her hand and sat back in her chair. "'Tis as foretold. A circle of three in the thirty-third generation. Emmaline, Maribeth, and Katrina McBride, you are the Chosen."

The sisters exchanged uneasy looks. Though Mari's newfound sense of peace continued to linger, foreboding once more gnawed at its edges. "I knew we should have gone to the Literary Society meeting instead," she muttered.

"The Chosen?" Emma asked.

"'Tis about opportunity, my dear. The opportunity for you and your sisters to be of invaluable service to those who follow. 'Tis about ending the Curse of Clan McBride."

"The Curse of Clan McBride?" Kat repeated.

Mari sat back in her chair. This. This was the news she'd been trying to avoid. A family curse. It fit.

"Wait a minute," she murmured, rejecting the notion despite the sense of rightness it engendered. "I don't believe in curses. It's nonsense."

The Scotswoman ignored her. "In ancient days, a fairy prince fell in love with a mortal woman. As fate would have it, she gave her heart to another, a McBride."

"Of course." Mari rolled her eyes.

"The prince was mightily displeased, and in an effort to prove the mortal unworthy of the maiden's love, he put McBride to a series of fearsome tests. To the prince's dismay, the McBride withstood every challenge, though at great physical cost. Finally, fearful for her beloved's safety and at substantial risk to herself, the fair Ariel called upon the prince and demanded he recognize that the love she and McBride shared was powerful, vigilant and true, and that no trial or challenge would change it."

"How romantic." Kat sighed.

Roslin smiled tenderly at Kat, then continued her tale. "Ungracious in defeat, the prince acquiesced to her demand with a caveat. Since the fair lady claimed her mortal love would outlast a union with a fairy prince, it must be proved. Her children and her children's children and their children, down through the ages, would be called upon to reinforce her claim."

Engrossed by the tale, Emma sat with her elbow on the table, her chin resting in her hand. "Could he do that, this fairy prince? How?"

"Aye, our prince has great power and he's used it in various ways through time. Physical trials. Emotional trials." She paused, eyed the girls significantly and added, "Runs of bad luck."

Kat gasped. Mari narrowed her eyes. Emma dipped her head in a considering tilt. "One moment. I assume you're referring to our father and his brother?"

"The Bad Luck Wedding Dress and the Bad Luck Wedding Cake," Kat elaborated.

Emma continued, "Both our father and our uncle are supremely happy in their marriages."

"Yes. But they earned that happiness only after great trial, did they not? They proved their love to be powerful, vigilant and true."

Apprehension swirled in Mari's stomach like sour milk. "So what are you saying here, ma'am? Our lives are cursed? You expect us to believe that?"

"Believe what you wish, Maribeth. I but offer the three of you the opportunity to end the curse for all time and save your children and grandchildren from trials and tribulations that otherwise would occur."

"What do we have to do?" Kat asked.

Nothing! We're not getting involved in this.

"Lady Ariel elicited a promise from the prince. When, in any one generation of McBrides, three sisters, three daughters marked with the sign of Ariel, find love to prove the claim of Ariel and accomplish a task of great personal import, the curse will be broken for all time."

"A task of great personal import?" Mari shot her sisters a pointed look. "This just keeps getting better and better."

Emma reached across the table and touched the seer's hand. "What is our task?"

"The tasks are different for each of you. You will choose."

From within a hidden pocket in her ice-blue gown, Roslin withdrew a blue velvet pouch. "Emma, as eldest, it is your obligation to choose first."

As the seer opened the pouch, Mari laid a warning hand on her sister's arm. Ignoring Mari, Emma cautiously reached inside. Slowly, she pulled out a long gold chain, a replica of the one worn around the Scotswoman's neck. Emma's stone, however, was a deep, warm red. "Oh, my. It looks like a real ruby."

Roslin looked at Mari. "Maribeth?"

"No, thank you. I don't think this is a good idea."

"Why not?" Kat asked.

"It feels…I don't know…dangerous."

Emma glanced up from her necklace. "It's jewelry, Mari. Not a rattlesnake."

Kat glanced at the seer and said, "She *hates* rattlesnakes."

"I just don't think this is something we should be dabbling in."

"I didn't think you believed in 'this,'" Emma said.

While Mari sought to frame a response to explain her conflicting emotions, Kat reached for the bag.

"I'll pick next," she said, then reached into the bag and drew out a second necklace, identical to Emma's but for the color of the pendant's stone. This one glowed a deep, mysterious green. "Oh, emerald is my most favorite color. It matches my eyes." To Mari, she said, "Go on. Your turn. Quit being a ninny. Let's see what you have."

Mari sent Emma a pleading gaze. Her older sister said, "Humor her, or you'll hear about it for months."

Emma was right. Maybe she should play along. After all, an ancient curse couldn't be worse than a daily dose of Kat's whining. Mari reached into the pouch and drew out the third necklace.

"Blue!" Kat exclaimed. "Sapphire-blue. I just knew that's what it would be."

Mari couldn't take her eyes off the pendant as Roslin rose from her seat. It was a beautiful piece of jewelry.

It scared Mari half to death.

The lady placed the appropriate necklace first around Emma's neck, then around Kat's. When she came to Mari, she rested her hand on Mari's shoulder. Again, a peaceful sense of warmth flowed through Mari's body and she remained relaxed as the necklace settled against her skin as if it belonged nowhere else.

The seer leaned over and blew out the pillars. "It is done."

For a moment, the McBrides sat in silence. Finally, Emma asked, "But what about our tasks?"

"Wear your necklaces at all times, my beauties. At the proper time, your task will be revealed."

Oh, no. What have we done?

"Wait," Mari said, as much to herself as the others. "I don't believe in this."

Ignoring her sister's musings, Emma asked, "Ma'am? A question. You said the daughters were 'marked with the sign of Ariel.' Are we marked in some way? Is that why you read our palms?"

"Aye, ye are marked. Extend your hands, all of you, and I will show you."

Emma and Kat followed the direction immediately. Mari acquiesced more slowly, following her sisters' glares. Roslin took Emma's hand and traced a thin line. "Look. This line is unique to you. It tells me you are a nurturer." She lifted Kat's hand. "Katrina, this is your unique line. It confirms my earlier sense that you have an adventurous soul. Maribeth, I was not at all surprised to read in your hand that you have the gift of intuition."

Mari simply frowned in reply.

"Your destiny, however—the mark of Ariel—is written identically upon each of you. Look." She pointed out a sickle-shaped line on each sister's hand.

"Why, she's right," said Kat. "It's exactly the same. We're just alike. All of us. I've never noticed that before."

"'Tis the mark of Ariel."

Emma's eyes went round with dismay. "The mark of Ariel."

Staring at her hand, Kat shook her head. "I guess I'm not really surprised. Somehow, it just seems fitting that the McBride Menaces would have a Bad Luck Love Line."

CHAPTER ONE

Fort Worth, two years later

LUKE GARRETT WORKED HARD TO MAKE sure the out-laws, scalawags, ne'er-do-wells and miscreants who frequented his Hell's Half Acre saloons recognized him as one of their own. He drank and gambled and gamboled with the working girls. He could cuss like a cowboy, and he specialized in two-hit fights—he hit a man and the man hit the ground.

The more upstanding citizens of Fort Worth knew of him, too. Luke had won a small fortune in railroad stock in a card game a few years back, and he used his money to support civic causes that endeared him to Fort Worth's city leaders, despite their disapproval of his hands-on involvement with his investments in the Acre. Staid society matrons bemoaned the fact that a man so well mannered, well educated and well financed made his living in Fort Worth's tenderloin, thus placing him beyond the pale. Restless wives sighed over the breadth of his shoulders, the swagger in his step and the smoldering look he sometimes tossed their way. Young women simply looked at him and swooned, both attracted and repelled by the danger in his wink, his smile, his notorious reputation.

The image served Luke well both within the boundaries of the Acre and without. The ability to mingle with both levels of society made it infinitely easier to do his job.

Luke wasn't worrying much about his job on this bright, late-May morning, however. Today, only the mundane tasks of everyday life concerned him. He needed to pay a call on his whiskey supplier in order to ensure that the watering-down incident was never repeated. Also, he wanted to order a new pair of snakeskins at the bootmaker on Main Street. Then after that, he figured he'd stop by the courthouse to publicly register his clandestine purchase of a lot in the high-toned neighborhood going up around Summit Avenue. That'd give the gossips something to chew on.

First, though, he was of the mind to indulge himself, to allow himself time from his busy day for a sensuous treat. He'd heard about a new establishment in town, run by a woman of superior talent and exquisite beauty who was passionate about pleasing her customers. Because Luke was a man who appreciated a variety of passions, he couldn't wait to take a taste of what the woman had to offer.

Strolling along Main Street, Luke whistled an Irish drinking song and flashed a winsome smile at a young mother guiding a pair of toddling twins toward the meat market around the corner. "Fine-lookin' family you have there, ma'am," he said, tipping his hat. "Your husband is a lucky man."

"Thank you," she responded, her eyes bright with pride and pleasure.

He gave her a wink, ignored the disapproving frown of an approaching battle-ax dressed in blue and carrying a smoked ham, and continued on his way. His destination was in sight.

The building was an attractive redbrick with green-and-white-striped awnings, located near the very heart of Fort Worth. Facing south, one could see the rising spires of the new St. Patrick's Cathedral being built just north of the old Catholic church, St. Stanislaus. Looking north, a man couldn't miss the trio of flagpoles that crowned another city landmark—Rachel Warden's Social Emporium, widely acknowledged to be the best whorehouse in town. Sin and salvation, with Indulgences in the middle.

Clever girl, Miss Mari McBride.

Doorbells chimed as he opened the shop's door, and one of the customers waiting in line in front of him glanced his way. Alarm lit the man's eyes. He took hold of the arm of the young woman standing next to him and tugged her close to his side, then his chin came up as he sent Luke a warning stare.

Daddy and daughter, Luke surmised, then dismissed him when the crowd parted, and he caught sight of the display cases. *Well, now.*

Indulgences sold confections, and its cases held the largest variety of sweets Luke had seen this side of the Mississippi. Two boys stood with their faces all but pressed against the glass, eyeing marzipan, chicken feed, candy eggs and sugar plums. They debated their choices between horehound drops and jellies, licorice ropes and peppermints, rock candy, lemon drops and dozens of other candies. Watching them, Luke grinned. Indulgences was a child's vision of paradise.

Adults appeared to like the view, too. They congregated in front of a second display case, this one containing chocolates. The visual appeal of the offerings in the case tempted Luke to do some face-against-the-glass pressing himself. What was it about sweets that appealed to the child in everyone?

Then he got a glimpse of the proprietress, and Luke grew up fast.

She had an angel's face and a strumpet's figure, blond hair and a bright, welcoming smile. Her deep blue eyes sparkled with intelligence. She wore a white apron trimmed in chocolate-brown over her dress, a modest design in a simple cotton print. Her sleeves were rolled up to the elbows.

Luke shifted out of line but moved closer, forgetting all about his sweet tooth as a more basic hunger swept through him.

She was speaking to a young matron. "...chocolates are my specialty, and they're all made here in the shop."

"What is this one?" the customer asked, pointing toward a dark brown square topped with a ripple of mint-green.

"That's one of Indulgences' creams." Mari McBride smiled. "I call it a Chocolate Tease."

"A Tease?" another customer repeated.

"The flavor is one that is rich and mysterious. You won't quite be able to place it, though you'll try. It lingers, and it teases."

"That's a challenge I can't resist," the customer said. "Please add Teases to my order."

Not only beautiful, Luke thought, but a damned good businesswoman, too. He folded his arms and leaned casually against the wall, enjoying the show as she pointed out other offerings. Temptations and Enticements. Heavens and Rainbows and Enchantments. Sinfuls.

Luke definitely wanted a couple of those.

Miss McBride reached into her display case and pulled out a flat medallion-shaped candy. "With a two-dollar purchase, today's customers all receive a bonus of three Kisses. Here's a sample." Her eyes gleamed wickedly as she handed the candy to the woman. "Now, don't go home and tell your husband you've enjoyed a kiss that's better than his."

A smile played on the customer's lips as she eyed the candy. "You say this kiss is better than my Harold's?"

"I've never kissed your Harold, but…" Mari McBride winked. "Why don't you try one and tell us?"

The woman accepted the piece of candy, bit into it and moaned. A long, full-throated, honey-I-saw-Jesus groan. "Oh, Miss McBride. Poor Harold's kisses are nothing compared to yours."

The other women in the shop giggled, while the lone man grumbled. Mari McBride smiled magnanimously. "I've been selling this particular chocolate for three weeks, and so far, no one has claimed to have experienced a superior Kiss."

Though the comment was obviously made in jest, Luke couldn't ignore the unspoken challenge. He stepped forward. "That's quite a claim, little lady."

"It's quite a piece of candy, sir."

"Reckon I'll have to give one a try."

Luke locked gazes with the beauty as he reached for a piece of her chocolate. Silently, she challenged him. He grinned, enjoying the moment, then he popped the piece of candy into his mouth and bit into it. Flavor exploded across his tongue. Cherry, smooth and creamy and so delicious that he had to concentrate to keep his eyes from rolling back in his head. It was like sex, really good sex. No wonder that customer had sounded as if she'd had her bell rung.

As was his habit with sensual matters, Luke took his time. He savored the chocolate, wrung every last bit of pleasure from the sweet. The customers waited anxiously.

Finally, he swallowed. Anticipation and expectation sparked in Mari McBride's eyes. Slowly, his eyes still on hers, Luke licked his lips. "That's mighty fine, ma'am. Mighty fine."

"Thank you."

"However…" He paused significantly, waited as she folded her arms and arched a curious brow, then continued. "I don't think my opinion is the one that matters. I'm not the one selling Kisses. As good as your chocolate Kisses are, I think you should try mine before you make that superiority claim again."

"You make chocolates, sir?"

"I'm talkin' kisses."

Now it was the man in the shop who chuckled. The beauty's eyes widened, then narrowed. Luke's blood stirred. When was the last time he'd bandied flirtatious words with a woman of good character? He couldn't recall.

When she didn't voice a protest, Luke reached for her sample plate and snagged a Kiss. Stepping close to her, he held the Kiss to her lips. "Are you confident enough to compare?"

Her mouth opened, and he fed her the chocolate, his thumb brushing slowly across her lower lip. Luke stared deeply into her eyes as she sucked on the piece of candy. It felt as though they were the only two people in the room.

When her tongue slipped from her mouth to rim her lips, he knew a surge of pure lust that transformed the moment from light flirtation to something much more intense. Everything within him went tight as he watched her finish the candy and swallow.

"Well?" he asked, his voice a low, rumbling taunt.

"Delicious."

Tension thickened the air. "Delicious, hmm? The best you've ever had?"

Licking her lips once more, she nodded.

"Then I think it's time to expand your sample base, don't you?" He trailed his fingers across her downy soft cheek, then gently cupped her chin. Leaning forward, he lowered his mouth toward hers...until an elbow jabbed him hard in the ribs and shoved him aside.

"Excuse me." A man's cold, hard voice cut through the tension like a hot knife through cold lard. "Maribeth, your mother needs you. I'll man your shop for now."

Mari jerked her attention away from Luke and color stained her cheeks. "Papa," she said, a hint of protest in her voice.

Well, hell, Luke thought.

The man was tall, broad, graying at the temples, and angry enough to chew nails. Trace McBride claimed a position at his daughter's side, then folded his arms and glared at Luke. "I didn't know you were back in town, Garrett."

"Yep. Got back a couple days ago."

Luke and McBride had worked together a time or two regarding issues in Hell's Half Acre, and McBride had been friendly enough whenever their paths crossed. Of course, this was the first time their paths had crossed while Luke was in the process of romancing one of his daughters. He could understand the man's reaction.

Still, that didn't mean Luke had to change directions.

Luke rolled his tongue around his mouth, tasted the lingering flavor of cherry cream, then winked at Mari

McBride and drawled, "You know, I do have a powerful sweet tooth, and those Sinfuls look to be right up my alley. Give me two dollars' worth."

Trace McBride smiled—or rather, bared his teeth—and bagged up the candy. "Maribeth, you get on home now."

The beauty shot her father a beastly glare. "These are *my* customers, Papa. I'll take care of them."

"Not him, you won't."

"Papa!"

Like any successful thief, Luke understood the importance of good timing. He tossed his money onto the counter and grabbed the small bag of chocolates from Trace McBride's hand. "Not to fret, sweet thing," he told Mari. "I'll return another time for my bonus Kisses. It'll give me something to look forward to. I find that anticipation for a particularly sumptuous treat just makes a man's appetite all the stronger."

Luke tipped his black hat toward Mari, then, accompanied by the sound of a protective father's growl, exited Indulgences, grinning all the while. That had been fun.

He opened the small white bag and fished out a piece of candy. He popped the chocolate into his mouth, then groaned aloud. Chocolate, caramel and nuts. "Sinnin's even better than Kissin'."

Luke glanced over his shoulder toward the redbrick building with green-and-white awnings, toward the gorgeous Mari McBride's Indulgences.

As a rule, he stayed away from young, unmarried females of good birth, no matter how pretty they were. But Mari McBride tempted him to make an exception. She tempted him, period. And she owed him three Kisses, by God.

Maybe he'd just make an exception this time. Maybe

he'd take her hint and indulge himself. Luke dug into his candy sack and removed another Sinful. He popped it into his mouth, savored it, then swallowed with a moan, his mind made up.

Any woman who could make him moan from a block and a half away was a woman worth knowing better. Plus, cozying up to her would have the added bonus of driving Trace McBride crazy. How could Luke resist?

He couldn't. He wouldn't. He'd see to his chores, then tend to his sweet tooth. She had Heavens and Rainbows and Sinfuls and Kisses. He was of a mind to inspire a brand-new candy. Something long and hard and tasty.

She could call them Lukes.

MARI BURST into the kitchen at Willow Hill and demanded, "Mama, you've got to stop him."

Seated at the kitchen table, her honey-colored hair slipping from a makeshift bun at the back of her neck, Jenny McBride glanced up from her mending. She closed her blue eyes and let out a long-suffering sigh. "What has Billy done now?"

"Not my brother. *Your husband!*"

Jenny's full mouth twitched with a smile as she patted the seat beside her. "Sit down and talk to me, honey. Tell me what mischief Trace has been up to now. I suppose he was being overprotective?"

"Overprotective? Ha." Mari flounced across the room. "He's the King of Protective. The Emperor of Protective. I'd say he was the God of Protective if it weren't blasphemous!"

Jenny McBride laughed softly. "Such dramatics. You sound more like Kat than yourself."

"I don't *feel* like myself. I'm harboring some serious anger toward my father." Mari plopped down into a chair at the kitchen table and buried her head in her arms. "Mama, he's making me crazy."

"Yes, Trace can do that." Jenny put a final stitch in the hem of the yellow gingham curtain, snipped the thread, then folded the cloth neatly on the table. She reached out and stroked Mari's hair. "What happened?"

Mari gave her stepmother a quick but thorough rundown of the afternoon's events at Indulgences. Jenny winced on Mari's behalf a time or two during the telling. When Mari finally wound down, Jenny sighed and asked, "So who was the gentleman?"

"I don't know. Papa called him Garrett."

"Garrett? Luke Garrett?"

Mari shrugged. "He never mentioned his given name."

"Describe him to me."

The man's image floated like a fantasy in Mari's mind. "He's tall with thick, dark hair that has a little wave to it. Brown eyes." *Wicked, hot-caramel eyes.* "Broad shoulders. A nice smile." *A devilish grin.* "He has a dimple, here." Mari placed a finger against her left cheek.

"A dimple." Jenny nodded. "That is Luke Garrett. You've heard of him, Mari. He owns the Blue Goose Saloon in the Acre. He's been in prison. In fact, I didn't know he'd been released. He's the one Idalou Whitaker…" Jenny allowed her sentence to trail off unfinished.

Mari's eyes widened at the mention of the year's most notorious scandal. She tried to imagine starchy Idalou with the intriguing man who had challenged Mari's Kisses, who had stared at her with such intensity, but her mind wouldn't picture it.

"As much as I hate to say it," Jenny continued, "I think that this time, your father was right to interfere. Luke Garrett's not the sort of man for a good girl to tangle with."

"Why? Because he owns property in Hell's Half Acre? Just like Papa did when you met him?"

"Now, Mari."

Mari pushed to her feet and began to pace the kitchen. "It doesn't matter whether my customer was a convicted criminal or a candidate for sainthood. He was my customer in my shop and dealing with him was my business. I am not a McBride Menace any longer. I'm an adult. I am responsible for my own actions, my own deeds. My own mistakes. I cannot—I will not—have Papa leaping to the rescue whether I'm selling a man chocolate or...or...or kissing him senseless on the courthouse steps!"

Jenny grimaced. "Please, Mari. Not the courthouse steps. That would revive your Menace reputation and you've worked so hard to shed it. Besides, you'd give your father apoplexy."

"He's giving me indigestion. And a headache. I'll probably break out in hives any minute."

"He's worried about you, sweetheart." Jenny rose and crossed the room toward Mari. She touched her cheek. "You're seldom home anymore. We hardly ever hear you laugh. Ever since Alexander—"

"I'm fine, Mama," Mari interrupted. She didn't want to talk about Alexander Simpson. She didn't want to even think about the man. "I'm happy. I've been busy opening my business. You know what that's like. When you opened Fortune's Design, didn't you work long days?"

"And nights," Jenny agreed. "Yes, I understand how much work is involved in launching a new business, and I know that you've been immersed in the entire process. Your father and I are so proud of what you've accomplished. But there's more to life than work, Mari. Even during the busiest times at Fortune's Design, I tried to maintain a social life. You, on the other hand, have done everything possible to avoid social engagements in recent months, and I don't believe Indulgences is the reason."

"Wait a minute. Didn't I speak at the Literary Society just last week?"

"Because you were promoting your business. When was the last time you did something just for fun?"

Mari had no answer.

Jenny's voice gentled. "Honey, to be frank, you've let the situation with Alexander affect your relationship with friends and family. That's part of the reason your father is so concerned about you right now."

"There's no need, Mama. Honestly. If Papa just has to worry, he should spend his energies fretting about my sisters. It's been almost two years since Casey died, and Emma still visits his grave every day. And Kat, I fear she's going to get herself in trouble with that actor. I don't trust him."

"Neither does your father. He worries plenty about both Emma and Katrina, believe me. He worries about all his children. He told me that when it comes to his babies, his neck has been niggling of late."

Mari frowned. She didn't like hearing that. If the niggle at the back of Trace McBride's neck told him he had reason to worry about his children, then she wouldn't argue. Her father was good at sensing trouble. Mari had long believed she'd inherited her intuition from him.

The challenging thing about one of her father's "neck niggles" was that it covered a lot of ground. He might know trouble was coming, but that trouble could be anything from physical safety to emotional pain to something as simple as one of the boys catching heck from the sheriff for one of their endless pranks.

Mari made a note to keep a closer eye on her siblings, then said, "He goes too far, Mama. I'm an adult. He needs to treat me like one."

"I know, honey. I'll talk to him. But you need to accept that he'll never stop worrying about you, no matter how old you get. However, there are things you can do that will ease his mind to an extent and, hopefully, make his visits to Indulgences fewer and farther between."

"Tell me, please. I'll do anything I can."

"First, start coming home at night before dark. Speak up at the supper table, share your day."

"I already do that."

"Do it more often. And don't disappear into your room after we eat. That behavior worries your father, too. Stay downstairs and visit with him. Or play tag or ball with your brothers. Nothing relaxes your father like watching his children play in the yard after supper."

"That I can do." Mari might be a grown woman with a business of her own, but she hoped she'd never be too old to play. "In fact, I'll organize a rousing game of blindman's buff this evening. I'll stop by Uncle Tye's house and invite the cousins."

"No, not this evening. Tonight we're all attending the ball at the Texas Spring Palace. I want you to join us, Maribeth."

Mari's stomach sank. Not that. Tonight's ball was the premier social event of the spring in Fort Worth. Alex was bound to be there.

"No, Mama. Not a ball. I'm not up to that. I'll stay home with Emma."

Jenny smiled and her eyes gleamed with pleasure. "Emma plans to attend the ball."

"What?" Mari said, shocked.

"She's even promised to dance if asked. She's wearing the yellow dress I made for her."

"That's wonderful!" Gladness and a full measure of hope filled Mari's heart at that bit of news. *Oh, Emma.* Maybe she was finally beginning to heal from her devastating loss.

Casey's death from pneumonia three months after his and Emma's wedding had almost destroyed Mari's elder sister. The two had grown up together, been friends before becoming lovers. They'd planned and dreamed and no sooner embarked on their blissful life together at Casey's ranch south of town than a summer cold turned ugly and took it all away. Emma's light had gone dark that day and remained so ever since.

Remembering the day that Casey died, Mari absently stroked a finger over the line that crossed her palm, the Bad Luck Love Line she didn't believe in, but of which, nevertheless, she was always conscious. "Did she finally cry, Mama?"

Jenny shook her head. "Not that I'm aware. Her eyes weren't red or puffy when she came to me this morning and asked to see the dress. She held it up against herself, looked into the mirror and said she was coming to the ball. No explanation. No excuse. Under the circumstances, I wasn't about to press the issue."

"No," Mari agreed. "No sense borrowing trouble."

Jenny picked up the window curtain and began threading it back onto the rod. "I'm hopeful this ball tonight will signal a new beginning for this family," she said. "I want to believe that the bad times are behind us and only good times lie ahead."

Mari nodded. "There's nothing else I'd like more."

Jenny fixed the curtain rod to its brackets, then stepped back. The two women took a moment to admire her handiwork. Then Jenny asked again, "So you'll join us at the Texas Spring Palace tonight, Mari?"

Mari sighed. "Yes. I'll be there for Emma."

And if she happened to run into the man who had jilted her at the altar, well, she'd act as friendly as a pup in a box.

Then, she'd sic her brothers on the scalawag and let Billy, Tommy and Bobby conduct a little McBride Monster mischief. *I wonder if I have enough time to whip up a special batch of chocolates? Ones made with prunes, perhaps?*

CHAPTER TWO

LUKE EYED the turnip-shaped cupolas and massive center dome of the Texas Spring Palace and wondered what the architect had been drinking when he designed the place. Intended to rival the Sioux City Corn Palace and the Toronto Ice Palace, the purpose of the regional immigration and agricultural fair was to attract settlers and investors to Texas. In its second season, the project appeared to be a rousing success, serving as an educational, cultural and entertainment center for visitors from across the country.

Nevertheless, Luke thought the Oriental-style building looked like something out of a fantasy world, more suited to the pages of a novel than the rolling Texas prairie.

As he entered the huge exhibit hall, Luke overheard a ticket taker claim that almost seven thousand people had crowded inside this evening. That could be a problem, he thought. With that many folks milling around the building, he might have a difficult time locating his contact.

And he truly did want to turn over the stolen diamond-and-ruby necklace hidden in his pocket.

He wandered through the agricultural hall pretending interest in the neatly classified samples of grains, grasses, fruits, vegetables and minerals produced

within the state while he developed his plan of action.
He figured the likeliest time to spy his quarry would be
during the Elgin Watch Band's performance. Besides,
Luke wouldn't mind dancing a waltz or two with a
Fort Worth lovely. It'd be a nice change from the un-
civilized company he'd been keeping the past few
weeks.

Having toured the length of the hall, Luke moseyed
on toward the art exhibit, where work either by Texas
artists or depicting an aspect of life in the Lone Star
State was on display. In this gallery, Luke didn't have
to feign interest. His stepfather had taught him to appreciate art, and during Luke's travels, he always made
it a point to visit local museums and galleries whenever
time allowed. The quality of the paintings and sculp-
tures on display here at the Texas Spring Palace impressed him. The bronze nude by Monique Day could
hold its own with anything he'd seen in the Louvre.

"Luke Garrett? Is that really you?"

Luke glanced away from a moody watercolor of
Galveston Bay to see Wilhemina Peters, society columnist for the Fort Worth *Daily Democrat*, bearing down
on him. She wore a candlelight silk shawl draped over
a bronze-colored evening gown and brought to mind an
image of a barquentine at full sail.

Luke stifled a sigh. Up until now, he'd enjoyed his
evening at the agriculture and immigration fair. Leave
it to Wilhemina Peters to destroy his peace.

Halting in front of him, she declared, "It *is* you."

"Good evening, Mrs. Peters. Are you enjoying the
gala?"

"Never mind the gala. What are you doing out of jail?"

Luke flashed a shark's smile, then drawled, "I've
been paroled."

"Paroled!"

"Yep. For good behavior." With a wicked wink, he added, "The warden's daughter testified on my behalf."

Mrs. Peters gasped and clutched at her voluminous bosom.

"For goodness' sake, Wilhemina, settle down." Mr. Peters walked up beside his wife and extended his hand toward Luke. "I heard you were here tonight, Garrett. Glad to know your conviction was overturned in time for you to attend the exposition. The Texas Spring Palace's second season has been a rousing success so far, and it wouldn't have happened without your substantial subscription."

Luke acknowledged the chairman of the Spring Palace committee with a nod. "Glad to have been of help."

Wilhemina sniffed. "It's been suggested that you considered your ten-thousand-dollar subscription to be simply good business. An influx of tourists to the city means more trains to rob, more horses to steal, more people to fleece in your Hell's Half Acre's saloons and brothels."

"Wilhemina, hush now," scolded her husband. "Mr. Garrett is completely innocent of any involvement in the slight increase in the city's crime rate since the exposition opened."

"That's right." Luke nodded solemnly. "I've been in jail."

While Wilhemina gasped, Mr. Peters continued, "The Spring Palace is the best thing that's happened to Fort Worth since electric lights, and Mr. Garrett is a big part of its success. I suggest you bury your animosity and—"

"Give the devil his due?" she interrupted, her smile false, her eyes narrowed and angry. "Very well." Before Luke or her husband realized her intentions, Wilhemina Peters took a step closer to him, drew back her hand and slapped him. "That's for Miss Whitaker."

The crowd around them gasped. Luke didn't so much as twitch an eyelash. Miss Whitaker? Did he know a Miss Whitaker?

Wilhemina Peters wasn't done. "What happened to you, Luke Garrett? I know who your people are. Miss Whitaker is my goddaughter, so I made it a point to find out. You were born to be a hero. Your grandfather died at the Alamo. Your great-uncle was killed in the Goliad Massacre. Your father defended Galveston against the Yankees, and your mother foiled a Comanche's attempt to steal her favorite horse. With that sort of honor and courage in your blood, how did you end up a low-down no-good—" she screeched the final word "—outlaw?"

Mr. Peterson's complexion bleached to a pasty white, and his focus slid down toward Luke's right hand as if expecting to see a gun.

Luke simply turned toward Mr. Peterson and pointedly arched a brow. That's all it took. Peterson placed his hands on his wife's shoulders and forcibly propelled her away through the throng of people who'd gathered to observe the scandalous exchange. With studied calm, Luke returned his attention toward the painting of Galveston Bay.

It truly was quite good. He'd been favorably impressed by all of the exhibits on display at the Spring Palace, not just the art. In his opinion the organizers had achieved their purpose of advertising the resources and opportunities to be found in the Lone Star State. He was glad to have contributed to the project.

After all, a man had to do something with his ill-gotten gains.

The buzz of conversation behind him slowly grew

louder and took on a mean tone as word of Wilhemina Peters's charges against him spread. Behind him, he heard a shrill feminine voice declare, "The nerve of the man, trying to mingle with polite society!"

"I think he should be shown the door," a man said.

A woman clucked her tongue. "I know this is a public event, but I don't feel safe. My daughters are here. What if he notices them?"

A breathy young woman's voice said, "He's so handsome. I wish he'd notice me."

"Elizabeth!" The woman gasped. "Alfred? Alfred! Do something."

Wonderful. Thank you, Wilhemina. As Alfred quietly argued with his wife about the advisability of tangling with a reputed gunslinger, Luke moved to the next painting in the gallery, a vibrant oil entitled *West Texas Sunset.* He'd seen that crimson-and-gold sky before. Worked cotton fields beneath it, at a place not far from here, in fact. The picture made him yearn for simpler times, back to the days before deceit had become the driving force in his life.

"All right, Garrett." Ol' Alfred's voice trembled just a little as he gathered his questionable courage and stepped forward. He grabbed Luke's arm. "It's best you move along."

"I suggest you remove your hand from my person," Luke said in a cold, dead tone.

"I know some townspeople are willing to put up with the likes of you because you spread your money around Fort Worth, but the fact remains you don't belong in polite compan—"

"Mr. Garrett! I'm sorry to keep you waiting so long. Thank you for your patience." A lovely young woman with honey hair and shining green eyes swept up beside him and slipped her hand around his arm. "The Elgin Watch Band has begun to play. Shall we join the dancers now?"

Luke hesitated but a second. "I'd be honored."

As he led her out of the art exhibit toward the ballroom, the whispers and murmurs and scandalized exclamations escalated to a near roar. At that point, he heard Wilhemina Peters exclaim, "Oh my heavens! Look at that. I knew it. I knew those Menaces would eventually come to no good. I wonder if Trace McBride knows his daughter has taken up with an outlaw?"

Trace McBride's daughter? Another one? Luke studied her features, recognized the similarities between the two young women and allowed himself the slightest of winces. Seven thousand people at this shindig, and he runs across another McBride Menace? This night was just getting better and better.

The rumbles faded behind them as he led her into the crush occupying the dance floor and joined in a waltz. "Miss McBride, I presume?"

"Kat McBride." She smiled sheepishly. "I was standing on the other side of the partition waiting for my beau to join me, and I heard the entire thing. I'm sorry, Mr. Garrett. It was presumptuous of me to interrupt that way, I know, but I was curious. I heard about your visit to my sister Mari's chocolate shop today, and of course, I'm well acquainted with both Mrs. Peterson and Idalou Whitaker. That harpy gossip columnist has been the bane of my existence for years, and as far as Idalou Whitaker goes, well, I know you're not the father of her baby."

Luke all but tripped over his own feet. "Baby?"

Kat McBride nodded. "Idalou said it was yours just to make her father crazy. Her mother ran off with a gambling man a few years back and ever since then, Mr. Whitaker has been downright mean. He said cruel things when he found out she was in a family way, and naming you was a way for her to strike back." She offered him an apologetic smile as she added, "I'm sure if she'd known you'd be paroled this soon, she'd have chosen another notorious man to name as the father of her child."

Dryly, Luke replied, "In the future, I'll be sure to publicize my travel plans."

Her eyes sparkled as laughter bubbled up, and in that moment, she reminded Luke of his sister Janna before life had sucked the joy from her soul.

"Are you really as bad as they say, Mr. Garrett?"

The question brought a grin to his face. Such an impertinent little filly. "What if I am? Shouldn't you fear being in my company?"

"La." She dismissed the question with a wrinkle of her button nose. "We're surrounded by hundreds of people. What damage could you do me in such a public place? Besides, I don't believe you're as wicked as people allow. You remind me a lot of my father, you know."

After a moment's pause, Luke deadpanned, "How flattering."

This time she giggled. "That wasn't an insult, sir. My father might be…well…mature, but he's still a very handsome man. Graying hair looks good on a gentleman."

"My hair isn't graying."

Her eyes twinkled at him. "Once upon a time, his reputation was almost as bad as yours, but he never was as bad as people believed. I think you're probably the same way."

"I think I understand why your father has graying

hair. You, too, have a certain reputation here in Fort Worth, Miss McBride. Correct me if I'm wrong, but I'm not the only alleged train robber in this conversation."

She lifted her chin. "Youthful indiscretions, long behind us. The McBride Menaces retired two years ago when my eldest sister, Mrs. Casey Tate, married." Kat McBride hesitated, her countenance dimming. "She lost her husband a short time later, and I'm afraid Emma hasn't felt like Menacing since then."

"My condolences to your sister."

"Thank you. It's been a difficult time, what with Casey's death and then Mari's heartbreak. Our family is cursed when it comes to love." Going dreamy eyed, she touched her necklace and added, "However, I'm going to change that."

Luke only partially listened as she rattled on about bad luck and palm reading and a fairy prince. His thoughts returned to the matter at hand. Perhaps he need not abort his plans. Perhaps he could turn all this attention to his benefit.

Kat McBride continued to prattle about her family, relaying stories about her younger brothers whom she affectionately referred to as the McBride Monsters. She captured his attention with a tale about sneezing powder in a church air vent and they shared a good laugh. When the joy in her manner abruptly died, Luke braced himself. "Trouble?"

"Definitely."

"Mrs. Peters?"

"Worse. It's Mari. We're in the midst of an argument regarding my beau. Ever since her fiancé jilted her, she's been a veritable shrew, and she thinks I'm headed for trouble by stepping out with my sweetheart. I was very much hoping to avoid her tonight. I thought she'd fix her attentions on our sister Emma and leave me alone. It doesn't look like I'll be that lucky." Kat McBride chewed at her bottom lip. "Mr. Garrett, in light of the briefness of our association would it be presumptuous of me to request your assistance?"

"What can I do to help you?"

"Slow her down?" she asked, her emerald eyes pleading as they began to move off the dance floor. "I need to get lost in the crowd for a bit. I'm supposed to meet Rory at the theater in twenty minutes."

Rory? Unease climbed like a spider up Luke's neck. No, surely not. It wasn't *that* unusual a name. And yet, he'd been hearing rumors about a man around town. Luke stopped her with a hand on her arm. "This sweetheart of yours. Where's he from?"

"Well, that's a matter of debate. He ordinarily speaks with the most wonderful Irish accent, but upon occasion, he'll slip into a luscious Southern drawl."

Well, hell. "How long have you known him? What does he look like? How old is he?"

Kat gave an exaggerated roll of her eyes. "My goodness, Mr. Garrett. Now you sound like Mari. I'll be fine, sir. Please don't worry. Just delay my sister. Ask her about her chocolates. That's all she talks since she opened her shop downtown. Oh, dear, here she comes. I must go. Thanks for the dance, Mr. Garrett."

Luke watched Kat McBride weave her way through the crowd and attempted to convince himself that his suspicions were groundless. If only the girl wasn't pretty, young and blond. *She's just Rory's type.*

"Excuse me, Mr. Garrett?" came a voice from behind him. "The woman you were dancing with is my sister, and I think it's only fair to warn you that my father is even more protective of her than he is of me."

Luke turned around. Dressed in fashionable sea-green silk, the woman took his breath away. *What kind of idiot would be stupid enough to jilt her?* He cleared his throat. "That's good. I get the impression she needs a keeper. You, on the other hand, appear to be a woman well in charge of her life, prepared to handle any challenge. Dance with me, Miss McBride," he said, offering his hand.

Refusal gleamed in blue eyes moody like the Galveston seascape, so Luke hurried to add, "I have concerns regarding your sister I wish to share with you."

Following a moment's contemplation, Mari McBride stepped into his arms, and Luke again felt a shimmer of unease.

The woman felt as if she belonged there.

MARI KNEW BETTER than to dance with Luke Garrett. With his dark chocolate hair and caramel eyes and spun-sugar smile, he tempted a woman to take a taste— even someone who'd sworn off his sort of sweets.

Mari had fallen for broad shoulders and a handsome face once before, and she'd be hanged if she'd go that route again. Never mind how appealing she found the wicked glint in Mr. Garrett's eye, the swagger in his step and the air of danger that surrounded him like a cloud of confectioner's sugar. Never mind that his physical form brought to mind her grandmother Monique's marble sculpture of Theseus, the Greek hero who slew the Minotaur, or that the sound of his slow drawl warmed her like smooth Southern whiskey. Luke Garrett had a reputation in town next to which hers paled in comparison. She'd be a fool to go anywhere near him. Yet, if Kat was in trouble…

Mari joined him in a dance. The moment his hand touched hers, that old, familiar sense of foreboding kissed the back of her neck.

"Chocolate is my sister's favorite treat," he told her as he swept her into a waltz. "As I travel about, I send her samples from different locales. Thus far her favorites are chocolates filled with coconut cream from a little shop on Jackson Square in New Orleans, followed closely by dark chocolates filled with an almond-and-honey nougat from a Parisian chocolatier."

Mari clumsily missed a step. "You send your sister chocolates? From Paris? France?"

His mouth twitched in amusement. "*Oui.* It's a place called Pierre's. On—"

"Rue Saint Michel," she exclaimed. "I've been there. His dark chocolate is fabulous."

"Janna likes it. However, I suspect she'll like your chocolate even more. I plan to send her a box of those Sinfuls I tasted this afternoon."

He wants to buy my chocolate to send to his sister. What kind of criminal was he?

One who loved his sister. Maybe that's why he wanted to talk to her about Kat. Maybe he had a soft spot for sisters. Or, maybe sisters had nothing to do with anything. Maybe he made up the sister-who-loves-chocolate just to sneak past Mari's defenses. Scoundrels did that sort of thing. She'd learned that hard lesson from her former fiancé, Alexander Simpson.

Mari's experience with Alex had taught her to be suspicious of men and their motives. However, she wasn't one of those silly twits who allowed the dishonorable actions of one man to color her opinion of an entire gender. No daughter of Trace McBride, no niece of Tye McBride, would be so stupid.

"Mr. Garrett—"

"Call me Luke, please."

She smiled politely. "Luke, then, and I am Mari. So, Luke, may I be frank with you?"

He winced in a charming manner. "A question such as that tends to make me wary, but yes, please feel free to speak your mind."

Mari's lips twitched with a grin. "My family would advise against such a blanket invitation."

"You father would tell you not to speak to me at all."

"True. However, he'd also tell me to keep an eye on my sister Kat whenever I suspect she might be headed for trouble. I'm worried about her. You said you had concerns…?"

Luke tilted his head toward the edge of the dance floor where Wilhemina Peters watched them while wagging her jaw to a handful of her cronies. "Let's walk, shall we? I've heard the exhibit of mosaics made from natural products is quite impressive."

Only too happy to get away from the gossip queen bee, Mari nodded her assent and allowed Luke Garrett to guide her off the dance floor.

Architects had designed the Spring Palace in the shape of a Saint Andrew's cross, with a dome 150 feet in diameter at its center. All the large gatherings, including tonight's gala ball, occurred beneath the dome. With a crowd as big as this one, people spread out to all parts of the building. With any luck at all, Mari wouldn't run into Trace while in Luke Garrett's company, a complication she'd just as soon avoid. She'd hate to have a public confrontation with her father, and unless Jenny could talk some sense into the man, Mari feared that a confrontation was unavoidable.

Neck niggle or not, the King of Overprotectiveness would have to abdicate his crown, for all his children's sakes. He could be watchful without being so dictatorial. Mari suspected that part of the reason Kat was playing the fool over the actor was their father's overbearing attitude.

"Your father appears more relaxed tonight than he did this afternoon," her companion observed, nodding toward the right.

Mari whipped her head around. Sure enough, her father stood near the entrance to the agriculture gallery, talking to his brother. Both men had smiles on their faces.

Obviously, her father hadn't seen her yet.

Mari ducked her head and picked up her pace. She didn't breathe freely until they had turned a corner and entered the mosaic exhibit. While Luke Garrett made a thorough inspection of a likeness of the Texas Spring Palace created entirely from seeds, tree bark and bits of stone, she silently fumed in self-disgust. She'd just run and hidden from her father. Could she act any more childish?

Seeking a distraction, she asked, "Luke? About those concerns of yours?"

He responded with a request of his own. "Tell me about this Rory fellow."

Mari grimaced at the name. "She's meeting him tonight, isn't she? I knew she was up to something." She sighed heavily. "She'd better hope that Papa doesn't find out or he'll lock her in her room for a year."

"He'd do that?"

"No." She waved her hand. "But he wouldn't be at

all pleased. He's forbidden her to see him, which was a big mistake, of course, because that only made Kat want to see him more. My sister adores drama, and she's cast herself as Juliet in this contretemps."

"And is Rory a Romeo?"

This time Mari showed her displeasure by wrinkling her nose. "I don't quite know what Rory is. He's outrageously handsome, undeniably charming, and obviously talented, but that's the problem. He's an actor, a very good actor, and I think he could play just about any role he wished. My fear is that he's playing a role for Kat."

"You don't trust him."

"Not one little bit." Mari lifted her head and challenged him with her gaze as she asked, "Why do you ask? Do you know him?"

"As far as I know, I've never met your sister's beau. I once knew a man by that name, however, and I wondered if Kat's Rory might be the same man."

"Was his last name Kelly?"

Luke took hold of Mari's elbow and led her toward the next mosaic on display, a street scene of San Antonio made of brightly colored tiles. "The Rory I knew changed his surname as often as he changed his socks."

"Was he blond, about twenty years old, six feet tall, with blue eyes and dimples in both cheeks?"

It was the dimples that did it. She could see it in Luke's eyes. "It's him, isn't it?" she asked, her thoughts racing. "Kat's Rory is your Rory, too." Before he could so much as nod, another thought occurred and she clutched the sleeve of his jacket. "Is he an outlaw like you? Is my sister in danger?"

"The Rory I know is a scoundrel, but I doubt Kat would find herself in any physical danger from him."

Luke angled his head and studied her a moment before saying, "It appears that my reputation has preceded me. Tell me, Miss McBride, does present company make you fearful for your own safety?"

Yes, but not for the reason you would think.

Mari lifted her chin and calmly looked into his eyes. "I understand that you are a convicted felon on parole, Mr. Garrett. Ordinarily in a town like Fort Worth, such a fact would make you a pariah at an event such as this, and yet, tonight I've watched you be greeted by the mayor, two aldermen, the editor of the newspaper, two preachers and a priest. That tells me that you must be an intelligent man. Too intelligent to harm the daughter of one of the town's leading citizens."

He flashed a grin, showing the dimple in his cheek. "You wield your father like a weapon, don't you?"

Mari nodded. "And he's just one part of my arsenal. Have you ever met my mother, Jenny?"

"Actually, I have. We have a mutual friend, Rachel Warden. You're right, your mother is a formidable woman. I quite admire her, and I wouldn't cross her on a bet."

"She keeps my father in line. Then of course there's my Uncle Tye and Aunt Claire. They'd walk through fire for any of us. So while I recognize that you are indeed a dangerous man, I believe myself to be safe in your company tonight."

"A dangerous man," Luke mused, his attention drifting to her lips. "I rather prefer that to being called an outlaw."

Mari felt the tangible force of his gaze and it sent a little thrill surging through her blood. Time hung suspended, and she licked her suddenly dry lips. His eyes narrowed, then his focus shifted and their gazes locked.

His caramel eyes heated. The air between them seemed to thicken and sizzle. Mari felt herself swaying toward him like…like…like an idiot.

She took a full step backward, then said in a shaky voice, "Dangerous."

After a moment's pause, he nodded, his mouth sliding into a smirk. "Yeah, probably so."

Mari drew a deep, calming breath, then said, "I'm worried about my sister. She's impulsive and she has a tendency to do infinitely foolish things. I think I should look for her."

"Probably that would be a good idea. I was supposed to meet a gentleman here tonight, but it can wait. I'd like to get a gander at this Rory of hers. We're easing up on half an hour now. Let's go."

He took her hand and led her rapidly away from the activity at the center of the Spring Palace, toward the sparsely populated far end of the exhibit hall. "Hold on," Mari said. "Wait a minute. Slow down. Where are you taking me?"

"To find your sister. She's meeting him at the theater."

"She told you this," Mari stated.

"Yeah. If he's the Rory I'm looking for, it'll be backstage."

"Backstage." Mari had a vision of dark, private nooks and crannies perfect for a scoundrel's nefarious deeds. Kat was primed to go along with it, too, the McBride Menace side of her nature up and flowing in the aftermath of her recent battles with their father.

Mari picked up her pace, her worry escalating with each second that ticked by. Maybe this was the reason for her father's apprehension. Maybe her sister was in danger of true ruination. *You're too young, Kat.*

"I knew she was cooking up trouble," Mari said as they approached the theater doors. "I didn't think it could be anything too serious. It's not like me to be that wrong. I usually have a hint."

"Don't borrow trouble," Luke advised, opening the door. "She might have better sense, or he might be another man entirely."

At first glance the dimly lit theater appeared empty, but as they moved down the aisle, Mari spied a thin line of light shining beneath the heavy red velvet stage curtain trimmed with gold tassels. Her muscles tensed. They climbed the wooden steps at the right side of the stage. Luke held up his hand palm out, motioning her to halt as he peeked behind the curtain. Mari held her breath.

He motioned for her to follow as he slipped behind the heavy veil.

Please let me be in time. Mari ducked backstage, swiftly scanning the set, part of the current production of *Taming of the Shrew.* No one.

Luke stood still, listening intently, then walked quietly stage left. A second later, Mari heard it, too—a rustle of petticoats and a soft, throaty moan.

Her stomach sank and just for a moment, Mari bowed her head and closed her eyes. *Oh, Kat.*

Then a sense of urgency overtook her, and she pushed her way past Luke and followed the sound around a castle wall made of wood. She stopped cold.

A pair of flickering candlesticks sat atop a small square table and illuminated the couple on a red velvet chaise longue. Her younger sister reclined against the chair, her gown and underpinnings pushed off her shoulders and pooling at her waist. A man lay atop her, feasting upon her bare breasts.

Once she caught her breath, Mari exclaimed, "Katrina McBride!"

The couple on the bed scrambled. Rory rolled onto the floor and began fumbling with the buttons on his shirt. Kat yanked up her dress, shielding her breasts, and sat up. Her face blushed crimson. "Mari. What are you doing here?"

"Me?" Mari braced her hands on her hips. "Me? What am I doing here? Isn't the question what are *you* doing here?"

"I think that answer is obvious." Luke's slow drawl had disappeared, replaced by a voice as hard and cold as the West Texas plains in February. "Hello, Rory."

The handsome young actor spit out an ugly curse. "Luke."

"You sorry son of a bitch," Luke said, advancing. "Do you have a clue as to the devastation you left behind in Galveston? Do you know—"

"Outside," Rory said, cutting him off, shooting him a fierce, demanding look. "Let's take it outside and allow the ladies a moment of privacy, shall we?"

Privacy, ha. Mari wrinkled her nose. Rory Kelly was the one who wanted privacy. No telling what "devastation" he'd caused that he didn't want publicly discussed. Not that Mari cared. "Luke, perhaps it would be best if you escorted him away from here before I lose my tenuous hold on my temper and shoot him right in the…"

"Mari!" Kat protested while Luke grabbed the scoundrel by the back of the neck and yanked him to his feet. After the men disappeared out an exit door that led to the alley behind the theater, Mari drew a deep breath and tried to calm her nerves.

"How dare you!" Kat said, her expression mutinous as she yanked her bodice up and her skirts down.

"Excuse me?"

"How *dare* you follow me and spy on me? Invade my privacy."

"Privacy?" Mari said, incredulous. "This is a public place, Katrina. Anyone could have walked in here. *Anyone*. Mrs. Peters. Reverend Erickson. *Papa*. Kat, think about it. If Papa had found you here like this, you'd be standing in front of a preacher repeating wedding vows this very moment."

Katrina's chin came up. "And what would be the problem with that?"

"Kat!"

"Well?" She scrambled to her feet, blinking her eyes rapidly as she fought back tears. "Why not? Maybe a shotgun wedding wouldn't be my first choice, but I'm beginning to think it'll be my only choice. There isn't a man in Fort Worth who'll risk romance with me. Not since *you* went and ruined my chances."

Mari blinked. "Since I *what?*"

"You know what I'm talking about."

"No, I don't. I haven't done anything to—"

"Alex talked," Kat boldly stated. "He told everyone that the reason he called off the wedding was because you are a cold fish, and that a man couldn't light a spark inside you with a smithy's furnace."

Mari sucked in a breath. Hurt was a cold spear to her heart. "Alex said that?"

"He told his friends on the baseball team and word got around. He blamed it on the McBride blood and the curse, so now everyone thinks I'm as frigid as you are."

Frigid? Frigid!

"Why did you have to go and tell him about the curse, Mari? You don't even believe in it."

Frigid. Anger churned like milk into butter. Why,

that sorry sack of wet sand! Just because she refused to anticipate their wedding vows, Alex had no right to spread such vicious gossip about her. Gossip that her younger sister obviously believed.

Of course, her sister believed anything.

Bitterness stung Mari's tongue as she said, "I didn't tell Alexander about the curse, Kat. *You* did. You told him the night of the Harvest Ball last fall when you got into the men's punch."

"I don't remember that."

"Of course not. You were drunk as a hoedown fiddler!"

"Nevertheless," Kat continued, "I wouldn't be in this predicament if not for you, so don't stand there acting all high-and-mighty on me. You may not want a husband, Miss High-and-Mighty Businesswoman, but I do. I want to be married and have a home and children. I don't dream about running my own chocolate shop like you or teaching children how to read and write and do sums like Emma. I'm a woman, and I enjoy the way a man can make me feel. I won't feel guilty because I'm not a dried-up old prune."

Like you. The unspoken words hung suspended in the air between them and wounded like an arrow. Mari reacted to the pain. "No, you should feel guilty because you're acting like a harlot. I'm ashamed of you, Kat."

This time, Kat was the one who gasped.

"How far have you allowed this to go?" Mari pressed on. "Have you given that scoundrel your virginity?"

Katrina burst into tears, and Mari's stomach sank to her knees. "Rory is not a scoundrel!"

Oh, no.

"He's a talented actor who will be famous someday.

I love him and he loves me and we're going to be married. Soon. You just wait and see, Mari McBride. I'm going to be so happy. I'll have a wonderful husband and wonderful children and a wonderful home and a wonderful life and you can just eat your words like that precious chocolate you sell."

Beyond the roaring in her ears, Mari detected the sound of a door opening, and she glanced over to see Luke Garrett and Rory Kelly standing in the doorway. In the thrall of her tirade, Kat remained oblivious to the fact they were no longer alone.

"You're ashamed of me?" she continued. "Well, I'm ashamed of you. You are a self-righteous, bitter old spinster, and you and your cold lonely heart deserve a cold lonely bed. Alexander Simpson did himself a favor by leaving you at the altar!"

The fact that her sister had said those ugly things was bad enough, but knowing the two men witnessed it made Mari's humiliation complete. She wanted to slink away and cry. Instead, she lifted her chin, squared her shoulders and said, "That's it, Kat. I'm done trying to protect you. If this is what you want…well…best of luck to you."

"Luck?" Kat snapped as Mari turned to walk away. "What do you mean by that? You're talking about the curse, aren't you?"

Attempting to depart with dignity, Mari nodded toward the men, doing her best to ignore the sympathetic look in the outlaw's eyes as Kat called, "Well, let me tell you this, Mari McBride. Rory and I will beat the bad luck. Our love is strong and true, just like Roslin said it needed to be. You just watch and see, Mari. You watch and see."

Mari knew she should keep her mouth shut and

make her exit, but humiliation and hurt loosened her tongue. At the stage curtain, she paused and glanced back over her shoulder. "No, Kat. Your *love* is nothing more than lust that will burn itself out in a flash. I'm the intuitive one, remember. That's what I see of your precious *love*. Dead, cold ashes."

CHAPTER THREE

"YOU BASTARD," Luke muttered to Rory when Mari McBride's proud, sad eyes shifted away and she hurried for the exit. "You must get a big charge out of causing women pain."

"You're the one making me do this," Rory murmured back.

"Damn straight. You have responsibilities, and by God, I'm going to see that you live up to them."

The moment Mari McBride disappeared from sight, Kat McBride burst into tears, ran toward Rory and threw herself into his arms. Rory held the young woman tight, offering comfort. He stared over at Luke, his expression wordlessly asking *What else can I do?*

Luke's fingers itched to form a fist and pop him in the face.

Kat sobbed against Rory's shirt. "She hates me. My sister hates me. She said she's ashamed of me."

"Shh, now, love."

Luke glared at Rory.

"This is awful. It's the worst thing. I wonder if she'll tell. I don't want her to tell. Papa will…oh, Rory. I said terrible things to her. I didn't mean it. Truly I didn't. I love Mari. She's my *sister.* But she doesn't understand. I love you, too."

Luke no longer wanted to punch Rory in the face, he wanted to pull his gun and shoot him. That poor girl. She didn't deserve Rory's kind of grief. Still, a sharp, clean cut healed the fastest.

"The train leaves in half an hour," he said to Rory. "Get it done."

Rory nodded and, shifting his hands on Kat's shoulders, tenderly pushed her away. She lifted an anguished face toward him. He sighed and thumbed a tear off her cheek. "You are so beautiful."

"I love my family, Rory, but I want to be with you."

"I want to be with you, too."

"For God's sake, Rory," Luke said.

The actor scowled at Luke, then led Kat to a chair placed near the chaise. "Please have a seat," he asked gently. "There's a few things I need to say."

Luke checked his pocket watch. Impatient as he was to be off, he recognized that Rory needed to let the girl down as gently as possible. Luke would give him five minutes but no more.

Ever one to appreciate setting of a scene, always ready to play to an audience, Rory shrugged into his jacket, then shot his cuffs. He clasped his hands behind his back and leveled a solemn stare upon the obviously anxious young woman. "You are a wonderful woman, Kat. You're bright, you're beautiful, you're entertaining. You make me...happy." He paused, frowned thoughtfully, then repeated, "Happy."

Kat blinked watery eyes. "You make me happy, too, Rory."

He cleared his throat. "This last month has been, well, it's been wonderful. I love knowing you're in the audience when I perform. You make me better, Kat, in many ways."

Luke folded his arms and scowled. Rory had always had a silver tongue with women, so he probably knew what he was doing. However, Luke thought he should get on to the leaving part.

"You make me a more honest man," he said, beginning to pace back and forth across the dull oak floorboards of the stage's back space.

Oh, brother.

Rory picked up a prop, a silver-knobbed cane, and tapped it against the floor as he walked. "You make me a more sensitive man."

Luke folded his arms and took a couple steps back so he could lean against the doorjamb. What a load of sheep dung.

"You make me more a more generous man." Rory twirled the cane in a slow, showy circle.

Luke couldn't smother his snort at that. The one thing Rory didn't need was more generosity where the ladies were concerned.

"My dear Kat, being with you makes me the man I've always wanted to be." Glancing at Luke, he added, "It's true."

"Doesn't matter."

"Rory?" Kat asked. "What is this all about?"

Rory tapped the cane against the floorboard, once, twice, three times. "I'm afraid I must…I need to…" He stopped, dropped his chin to his chest and closed his eyes. "It's all so difficult."

"Two more minutes," Luke warned.

Kat shifted anxiously in her seat. "Rory, you're making me nervous."

"I'm rather nervous myself," he murmured. "The idea of returning…" His voice trailed off.

"Returning?" Kat's eyes rounded. "Returning where?

You're not leaving Fort Worth, are you? You're not leaving me?"

Rory hesitated, fixed on the uneasy young woman. Following a long moment of silence, he slowly began to speak. "My situation has grown complicated, love. I am pursued by forces difficult to resist."

Kat turned to Luke. "Him? Rory, are you tangled up with outlaws?"

Rory's mouth twisted. "Am I tangled up with outlaws?" he repeated, walking toward Luke, tapping the cane against the floor as he approached. "Now there's a question. What does the infamous outlaw Luke Garrett want with the likes of me?"

Noting the faint edge in Rory's voice, Luke went on guard. He straightened, flexed his fingers, watched the other man closely, paying special attention to the cane, a potential weapon. Not that he honestly believed Rory would resort to violence. That wasn't his way. He'd lie, sneak, cheat and steal, but unless he'd changed dramatically in recent months, he avoided physical confrontation like the plague.

"The answer is simple, my lovely Kat." Rory swung the cane slowly back and forth. "Luke Garrett wants to send me…"

Just being cautious, Luke reached to grab the end of the cane. Before he had a grip on the stick, Rory let go and the cane dropped to the ground. Luke bent to pick it up.

He never saw the whiskey bottle until it crashed against his head.

"Rory!" Kat squealed.

Magician's sleight-of-hand, Luke thought as his world went fuzzy and he dropped to his knees. *I should have remembered.*

As if through a mist, he saw the young woman shove to her feet, her elbow brushing one of the candlesticks as she rose and rushed toward him. The burning candle teetered, fell to the ground, then rolled beneath the chaise. Luke tried to warn her and Rory, but his mouth didn't seem to want to work.

Everything went black.

MARI BLENDED sugar and cocoa and cream for a living. She'd developed her own personal recipes for her chocolates' cream fillings, using her Aunt Claire's special flavoring, Magic, in many of them. She considered candy-making part science, part art. Baking oatmeal cookies was pure comfort.

After the scene with Kat, she'd fled the Texas Spring Palace for her shop. There she fired up her oven, pulled out the butter, sugar and flour, and went to work. Blending the thick, heavy cookie dough with her favorite wooden spoon was just the physical work she needed.

"Frigid," she grumbled. "The next time I see Alexander Simpson I'll teach him a whole new definition of the Curse of Clan McBride. Spreading such nonsense to his friends. How dare he!"

It hurt. It hurt to know that she was being talked about in such a personal manner. It hurt to know that the good reputation she'd worked so hard to establish was being tarnished by ugly accusations. It hurt that the man she'd loved and intended to spend her life with, raise a family with, would do such a thing. It hurt that her sister would believe him.

"She's supposed to be on my side. She's supposed to stand up for me. That's what family does. That's what the McBrides do."

That's what the McBrides used to do. Ever since

Casey's death, it seemed as if the family was falling apart. Emma was difficult to reach. Even tonight, dressed in yellow and out in public and obviously making an effort, grief wrapped Emma like a shroud and insulated her, isolated her, from her loved ones.

Mari missed her.

"Kat's another story," Mari muttered, giving her wooden spoon a whack against the side of the bowl. At the moment, she'd like to see her youngest sister take an extended trip somewhere far away. She could go visit their cousins, the Rosses, in Scotland. She could stay through the winter, a bitter cold Highland winter. "Maybe that would cool her lust-fevered blood."

Thinking along those lines, Kat would probably recommend Mari head for the Sahara Desert.

"I don't need a desert sun to warm me up." Hadn't her blood run plenty hot this very night while dancing with Luke Garrett?

Luke Garrett. She wondered how he and Rory Kelly had crossed paths in the past. Something to do with money, she'd bet. A robbery? One of those legendary high-stakes poker games they have down in San Antonio? Maybe Rory once worked for Luke. She couldn't imagine it being the other way around.

If not money, then a woman. It wasn't difficult to imagine a woman deserting Rory for the likes of Luke. Maybe she shouldn't have left Kat alone with the two men. She'd jump from the frying pan into the fire.

Mari wondered what it'd be like to play with that kind of fire. She wondered if Luke Garrett would tell all his outlaw friends that she was a cold fish. She wondered if he and all his outlaw friends had already heard that about her. Could she be as infamous in her own way as Luke Garrett was in his?

"How humiliating."

Eyeing the cookie dough in her bowl, Mari imagined hearing the tinkle of her door chimes. She'd glance up to see Alexander Simpson walk into her shop, a penitent look on his face. She'd pick up the bowl—no, just scoop up a big wad of dough—and send it flying. It'd splat against his face in gooey, gummy wads. He'd drop to his knees and beg her forgiveness. He'd tell her—

The fantasy dissolved when a thundering explosion rattled her shop windows. "What…?" she murmured, reaching for a damp towel to wipe her hands as she moved from behind her worktable, pausing just long enough to turn off her oven before hurrying to the front of her shop. Outside, alarm filled the faces of the people spilling into the street and the fading light of evening and rushing south.

South? What could have exploded to the south? Her first thought had been the meatpacking plant, but that was on the north end of town.

She smelled burning wood the moment she stepped outside. Fire bells clanged their way down Main Street and, hearing them, Mari experienced her first glimmer of true fear. The Texas Spring Palace stood on the south end of town.

She joined the flood of people making their way down the street and almost against her will, tuned into the conversations taking place around her.

Train wreck…boiler explosion…whorehouse in Hell's Half Acre. The Palace. The Spring Palace. Gotta be the Texas Spring Palace.

A cowboy exited the dry-goods store saying, "Heard they expected a big crowd there tonight. Hope some folks got out of there alive."

Mari heart shot up to lodge in her throat as she broke into a run. *No. No. No. My family. Oh, God. Please.*

It took forever to reach the end of the street, and yet, she arrived far too soon. Bracing herself, she looked left. Her blood ran cold and terror froze her footsteps.

Fire engulfed the Texas Spring Palace. Black smoke billowed into the sky. Flames danced everywhere she looked. The roof of the west wing collapsed even as the east wing's walls disappeared behind a wall of red and yellow fire. Fingers of flame clawed across the huge dome. The northwest cupola teetered, then fell with a groan.

It was the sounds that finally penetrated Mari's horror. The cracks and crashes, the clanging of fire bells. The screams. Oh, God, the screams.

As she watched, a woman dropped a child from a second-story window into willing arms waiting below. Then, she made the leap herself.

The huge crowd outside the building gave her hope. The Spring Palace had many exits, something her architect father had noted with approval. People had escaped. Surely her family had escaped.

Please, God, let my family have escaped.

How could she know? The scene was chaotic. People rushed away from the building, toward the building, from one side to the other. Husbands called for wives, mothers for children. Children cried for their mommies and daddies and broke Mari's heart.

She stopped beside a boy of five or six who sat sobbing on the ground. He had sandy hair and big, teary brown eyes and a trembling mouth that revealed two missing front teeth. He wore a cute little fringed leather jacket with the Lone Star flag embroidered across the back. Kneeling beside him, she asked, "Can I help you?"

"I can't find Pa."

"Were you inside the Spring Palace?"

"Uh-huh. We was in the farmin' section lookin' at plows and there was a big boom and Pa hauled me out but then he stopped to help somebody and I don't know what happened. He was right there and then he was gone. I'm scared, lady."

"I know, honey. What's your name?"

"Billy. Billy Waddell."

"Billy is a good name. One of my brothers is named Billy. He is ten years old and I'm looking for him. How about you and I look together?"

"Okay," he replied, sniffing as he climbed to his feet.

"Let's get you up where you can see." Mari scooped him up into her arms. "What does your father look like?"

"He's big and he has black hair."

"What was he wearing tonight?"

"His good boots."

Obviously, she needed to take a different tack. Chances were, given the chance, Billy's father would spy him before Billy spied his father. She'd find a prominent spot and wait and…

"Wait. That's it." She smiled as a childhood memory provided plan. "When I was young like you, my papa told me and my sisters that if we ever became separated in a crowd, we should look for the tallest thing around and go stand by it. Has your papa ever told you anything like that?"

"No."

"Let's try it for a bit, anyway, shall we?" While she'd continually scanned the area for familiar faces, now she shifted her attention to locating a tall, safely located landmark. There, the flagpoles in the park across the street from the Spring Palace. If members of the McBride family remembered Trace McBride's instructions, that's where they'd go. "In fact, I have an idea. You keep a sharp eye out for your daddy, now."

Mari threaded her way through the panicked crowd toward the park. She was halfway there when, with a loud crackle and roar, the dome of the Texas Spring Palace collapsed. Little Billy Waddle began to cry. "I want my daddy."

"I know just how you feel."

Anxiously, she scanned the park area. Of the seven other members of her family in attendance at the Texas Spring Palace tonight, surely someone recalled Papa's instructions. Surely, someone would be there. Someone would be...

"Mama!"

Jenny McBride whirled around at the sound of her daughter's voice. Joy lit her face as she spread her arms wide. "Mari! Thank God."

Tears spilled from both women's eyes as they embraced. "What about the others, Mama? Where are the others?"

"Isn't Billy with you?"

"No."

"Oh." Jenny drew back, a wobble in both her voice and her forced smile. "Emma took Tom and Bobby home. Your papa is looking for you and Billy and Kat. I'm sure he'll arrive with them in tow any moment. And who is this handsome fellow?"

Kat and Billy. Mari's troubled focus shifted toward the burning building. She swallowed hard, then summoned a casual tone to say, "This is Billy Waddell. He got separated from his father in the crowd, and he's going to wait with us until his papa finds him." To the boy, she said, "Once when my brothers were younger they stole a lady's petticoat off the clothesline and ran it up the flagpole outside the county courthouse. Everyone in town saw it. I'll bet if we send your jacket up this one, your papa will find you real quick."

"That's a wonderful idea," Jenny agreed as a shifting wind brought a cloud of gray smoke billowing over them. They coughed, and their eyes stung. They shifted position as little Billy said, "That stinks like the dump."

The smell was bitter and acrid and awful—the aroma of destruction. Mari thought she'd remember this stench all her life.

The pulley on the flagpole squeaked as Jenny lowered the Lone Star banner while Mari helped the boy take off his jacket. Jenny produced a pair of safety pins from the hem of her skirt, frowned and said, "I think we'll need another. Hand me one of yours."

A seamstress, Jenny had taught her girls always to be prepared. Mari turned up the hem of her dress and removed one of her extra pins.

They secured the distinctive jacket through the grommets in the Lone Star flag and ran both objects up the pole. To give him a better view of the crowd, they lifted Billy to sit at one corner of the pole's square granite base. While he watched for his father, Jenny and Mari leaned against the base and continued their own vigil. "What happened, Mama?" Mari asked. "What started the fire?"

"I don't know. Your father and I were dancing when the band director abruptly halted the music and announced the building was being evacuated due to a fire in the southeast wing.

The southeast wing? Mari's heart climbed to her throat. *Oh, God.*

"There was a stir," Jenny continued, "a few panicky people, but for the most part, the crowd moved in an orderly manner. I was in a terror over you children, of course. The boys were supposed to be in the next room, the Texas History exhibit, but I knew better than to believe they'd actually be where they said they'd be. We had headed that way when Emma found us and told us she'd seen the two younger boys run outside. That's when the boiler exploded and knocked us all to the ground. What about you, Mari? Where were you?"

"I'd left," Mari replied. "I was at the store making a batch of cookies when I heard the explosion."

"Cookies? You left a dress ball early to go make cookies? Oh, dear." Jenny touched her daughter's arm. "What happened, honey? Did that rat-bounder Alexander Simpson say something to you? I saw him here tonight. You know, I do believe his hairline is beginning to recede."

Mari offered a weak smile. Jenny McBride's mother antenna quivered even in the middle of a crisis. "Alex Simpson isn't worth the cost of cookie dough, Mama. Don't fret, I…oh, look. I'll bet that is Billy's—"

"Daddy!" the little boy cried.

The reunion of father and son brought tears to both McBride women's eyes. Billy's grateful father, a butcher, promised them free beef for the rest of their lives. Watching the two depart, Jenny sighed and said, "It seems just yesterday my Billy was that age."

Hearing the tremble in her mother's voice, Mari reached out and grasped her hand.

Around the Texas Spring Palace, chaos continued to reign. Those fighting the raging flames had abandoned the building and instead, worked to prevent the fire from spreading to nearby structures. Further rescue attempts of any person trapped inside apparently had been abandoned. "Did the boys say where they last saw Billy?" Mari asked.

"Tommy said he followed you out of the ballroom when you left with Luke Garrett."

"Billy followed me?" Mari's mind raced back over the scene her young, impressionable brother might have witnessed. *Oh, Kat. If Billy saw what I saw....*

"I imagine he was worried about you. He's protective of his big sisters, and you were with a known outlaw. I haven't a clue where Kat ran off to. What part of the building were you in?"

The southeast wing. Where the fire started. Oh, God. "I was in the theater, but that was long before the fire started. I never saw Billy. I'll bet something else distracted him and he went off somewhere else entirely."

Or else, he stayed to watch Kat after Mari fled the building. Maybe he's with Kat even now. "Maybe he went home. Maybe he and Kat are waiting at for us at Willow Hill."

"I pray that's so. Emma promised to send Tom to tell me the minute anyone comes home."

Tension churned in Mari's stomach. She wanted to snarl at the bystanders nearby who oohed and aahed with excitement. One barrel-bellied cowboy actually said it'd be something to see a burning body dash from the inferno. "What's wrong with people?" she murmured.

Her mother squeezed her hand in silent agreement.

Then a voice resonant with joy called out from the crowd. "Maribeth!"

Seconds later, she was wrapped in Trace McBride's strong embrace. "My baby, baby, baby," he murmured into her hair. The tremor in his voice made her want to weep.

Abruptly, he stepped back, surveying her from head to toe. "You're all right. You weren't hurt."

"I'm fine, Papa." He, however, looked as if he'd aged a dozen years in the past two hours. The lines feathering from around his eyes had deepened, and his salt-and-pepper hair appeared heavier on salt. He looked weary and worried and wounded.

Almost as if he knew something. Something bad.

Oh, God.

Jenny touched her husband's sleeve. "Trace? Kat and Billy?"

Distress flashed across his face. "No sign. No one has seen them. It's a madhouse, though, and locating anyone is just a matter of chance. I had hoped to find everyone here." To Mari, he said, "You remembered my rule about getting lost in a crowd."

"I did."

"The younger boys remembered," he continued. "Billy should. Kat, too. I could see Billy getting caught up in the excitement of the fire and not thinking how worried we'd be, but Katrina should know better. She should know better, and she should remember and she should be here right now."

Mari didn't know what to say to her father. Should she tell him about seeing Kat with Rory? How could she not? "Papa, I—"

"Papa! Mama!" came a welcome, though teary, voice. "I hoped you'd be here."

Billy. Joy and relief filled Mari's heart as her mother and father rushed forward and she turned to see…a most unexpected sight.

Luke Garrett carried her brother in his arms. Though scuffed and dirty with red-rimmed eyes, Billy appeared to be in good health. Luke had a bloody gash on his cheek and a bruise on his temple. His smile was grim, the light in his eyes flat. He handed Billy over to her mother, then stepped back while her parents made a fuss over their son.

Watching him, Mari's blood ran cold. She knew. *No. Please, God. No.*

Kat.

Mari's knees went weak and her head started to spin. She leaned back against the flagpole base for support.

Having greeted his son, Trace turned to Luke Garrett. "Where did you find him?"

"He found me." Then Luke stunned them all by adding, "Mr. McBride, your son saved my life. I am in his debt."

Now standing at his mother's side, Billy buried his head in her skirts and started to sob. The sound brought a lump to Mari's throat and triggered tears of her own.

Roughly, Trace demanded, "What happened?"

Luke looked briefly at Mari and she knew from the brief exchange that they'd hear a censored version of events. "I'd met with an accident and as the fire spread, I lay unconscious in an out-of-the-way place. After his attempts to rouse me proved unsuccessful, Billy ran for help."

Trace placed two fingers under his son's chin and tilted his face upward. In a voice brimming with emotion, he said, "I'm proud of you, son."

Billy jerked away and closed his eyes. "No, Pa. I'm bad. I'm a sorry, awful person!"

Trace and Jenny shared a baffled glance. Mari's stomach took a nauseous roll. *Kat.*

Jenny knelt before her son. "What's wrong, Billy? Tell us."

"Mrs. McBride," Luke began. "I don't think—"

Billy interrupted with a tormented torrent of words. "The man hit him with a whiskey bottle and Kat screamed and she thought he was dead and she bumped the table and the candle fell but she didn't see. I know she didn't see. The man made her go behind the curtain and I ran up to the stage but by the time I got there it was on fire. It was on fire, Mama, and I was afraid to go get her, to tell her it was burning. I was *afraid*." His voice broke on a sob. "It was smoking and crackling and burning and I was so scared. I'm sorry. I'm so sorry. It's my fault. It's my fault!"

Jenny cried out softly like an animal in pain. Trace's face bleached white. "Ka—" His voice cracked. He cleared his throat, then tried again. "Katrina?"

Luke said, "I don't know, Mr. McBride. I didn't see them leave. It's possible they found an exit."

"They?" Jenny repeated. "Who's they?"

"That actor," Mari said, in doing so admitting her involvement. "Kat met that actor in the theater. I followed her and she and I had…words."

After a moment's silence, Jenny murmured, "The cookies."

Her heart breaking, Mari took a step toward her father. He appeared as if he'd taken a mortal blow. "The fire began in that wing. Kat." He reached for Mari's hand. Squeezed it hard. "Kat started the fire. Kat started the fire and no one's seen her since."

"I saw it too, Mr. McBride," Luke said. "It definitely was an accident."

Mari felt her father shudder, then he turned a stricken look toward his wife. "I had a feeling, Treasure. I've had this goddamn feeling for months!"

In the face of her husband's despair, Jenny seemed to draw upon some inner strength. Her spine straightened, her shoulders squared. She rose to her feet and looked her husband straight in the eyes. "Leave it be, McBride. It's too early to assume the worst."

"If she's not hurt, then where is she?"

Billy began sobbing anew, and Mari moved to take him into her arms to offer both of them comfort. "Maybe she knows about knocking over the candle and she's afraid to come home, afraid to face us."

"No!" Billy cried. "She didn't know, I tell you. It was an accident and it rolled under the chair and she didn't even know! She didn't come out. I asked that man if there was another door and he said no. She didn't come out!"

"What man?" Trace snapped.

Luke responded. "The fella Billy found to haul me out of the theater. A guy named Wagner. He knows the building and said that stage door was the only back door out of the theater. That doesn't mean they didn't leave another way."

"But I didn't see them. I'd have seen them. Kat didn't come."

"Stop it." Jenny pinned them each in turn with a fierce, determined look, then took charge. "I'll have no more negative talk. Now, I think we can conclude that had Kat remembered her father's edict regarding crowds and tall landmarks, she'd have been here by now. Therefore, Mari, I want you to take your brother home. I'm sure your father wishes to remain at the site and assist in the…um…efforts. I'll stay with him."

Trace shook his head. "Jenny, you should go home, too."

"I'm staying," she stated flatly. "Mari, if your sister arrives at Willow Hill, one of you come down and let's do like we did for Mr. Waddell. Run something of Kat's up this flagpole. Her yellow shawl, I think. That's bright. We'll spot it."

She turned to Luke and offered him her hand. "Thank you for bringing my son to us, Mr. Garrett. I'm glad he was able to be of assistance to you. Perhaps when this is all over, you could come to tea and share more of the details with us."

"Certainly, Mrs. McBride. Whatever you like."

Luke Garrett, however, wasn't ready to be dismissed. He glanced at Mari once more, then said, "Considering this evening's events, you should know that I intend to participate in a search for your daughter and Rory."

"Thank you, Garrett." Trace cleared his throat gruffly. "All hands are appreciated at a time like this."

Mari sensed more to his offer than gratitude for Billy's assistance, and under the circumstances, she thought she should call him on it. "Who is he to you, Luke?"

He shoved his hands into his pockets and looked away for just a moment. Then, staring her straight in the eye, he said, "His real name is Callahan. Rory Callahan is my half brother."

Unsurprised, Mari nodded once. "Find them."

"I will."

At Willow Hill, Mari, Emma, and their three younger brothers gathered on the front porch in the gathering darkness, their mood quiet and subdued. Billy sat off by himself, his back turned toward the driveway. Mari tried to keep the other boys entertained with a game of cards, but in a rare occurrence, no one cared about competition.

A little after ten, the youngest McBride, seven-year-old Bobby, fell off to sleep and Emma carried him upstairs to bed. Nine-year-old Tommy made it until just after midnight. Billy was still awake at half past three when the McBride family carriage rattled slowly up the hill.

Light from a three-quarter moon cast a ghostly silver light across the scene, and though her parents' faces remained in shadow, the very stillness of their bodies foretold the news they bore.

Simultaneously, Emma and Mari reached for each other's hand. Without uttering a sound, Billy McBride leaped up and ran inside, the front screen door shutting with a bang behind him.

Their expressions ravaged, their cheeks tear-streaked, Trace and Jenny McBride lifted leaden feet to climb the steps of their home and face their two eldest children.

Beside Mari, Emma swayed. "Mama?"

Jenny looked at them, and tears spilled from reddened eyes. She slowly shook her head.

"No-o-o-o." Emma melted into her mother's arms and the two women collapsed into quiet weeping.

Mari stared up at her father, the strongest man she'd ever known. Her hero. Her champion. Her daddy. "Your Katie-cat?"

Broken, Trace McBride pulled her into his arms and wept against her hair. "I'm afraid she's gone, Mari. God help us, but I'm afraid that damned explosion took our Katie-cat away."

CHAPTER FOUR

Three months later

BACK IN THE DAY, Luke's grandfather referred to Texas's August heat as sick-dog weather, meaning the way a sick dog's nose was hot and dry instead of cold and wet like usual. Luke recalled afternoons when his father would stroll onto the front porch of the ranch house, sipping on a steaming cup of coffee. He'd stare out over his land, where the only movement to be seen was the ripple of heat rising from brittle brown grass, and drawl, "It's hot enough to loosen the bristles on a wild hog." Then he'd sip his coffee, throw his wife a wink, and walk out into the blazing heat to tend a horse or fix a fence.

Buck Garrett had thrived on summertime in Texas. He'd died one bleak and bitter February morn when a blizzard blew in off the West Texas plains and collapsed the roof of the line shack where he slept. From that day forward, Luke detested cold weather.

Of course, that didn't mean he liked sweltering in his bed trying to get some shut-eye following a surveillance operation that had lasted all night.

He rolled onto his back and scowled up at the ceiling fan that did little more than stir hot stagnant air. He was a Texan born and bred and proud of it, but on a day like this, livin' in Alaska sounded like a damned fine idea. *Grandpa would have me hanged as a traitor for such a thought.*

Luke's mouth twisted in a rueful grin. Someday, somebody would invent a machine that blew winter-cold air into a summer-hot room. When that arrived, living in Texas would be like living in paradise. But in the meantime, he didn't figure there could be a more appropriate name for the place where he currently lived than Hell's Half Acre.

Giving up on getting any sleep, he rolled from the bed and stepped naked across the room toward the second-story window, hoping to catch a little breeze. Bracing his hands on the windowsill, he leaned out, looked up the street, then down.

"Well…well…well," he murmured. Now there was an unusual sight. The lovely Miss Mari McBride was paying a visit to the Acre.

She wore a demure dress in a goldenrod print and carried a matching parasol and small handbag made of straw. She walked along the sidewalk with a purposeful sashay that drew a man's eye, giving her parasol a twirl every third or fourth step. Luke wondered what business brought her down to the Acre.

From what he'd heard, it had been a bad summer for the McBride family. Kat McBride's death had hit them all hard. Luke hadn't seen Mari or her sister Emma since the fire, but he'd caught sight of the boys a time or two. The towheaded pullets seemed to have lost their spirit.

Their father didn't look any better. Trace McBride appeared to have aged a lifetime since his daughter's death, and they said his wife spent a good share of each day tending to the young woman's grave.

Not that there was a body buried beneath the marker. Against his will, Luke's thoughts returned to that awful night. Digging through the smoldering rubble. Finding that damned doll. At first glance, he'd thought it was a child. The sights, sounds and smells would haunt his nightmares for years to come. As would memories of that last encounter with his brother.

Rory. Charming, crafty, cunning, Rory. The son of a bitch. Luke would miss him the rest of his life.

He watched as Mari McBride stopped a whore on the street and struck up a conversation. Most respectable women in town wouldn't dream of speaking with a light-skirt, but the McBride women were different. Mari's mother had been sewing costumes for the ladies of the Acre for years. The soiled doves in town had come out in force for Kat McBride's funeral.

The street girl lifted her arm and pointed toward the window where Luke stood. Mari turned her head and their eyes met and held. Then her face broke out in a brilliant, though puzzling, smile.

Me? Why in the world would she be shooting a smile like that toward me?

Her focus slipped, skimmed over his bare chest, and she visibly hesitated. Then, after giving those delicate shoulders a little shrug, she spoke again with the sporting girl, stepped down from the sidewalk and started across the street. Toward his saloon. *She's coming to see me.*

Luke moved away from the window and tried to deduce what the candy maker might want with him. However, since he had been working for a thirty-six-hour stretch without sleep, his mind processed sluggishly. Basically. *I'm naked. She's beautiful. Wonder if she'd...*

He startled as his door opened and Mattie Porter, the

manager of the Blue Goose Saloon, poked her head inside. Her eyes shifted from the empty bed to where he stood beside the burled oak wardrobe and amusement sparked in her face. "Oh, I see you're already up."

Ignoring the glare he shot her before turning to face the wardrobe, she continued, "There's a lady downstairs wanting to speak with you. A real one. Trace McBride's girl. Must be something important. She hasn't shown her face in the Acre in quite some time."

Luke grabbed a pair of pants. "Tell her I'll be right down."

"All right."

Hearing no sounds to indicate her departure, Luke glanced over his shoulder and arched a brow.

"Just admiring the sights," Mattie explained. "Now that I'm retired, I don't get to see such pretty things very often. Come to think of it, I seldom saw an ass as fine as yours when I was working. Might not have retired early if fellas like you came lookin' for my services."

"Please, Mattie, you're embarrassing me."

The madam snorted a laugh, then left, chuckling gaily as she made her way downstairs. Luke quickly dressed and followed her.

The Blue Goose was typical of most saloons in the Acre. An oil painting of a well-endowed miss dressed only in gossamer scarves hung over a polished, ornately carved bar. A piano sat against the opposite wall. Spittoons graced every corner and sawdust blanketed the floor. Mari McBride sat at a round card table near the bar sipping a lemonade. Luke signaled the barkeep for a whiskey and joined her. "Good morning, Mari McBride."

"Yes, it's a glorious morning, isn't it?"

Her smile could have lit up a crypt, and her eyes

sparkled like sunlight on the Caribbean Sea. She beamed, she bubbled, she blushed. He halfway expected her to break into song.

Luke grew suspicious. He could think of only one thing that would both have this effect on her and bring her here to him, and by God, that was impossible. Abandoning social niceties, he demanded, "What is it?"

"They're alive."

Anger flared like a matchstick. If some joker thought to prey upon this poor family's grief, he would by God make him pay. They'd been through enough. "Mari, is someone trying to get money out of you?"

"No, no. That's not it." She flipped open her handbag and withdrew an envelope. "This arrived in the mail at Willow Hill. It's from an old friend of mine whose family moved to San Antonio. Read it."

Skeptical, Luke took the envelope and removed the folded pages inside.

"You needn't read it all, actually. It's on the second page. The third paragraph." She pointed out the passage.

I thought of the McBride Menaces last week when a gentleman brought a necklace into my father's store for an appraisal. It looked exactly like the ones the three of you wore—a large emerald set in an ornate gold filigree pendant. The man said it was a family heirloom, and that he and his wife feared they might need to sell it if their situation failed to improve.

"See?" she said. "That's Kat's necklace, and the man is Rory Callahan. They didn't die in the fire. They ran off and got married."

No. They absolutely had not. Luke lowered the letter. "Mari, I'm sorry to say you're reading a lot into very little. All this says is that someone has a necklace similar to yours."

"To Kat's. Hers is the emerald. Look." She reached past her neckline and pulled out a necklace.

Luke leaned forward, caught a whiff of rose water as he reached for the pendant. The metal was warm from having nestled between her breasts. For a moment, Luke lost his train of thought.

"Our necklaces are a trio, and they're unique. If my friend saw a necklace like one of ours, it *was* one of ours. It was Kat's. She's alive. I've always felt it in my heart. I never believed she was gone."

"Your father found her body."

Mari shook her head. "No, he didn't. He found a body part, a woman's leg wearing a dancing slipper like Kat's. Seven women are on the list of those missing following the Spring Palace fire. It's more believable that one of those women had the same shoes as Kat than that another woman is running around Texas with a necklace like hers."

Luke shook his head. "I was there that night. I saw. Neither your father nor your mother wanted to believe they'd found proof of your sister's death, but the facts convinced them."

"I know, I know." Mari waved a dismissive hand. "He found someone who saw her and Rory after they left the theater, and he concluded she was near the boiler when it blew. But my father is wrong, thank God. This letter proves that what I've known in my heart all along is true. My sister didn't die that night. She ran off with a scoundrel instead."

Luke wondered if her argument could possibly have any validity. He could accept the notion that Rory ran off with the girl. He could even believe that Mari had her facts straight regarding the uniqueness of the necklace. Yet, knowing the close-knit reputation the McBride family enjoyed in Fort Worth, he could not believe that the young woman who rescued him from Wilhemina Peters would allow her family to mourn her death in error.

Luke leaned back in his chair. "If that's so, then why hasn't she contacted you?"

"I don't know," Mari said with a frown. "That concerns me. It's part of why I've come to you today. Tell me about your brother, Luke. Do you know of a reason he wouldn't want my sister contacting her family to assure us that she's safe?"

Off the top of his head, Luke could think of ten thousand reasons. Make that ten thousand four hundred fifty-two reasons. "The night of the fire was the first time I'd seen Rory in over three years. I didn't know him well."

"Really? Why?"

Now there was a question that could take weeks to answer. "We were…different."

After waiting in vain a few moments for him to elaborate, she said, "But you know he's a scoundrel."

"He was."

"He *is*. He's alive and he was in San Antonio four weeks ago attempting to sell my sister's necklace."

The glint of determination shining in the ocean of her eyes told Luke not to waste his breath trying to convince her she'd wrongly interpreted the situation. Besides, what if she was right? What if the necklace referred to in the letter was, in fact, Kat McBride's? What if the couple had left the building before the explosion? What if her sister and his villainous brother were still alive?

I guess I need to find out the truth.

"You're certain of this."

"I am."

"If you're wrong, you could be setting yourself up for a terrible disappointment."

"I realize that. It's why I must confirm my suspicions before I say anything to my family. Well, except for Emma. I already showed her the letter."

"Oh? And what was your sister's reaction?"

A shadow drifted across Mari's eyes. "What you must understand about Emma is that widowhood has changed her view of the world."

"She thinks you're wrong."

"She can't see past her grief."

And Mari McBride didn't want to accept it. Luke drummed his fingers on the table and considered the beauty seated across from him. Maybe it was the distracting lack of sleep, or more likely, the scarcity of female companionship in his life of late, but damn, she sparked his powder.

He cleared his throat. "So, you came to me today for what purpose? You want me to search for them?"

"Oh, no, thank you. I'm doing that myself. I leave for San Antonio this afternoon. As I said, I want you to tell me about your brother, any clues you can provide that might assist me in my search."

"Wait a minute." Luke sat up straight in his chair. Ever since the fire, he'd kept his ear to the ground where the McBride family was concerned. He knew damned well that her parents had taken their boys to visit relatives in Britain with the hope of distracting young Billy from his guilt-fed grief. "*You're* leaving for San Antone? Is your uncle taking you?"

"Uncle Tye? No. I don't plan on telling them this

news. They're mourning Kat as much as the rest of the family."

"Who's going with you? Your sister?"

"No." She frowned. "Emma cannot leave Fort Worth at this time due to a professional commitment. I'm going alone, sir. Not that it's any of your concern."

"Alone? You can't travel alone. It's not safe."

"Why?"

"Because you're a woman!"

"That's ridiculous. Women travel by themselves all the time. My grandmother travels all over the world by herself, and she's never encountered serious trouble."

"Your grandmother's not young and beautiful."

"Monique is extraordinary, I'll have you know," Mari said, a softening in her eyes showing that she'd noted his backhanded compliment. Then she lifted her chin. "Besides, I can take care of myself."

Luke snorted. "It's a wonder your father hasn't gone completely gray by now."

"My father has changed. He blames himself for Kat's 'death' because he feels he drove her into your brother's arms. He's sworn to trust my judgment."

My God. Grief could do strange things to a man.

"We have drifted off topic," Mari continued. "I called upon you to speak about your brother. Now, I intend to research any acting troupes who may have played San Antonio in recent weeks, but does Rory Callahan have any other talents, interests, or vices I should pursue? Is he a gambler, perhaps? Should I investigate gambling establishments in whatever area of San Antonio is equivalent to Hell's Half Acre?"

"Hell's Half Acre." Luke pushed aside his lemonade and got up to get a whiskey. "Miss McBride, San Antonio's red-light district is called Hell's Half Acre, just like ours, only it makes this Acre look like church-house row. You can't go there. Period. Do you want your father to be mourning two daughters when he returns to town?"

"What I want," she quietly stated, "is for my father to come home to the news that his Katie-cat has been restored to him. Now." She pulled a notepad and pencil out of her handbag. With her pencil poised above the paper, she asked, "Is your brother attracted to cock-fights and the like?"

The question pushed him right over the edge. Luke glared at her, then slammed back his whiskey. Fire scorched a path down his throat as he banged his empty glass on the bar. "Fine. What time do we leave?"

"We?" Her brows rose. "Oh, no."

"Oh, yes."

"Oh, *no*. Luke, I cannot travel with you."

"Why not? If your theory has any legs, then your sister is traveling with my brother."

"But they eloped!"

Luke held up his hand, palm out. "Now that's where I draw the line. Don't be getting any marriage designs on me, Miss McBride. I'm strictly your bodyguard."

"But you're a gunslinger, an outlaw!"

"Who better to protect you from other outlaws and gunslingers? What time did you say our train leaves?"

Luke dragged his hand down his face, his thoughts skipping forward to tasks he'd need to accomplish before leaving town. He badly needed sleep, but that would have to wait.

"I didn't. I won't. I never should have come to you. I should have just gone to San Antonio and worked from my own knowledge of Rory Kelly-Callahan. Why are you doing this?"

Because if Rory is alive, then I want to be the one to find him, by God. "I owe your family a debt."

"Well, that is true." Mari McBride tapped her lip in a considering manner. "My little brother did save your life. You'd have died in that fire, Luke. My father spoke to the man who helped carry you from the building, and he said you'd have burned to a crispy critter in another five minutes if Billy hadn't sounded the alarm."

She said it with such relish that Luke drew back.

"I understand the importance of paying one's debts," she continued. "Are you certain about this, sir? You're agreeable to traveling with me to find our siblings?"

"*Agreeable* probably isn't the word I'd choose, but yes, I'm willing to go."

She clicked her tongue as she mentally chewed the idea. "Well," she said finally with a sigh. "All right. You may accompany me as my bodyguard. However, I expect you to remember that this was your idea."

Narrowing his eyes, Luke studied her. Mari McBride boldly returned his stare. Hmm…something else was going on here, some detail that in his weary state, he wasn't picking up. Sensing he might be making a mistake, he nevertheless said, "Fine. So what time's the train?"

"Four o'clock."

"What time is it now?"

"Quarter till noon."

Damn. No rest for the weary. Luke sighed heavily, then nodded. "I'll meet you on board. Go early and get us a good seat. We want to be on the west side."

"The west?" Her pert nose wrinkled. "But won't that be hotter in late afternoon?"

"Yeah, but it'll be safer."

"Safer? Why?"

"On the flatlands between here and San Antone, train robbers like to use the setting sun to shield them from sight."

"Oh. Well." She shrugged. "I guess you'd know."

Blandly, he drawled, "I guess I would."

"Very well, then." She slipped her arm through the handle of her handbag and picked up her parasol. A light that looked suspiciously like satisfaction gleamed in her eyes as she dipped her head in a nod and turned to leave. "Until later, Mr. Garrett."

"Later, Miss McBride," he said to her departing figure.

While Luke took a moment to mentally make a list of things to do in the next few hours, he strolled over to the window and absently watched Mari McBride sashay her way up the street. She distracted him from his thoughts when she gave her parasol a jaunty twirl. She got his total attention when she stopped and blew a kiss to a pair of catcalling cowboys. Finally, just before she turned the corner and disappeared from sight, she glanced back over her shoulder toward the Blue Goose and let loose a honey of a smile.

In that moment, Luke knew for certain. He didn't know precisely why and he didn't know exactly how, but one way or another, he'd just been had. The woman was a fraud, a bamboozler.

Mari McBride was a Menace.

CHAPTER FIVE

"HE BOUGHT IT, Emma. It worked!" In the kitchen at Willow Hill, Mari grabbed her sister in a heartfelt hug. "I haven't lost my touch. Luke Garrett insisted on escorting me to San Antonio to search for Kat and that rat Rory Callahan."

"And this is good news?"

"Oh, Emma," Mari said, a sigh in her voice.

"I don't care. I don't like this plan. The man is a convicted criminal. He's Rory's *brother.* How can you possibly believe a word he says? What's to keep him from robbing you or abandoning you or…or…taking advantage of you?"

An image flashed through her mind of Luke Garrett nibbling at her throat. She gave herself a little shake, then said, "I need to finish packing. Come upstairs with me, would you?"

Once in her bedroom, Mari opened her bureau drawer, removed a stack of clean lingerie, and added it to a half-filled trunk. "We've been through this before, Em. I can't do this alone. As much as I hate to admit it, it wouldn't be safe for me to undertake this search without a man's protection."

"Then hire someone to be your escort, or ask Uncle Tye."

"Aunt Claire's baby is due in little more than a

month. I refuse to drag Uncle Tye away from Fort Worth at a time like this. As far as hiring an escort, who could possibly be better for the job than Luke Garrett? I promised Papa that I'd stay out of trouble if he left me behind, and that's what I'm trying to do."

"By going off with the most notorious man in town?" Emma threw out her hands. "And to think that *you're* the one who worked so hard to leave your McBride Menace reputation behind you."

Mari waited a moment, then said softly, "He's the best man for the job, Em."

Emma sat on the edge of Mari's bed, closed her eyes and rubbed her temples. "It scares me. Mari, if something were to happen to you…"

Mari's shoulders dipped beneath the weight of her family's grief. She sat beside her sister and took her hand. "I give you my solemn word that I'll be as careful as possible. This isn't a mischievous McBride Menace escapade. In fact, this is just the opposite. This is acting responsibly in the best interests of our family."

Emma smiled, her eyes pooling with tears. "I know I'm being a ninny. I know that it's best for the family for you to pursue this personally, now, rather than to wait for Papa to come home or for Aunt Claire to have her baby so that Tye is free to leave. I'm frightened for her, too. She had such a difficult delivery the last time. It just scares me. Everything scares me these days."

"That's because you live a frightening life these days, Emma, tutoring those Harrison twins," Mari said, attempting to lighten the mood. "Those boys are terrors."

Emma smiled. "They're darlings and you just watch, I'll have them ready to impress their stuffy old grandfather when he comes to town next month. He'll have no excuse to try to take those children away from Mr. Harrison. None at all."

A glance at the wall clock told Mari she'd best return to her packing. Standing, she moved to her wardrobe. "Think how wonderful it will be when I bring Kat home, Emma. Imagine Papa's and Mama's faces."

"It's a lovely dream."

"I think it will happen. I truly do. And I think Luke Garrett will play a pivotal part in making that dream come true."

Emma eyed her thoughtfully. "One of your hunches, Maribeth?"

"Maybe." She shrugged. "But it's a logical conclusion, too. Think about it. Because of the family connection, he's motivated. Because of his…um…occupation, he has a certain expertise which might possibly come in useful. And he passed my character test."

"I still think that was a stupid idea."

"It worked, didn't it? He acted just like Papa would have, Emma. It was obvious that he thought I was acting like a foolish twit."

"Which you were."

"Yes, well. That's beside the point. Luke didn't react like a criminal, he responded like a protective male. Just like when he brought Billy to Mama the night of the fire. I know about Luke Garrett's criminal history and infamous reputation, but from what I've seen personally, I believe him to be an honorable man."

"Maybe you're right. I hope you're right. I hope he hasn't fooled us all just like his brother."

"Kat was the only one fooled by Rory Callahan. The rest of us knew he was no good. Papa forbade her to see him, remember?"

"I remember that he wasn't all that happy that you

batted your lashes over bonbons with Luke Garrett the day of the fire."

Remembering the incident, Mari grinned. She had been rather overbold that afternoon. "Papa doesn't like his girls flirting, period. He'd have acted the same way had I been smiling at that handsome, unmarried Methodist minister who's just moved to town."

"True. Still, if he knew what you're planning…"

"I'm planning to bring Kat home. Papa wouldn't argue with that."

Mari finished packing while Emma filled a picnic basket for her and Garrett to share on the train. Then the two women wrestled Mari's suitcase and trunk downstairs shortly before the baggage man she'd hired arrived to ferry the items to the rail station. He loaded the items in his wagon and departed minutes before potential trouble arrived in the form of their father's twin.

"Uncle Tye!" Emma called upon answering the door, making sure to speak loud enough for Mari to hear. "This is a nice surprise."

"Why is it a surprise?" came the beloved masculine voice. "I check on you two every day, don't I?"

Mari set down her large travel handbag and took off the hat she'd just donned. It wouldn't do at all for Uncle Tye to discover her plans, and he had a sharp eye. She'd best play this meeting with care.

"You check on us every evening," she said, breezing into the entry hall. "Although I think that's an excuse to sample whatever sweets I've brought home from the shop that day."

He grinned sheepishly. "Pregnancy is difficult on a man when his wife is a baker confined to bed and unable to bake. I'm accustomed to my desserts."

"So is your sweet tooth acting up early?" Mari

asked as he bent to kiss her cheek in greeting. "It's only midafternoon."

"Your shop is closed today. I'm concerned."

Darn. She'd hoped to get away before he noticed. "No need for concern. I felt poorly this morning, but I'm doing better now."

"Poorly?" Worry dimmed his moss-colored eyes. "What's wrong? Should we call a doctor?"

"I'm fine."

"Are you sure? Should you be in bed? Do you have a fever?"

Mari patted his hand and employed the excuse sure to shut him down. "Female troubles, Uncle Tye."

"Oh. Well. All right, then."

"I have a batch of fudge I brought from the shop to send to the Harrisons with Emma. Would you like some to take home?"

"Chocolate fudge?"

"Yes."

He wrapped her in a loving hug. "Mari McBride, you are my favorite niece."

"Well," Emma said with a huff, though the amused light in her eyes belied her tone. Tye McBride habitually declared all his nieces and nephews his favorite. "I like that. And to think I intended to stop by your house this evening and take all the children out for ice cream to give you and Aunt Claire some time alone."

Tye released Mari and pulled Emma into his arms. "Emma McBride, you are my favorite niece."

The sisters managed to reassure their uncle and hustle him on his way within a few minutes' time. Despite their hurry, Mari reached the depot later than she'd intended. Luke Garrett might have to do without his westside seats.

White smoke puffed from the locomotive on the track and the sounds of goodbyes filled the air. Her heart thrumming with excitement over the possibilities of the upcoming trip, Mari set her satchel on the platform and embraced her sister. "You be careful," Emma said, tears in both her eyes and voice.

"I will. I promise." Mari batted her lashes rapidly to blink back her own tears. "I'm sorry to leave you to face Uncle Tye by yourself, but tell him I'll write every day and report in by telegraph as often as possible."

"I'll be fine. Don't worry about me or the family or your shop. I'll hold the fort while you're gone." Emma gave her sister one last squeeze before stepping back.

Mari reached up and clutched the sapphire pendant of her necklace. "I'll bring her home, Emma."

"I know." Emma clasped her own ruby pendant. "If she's alive, I know you'll find her."

"She's alive," Mari declared. After blowing her sister one final kiss, a scant ten minutes before the scheduled departure, she boarded the passenger car next to the caboose.

The train was crowded. In light of her tardiness, Luke might well be on board already, so Mari decided to make a quick walk through of all the cars before choosing a seat.

Holding her satchel in front of her, the picnic basket behind her, she made her way down the narrow aisle past businessmen in suits who sat beside farmers wearing denim overalls. She smiled at a demurely gowned lady who sat across the aisle from a gaudily dressed woman busy sending bawdy winks toward a cowboy searching for a seat. Mari spied an empty west-side seat and considered claiming it by setting down her satchel. Upon noting that the seat behind it contained a trio of boys remarkably reminiscent of her brothers, she decided to try another car.

It took her at least five minutes to make her way through three of the railcars. Summer heat created a stifling atmosphere inside, the odor of unwashed bodies mingling with the aroma of fried chicken rising from picnic baskets, floral perfumes, and a toddler's dirty diaper. Mari fanned her face and hoped that the three long toots of the train whistle indicated an on-time departure. Having fresh air blowing through the windows would be a relief.

In the fourth car, she was hailed by an acquaintance of her mother's. She dodged probing questions, then quickly took her leave. The train was starting to roll and her nerves had gone tense by the time she entered the passenger car nearest the locomotive. Had Luke Garrett stood her up?

"Not real good at following directions, are you, Miss McBride?"

He lounged like a sleepy mountain cat across two seats at the very back of the car, the broad brim of his black felt hat pulled low on his brow, his arms folded over his chest, his long denim-clad legs outstretched and his booted feet crossed at the ankles. The seat across the aisle from him and the four directly in front were occupied by, of all people, nuns.

Nuns who knew her. Knew her well.

"Maribeth McBride," said Sister Gonzaga. "I understand you haven't attended church since your parents left town."

That caused Luke Garrett to sit up and push his hat back. Interest gleamed in his tawny eyes.

"I...um..."

"Your sister is in church every Sunday."

"Yes…well…"

Luke Garrett's lips twitched.

"Father King hears confessions on Saturday afternoons. I'll tell him to expect you. Will you and Emma be back from your travels this coming weekend?"

Mari couldn't think of a single response that wouldn't get her into trouble, so she shot Luke a "help me" look. He was supposed to be her bodyguard, wasn't he? He should do something to save her!

When mischief sparked in his eyes and his dimple creased his cheek, she figured she'd made a big mistake. Watch him say something outrageous, something sure to ruin her reputation at home. Something that would ruin her business. *I should have anticipated that I might see someone I knew on this leg of the trip. I should have had an excuse or explanation at the ready.*

I'm so out of practice at Menacing.

Mari held her breath as Luke unfolded from his slouch and leaned forward. "Sister? Miss McBride could use your prayers in the coming days, your prayers and your discretion."

Sister Gonzaga twisted in her seat and shot him a suspicious look. Luke continued, "Miss McBride has received information that her sister might have survived the Spring Palace fire after all, and she's traveling to San Antonio in an attempt to confirm it."

The truth? He's using the truth for an excuse?
What a novel idea.

"Little Kat? Alive?"

"It's possible, but in my opinion, unlikely." Ignoring Mari's little murmur of protest, he continued, "However, Miss McBride must do all she can to put the matter to rest one way or another as soon as possible, certainly before her family returns to Texas. The

McBrides have suffered tremendously from the loss of their Kat. If this rumor proves false, the fewer family members who have their hopes raised then dashed, the better."

"Of course. Young Billy especially has had an awful time of it." The elderly nun looked at Mari, her eyes brimming with compassion. She reached over and patted Mari's hand. "You're a good girl, Maribeth. The sisters and I will pray for God's blessing upon your quest."

"Thank you," Mari replied with complete sincerity. "I trust you'll be discreet with this information?"

"Of course, dear." Then the nun's eyes narrowed and she turned toward Luke. "And just who are you, sir?"

He removed his hat. "My name is Luke Garrett, ma'am. Miss McBride has asked me to provide her protection during her search."

"Garrett? Yes. I should have recognized you." She gave him the look Mari and her sisters had dubbed "The Evil Eye" in their youth. "You're the wicked lost soul who leads God's wayward children into sin in Hell's Half Acre."

He winced, scratched the back of his neck, then sighed. "I shouldn't do this, but…" He leaned forward and lowered his voice to just above a whisper. "That's not my true identity, Sister Gonzaga. I'm actually a Texas Ranger working incognito in Hell's Half Acre."

Mari rolled her eyes.

The nun clasped her hands above her prodigious bosom and studied him. Mari thought he must have inherited some of his brother's acting talent, too, because he managed to appear totally sincere.

Watching him, Mari knew a brief moment of doubt. Surely he wasn't telling the truth about that, too!

No, the idea that Luke Garrett could be a Texas Ranger was too big a stretch to believe. Incognito, indeed. Why, to pull that off, he'd need acting skills to put ol' Rory's to shame. Besides, Mari personally knew two Texas Rangers. They traded in her shop. One was tall, thin and talkative, the other short, stocky, quiet and shy. They were different as night and day. Yet both men possessed a certain quality, a quiet confidence, which identified them as members of the Ranger corps.

Luke Garrett, on the other hand, had the brazen swagger of a criminal. He was nothing like the Texas Rangers of her acquaintance.

Sister Gonzaga must not have known any Texas Rangers, because apparently she bought into his story. Nodding, she said, "I will pray for you both."

"Thank you." To Mari, Luke said, "Do you intend to stand all the way to San Antonio?"

Mari didn't really want to sit behind the nuns for the next three hundred miles. A quick scan of the car for an available seat told her she didn't have much choice. By now, undoubtedly, the seats in the other cars had been filled. She smiled wanly and sat beside her bodyguard on the hard wooden seat.

Luke put his hat back on, tucked his chin against his chest and promptly fell asleep. Without an excuse or apology, he just closed his eyes and started to snore.

Mari marveled at his ease. The man had just lied to a nun—not just any nun, but *the* nun—then drifted off to sleep like an innocent. Even in the worst of her Menace days, she'd never worn guilt so easily. It was something she'd do well to remember as she traveled with Luke Garrett.

Mari shifted in her seat, trying to get comfortable. She took one deep breath, then two, and willed herself to relax. She was on the train, on the way to San Antonio. On the way to find her sister. She could do nothing more about anything until they arrived at their destination. In the meantime, she should follow Garrett's example and rest and conserve her resources.

Weariness tugged at her bones, the result of overtaxed emotions and very little sleep. Though the letter had arrived in yesterday's post, she hadn't opened it until half past eleven. After absorbing the shock, pondering the possibilities, she'd awakened Emma and they'd discussed possible courses of action until the wee hours of the morning. Even after she'd climbed into bed and switched off the lamp, sleep remained elusive as her blood hummed with excitement. She'd dozed until dawn, then watched the sun rise with a heart overflowing with hope.

Mari turned her face toward the warm, though welcome, breeze streaming through the open windows and smiled. She shut her eyes and relaxed into the gentle sway of the railroad car, lulled by the constant click of the wheels on the track and the soft murmur of voices reciting the familiar prayers of the rosary.

Somewhere south of Fort Worth, Mari fell asleep.

SOMEWHERE NORTH of Waco, Luke awoke with his arm around Mari McBride's shoulder, his hand cupping her ample breast. Her head rested against his chest, and the heady scent of roses teased his senses. After a moment's thoughtful consideration, he decided not to move. He couldn't risk waking her. The poor woman obviously needed her rest.

Damn, but he was noble.

Luke looked out the window into the setting sun and tried to pinpoint their location. He'd journeyed this way often enough during the past five years that he felt he knew every mesquite tree and cotton field along the way. The road between Fort Worth and San Antone was well traveled both by those with legitimate interests and those attempting to stay one step ahead of the law.

Luke had made the trip under both circumstances.

Miss Mari made a little sniffle and burrowed deeper into his chest. Luke took a moment to appreciate the sensation of holding a true lady against him, and tried to recall the last time he'd had his arms around a virtuous woman.

Then, because he was anything but virtuous, Luke flexed his fingers and tested the pillowed softness of her breast. The globe seemed to swell against his hand. His fingers itched to delve into her bodice and touch her skin to skin. *Hell, she's a sweet little thing.*

Her eyes flew open and her chin dropped in shock. Quickly, because he was no idiot, Luke shut his eyes and feigned sleep.

Damned if she didn't hesitate—just for a moment—before moving his hand and ducking out from beneath him.

Luke made a show of waking up, then he gave her a casual glance. She sat prim as a spinster, her shoulders squared, her hands folded in her lap. He wanted to lean over and bite her neck.

Whoa, there, Garrett. You need to put a lid on your lust. He'd be hanged if he'd treat this girl the way his brother had undoubtedly treated her sister.

"Where are we?" he asked, even though he knew they'd be coming up on the little town of Trickling Springs in half an hour or so.

"I don't know. I fell asleep."

"Hmm…" Luke flipped open his pocket watch and checked the time. "I expect we'll reach a meal stop before long. We'll have forty-five minutes."

"Good. I want to use the time to check the marriage registry in the local churches. If Kat took the train out of town that night, Trickling Springs would be the first place they stopped."

Luke knew her effort would be a waste of time. She wouldn't find any evidence of a marriage between her sister and his brother. However, if he told her so, she'd want to know why and he didn't want to get into that. Not if he could help it. Luke tried another tack. "That evening train wouldn't have come through town until late. Churches would have been closed."

"Believe me, under the circumstances, that wouldn't have stopped my sister."

Luke thought about it, nodded. He couldn't see what such an exercise would hurt, not as long as it didn't cost him his supper. "So, what did you bring us to eat?"

"Fried chicken."

"Yeah?" Luke eyed her wicker satchel with interest. "What else?"

"Potato salad. Green tomato pickles. Some nice Parker County peaches. Candy for dessert, of course."

"Candy? What kind of candy?"

She offered him a dry smile. "I'm a chocolatier, Mr. Garrett."

"Kisses? Sinfuls? Maybe some Temptations?" Suddenly starved, Luke reached for the satchel. The confounding woman slapped the back of his hand. "Not yet. We'll eat after the stop."

"But I'm hungry now."

She laughed. "You sound just like my little brothers. Here." She reached into the basket and pulled out a pair of peaches. Handing him one, she said, "This will tide you over."

Then she bit into her fruit, and Luke's hunger dropped from his belly south.

As a rule, peaches from Parker County were plump, juicy and sweet. A person could hardly eat one without getting a little messy. Mari McBride got more than a little messy.

Peach nectar coated her fingers, glistened on her lush red lips, beaded at the corners of her mouth. Flesh from the fruit clung to her full lower lip. Her tongue flicked out and licked it away.

Luke almost groaned aloud.

She glanced at him, all innocent and virginal. "I thought you were hungry? Don't you care for peaches?"

"I love peaches. I'm just…savoring the moment."

She gave him a curious look, then continued with her snack. Luke's denim britches grew uncomfortably tight and he decided right then and there that he'd gone too long without a woman. While he didn't ordinarily consort with whores, he suspected that by the time this train hit San Antone, he'd be ready for a cowboy four-get: get up, get in, get off, get out.

Finally, she finished her peach. When she sucked the ends of her fingers one by one, Luke decided to stretch his legs. "Guess it wouldn't hurt to stroll through the other cars, check out the other passengers. If the train arrives at Trickling Springs before I get back, you wait here for me."

She opened her mouth as if to protest, then obviously thought better of it. Luke marched down the aisle as if he had a demon at his heels.

In truth, he had a nun nipping at his boots.

Sister Gonzaga caught him on the landing. "Mr. Garrett?"

Great. Now he'd catch hell for lusting after an angel. "Yes?"

"I require a moment of your time. While you were sleeping, I desired exercise so I walked to the other end of the train. Considering the information you shared earlier, I believe you might be interested in someone seated in the third passenger car from the back."

No scolding? That was disconcerting. "Who's on board?"

"Finn Murphy."

Luke's pulse spiked. "Who?"

"Also, Kid Carver. Frank DeBuque and Hoss Ketchum. Clay Burrows and Harry Mortimer."

"That's the entire Brazos Valley gang." She had to be mistaken. How would a nun recognize the Brazos Valley gang? "What makes you think it's them?"

"I periodically make a study of wanted posters, which is why I should have recognized you right off, even though your poster is dated and shows you sporting a mustache. At times our charitable work takes us to unsavory places, and I think it's important that one always remains aware of potential dangers."

That made sense. Come to think of it, Luke recalled seeing a nun's habit upon occasion down in the Acre.

He glanced toward the front of the train. The Brazos Valley gang. All together in one spot. Good Lord, the law had been after them for years. They were near the top of the wanted list for everyone from Pinkerton to Wells Fargo to, yes, the Texas Rangers. More importantly, Luke had a personal score to settle with Finn Murphy. A very personal, very serious score.

One he couldn't ignore.

"Thanks for the information, Sister," he told her, tipping his hat as she prepared to return to her seat. Now he'd have to decide what to do with it.

A stroll through the car in question wasn't a good option. Murphy would take one look at him and go for his gun. Yet, Luke should make certain Sister Gonzaga had her facts right before he made a plan of action. He needed to see inside that car, preferably before they reached Trickling Springs.

A diversion was in order.

He didn't want to do anything that might endanger the other passengers, so that limited his choices. What he needed was…an assistant.

"Yeah," he murmured. A blue-eyed, blond-haired, sashaying-hips assistant.

Quickly, Luke formulated his plan, then returned to his seat where he found Mari making notes in a journal. He slipped his gun belt from his travel bag and strapped it on. Giving Sister Gonzaga a significant look, he requested the loan of her suitcase. Then he picked up both his and Mari's satchels and the picnic basket saying, "Mari, I need you to follow me."

"What? Hey, wait. Where are you going with our supper?"

He glanced over his shoulder to see her scooting out of her seat. Burdened by the bags, he kept going, making his way through one car, then another. He heard her call his name, but he kept on going.

Finally, he stopped at the vestibule outside the car where, according to the nun, the Brazos Valley gang had seats. Mari was only seconds behind him. Her blue eyes snapped with temper. "Luke, what are you doing?"

"I need your help."

Surprise supplanted irritation. "My help?"

"I need to get a look at someone inside this car, but it won't do for them to identify me. I intend to walk up the aisle using these cases to shield my face. I'd like you to walk ahead of me and do whatever you can to draw the passengers' attention so no one pays me much mind. I'd rather not go all the way through the car, because then we'll be stuck at the back of the train. When I see who I need to see, I'll nudge you and turn around, and then you follow me. Will you do that?"

"Who is this person?"

"You don't need to know."

Mari folded her arms. The booted foot peeking from beneath her skirt began to tap. "I realize we're just getting to know one another. However, you will be well served to understand that dismissing my question in such a manner is not the way to secure my cooperation. Now, let's try it again, shall we? Who is this person?"

Troublesome bit of baggage. If she expected him to explain himself every time he turned around, she had another think coming. Yet, now was not the time to point that fact out to her, not when he needed her help. Nor was it time to be truthful. Finn Murphy was a cagey son of a bitch, and the last thing Luke needed was for Mari McBride to say or do something that might cause the outlaw to realize he'd been spotted.

"It's a woman, isn't it?" she concluded, interest lighting her eyes. "Who is she? An old lover? What makes you think she might be on the train? Why don't you want her to see you?"

After a significant pause, he followed her lead. "Please, it's painful for me."

"Oh." Sympathy softened her eyes. She reached out and touched his arm. "I understand."

Surprisingly, Luke felt a twinge of guilt for this particular lie considering her recent romantic troubles, but he shook it off. "She may be traveling with a man. About ten years older than me."

"How old *are* you?"

"Thirty. Now, this fellow has a full head of gray hair. In a suit, he looks distinguished. He's the one I'm curious about."

"Someone safe, then. You were her love, but you're dangerous." Apparently satisfied by her conclusions, Mari folded her arms and thoughtfully tapped a finger against her mouth. "Well, then. You want me to draw attention to myself. How best to go about it? Hmm… back in our Menace days, this part always went to Kat. She's always harbored a love for drama."

Luke would bet that if Mari's sister did the acting, Mari wrote the script. "I don't care how you do it. Let's just get it done. We'll be arriving in Trickling Springs before too long." He wanted to be ready with a plan by that time.

"All right." She brushed her hands together. "Don your boxes, Mr. Garrett, and let's proceed."

Luke tugged his hat low on his head, then stacked Mari's picnic basket and satchel on top of Sister Gonzaga's suitcase, and hoisted them into his arms, effectively concealing his face. "After you."

Mari opened the door, lifted her chin and sailed into the car. "Come along, Virgil," she said in a sharp, shrill tone. "I refuse to share a passenger car with that woman one minute more. I know she's your mother, but honestly, how dare she claim you'd rather eat her fried chicken than mine? Everyone knows I make the best fried chicken in Wichita County. Why, haven't I won the blue ribbon three years in a row?"

Peering around the boxes in his arms, Luke surveyed the left side of the passenger car. Many of the women had turned to look at Mari. The men paid her little mind. He couldn't see faces to identify Murphy or any of the Brazos Valley gang.

As Luke shifted to peruse the passengers on the right side of the train, Mari raised both the volume and pitch of her voice. "And if *that* isn't enough, how dare she make such a critical comment regarding the size of my bosom? I'm not ashamed of being generously endowed!"

Every head in the place twisted around to take a gander at Mari McBride's endowments. Luke immediately spied Kid Carver and Harry Mortimer. A quick glance back to the left revealed Hoss Ketchum seated next to Finn, himself. So, Sister Gonzaga was right. Careful to keep his burden balanced, Luke turned and retraced his steps. *Pay attention, Mari.*

"I think your mother is a mean, old, jealous biddy," Mari continued, continuing up the aisle. "She doesn't like it that you're sweet on me. She doesn't—Virgil? Virgil! Where are you going? Come back here."

He managed to step out onto the platform without tipping his burden. Through the opened doorway, he heard Mari exclaim, "Well, of all the nerve!"

A man near the back of the car drawled, "Guess he's run back to his mama. Here, dumplin'. Why don't you share my seat with me. I'll be happy to—" slap "—yeow!"

"Villain," she snapped, then let Luke know she was following him by calling, "Virgil? Virgil!"

Deciding it prudent to put some space between himself and the Brazos Valley gang, Luke backtracked through two more cars before stopping to wait for Mari. He set down the suitcases, then rummaged through the picnic basket. He took his first bite from a chicken leg just before Mari stepped out onto the platform.

It required conscious effort for Luke to keep his eyes from dropping to her…endowments. Looking at her face proved distracting enough. Her blue eyes sparkled and color painted her cheeks. Her beauty shone like morning dew on spring green grass. She'd obviously enjoyed her stint on stage.

Noting the raided picnic basket, she sent him a chastising look. Luke swallowed, held up the chicken leg and said, "I'll be sure to tell Mama how good this was."

She grinned. "Blue ribbon."

This time, he couldn't keep his attention from dipping below her shoulders. *Definitely blue ribbon.*

"She was the beautiful redhead halfway down on the right side, wasn't she?" Mari asked as he concentrated on finishing his snack.

"Hmm?"

"The woman wearing green who sat next to the banker. Was she your, um, old friend?"

After thinking a moment, Luke recalled the redhead sitting next to Kid Carver. So Mari thought Carver looked like a banker. Considering his occupation, that assumption wasn't far from wrong.

"I don't know the redhead," Luke told her. Then, in an attempt to distract her from any more talk about the identity of his quarry, he added, "You did a good job. Bold, but effective."

She shrugged. "The men weren't paying attention. My grandmother always says the quickest way to catch a man's notice is to lead with your chest."

"Something tells me I'd like your grandmother."

"Most men do." Like a terrier with a bone, she returned to her questions. "So, the couple you were look-

ing for wasn't in that car? We put on that show for nothing?"

"No. They were there. They…" Luke let his voice
trail off as the railcar door behind Mari began to open.
The hand on the doorknob sported an Irish Claddagh
ring Luke recognized at once. "Damn."

With no time to plan, he did the only thing he could
do.

He pulled Mari into his arms and kissed her.

CHAPTER SIX

MARI'S HEART SKIPPED a beat when Luke's mouth covered hers. Her entire body pulsed with surprise, then sensation. So much sensation that she lost all sense of time and place.

A delicious warmth flowed through her as his hands cradled her head. Restless longing seeped into her veins as his fingers threaded through her hair. His tongue skimmed her lips, probing, then plunging. Shocking her. Thrilling her. No other man's kisses had ever made her feel like this.

Tentatively, she followed his lead and touched his lips with the tip of her tongue. The heat within her intensified as their tongues met, teased and stroked, and their mouths clung. Her arms rose, and she clutched his shoulders while his hands slid lower, made slow circles down her back. He angled his head one way, and then the other, until she didn't know when one kiss ended and the next began.

Urgency gripped her, a wild, reckless yearning that allowed her to melt against his hard muscular form. To surrender.

Then an amused voice drawled, "Attaboy, Virgil."

She stiffened, tried to break away, but he held her in a viselike grip. "No," he murmured against her mouth. "Wait."

Then he kissed her again.

This time she managed to resist the spell he wove. Barely. The only thing keeping her from falling was the knowledge that their actions were being observed.

"Think he'd come up for air, wouldn't you?" asked another voice, different from the first.

"I don't know, Kid. If it were me, I'd be in danger of burying myself in that bosom and smothering to death. You know I'm partial to a nice set of tits."

Mari stiffened, then buried her head against Luke's chest. Luke went completely still, a sense of menace radiating from his body. His right hand released its grip on her hip and slid to his own thigh, resting on his gun belt.

Holy Moses. A lump rose in Mari's throat. She didn't like the insult either, but considering the circumstances, it certainly wasn't a shooting offense.

She gripped his arm in warning. He ignored her.

Yet, he didn't turn around.

He doesn't want these men to see his face. It wasn't a woman at all. It's these men. Who are they?

Luke cleared his throat, then spoke in a raspy tone. "I'd appreciate it if you fellas would excuse me and the lady."

"I'm sure you would," the one called Kid replied.

"Sounds to me like he's wantin' to stick it to her real bad. Go ahead, Virgil. I don't mind watchin'."

Mari knew the instant he made up his mind to act, because his hard, taut body suddenly went fluid. Loose.

He's going to shoot them!

Reacting instinctively, she wrenched herself away from Luke and advanced upon the strangers in full harpy mode. "How dare you speak that way! Why, I've never been so insulted in all my life. Your mothers would be so ashamed of you. Virgil? Escort me away from these villains."

She took hold of his arm and attempted to propel him forward. She'd have had better luck moving a mountain. "Virgil," she said again, stressing the name.

Still, he didn't move.

"Virgil Beaudine! There's a time and a place for everything and this isn't it."

After a long moment's pause, he rasped, "Yes, dear."

Mari's knees went weak with relief. She tucked her arm firmly around his and attempted to lead the way back toward their seats. Instead, keeping his head turned away from the men, he led her back the way they'd come.

Once inside the car, he found an empty seat, shoved her into it and said, "Don't move."

"Wait!" She clutched his sleeve. "Where are you going? What are you going to do?"

"Sit. Stay. Hush." He pulled free of her and turned, headed for the door.

Sit? Stay? Hush? *What am I, a cocker spaniel?*

Never one to submit to such autocratic demands, she started to rise, but an unexpected lurch in the motion knocked her back into her seat. Brakes screeched and the train began to slow. Mari glanced out the window. No town. No station. Why were they stopping?

Before she could reason it out, Luke was back at her side, his expression grim, his manner rushed. "C'mon," he said, grabbing her arm and pulling her to her feet. "Let's go."

"You just told me to sit and stay."

"Don't be difficult."

"Me? You're calling *me* difficult?"

He didn't speak again until they'd once again exited

the car onto the vestibule. Then he looked her dead in the eye and said, "They're robbing the train. They'll kill me if they get a good look at me, and since they've seen us together, they'll probably kill you, too."

"Kill me?"

"After they rape you."

Despite the fact she'd been acting as silly as her younger sister, Mari wasn't stupid. "Where shall we hide?"

Luke slipped the guard chain from its mooring then pointed off toward a section of high grass. "There."

"We're jumping from the train?"

"Leave your knees soft when you land, then roll. Once you have control, get up and run like hell."

Mari watched the ground roll by and her stomach churned. "All right. It's all right. I've jumped from a train before. Of course I was a child then. A limber child. I—"

He put both hands on her rear end and lifted her, sent her sailing from the train. Mari hit the ground hard, bottom first, then she rolled like a tumbleweed across the rocky dirt. Stones skinned her hands and one elbow. Something sharp pierced her skin. But when she finally came to a stop, a quick survey of arms and legs confirmed she'd escaped relatively unscathed.

Scrambling to her feet, fearful of hearing a gunshot at any moment, Mari darted toward the shelter of the waist-high grass. Luke caught up to her, grabbed her arm and forced her to run faster. They spilled into the grass, snapped the stems of a half dozen sunflowers, then lay flat against the ground. "Keep your head down," Luke warned.

"I intend to."

She attempted to observe the developments by

watching him, but he proved impossible to read. He lay still as a stone, moving nothing but his eyes. Long minutes dragged by.

Finally, Mari could stand no more. "What's happening?" she whispered. "Who are these people?"

He waited a long moment before responding. "Train's stopped. Had to have been a prearranged rendezvous. Their horses must be on the other side. I can't see 'em from here."

"How long does it usually take to rob a train?"

"Depends."

She waited for him to elaborate, but he remained frustratingly silent. When this was all over, they needed to have a talk about his infuriating lack of communication. Finally, she lost control of her patience. She carefully, cautiously, lifted her head.

Well, she didn't see anyone with a gun pointed in her direction. In fact, she didn't see anyone at all. Not outside the train, anyway. Everything appeared normal, but then a bend in the track leading away from them prevented her from seeing the locomotive, coal car or the first two passenger cars.

"Lie still," Luke said. "I'll be right back."

Keeping low to the ground, he rose. He moved parallel to the railcars, making his way forward with silent, deliberate grace that made Mari think of a mountain lion stalking his prey. Even under difficult circumstances like this, she couldn't help but notice that Luke Garrett truly was a magnificent animal.

He kissed like a dream.

Oh, stop it, Mari silently chastised herself. He's an outlaw. That kiss was nothing more than a diversion, a way for him to hide. She should forget it.

She knew she'd never forget it.

"Fine. But think about it later," she murmured, her breath sending seeds from a dandelion pod flying. Somehow, it didn't feel seemly to worry about a simple kiss during a train robbery.

Except that kiss wasn't at all simple.

Luke reached the bend in the track, then suddenly, he abandoned his attempt at stealth and stood. He took three long strides toward the train, then glanced her way and motioned her to join him.

As she began to move, an ominous sound to her left caught her notice, and she glanced in that direction. And froze.

The snake lay coiled atop a large flat rock. It was tan in color, with dark diamond-shaped patches running from its broad, flat, arrow-shaped head down its back to its tail. Its rattle-tipped tail.

Dear Lord.

Mari's mouth went as dry as the dirt beneath her, and her blood ran cold. Instinct told her to remain totally still as she tried desperately to recall anything she'd ever learned about diamondback rattlesnakes.

She'd helped Emma take her class to a rattlesnake "milking" demonstration at the Texas Spring Palace about a week before the fire last spring. According to the lecturer, diamondbacks were large, fearless and aggressive snakes that were apt to stand their ground and fight rather than retreat from a threat.

I'm no threat.

A bite wasn't always fatal, either. With prompt and proper treatment, many victims of a rattlesnake bite will live.

And I could get prompt, proper treatment here in the middle of a train robbery in the middle of nowhere.

They eat rats and rabbits. Whole.

I'm too big to digest.

The snake's tail began to vibrate, the rattle buzzed. *Oh, dear Lord.* Mari wanted to scramble back, to rise and run away. She wanted to scream. Instead, she lay quiet and still but for the pounding of her pulse. She'd wait him out. Maybe he'd get tired of holding his head up like that. Maybe he'd just slither away. Maybe—

The train whistle blew just as the crack of a gunshot sounded. Before Mari's eyes, the snake's head separated from its body, slinging blood and gore. While the head was still in the air, Luke shouted. "Get away. It can still bite."

The rattlesnake's head landed with its mouth open, its fangs extended, mere inches from her face.

Mari's world went black.

LUKE WAS IN a world-class temper.

Here he was afoot in the middle of nowhere, an unconscious woman slung over his shoulder, trying to run down a wagon filled with pigs so he wouldn't have to walk ten miles or farther to the nearest town. Meanwhile, his mortal enemy rode safely out of Luke's clutches in the relative comfort of a Texas & Pacific passenger railcar.

All in all, it had been one blue-ribbon lousy day.

And it wasn't over yet.

The weight on his shoulder shifted as Mari awakened from her faint. "What..?" she said, starting to struggle. "Put me down. Oh, wait. That snake. Maybe you should carry me back to the train. Could we shift position, though?"

Giving in to his temper, Luke gave her butt a swat. "Be still," he said over her gasp of offense. "The train left without us."

"It left?" she said with a squeak.

"We gotta catch that wagon."

"Wagon? What wagon?"

She wiggled and squirmed like a sand bass on a hook, forcing him to slow. Deciding it'd be faster to put her down, Luke set her on her feet then pointed toward a cloud of dust a couple hundred yards away. "That wagon. The one we've got to run and catch up with if we don't want to walk to Trickling Springs."

Mari looked toward the empty train track. "Walk. We can't walk. I'm not walking." Shuddering, she added, "That was a rattlesnake."

"I noticed."

"The robbers." Wide-eyed, she glanced up at Luke. "What about the train robbers? Where did they go?"

Luke scowled and started walking in long, angry strides after the wagon. "They didn't get off."

She hurried after him. "They robbed a train, then stayed on it?"

"They didn't rob the train," Luke responded, breaking into a slow run.

"What?"

Damn, this was humiliating. Luke seldom felt like a fool, and he didn't wear the sensation well. "Better get a move on. I figure it's at least ten miles to town."

He gave it half a minute then checked over his shoulder. He couldn't help but appreciate the delicious amount of leg she displayed as she hefted her skirts knee-high and started after him. Though he was tempted to pick up his speed and maintain a distance that made discussion impossible, he didn't have the heart to make this any more difficult for her than it already was. He couldn't forget the look on her face as she stared down that diamondback. The girl had grit. He respected that.

"Luke Garrett! What do you mean they didn't rob the train?" she called out.

But she also had a damned sharp tongue. *Well, hell.* Luke halted, whirled around and spit his words like bullets. "The train stopped because the pig wagon was stuck on the tracks. The wagon moved. The train left." He shrugged.

Mari stopping running. She braced her hands on her hips. "So you were wrong? We went through all this for nothing? I risked my life for nothing?"

"You didn't risk your life," he said, resuming his long-legged lope.

She put on a burst of speed and came around in front of him. "No? I jumped from a moving train. I was a hairbreadth away from being bitten by a viper. All because you made a mistake and told me I was in danger from a bunch of train robbers! What kind of an outlaw are you that you can't tell when a train is being robbed?"

Her sapphire eyes flashed, and her cheeks flushed rosy. Luke was glad to see the color back in her complexion. He didn't feel near as guilty now. So he gave her a wink, then said, "Hey, you got a damn fine kiss out of it."

She gasped, glared, then whirled around and increased her pace. Luke eyed her pumping legs, matched her stride, and his mood went almost mellow.

When they drew within hailing distance of the wagon, he increased his speed and ran around her. "Howdy, sir," Luke called. When the driver, a weathered man of around sixty, turned to look, Luke jerked a thumb over his shoulder toward Mari and continued, "My wife and I are in a speck of trouble. Would you be of some help to us?"

"Whoa there," the driver called as he reined in his horses. In the back of the wagon, a pair of hogs snorted and snuffled. "Where did you come from, stranger?"

Mari caught up with Luke as he began to spin his yarn. "I'm afraid we stepped off the train when it stopped. The little lady here was feeling a bit green around the gills from all the swaying." He put his arm around Mari's waist, gave her a squeeze and a smile, ignoring the way she stiffened at his touch. "Caught us by surprise when the train took off rolling again. My little darling was busy puking her guts up, so we couldn't run to catch it. She's carryin', you see."

"Congratulations," the driver said.

"Thank you. We're hoping for a boy. We're the Beaudines. I'm Virgil and this here is Ethel. We're hoping you'd be so kind as to give us a ride into Trickling Springs."

The fellow tipped back his hat. "That's a problem, young man. I'm late gettin' where I'm goin' 'cause of my wagon gettin' hung up on the railroad tracks. I've gotta get home by sundown 'cause today's my wife's birthday, and these hogs are her gift. Now, y'all are welcome to ride along with me. I'm Dennis Hill. My wife and I have a cotton farm a short piece from here. Y'all can stay the night at the farm, and I'll carry you into town tomorrow."

"But the train," Mari said, casting Luke an anxious look. "It's stopping for dinner. We could catch up with it. We must catch up with it. My bags are on that train!"

Luke frowned and scratched the back of his head. "Now, Ethel, you do have a point. Sir, I'd be happy to pay you a good wage for the ride tonight. You could buy the missus some little purdy to go along with her hogs. And allow me to mention what fine hogs they are, too."

Now it was the farmer's turn to frown. He pursed his lips, scratched his full beard, then shook his head. "No, I'm sorry. Can't rightly do that. I forgot her birthday entirely last year, and she'll be hotter than a pot of boiling collards if I don't get my hogs home tonight. Y'all come on and climb up into the wagon. The wife will be pleased to have company. We'll get you into town in plenty of time to catch tomorrow's train."

Mari opened her mouth as though to protest, then obviously thought better of it. She flashed Hill a grateful smile, then stepped up into the wagon and settled broadly into the seat. "Oh, my. There's not much room. It looks like you'll have to ride in back with the rest of the pigs, Virgil."

Good try, sugar.

"That's all right." He stepped up into the wagon, scooped her up, then sat and settled her into his lap. "I don't mind you sitting on me, even if you have put on some weight with the young'un and all."

She sat stiff as a new rawhide rope, and her elbow jabbed him hard in the breadbasket. Damn, but he liked her starch, not to mention that yellow-rose scent that clung to her skin despite her recent brush with dirt, dust and death. "Besides, you smell a lot better than the hogs."

She retaliated by "accidentally" kicking his shin. Grinning, Luke relaxed against the backboard and prepared to enjoy the ride.

HILLSIDE FARM WAS a pretty place snuggled up against the banks of the Brazos River. Post oak and cedar dotted the gently rolling hills, and in the fields, fluffy white cotton dotted the ground like snowballs.

The farmhouse had been around awhile. Built in the

traditional dogtrot style, the original house consisted of two log rooms with a central connecting passageway, a porch at either side, and a chimney at both ends. "What a pretty place," Mari told the farmer.

"It's a hodgepodge," he replied, although his voice brimmed with pride. "My father built the original cabin, and we've added on over the years. My Penny is right proud of her new kitchen and dining room. If you like it, Mrs. Beaudine, it'd be a kindness for you to mention it to her."

Because he wanted to keep his wife's gift a secret until the appropriate time, he pulled the wagon into the barn and they approached the house on foot. Glancing through a window, Mari spied Penny Hill at the stove in her kitchen with a wooden spoon in hand stirring, judging by the smell, a pot of beans. At first glance, Mari thought she appeared to be younger than her husband by at least ten years.

Dennis Hill waved them onto the porch, then opened the door and asked, "How's the birthday girl?"

"You remembered!" Her smile bloomed and delight filled her eyes as she turned around. Then, seeing strangers at the doorway of her home, she paused. Delight shifted to curiosity. "Why, hello."

"Come on in, folks," Dennis said, waving them inside. "Penny, this here's Mr. and Mrs. Beaudine. They had a travel mishap on account of the missus is in the family way. They're gonna stay with us tonight, then I'm gonna carry them to town tomorrow in time to catch the southbound train."

Luke took off his hat and ushered Mari inside. "We're sorry to impose on your celebration, ma'am."

"Oh, company is never an imposition. In fact, this is a delightful surprise. Welcome to our home."

The farmer's wife offered Mari the opportunity to freshen up, and upon hearing the details according to Luke the Liar about their "travel mishap," offered "Ethel" a clean dress to wear.

"Please, call me Mari," she said, gratefully accepting the change of clothes. "It's the name I ordinarily go by. Virgil is the only one who uses the other."

The dress fit snug in the bust, loose in the waist, and showed an impolite amount of ankle, but Mari was pleased to have it. She joined Penny in the kitchen and assisted with supper preparations. Soon the two women chatted away like old friends. She learned that the couple had two sons, one who lived and worked in Dallas and the other who helped his father on the farm, but lived with his wife and young daughter in a house on another section of land they owned a short distance away. "They'd intended to come for supper tonight, but the baby came down sick. My son rode over this afternoon and brought me my gift. Can I show you?"

It was a photograph of her son's family, and the two women spent some time oohing and aahing over the Hills' granddaughter. Mari did her best to shift the conversation away from children when Penny asked a question or two about her pregnancy. While she did have some experience at shading the truth—that McBride Menace influence, she was afraid—she didn't feel right about misleading people as nice as Dennis and Penny Hill.

Luke, however, seemed to revel in it. The cad.

Over supper, he spun a yarn about the reason for their trip that had nothing to do with the truth. It did, however, manage to charm their hosts completely. Who wouldn't be impressed by a man who spoke so passionately about his desire to preserve Texas history by recovering historical documents and establishing a museum to exhibit artifacts from the days of the Republic? Obviously, Luke had as much a talent for acting as did his brother.

He revealed yet another facet of his talents after Dennis presented his wife with her gift when supper was over. Penny's delight in the hogs was infectious and Mari found herself wishing she had a gift of her own to give. Apparently, Luke felt the same way. Reaching for Mari's hand, he gave it a warning squeeze and said, "It's a poor guest who attends a birthday party without a gift. Since we can't exactly run down to the general store to purchase you tea towels, would you accept a bit of entertainment from my wife and me as our birthday contribution?"

While Mari looked at Luke in shock, the farmer piped up. "You wantin' to sing? I have tender ears. Can't abide poor singin'."

"No. No singing." Luke stood, pulled Mari to her feet, then continued in a theatrical tone. "Mr. and Mrs. Hill, allow me to present Beaudine the Magnificent and his lovely assistant, Ethel!"

He made a flourish, then tugged a handkerchief and a coin from his pocket. For the next ten minutes, he performed one parlor trick after another with only those two items. He made the coin disappear and reappear in various places of the room and on his "assistant's" body. He tied the kerchief in knots, made the knots disappear, made the kerchief disappear…and reappear from the dip in Mari's neckline.

Mari's contribution to the act became one of reacting to his tricks. Every time she slapped his hand away for brushing her body inappropriately, each time she reacted with shock or surprise to his antics, the Hills' amusement increased. Soon Mari found herself playing to her audience, and when Luke ended the act by pulling a yellow rosebud from her bodice, then bending her back over his arm for a boisterous kiss, she participated enthusiastically.

She was still floating on a performer's high spirits a short time later when she found herself alone in a room with Luke. Alone in a bedroom. Their bedroom. The one with the bed. Only one bed.

Oh, my.

Luke unbuckled his gun belt and draped it over the back of the one other piece of furniture in the room, a wooden ladder-back chair. Then he sat on the edge of the bed and began to pull off his boots. "That was fun," he observed. "I haven't performed my magic act in ages."

Mari stood stiff as a fence post in the middle of the room.

One boot fell to the wooden floor with a thud. Mari startled, then nervously cleared her throat. "Do...um... did you...um...where did you learn those tricks?"

The second boot fell to the floor. "My stepfather taught me when I was a boy. Helped me learn to be good with my hands."

Oh, my goodness.

"They're nice people, the Hills. Did you notice that painting above their mantel? The cowboys around the campfire? The artist is Charles M. Russell. Dennis said he bought it out of a Fort Worth bar. Russell is starting to earn a real name in the art world. My bet is that painting will be worth a pretty penny someday."

"You're not going to steal it from him, are you?"

He shot her a chastising look. "You can be a real shrew, Mari McBride."

"Only with you, Luke Garrett."

"You gonna stand there all night or are you coming to bed?" He started unbuttoning his shirt.

Mari's pulse jumped. "Hold on. Just hold on one minute. What do you think you're doing?"

"I'm going to bed. I haven't had any real sleep in three days."

"But you can't...we can't..."

"We won't." He sighed heavily. "Don't be silly about this, Mari. You must have known when you asked me to travel with you that we'd find ourselves in close proximity upon occasion."

"Yes, but there's close, and then there's *close.*"

"Well, this isn't *close.* I'm too tired for *close.* I hate to disappoint you, but all I intend to do tonight is go to sleep. In this bed. Now. You can either join me or sleep on the floor. Whatever trips your trigger."

Sleep on the floor? Me? "A gentleman would offer me the bed and sleep on the floor himself."

Luke sent her a droll look, then slipped off his shirt. When his hands went to the buttons on his denims, she whirled around. "You can't take off your pants!"

"Just watch me."

"Luke!"

"I'm not putting these britches against Penny's clean sheets. They're filthy. One of the pigs gave me a gift when I was helping Dennis unload the wagon."

Mari wrinkled her nose. She'd thought she smelled something off a time or two this evening.

She heard his pants hit the floor, then the rustle of bedclothes and the creak of bed ropes. Glass rattled, then the lamp went out.

Standing in the darkness, Mari asked, "It didn't get your drawers, too, did it?"

"G'night, Mari."

She felt her way over to the chair—the hard, unpadded, wooden chair—and took a seat. She slipped off her shoes and tried to get comfortable.

After a few long minutes, she scowled into the darkness. No. Comfort wasn't going to be possible in this chair. Maybe she should try the floor.

Mari grabbed a pillow and the quilt folded at the bottom of the bed and settled onto the floor in front of the fireplace. She shut her eyes and willed herself to relax. She was tired. That nap on the train hadn't been enough to combat the energy-draining ups and downs of the past twenty or so hours. She should be able to drift right off to sleep, hard floor or no. Except her mind kept returning to that moment in the grass when she stared into the rattlesnake's soulless black eyes.

That made her think about things that slither and crawl on the ground.

I'll never get to sleep down here.

She gave up and returned to the chair. Hugging the pillow to her chest, she closed her eyes and started counting sheep. Then Luke let out a snore, and the sheep transformed to complaints.

This was all his fault. He's the one who mistook a wagon accident for a train robbery. He's the one who told the Hills that they were married. He's the one who called her Ethel. Ethel!

He's the one who touched her, who teased her. Who kissed her. Luke Garrett was the one who heated her blood and made her afraid to seek the innocent comfort of a mattress just because she feared her own reaction to his wicked allure.

Why in the world did she find him so attractive? Sure he was handsome and charming, but he was a criminal, for goodness' sake. He stole from people. Maybe killed people, even. He'd proved his talent with a gun this very day, hadn't he? She had absolutely no business being attracted to him. None.

So stop it. I'm a willful woman. I can be stubborn. I can turn off these feelings like a gaslight.

I can get a good night's sleep.

She stood and approached the bed. She took two deep breaths, then crawled gingerly in beside Luke.

LUKE DREAMED about lovemaking.

He lay upon a blanket of green grass beside a riverbank, naked and hot, arousal pulsing through his veins like whiskey. The woman rose above him, straddled him, her full, pink-tipped breasts mere inches from his mouth. He ached with the need to take, to possess. He heard himself moan.

The moan prodded him awake.

Luke's eyes opened, blinked into the darkness. Again, he heard a deep-throated, in-the-throes-of-good-sex groan. Except, it wasn't coming from him.

As sleep's fog began to clear from his mind, Luke recognized that the sounds he was hearing emanated from their host's bedroom. Luke's lips stretched into a grin. Looked like the birthday gift-giving didn't end with a pair of sows.

Even as that thought drifted through his mind, another fact occurred. He wasn't alone in bed. In fact, if he wasn't mistaken—and he never was about such things—Miss Mari's hand rested mere inches from his pecker.

His hard, raging, rarin'-to-go pecker.

From across the narrow passageway came a muffled feminine scream. Beside him, Mari startled and came awake. "What…?"

A man's voice said, "Mmm…oh, oh, oh."

"Oh…" Mari murmured, her tone ripe with understanding.

Ripe. Damn. Now there was a word he shouldn't be thinking under current circumstances. Ripe. Primed. Ready.

He was damned well ripe, primed and ready. Hell, wouldn't take much at all to set him off. Maybe…

He wondered if she'd taken off her clothes when she came to bed.

"Oh...aah…aah…aah."

Beside him, Mari shifted restlessly. Luke turned his head and tried to see her in the darkness. The tension thickening the air told him that she was as aware of him as he was of her.

"Well," she said. "I think I'll just…um…go back to sleep."

Luke let a moment pass before the ache in his groin prodded him to ask, "Are you still a virgin?"

"Excuse me?" She sat straight up in bed. "Why in the world would you ask me such a question? What are you doing thinking about my virtue?"

"It was just a thought," he defended.

"A thought? Like you *thought* the train was being robbed? I've had quite enough of your thoughts, thank you very much."

With a huff, she bounced back down, and though he couldn't see her, he knew she'd rolled onto her side facing away from him. After a moment and another long moan from the other bedroom, Luke said, "It's a natural reaction."

She sniffed.

Then, because he was a man, he went on the offensive. "Don't try to tell me you weren't thinking about it, too."

"I most certainly was not."

"Liar."

"All I'm thinking about is trying to get some sleep. Now good night!"

He was so tempted to reach out and caress her hip.

"Oh...oh...oh...oh...oh!"

"Aargh!" Mari put the pillow over her head.

Luke tried to wrestle control of the images running through his mind. He concentrated on cold things—icebergs, North Pole snow. Iced tea. Ice cream.

Strawberry ice cream.

Resting in the hollow of her stomach just above her navel.

Where he could lick it up.

Oh, hell.

Luke rolled onto his side facing away from her, hard and aching and cranky. He draped his arm above his head, covering his ear and succeeded to some extent in muffling the sounds of lovemaking coming from the other room. Still he waited, tense and anxious, as the sound built to a crescendo, then climaxed with a pair of intensely satisfied, full-bodied groans.

Luke rolled onto his back, then pushed himself into a seated position. He drew a deep breath, then exhaled in a rush. Damn, he was glad that was over. Now maybe he could relax and get back to sleep. Tomorrow promised to be another challenging day.

Beside him, Mari let out a soft giggle. Hearing the sound, Luke's tension drained like beer from a newly tapped barrel. He turned his head toward the sound and grinned into the darkness. "Hey, Mari?"

"What?"

"Do you have a cigarette on you?"

She hit him in the face with her pillow.

CHAPTER SEVEN

THE TOWN OF Trickling Springs owed its prosperity to the railroad. Three times a day trains stopped for forty minutes, spilling restless passengers from cramped cars to mill about Main Street, stretching their legs and spending their money. Merchants, restaurateurs and even service establishments like barbershops and bath-houses made a fine penny from the travelers. As a result, Trickling Springs residents made a concerted effort to welcome strangers to their town with open arms.

Personally, Mari would just as soon they stopped all that smiling. She wasn't in a good mood, and she didn't want to be nice to people.

It hadn't been the most pleasant of days.

First, following a fitful night's sleep, she'd awoken spooned against Luke Garrett, entirely too comfort-able. Next, Mr. Hill and Luke had amused themselves by claiming to spot snakes and scorpions and various other wildlife on the way into town. Once in Trickling Springs, Mari had to badger Luke into checking church records for a listing of Kat's marriage to Rory Kelly-Callahan. Each time they entered a church and spoke to the pastor about the marriage records, Luke got a strange look on his face. Mari wondered if his aversion was to places of worship, or the institution of marriage.

"That's every church in town, Mari," Luke grumbled as they departed First Presbyterian. "I told you we wouldn't find anything."

"We haven't checked with City Hall yet. Maybe they had a civil service."

"This town isn't big enough to have a City Hall!"

"A judge, then. Or the mayor. Can a couple be married by a mayor in Texas?"

"How would I know? Mari, be reasonable. The only places open when the nighttime train rolls through are restaurants and the whorehouse."

"Which shall we try first?"

Luke scowled and rolled his eyes. "You can do what you want. I need to send a telegram."

"Luke…please?"

He sighed heavily. "All right, fine. Telegraph office first, though. We'll try the restaurants after that. I could use some lunch. I'm not taking you into the Trickling Springs Social Club."

"I've been to brothels before, Luke. I went to yours yesterday, if you recall."

"Do you honestly believe your little sister would agree to get married in one?"

Mari wrinkled her nose but didn't argue. Luke was right. Kat wouldn't settle for a whorehouse wedding, not even under dire circumstances.

At the telegraph office, Luke took pains to ensure the privacy of the message he sent. Mari was mildly curious about his manner, but she didn't challenge him on it. She was anxious to question workers at the restaurants in hopes of finding someone who might remember seeing Kat McBride the night of the Texas Spring Palace fire.

Unfortunately, the photograph she'd brought along

to aid in her search was in her handbag—the one she'd stuck inside the satchel left behind on the train. Still, she had hopes that someone might recall seeing Kat. Mari knew her sister well enough to believe that she'd have been sparkling with excitement from the elopement. A sparkling Kat was a memorable Kat.

Trickling Springs had three restaurants, but Mari and Luke quickly discovered that two of them opened only during train stops. The third served up bad sandwiches and no useful information. Mari left the building discouraged.

"Come on, now." Luke tucked a loose strand of her hair back behind her ear. "Buck up. You knew it was a long shot."

She shrugged. "I know my sister is alive, but I'd hoped to get confirmation."

"Investigations rarely get results right out of the chute, Mari. Sometimes it takes months of dogged work to glean even the slightest piece of information."

Mari shot him a curious glance. "I didn't realize train robbers made it a practice to conduct investigations."

He hesitated, annoyance flashing across the his caramel-colored eyes, but Mari sensed the emotion was self-directed. What had put a burr under his saddle? Her reference to his criminal past? Was he ashamed of his criminal past? He'd never appeared to be before.

"Those men on the train yesterday. Who were they to you, Luke?"

He shook his head and tried to evade the question, but Mari wasn't giving in this time. In a warning tone, she said, "Luke?"

Finally, he shrugged and said, "Ghosts from my past, Mari. That's all. And as far as investigating goes, you'd be surprised how train robbers spend their time. Right now, in fact, this train robber needs to stop back by the telegraph office."

He reached into his pocket and pulled out his wallet. Removing a handful of bills, he handed them to her saying, "Why don't you go ahead to the general store and get what you need to hold you until we catch up with our bags? Pick up a change of clothes for me, too, please, if you would. The train is due in at two. I'll meet you at the station by one-thirty."

Before she could form a protest or even ask his size, Luke turned and walked away, his long legs moving quickly. She frowned after him. That was a strange bit of behavior. It was almost as if he'd revealed something he shouldn't have.

Mari turned from his retreating form and considered the handful of cash in her hand. Noting the denominations, she blinked. "Goodness, I could buy an entire wardrobe with this much money."

She tucked it safely away in her pocket, then with one last glance toward Luke, who was disappearing into the telegraph office, Mari headed not for the general store, but for the sweet shop she'd noticed upon her arrival in town.

A good businesswoman could always learn from the competition.

The shop specialized in saltwater taffy rather than chocolate, but similar to Mari's shop, refreshments were served at a half-dozen small round tables placed both inside and out on the boardwalk in front of the store. Mari ordered mint iced tea and a small assortment of taffy, then took a seat outside in the pleasant breeze. She questioned her server about the night of the fire.

"Yes, I'm sure we were open that night. We do more business during the nighttime stopovers than the day-time ones. You'll want to speak with my sister. She works that late shift."

"Where can I find her?" Mari asked, hope blossoming anew. Kat absolutely adored saltwater taffy.

"She'll be here before long. Twenty minutes at the most. Why don't you just sit back and enjoy your tea and candy, and I'll have her visit with you the moment she arrives?"

Happy with that plan, Mari sat back in her chair, sipped her tea and watched the bustle of Main Street, Trickling Springs, Texas.

In front of the livery, a boy threw a stick for a long-eared mutt to chase. Young matrons exchanged pleasantries on the sidewalk outside the seamstress shop, and a pair of elderly men set up a checkerboard beneath the red-and-white-striped barber pole. Young girls giggled and horses snorted, dogs barked and from the steps of a church house at the north end of the street came the a cappella chords of a men's choir singing "Amazing Grace." It was, Mari thought, a nice little town.

She took a bite of peppermint taffy and nodded with approval as creamy flavor melted throughout her mouth. She twisted her head to ask the shopkeeper a question about her flavoring when, from the corner of her eye, she caught sight of Luke Garrett exiting the telegraph office. He stepped out into the street, glanced toward the general store, then, to her surprise, turned in the opposite direction.

Mari forgot all about peppermint as she watched him head south down Main. Soon he'd passed every building in town except for the two-story house constructed just beyond the outskirts of Trickling Springs.

As her bodyguard climbed the steps of the Social Club, Mari wondered why Luke would pay a call on the whorehouse. Had he decided to check there about Kat and his brother, after all? Did it have something to do with his mystery telegram?

Or was the purpose behind his visit of a more ordinary variety?

Her mouth went tight. Her stomach did a roll. How dare he go from her bed to a whore's!

In a manner of speaking.

Mari drummed her fingers on the table and told herself not to jump to conclusions. She should be patient. He'd have an explanation for leaving her alone and unprotected despite the fact that he was supposed to be her bodyguard. Besides, she didn't truly want him hovering around her all the time, did she?

She didn't want him hovering around other women, ever.

"Miss McBride? I'm Polly Hartwick. My sister said you wanted to ask me a few questions?"

"Yes. I do." Dragging her attention back to *important* matters, she motioned toward the opposite chair. "Please join me."

Polly Hartwick was an attractive brunette with lovely green eyes, near Mari's own age. They exchanged brief pleasantries, then Mari got down to business. "On May thirtieth, the night of the Texas Spring Palace fire, I believe my younger sister eloped with an actor who used the name of either Rory Callahan or Rory Kelly. They would have arrived in Trickling Springs on the late-night train. I'm trying to find evidence that she was indeed here that night. She has a strong sweet tooth, so it's logical she might have made a purchase here."

Miss Hartwick shook her head. "That was a long time ago and we get so many people through here."

Nodding, Mari said, "She's eighteen years old, with hair color similar to mine and eyes the color of yours. She'd have been wearing a necklace similar to this."

Mari tugged on the chain around her neck and revealed her sapphire pendant. "My sister's was—"

"Green," Polly Hartwick finished. "I remember it. I've never seen an emerald that big before."

Her voice trembling, Mari asked, "You remember her?"

"I recall thinking that the necklace matched her eyes. That was the night the train was delayed for repairs. She was with the most handsome man. They stayed here quite a long time, and they bought an entire pound of butterscotch taffy."

Butterscotch taffy. That sealed it. Goosebumps shuddered their way up Mari's arm. "It *was* her. She *is* alive. My sister is alive!"

Mari flung herself across the table and gave Polly Hartwick a quick, hard hug. "Thank you. Oh, thank you so much. All this time, my family thought she died in the fire."

"Really? Oh, I'm glad I could help."

"Do you remember anything else? Anything she said? Did she seem happy? Did she mention their destination?"

The other woman thought a moment, then regretfully shook her head. "I'm sorry. I just don't recall anything else."

"That's all right. It's fine. Everything's wonderful!" Joy bubbled inside Mari like champagne, her mind whirling as she tried to decide what to do next. "I knew she was alive, but it's so good to have confirmation. I need to tell Emma. Send her a telegram. And Luke.

He'll want to know about Rory." Standing, she gave Polly another hug, then reached into her pocket and pulled out Luke's wad of bills. Peeling off a couple larger denominations, she set them on the table saying, "Let me—"

"Oh, no. I can't take your money for this."

"Then take it for…for…" Mari spied the boy playing with his dog. "I'll buy candy for the children. It's a celebration. Katrina McBride is alive!"

Mari laughed aloud as she hurried toward the telegraph office. She pictured Emma's expression when she opened the telegram, imagined the thrill her sister would feel upon realizing their hopes had come true.

Mari fantasized her parents' reaction when they first laid eyes on the daughter they thought they had lost.

"But first I have to find her," she murmured, and as her mind returned to the purpose of her journey, a sense of urgency gripped her. She wanted the train to get here. She wanted to get on with the search. She wanted to find her sister *now*.

And she'd lost a full day because her bumbling bodyguard had thought the train was being robbed.

She stopped mid-step, her attention shooting toward the Trickling Springs Social Club. Was he still there? Still…busy? Maybe not. Maybe she'd missed his leaving. She had been distracted, after all.

Oh, well. She wouldn't think about that now. Why waste any of this happiness on feeling angry?

She bounded up the telegraph-office steps, then breezed inside. "I need to send a telegram, please. To Mrs. Tate at Willow Hill in Fort Worth, Texas."

The operator, a bewhiskered gentleman with kind brown eyes, smiled at her, set a blank sheet of paper on the counter, then gestured toward a pencil. "Happy to help you, pretty miss. Just write out your message and we'll get it sent."

Mari took but a moment to frame her news, then wrote: *Kat confirmed alive in Trickling Springs morning of May 31. Hurrah!* She handed the paper to the operator with a flourish, then paid the fee from Luke's roll of cash.

She watched as the operator tapped out her message to her sister, then, filled with a sense of satisfaction, departed the telegraph office.

Warm summer sunshine beamed down upon the street. Today promised to be a scorcher. Mari made a mental note to add a parasol to her shopping list, then checked her watch. Less than an hour before the train arrived. She had just enough time to visit the general store and purchase supplies.

As she walked toward the store, she again noted the whorehouse. *Was* he still there? Why did she care? She shouldn't care if he wanted to disport himself with painted ladies. She *didn't* care. She didn't!

With a toss of her head, Mari decided to spend all the money he'd shoved at her before sauntering away. On herself. If he wanted fresh clothes, he could have his "hostess" wash the ones he was wearing.

Upon entering the Trickling Springs general store, she headed directly for the small section of ready-mades. She paid little attention to the other customers in the building as she selected lingerie, then worked her way outward, choosing three complete changes of clothing and two pairs of shoes. She experienced not one bit of guilt. It was Luke's fault she needed clothes, after all. Train robbery, indeed. He could darn well pay for them *and* the new suitcase she purchased to carry them in.

Wearing one of the new outfits, a pretty blue print

that matched her eyes and fit loose for comfortable traveling, Mari paid for her purchases and thanked the female salesclerk for her assistance. She carried the new carpetbag in her left hand as she stepped outside and turned right toward the train depot.

As she crossed a narrow alley between the dry-goods store and an apothecary shop, a man sidled up beside her on the left, surreptitiously took her arm and forced her into the alley. "Hey!" Mari protested.

"Where's Luke Garrett?"

She looked him in the face, took in the bushy red eyebrows and the long, thin scar running diagonally across one cheek. He was one of the men from the train. One of *the* men. The train robbers.

Oh, no. Mind racing, she tried to delay by asking, "Pardon me? I don't know what you're talking about, and I don't appreciate being manhandled."

A second man—the silver-haired fellow with the Irish ring on his hand—appeared on her right and spoke in a low, threatening tone. "Answer the question, lady. We know he's in town, and we've pieced it together. You're the harpy from the train. The man you were henpecking was Luke Garrett."

"I don't henpeck," Mari said with false bravado. She couldn't believe this was happening. What should she do? How should she react? Where was Luke when she needed him? Then, just as she decided to fight back by swinging the suitcase, she felt the barrel of a gun press against her side.

The second man added, "Now tell us where he is."

"A gun," she muttered in disbelief. He was pressing a gun against her body. Her body that was supposed to be being guarded. Only her guard was off dipping his wick at the local whorehouse.

Suddenly, Mari had had enough. She struggled fiercely in their grip. "You know what? I don't know where Luke Garrett is, but if you two are out to kill him, you'll just have to wait in line behind me."

She wrenched from their hold and managed two steps away before they grabbed her and hauled her back. She continued to thrash about and drew a breath to scream, but one of them clamped a hand over her mouth. She bit him.

"Goddammit," he cursed, then shoved her against the building. She got out a squeal before the one without the gun pressed a knife against her cheek. "Settle down or I'll cut you. It'd be a cryin' shame to scar up that pretty face of yours. Now, where the hell is he?"

Fear sizzled down her spine. "I don't know."

She felt pressure against her cheek, a sting. "Honestly, I don't know! He said he'd meet me in a little while at the train station."

The knife eased away. "Train station is too public," the silver-haired man said to the other. "I'd prefer this to happen away from town."

"All right."

He'd prefer *what* to happen? Mari thought about asking the question aloud, but then she figured out she didn't really want to know.

"Yeah, go ahead and take her."

Take her? Take *me?* Where? Why? "Why would you take me?"

"So he'll come after you."

Oh. Mari blinked twice. Thought about it, then shook her head. "He won't come after me. He'll be glad to be rid of me. He doesn't even like me."

"Doesn't matter. You're his, and I'll have you. Luke Garrett won't like that one bit. He'll come after you.

And then..." His mouth stretched in a wicked smile as he took the pendant of her necklace in his hand. He yanked hard, broke the chain and added, "Then I'll kill him."

LUKE CHECKED his pocket watch, then made one more stroll around the station, his unease growing with every minute that passed. The train had arrived at the station over half an hour ago. It was due to depart in less than ten minutes. Where the hell was she?

He dared not leave the station himself to go looking for her. Knowing his luck, he'd walk out one door while she walked in another.

He had a bad feeling about this. When he'd arrived on time to find he'd beat her to the station, he didn't think much about it. When fifteen minutes passed and she still hadn't shown, he decided she must have gotten tied up shopping and lost track of the time. He'd made a quick run to the general store to look for her, but his effort proved fruitless.

That's when he'd felt that first niggle of worry. Something wasn't right. Mari wouldn't miss this train unless she had found her sister or something bad had happened.

Life had taught Luke to bet on the bad.

Yet, he wasn't ready to give up. He paid the conductor to board the train and walk every car paging Mari McBride. He paid a teenage boy to do the same, in as loud a voice as he could manage, up and down Main Street. Then, because he knew those efforts would prove futile, he planned his course of action, all the while mentally cursing himself for his poor decision to leave her on her own while he took care of business regarding the Brazos Valley gang.

He'd discovered that yesterday, the gang had left the train at Trickling Springs. Kid Carver had purchased six horses at the livery stable, but only he, Frank, Hoss and Harry had been seen riding out of town. That left Finn Murphy and Clay Burrows unaccounted for.

That meant trouble. Luke sensed it from the tip of his hat to the toes of his boots. Murphy was in town, and Mari had gone missing. If Murphy had learned that Luke was in Trickling Springs asking questions about him, then made the connection between the man he'd seen with Mari on the train, the answer as to Mari's whereabouts was obvious. Murphy had her.

And Luke's reinforcements wouldn't arrive until this evening.

The conductor approached Luke, shaking his head. "She's not on the train, Mr. Garrett."

"I appreciate your checking for me."

Moments later, the train whistle blew and the conductor called, "All aboard."

Luke leaned against a post, crossed his arms and waited, hoping, but not expecting, to see Mari rush onto the platform. His tension built with each passing minute. Three passengers arrived late, a mother with a crying toddler and an elderly couple vocal with the excitement of beginning their journey to visit beloved grandchildren. Luke saw neither hide nor hair of a beautiful blonde anxious to continue the journey to her missing sister.

The moment the train wheels began to roll, he headed out, planning to gather facts and pick up her trail. A woman like Mari McBride wouldn't go unnoticed.

He tried the general store again and learned she'd spent a chunk of his bankroll and purchased a floral carpetbag in order to tote her loot around. Quickly and methodically, he canvassed every business in town. His stomach sank upon learning that a mare had gone missing from the livery. Mari definitely had been noticed, but no one had seen her carrying the suitcase. Murphy must have snatched her after she left the general store.

Luke returned to the store and set about retracing Mari's steps. The alley beside the apothecary shop provided a prime spot for an ambush, so Luke decided to give it a thorough search. He spotted signs of a scuffle immediately.

Hunkering down, he studied the patches of bent grass and disturbed dirt. Two men and a woman. Luke muttered an ugly curse. He'd proved a damned sorry excuse for a bodyguard.

He tracked the trio along a southwest path away from the center of town. As he followed the trail, a hard, hot rage began to churn in his gut. He was frightened for Mari, furious with himself, and he fantasized of drawing a bead on Finn Murphy and blowing the murdering snake away. He should have killed the son of a bitch years ago.

Recognizing that he needed to maintain his focus, Luke consciously locked away his fears and concerns and studied the trail with a practiced, professional eye. He followed the signs of the trio's passage for approximately five minutes, and then, beneath a cottonwood along the bank of a dry streambed, he made a disturbing discovery.

Mari's necklace hung from a leafy limb and swayed slowly back and forth in the gentle summer breeze. The chain was broken, knotted and threaded through a small piece of paper.

Luke's hand trembled ever so slightly as he reached up and removed the necklace from the tree.

The note consisted of a single sentence: *She sure is a pretty one.*

Luke's blood ran cold.

CHAPTER EIGHT

MARI WAS HOT. She was hot and thirsty and alternately angry and afraid.

They had her mounted on a docile sorrel mare led by the silver-haired man's more spirited gelding. Her hands were crossed at the wrist and tied to the saddlehorn. They'd taken her shoes and made unsettling promises about the consequences she'd face should she act in any way to impede their progress.

They rode for hours beneath the blazing sun, their route taking them deep into the Texas Hill Country. They forded creeks and trotted across meadows painted orange and yellow with butterfly weed and Mexican hats. They pushed their way through a thicket of blackberry vines that snagged and stained her new dress. Pain radiated from Mari's thighs, hips and bottom—it had been years since she'd spent this much time on horseback—but it took the ruin of her new dress to actually bring her to tears.

Since one man rode in front of her and the other behind her, little conversation took place. It wasn't until they finally stopped to rest that the men spoke of anything of consequence. Then she wished with all her heart that they'd kept their mouths shut.

"We'll lead him into Cedar Canyon," said the silver-haired outlaw. His name was Murphy, Finn Murphy, and Mari had realized early on in her abduction that he was the obvious leader of the pair.

The second villain, Clay Burrows, scratched his neck and pursed his lips. "Lookout Rock," he mused. "You thinking to take the high ground, then shoot him when he rides by like we did with that Pinkerton fella?"

"No." Murphy glanced over at Mari and smiled. The gleam of anticipation in his pale gray eyes sent a shiver coursing up her spine. "That's too easy. I have something more…personal…in mind for Luke Garrett."

"Yeah?" Burrows followed the path of Murphy's focus, then smirked. "Leave it to Murphy to figure a way to work a woman into his plans."

"Not just a woman. Garrett's woman." He chuckled softly. "I'm going to enjoy this."

Mari's stomach sank, and the fright that had been numbed by the rigors of their journey erupted anew, fresh and sharp and bigger than basic fear for her life. This time, for the first time in her life, Mari knew a woman's fear as the threat of sexual violation loomed.

That fright propelled her to speak up. "I'm not his woman."

Murphy arched a brow. Burrows snorted with disbelief.

"I'm not. I told you before he's just as likely to leave without me as to come look for me."

"Nice try, honey, but he had his tongue down your throat, and he took you with him when he sneaked off the train yesterday. You're his woman, all right."

I wish that were true, Mari thought. Better to have given her virginity to a man of her choice than to have it stolen from her by a villain.

Murphy's smile turned predatory as he ambled toward her. Mari forced herself to ignore the instinct to back away. He reached up, trailed a finger down her cheek. "That's why making you mine will be all the more entertaining."

Oh, heavens. Mari straightened her spine and squared her shoulders. "No matter what you do to me, sir, I will never be yours."

He chuckled. "Spunk. I like a gal with spunk." He put his hands at her waist, hoisted her up into the saddle and retied her wrists. "Breaking you is gonna be a pleasure."

He mounted his horse, and they resumed their journey, Murphy leading and Burrows at her back. Mari's thoughts whirled, a storm of anger and dread and determination. The echo of his threat boomed like thunder. *Breaking you. Breaking you. Breaking you.*

Mari vowed it wouldn't happen. She'd do whatever was necessary to prevent it. For herself, for her family. *I won't break. No matter what, I won't break. I'm a McBride of Willow Hill. If he does his worst, I'll be a willow. I'll bend, but I won't break.*

First, though, she'd do her level best to prevent Murphy from accomplishing any more mischief than he'd already managed.

Fortified by the exercise, Mari realized she needed to make her own plan. A battle was at hand and right now, her only weapon was her wits. Not an insignificant weapon, she told herself, but at this particular moment, she'd just as soon have a gun.

All right, Mari, think. For him to accomplish his threat, she'd need to be out of the saddle. On the ground she had her feet for weapons, her knees. Papa had taught all his daughters long ago the way to use their knees to disable a man.

Good. That's one weapon to keep at the ready. What else?

She needed her hands free. That would open up many more options. During the long ride, she'd tried repeatedly to free them, but she'd had little luck.

Mari studied the rope binding her wrists. Strong. Sturdy. A simple but effective square knot. While the knot wasn't as tight as it had been before their rest stop, she shouldn't expect it to come undone on its own.

Burrows interrupted her musing by calling out, "Hey, boss? You gonna let me take a turn with her?"

Murphy glanced over his shoulder. "I'm a generous man."

Mari shuddered, and though panic hovered at the edge of her consciousness, she managed to keep her focus. Her teeth. Maybe she could use her teeth to pick the knot loose. It was worth a try. So how to go about it in such a way that they wouldn't notice?

This would take some pretense. Some acting. What would Kat do in a situation like this?

Hunching her shoulders, hanging her head, Mari began to sob. It was an easy bit of acting.

"Now, don't be scared, honey," Burrows said, a grin in his voice. "It's just a screw. We're not gonna kill you or anything. Right, Murphy? Were you figuring on killing her?"

"Probably not. Unless she does something stupid."

"See?" Burrows continued. "Hell, you're liable to like it so much you'll want to join the Brazos Valley gang. That's happened to us before, you know. Women go for Finn Murphy."

I'll go for him, all right. I'll go for his gizzard with his very own knife.

Doubled over in the saddle, Mari continued her pretense of crying and surreptitiously put her teeth to the knot. The dry hemp tasted salty with sweat, and her thirst grew even more pronounced.

Behind her, Burrows continued to talk. "Remember those gals in Tucson, Murphy? A couple of redheaded sisters. They grabbed hold of ol' Murphy and didn't let him out of their house for damn near a week."

The prospect of rape obviously excited the outlaw, because he continued to rattle on about the gang's sexual conquests for a good ten minutes. As disconcerting as Mari found the topic, she was glad he had found something to keep him occupied, because it kept his attention in the past and away from her long enough for her to accomplish her goal.

With one last tug of her teeth, the knot slipped and the rope loosened enough for her to pull her hands free. She choked back an exultant cry.

Good. This was good. Now, what next? She was tempted to make a break and ride hell-bent for safety, except she recognized the foolishness of such an action. Their horses were faster, and they'd undoubtedly catch her before she traveled a hundred yards.

No. Better to wait for an opportunity to go for one of their guns. Mari knew how to shoot. She was, in fact, a better-than-decent shot.

In front of her, Murphy lifted his right hand, signaling a stop. Mari's gaze flicked down to her wrists, checking to make sure she still appeared bound. *Be ready. Think quick and be prepared to act.*

Finn Murphy gestured toward a hill rising no more than a quarter mile in front of them, the highest elevation Mari had seen that day. "Clay, ride ahead and check our trail. Need to make sure Garrett isn't following faster than I expected."

"Sure thing, boss."

Excellent idea, Mari thought. She much preferred dealing with villains one at a time.

"You can meet us at Cedar Canyon." Murphy glanced at Mari, then added. "Take your time."

Burrows's knowing leer made Mari's skin crawl. He spurred his horse, kicking up a cloud of red dirt as he cantered toward the hill. Murphy whistled "Yellow Rose of Texas" as they continued on their way.

They rode due west into the late-afternoon sun. Thirst became a vicious companion, but Mari refrained from requesting water out of fear that he'd notice the loosened rope.

She suspected her best opportunity would come when he went to lift her down from the saddle. She'd have the advantage of height, and he wouldn't be expecting her to launch herself at him. She could knock him down, go for his gun. Then…what? Shoot him? Could she do it? Did she have it in her to murder a man?

Except, it wouldn't be murder. It'd be self-defense and she needed to remember that. When the time arrived, she'd only get one chance. She couldn't afford squeamishness.

She wouldn't allow her parents to face the loss of another daughter.

Mari realized that no matter what he said, if Finn Murphy succeeded in his quest to kill Luke Garrett, then he'd likely kill her, too. It made no sense for him to allow her to live. Not only could she testify against him, she'd have knowledge of the general direction of his Texas hideout. No, this was a fight for her life. Mari had to be ready to kill.

Damn you, Luke Garrett. This is all your fault.

TENSION COILED in Luke's belly like a rattlesnake, cold-blooded and mean. It was done. The die had been cast. Finn Murphy was a dead man.

Luke had put the task off long enough.

Eighteen years he'd known the man. Eighteen years he'd despised him. Ten years since the first time he'd seriously contemplated killing him but refrained, because his sister had begged him not to do it. Today she'd probably load his gun for him.

Luke rode hard, following a trail they'd made no attempt to conceal. At the beginning of the chase he'd expected an ambush, and he'd proceeded with appropriate caution. But after passing without mishap three separate areas perfect for attack, he'd concluded that Murphy was leading him somewhere specific for a particular purpose.

He didn't like that idea one bit. He knew in his gut it meant trouble for Mari. "Damn me for letting her out of my sight for even a minute."

Luke spied a spot where they'd stopped. He dismounted, studied the signs. Three horses. Footprints, two men and—thank God—a woman. They were still a good hour ahead of him.

He remounted and moved out, determined to make up the time. Mari McBride was in trouble, and it was all his fault.

If Murphy hurt her, Luke would never forgive himself.

MURPHY REINED his mount to a stop beneath a cottonwood growing on the bank of a creek-fed pool. Had she not been busy plotting how to save her life, Mari might have appreciated the beauty of the spot. As it was, she quickly scanned the area, looking for loose rocks, fallen limbs, anything she might use as a weapon should her plan to knock him down and grab his gun fail.

Murphy swung his long leg over the saddle and slid to the ground. He tied his horse to the cottonwood trunk then turned and looked at her. He folded his arms, his gray eyes smoldering. "I've been looking forward to this all afternoon. Get down."

Mari went still. Down? That wasn't the plan! "I can't. My hands…"

"You got that rope untied an hour ago. Nice bit of acting there, though. Burrows never noticed you were free. Now get down from your horse, little lady."

No! He was too far away. She couldn't throw herself that far to knock him down. Besides, without the element of surprise she'd never be successful.

All right, Mari. Go to Plan B.

"I will as soon as I think of a Plan B," she murmured beneath her breath.

"C'mon, honey," he prodded. "Let me see a little leg while you're at it."

I'll show you my leg. Right before it kicks your private parts up to your ears.

Despite her silent bravado, fear rode her blood as she slid her leg over the saddle and slipped to the ground. She did her best to ignore it. She needed to focus all her energy on defeating her enemy.

Spine straight, shoulders back, Mari faced Finn Murphy. He'd moved closer. Mari eyed the distance, noted the gun at his hip. If she moved fast, could she—

"Strip."

"Excuse me?"

"Take your clothes off."

She licked her lips. "You want to go swimming?"

"I want to see those nice plump tits. Now. We'll take a dip afterward to cool off. Sex is sweaty work."

Now, fear not only rode her blood, it gnawed at her like a hungry dog on a juicy bone. She didn't want to be a willow that bends. She didn't even want to be a strong oak tree. She wanted to be a bird that could take wing and escape.

Without taking his heated gaze off her, Murphy reached into his boot and drew out a stiletto. "Don't be difficult," he warned, his voice resonant with threat. "I'm losing my patience."

Mari backed up a step and attempted the only Plan B that occurred to her at the moment. "My father will pay you. He's very wealthy. You may have heard of him. He's a famous architect, Trace McBride. If you return me unharmed, he'll pay you a substantial reward."

"Hmm…" Murphy scratched his jaw. "A rich daddy. That's an interesting tidbit of information. He likes you, hmm?"

Mari nodded briskly. "He loves me very, very much."

"Well…that's something to think about." He used the knife to point toward the buttons at her bodice. "Now, the clothes. If I'm forced to cut your dress off, you won't have anything to wear afterward."

Afterward. Mari shuddered. "But what about my father?"

"I'll think about it. Later. If he loves you like you say, he'll pay to have you back no matter what shape you're in. Even dead, for that matter. It's my experience that people like to have bodies to bury. Actually, just knowing where the bodies are already buried makes a difference."

Bodies. Oh, my. Mari closed her eyes.

"Show me your bosom, woman."

Mari's trembling fingers went to the buttons on her bodice. So much for Plan B. Yes, the logic had been weak, but it had been worth a try. If Murphy were stupid, it might have worked.

If Murphy were stupid, he wouldn't be the leader of one of the most notorious outlaw gangs in the country.

Plan C. I need a Plan C.

You better hope you come up with something better than Plan B.

The gentle breeze kissed her bare skin and she shuddered as the dress parted, revealing the thin linen chemise beneath it. Mari regretted her decision earlier at the general store to forgo a corset and travel in comfort until she caught up with her baggage and her own custom-fitted underpinnings.

Murphy's voice held a husky note as he took another step toward her saying, "Hurry up."

His urgency was apparent, and Mari knew she was running out of time. Plan C. Plan C. She still had the knee-to-the-groin move to employ, though she'd just as soon Plan C involve a weapon for use in quarters less close.

She looked down, ostensibly to aid in drawing her arm through her sleeve, but in reality, she searched the ground for a weapon. She saw nothing but small stones, a few sticks, a clump of flowering lantana, and a cactus shaped like a baseball bat.

An idea flickered, hovered just beyond reach. Then she heard her flamboyant, bohemian grandmother's voice, speaking clear as springwater in her mind. *A woman carries two potent weapons with her at all times; her body and her mind. Wielded together, they can make her all but invincible.*

Invincible.

Plan C burst fully formed like San Jacinto Day fireworks in Mari's brain. Without hesitation, without second thoughts, she made quick work of stripping off her dress. *My body. My mind. Invincible.*

She stood proudly before him dressed in only a thin chemise and drawers. His stare never lifted above her neck. His hand reached down between his legs. and he gave himself a vulgar stroke.

Mari swallowed hard, then said, "That works better with your britches off, you know."

Now he did look up, obviously surprised. Mari summoned every lesson she'd ever learned at the feet of her grandmother, Monique Day, Texas's most infamous flirt, and allowed her eyes to melt with sultry warmth. Then she smiled at him with wanton invitation and shrugged. "If this is inevitable, I might as well enjoy it. You are a handsome man, Finn."

Lust flared like a wildfire in his eyes and he took a step toward her, then abruptly stopped. Suspicion hung ripe in his tone as he asked, "What trick is this?"

Be bold. Be smart. Be invincible. Mari grabbed the hem of her chemise. "No trick." She whipped the garment over her head, baring her breasts to his hungry eyes. "Are you all talk, Finn? Or a man of action?"

He took two more steps toward her before his brain caught up. He unstrapped his gun belt, then set it on the ground and repeated the action with his knife.

Mari hated to see the weapons go—she'd have preferred using one of them. Yet, she still had options. She had a plan. She'd be invincible…or, if worse came to worst, a willow. She'd be fine. Just fine.

Murphy started toward her.

Oh, God.

"Wait!" She held up her hand, palm out, then threw him a smoldering look and repeated his earlier demand, "Strip."

He arched a brow. Amusement joined the lust gleaming in his eyes.

Mari needed him to be excited, distracted, so she put a purr into her voice. "Take your clothes off. I want to see you, too. You're such a…big…man, Finn. Let me see how big you really are."

Leering, he yanked off his shirt, then tugged off his boots. Mari's blood pumped with nervous determination. She chanced a glance toward her weapon of choice, judged the distance, planned her timing.

Finn Murphy shucked down his britches. It took all of Mari's acting ability not to recoil at the sight of his jutting penis.

She'd never seen one before, not an adult one, anyway. It looked a whole lot different than her brothers' tallywhackers did when she used to change their diapers. In no way did she find it appealing.

But it was imperative she pretend to like it, to be impressed, so she widened her eyes and said, "Aren't you a fine-looking man?"

He preened like a peacock. "Your turn. Scoot outta those bloomers, honey."

This time, Mari couldn't suppress her shudder. Seeing it, Murphy chuckled. "You're a hot one, aren't you?" He reached down again and stroked his cock. "Hell, if I'd known you wanted it this bad, I'd have stopped hours ago."

Now, Mari. Now's the time.

Though Finn Murphy didn't know it, the predator had just become the prey.

She hooked her left thumb in the waist of her drawers, then, giving her hips a wide, eye-summoning swing, walked toward him. With a tug of her thumb, she exposed just a little more skin. He all but salivated. She took two more steps toward him, then stopped within reach of her goal.

Mari braced herself. She wanted his attention on her left hand, not her right, so she tugged her drawers well below her navel.

"Goddamn," Murphy breathed.

Do it!

With a fast, smooth flurry of movement, she bent her knees and grabbed the cactus close to the ground. Needle-sharp spines gouged into her palm and fingers as she yanked the plant from the dirt and windmilled her arm. Swinging with all her might, Mari hit him with the cactus exactly where she'd aimed.

Right between the legs.

Howling, Murphy dropped to his knees, then onto his side. Shrill screams emerged from his throat.

Mari dropped the cactus and shook her hand hard. The spines burned. Her hand felt as if it was on fire. The rest of her felt like a warrior goddess. Invincible.

While Murphy writhed on the ground, Mari quickly confiscated her captor's gun and knife, then scooped up her clothes and hurried to the bank of the pond. Ignoring his curses and moans, she knelt and doused her burning hand into the water and whooshed it around, hoping to wash the cactus spines from her skin. With her good hand, she scooped up water and brought it to her mouth to drink. Once she'd quenched her thirst, she straightened and studied her hand. Though she'd managed to dislodge a fair number of needles, at least half of them remained embedded in her skin.

She found the pain reassuring. If her hand hurt this badly, Finn Murphy wouldn't be going anywhere anytime soon. Of course, Clay Burrows could show up at any moment, so she dared not waste too much time before getting out of here.

Still, the water looked inviting and she was already nearly naked. A few minutes delay surely wouldn't hurt. Mari glanced over her shoulder at the thrashing man on the ground and decided to risk it. She raided his saddlebags for a clean shirt with which to dry herself, then waded into the pond. The water soothed her, refreshed her, and the normal act of cleansing her body allowed her to relax. She emerged rejuvenated from the pond.

"You bitch," Murphy gasped. "You goddamn bitch."

Mari turned away from him, and calmly dried herself, then dressed. He continued to spit even more vile invectives, but she ignored both him and the twinge of guilt she felt for causing him such pain. Considering what he'd intended for her, he deserved her fury, not her sympathy. Still, it went against her nature to cause any living being pain—even a being as villainous as Finn Murphy.

Once she managed to button her gown, Mari turned her attention to finding her missing shoes. A search of Murphy's saddle proved fruitless. Either Burrows had them or they'd discarded them somewhere along the trail. Mari slipped her feet into Murphy's boots. They were big on her, but they'd do.

More than ready to continue her escape, she glanced at the two horses and made a swift decision to take them both. While she seriously doubted he physically could manage to follow her anytime soon, she'd rather be safe than sorry. Working one-handed, she adjusted his stirrups to fit her.

Hearing a stirring behind her, she glanced toward Murphy and saw him attempt to rise onto his knees. Groaning, he slumped back onto the ground.

"I imagine Mr. Burrows will arrive soon to help you," she told him matter-of-factly.

"You bitch." Murphy glared at her through pain-racked eyes. "You'll pay. I swear I'll make you pay for what you've done to me."

His threat was the spark that set fire to Mari's fury. "What *I've* done to *you?*" she snapped, stepping toward him, her hands braced on her hips. "You've got some nerve, Finn Murphy! You're the one who kidnapped me off the street. You're the one who intended rape. You brought this all on yourself."

It was as if he hadn't heard a word she said. "One way or another, I'll make you pay," he vowed. "Whatever I do is gonna hurt you far, far worse than this hurts me now."

He certainly sounded like he meant it. Did she want to have that threat hanging over her future? No, not at all.

But eliminating the threat meant eliminating Murphy. Mari raised the gun, leveled it at her attacker. Could she do it? Could she shoot the man now, in cold blood, with her life not immediately at risk?

Yes. Yes, she could pull the trigger. She could end the threat, end his life, with a bullet through the heart. Right here, right now.

Anger churned inside her as Mari stared down the barrel of Finn Murphy's gun.

"You're not gonna do it," he said, his tone filled with scorn.

For a long moment, Mari's finger twitched against the trigger, then slowly, she lowered the gun to her side. "No, I'm not. That would make me no better than you."

Slipping her foot into a stirrup, Mari swung up onto his horse. She wrapped the sorrel's reins around her right wrist, then took up the black's reins in her left hand and gave him one last look. "I guess I'll just have to hope somebody else manages to give you what you deserve."

He spit more curses at her as Mari gave the horse a kick and calmly rode out, following the trail they'd made coming in.

Once away from the villain's sight, she indulged in a groan of pain. Her hand burned. Her bottom, already sore from hours on horseback, ached with every bounce upon the saddle. Her nose was sunburned, her lips dry and cracked. The borrowed boots rubbed blisters on her feet. As if that wasn't enough, she was now a target for retribution from a silver-haired, gray-eyed, black-hearted villain.

Luke Garrett had plenty to answer for.

Maybe she *would* shoot someone in cold blood, after all.

CHAPTER NINE

LUKE EYED THE SPOT on the trail where one of the three horses veered off. Not Mari, he noted with disappointment, but not surprise. The smaller mount remained with the biggest horse. This wasn't sign of an escape, but a separation. He followed the trail of the single horse a few feet, then surveyed the landscape.

The high ground. Odds were Murphy sent Burrows to the high ground to watch for Luke. That meant a couple of things. One, Burrows must have seen him coming by now, and two, their destination likely was close.

So, how should he approach? They knew he was coming. No sense trying to sneak in. He might as well ride in bold as brass, guns not blazing but at the ready. Murphy wanted him there for a reason.

Spurring his horse, he followed Mari's trail, energized by the knowledge that the confrontation was undoubtedly near at hand. Knowing he'd need cool, calm control during the showdown, Luke allowed himself a few minutes to give his rage toward Murphy free rein and get it out of his system.

Fury, hatred, a fierce need for vengeance—all roared through him like a springtime tornado. This time, finally, he'd make Finn Murphy pay. For Janna and the girls. For the finest Texas Ranger who ever wore the badge, his friend Harvey Rowan. For Luke's stepfather,

Brian Callahan. For Rory. For the countless innocent people Murphy had wronged, robbed or murdered.

And now, for Mari McBride.

He prayed that this time he wouldn't be too late.

So caught up was he with the intensity of his loathing, when he first spied the figure up ahead of him on the trail, he thought the virulence of his emotions must have caused him to hallucinate. That couldn't be Mari McBride perched atop a boulder, arms folded and foot tapping impatiently against the rock.

"It's about darn time you got here," the apparition snapped as he approached.

"Mari?"

"You and I need to have a discussion regarding the duties of a bodyguard. I must tell you, Luke Garrett, so far your job performance is less than stellar."

Mari. Relief rolled over Luke like a wave. She looked tired and worn and torn and tangled—more beautiful than any woman he'd ever seen.

He swung from his horse, grabbed her around the waist and lifted her off the rock. He twirled her around, once, twice. "Dammit, woman. I was worried about you."

"As well you should have been. I was in serious dang—"

Luke stopped her words with a kiss. He didn't plan it, he just did it. He swooped down and took her mouth in a happy-to-see-you, don't-say-that-word-and-remind-me friendly smack. Only, somewhere along the way, the kiss changed to something else. Something different.

Something more.

She tasted of blackberries and felt fragile as blown glass in his arms. A great, aching tenderness welled up inside Luke, and his mouth softened on hers. So sweet. Innocence and a warmth that called to the coldness that dwelled in his soul.

When she responded to him, answering the gentle tug of his teeth against her bottom lip with a low, throaty groan, he knew a fierce rush of pleasure. His lips drifted across her face, and his tongue traced the delicate whorls of her ear. She shivered when he nibbled at her lobe, then nipped his way down her neck. Her breathless sigh had him spreading his legs and pulling her even closer. He covered her mouth with his once again, only this time, his kiss was hungry.

Luke feasted on her lips, invaded her with his tongue. Plundered the sweet, delicious mouth over and over and over again. He simply couldn't get enough. Urgency rose within him and threatened his control. He wanted—no, he *needed* his hands on her. He needed her hands on him. He needed…well, hell.

He needed to make sure they were safe.

He lifted his head, took a step back. She stared up at him, her eyes wide and filled with shock.

Luke thought he should probably apologize. For the kidnapping, not the kiss. Be damned if he'd apologize for kissing her. Instead, he asked, "Did they hurt you, honey?"

Tears flooded her eyes. "Yes."

No. God, no.

"Not bad, though," she added, her bottom lip trembling. "I was so scared. He was going to hurt me really bad, and I was so afraid."

"Ah, Mari." He wrapped her in a comforting hug and held her against him. "Where is Murphy?"

"Thataway." Her head buried against his chest, she waved her left hand. "About a twenty-minute ride."

"What about the other man?"

"Burrows? He's probably helping Murphy by now. He came riding through here awhile back. He was watching for you. That's how I knew you'd be along sometime soon."

"Helping Murphy do what?"

"Pull needles out of his…um, well, he's hurt. I hurt him. I…oh, Luke. It was awful."

The story that poured out of her during the next few minutes angered Luke, amazed him and filled him with admiration. The male in him couldn't help but feel a twinge of horror at Murphy's fate. One good thing, he needn't keep an eye out for Murphy and Burrows tonight. No way could the bastard ride a horse, and he'd undoubtedly keep his henchman close by to help.

It impressed Luke that Mari had had the temerity to attack Murphy.

He'd known from the first that the woman had spunk, but to see it put into action…well… "I wish my sister had your guts."

She burrowed her head even closer and spoke into his shirt. "I wasn't brave. I was scared of being a willow."

Luke didn't understand that, but the way she said it made him smile. Her shoulders shook as she continued to weep against his chest. Luke patted her back and spoke soft, soothing words into her ear, and wished he could do more to comfort her.

Ordinarily, he didn't like dealing with a woman's tears, because too often they were used to manipulate a man. These tears were different. These tears were being wrenched from the heart of a strong woman, and that gave them power to bring a man like Luke to his knees.

"Hush, now, Mari," he murmured. "You're all right now. Everything's fine."

"No it's not," she insisted. "We're out in the middle of nowhere and I don't want to get back on a horse because my bottom is killing me and I'm hungry and I'm going to have nightmares about the way Murphy looked naked and my hand hurts from cactus spines!"

Luke took them in order. "I know this country and there's a nice spot to camp nearby—a different place from the one Murphy took you to. I have some jerky in my saddlebag and as soon as we're settled, I'll hunt us up some meat for our supper. Now, I'm afraid I can't stop your nightmares, but I will promise to be close if you need me in the night. As far as your hand goes, let's see what I can do to make it better."

Gently cradling her right hand in his, Luke turned her palm up and winced. Blood smeared her hand from innumerable pinpricks. Luke counted half-a-dozen substantial thornlike spines still embedded in her skin. "My poor, brave little warrior."

"Don't touch it," Mari said, a pout in both her voice and expression. Remnants of her tears clung to her thick, curling lashes. "It hurts too much to touch. I got most of them out, but those…it hurts."

"They have to come out or they'll fester. I'll be gentle, honey." Then he brought her hand up to his mouth and clamping a cactus thorn between his teeth, gently and carefully tugged it free. He turned his head, spat out the spine, then repeated the action five more times. Then, his eyes fixed on hers, Luke used the slightest brush of his tongue to test every inch of skin on the inside of her hand. "Did I miss any?" he asked, his voice husky and low.

Eyes wide, Mari shook her head.

"Good." Luke again brought her hand to his mouth, only this time, instead of barely touching her, he licked at all the tiny pinpricks on her palm, then sucked at the wounds, staring deeply into her eyes as he did so.

Mari's eyelids grew heavy and she shuddered. Luke drew her entire index finger into his mouth, rubbed it with his tongue, and sucked, then repeated the action with her other fingers and lastly, her thumb.

"What are you doing?" she breathed.

When finally he released her, he winked and said, "Kissing it and making it better. Did it work?"

She swallowed hard, blinked twice and nodded.

"Good." Luke fought his instincts to take his ministrations to other parts of her body that might benefit from his attentions. Still, he couldn't help but ask. "Anyplace else need kissin'?"

She wet her lips, then once again, nodded. Her movement slow and graceful, she brought up her left hand and offered it up to him.

Luke arched a brow and glanced at the hand. He didn't see any cactus spines, nor any scrapes or cuts or bruises. Her hand looked...virginal. The look in her eyes, however, was pure temptation, and Luke surrendered to it. He licked and nipped and nibbled and sucked until they both were breathing hard. When she finally drew her hand away from him and took a step back, Luke had to shove his own hands in his pockets to keep from reaching for her again.

Mari cleared her throat. "Maybe I'm not too sore to ride, after all. Maybe we should ride on to Trickling Springs."

"No." Luke rocked back on his heels and tried to ignore the ache in his loins. "It's too late. We couldn't get even halfway before dark, and tonight's a new moon. It wouldn't be safe for you to travel."

She hesitated a long moment before asking, "Will I be safe staying with you?"

Luke went still. "Do you want to be?"

The seconds dragged by like hours until she answered. "Yes. I guess I do."

Damn.

"It's been a traumatic day, and my emotions are in flux. I'm probably not thinking straight."

Personally, Luke was fine with the direction her thoughts were taking. More than fine, in fact. He knew from experience that a brush with death sometimes left a person with the desire to reaffirm life. At the moment, he could think of nothing he'd like better than helping Mari McBride celebrate being alive.

However, because she had basically said no by saying yes, and because he refused to allow his pecker to make decisions for him, Luke had but one course of action to take. "So," he said, stepping away. "How about that jerky?"

THE AROMA of roasted rabbit lingered on the air like a song as the sun sank toward the treetops that hugged the banks of the Perdenales River. Mari sipped cool, sweet water from a tin cup and watched the western sky explode in a pallet of vermillion, rose and gold. With her hunger assuaged, her thirst quenched, and her body enjoying a reprieve from the saddle, she expected to be able to relax. Instead, she hummed with tension that simply wouldn't stop.

Her nerves were a jumble. She jumped at every rustle in the bushes and startled at every crackle of the campfire. By rights, she should be drooping from exhaustion, ready to lie upon the bedroll spread out beside the fire and lose herself in the oblivion of sleep. Instead, she felt jittery as a cat on ice.

"Pretty sunset tonight," Luke observed, coming up to stand beside her. "Seems I spend so much time in town, I forget to look up and enjoy the show."

"It's been my parents' habit to watch the sunset together every evening," Mari said wistfully. "A year after Papa married Jenny, he added a widow's walk atop Willow Hill so they could have a better view of the sky. It's their private time, and the children aren't allowed to interrupt."

"Bet the McBride Menaces hated that."

She smiled wistfully. "My sisters and I used to climb the neighbor's cottonwood tree and spy on them. Sometimes we'd catch them sparking, but mostly they'd sit in their chairs holding hands and talking. Sometimes, they didn't even talk. Yet, every time they come back downstairs, they always seem more…I don't know… more connected." After a moment's pause, she added, "I don't recall them watching the sunset together once since the Spring Palace fire."

"Losing a loved one is always tough."

The edgy element of Mari's mood sharpened into temper at his observation. "And shame on our loved ones for getting themselves lost. I swear, when I get hold of Kat, I'm gonna wring her neck."

"That would be a more believable threat were you not working so hard to prove she's not already dead."

"I've already proved that." Mari glanced up at Luke. "With all the excitement, I didn't tell you what I learned in Trickling Springs. They were there, Luke. The night of the fire. A woman at the chocolate shop remembered them."

Surprise widened his eyes. "You're not serious."

"Oh, yes I am. She definitely remembers them. She remembered Kat's necklace, and she described Rory and Kat right down to her love of butterscotch taffy. It proves that my sister and your brother didn't die in that fire."

He thought about that a moment, then said softly, "I'll be damned."

"They're the ones who need to worry about damnation," Mari snapped. "Their selfish elopement has caused serious harm."

Luke rubbed the back of his neck as she continued, "Kat needlessly subjected our family to devastating grief. Finding her alive will not erase that. Nor will it bring back months of sunsets for my parents to share or the days Billy went without cracking a single smile or the weeks Emma spent in bed with the covers pulled over her head, laid low by the loss of her sister just as she was beginning to heal from the death of her husband. Don't get me wrong, I'm thrilled clear to my bones that Kat is alive. Nevertheless, that doesn't change the fact that because she ran off with your brother, I had to use a cactus for a baseball bat to defend my virtue."

Agitated now, Mari paced back and forth along the riverbank. "I'm so *angry* at her. I've mourned her so deeply. Today, I was so afraid. I was terrified."

"My fault." Grimacing, Luke faced her. "I'm sorry, Mari. I never should have left you alone."

She winced and closed her eyes, shaking her head. "Yes, your bodyguard skills could use some work, but I'm not blaming you, Luke. Not really. The fault lies at our siblings' feet. They fell in love and acted foolishly, and that's what led to us having the bad luck to meet Finn Murphy on the—"

She broke off abruptly. *Love. Bad luck. Love and Bad Luck.* Mari glanced down at her hand. *The Bad Luck Love Line.*

"No. I won't believe it."

"Believe what?"

That I was wrong to deny my own intuition. That I was wrong to dismiss Roslin as a charlatan. Her thoughts drifted back to the gypsy's room that night in Hell's Half Acre, and the unsettling sense of awareness that overcame her the first time the stranger placed the sapphire necklace in Mari's hand.

"The necklace." She clapped her hand against her breast, reaching for the pendant that wasn't there. "Oh, no. He took it, and I forgot. I don't wear it all the time like my sisters and I forgot. Oh, no."

Mari's teeth tugged at her lower lip as despair poured through her. "I've got to go back. If the curse is real, then I must have my necklace. I've got to track down Murphy and—"

"Hush," Luke said, pressing a finger against her mouth. He reached into his pocket and pulled out her necklace. The sapphire pendant dangled from a broken chain, glowing a brilliant blue in the soft light of the setting sun.

Relief rolled over Mari like a wave. "How did… Murphy sent it to you?"

"With a little note. So what's this talk about a curse? Look, I've known that Irishman a long time, and you can't let him scare you with his yammering on about banshees and the like."

Holding the pendant in her left hand, Mari traced the facets of the stone with her right index finger. "Do you believe in curses, Luke?"

"Not coming out of that son of a bitch's mouth."

"I'm not talking about Murphy. I mean fairies and ancient prophecies and—" she gathered up the broken necklace and dropped it down her bodice "—legendary jewels."

"Legendary," he murmured, his regard steady on her chest. Then he gave himself a shake and said, "Fairies, hmm? Well, I don't know that I've given it much thought. I'm as superstitious as the next fella, I guess. I appreciate a run of luck at cards, and I shy away from black cats. I've never put much store in fortune-tellers who claim to read the future from tea leaves at the bottom of a cup."

"Me neither." Mari's mouth twisted in a rueful smile. "Believe me, holding that opinion hasn't been easy. Not in my family. Imagine being a McBride in a town where the Bad Luck Wedding Dress or the Bad Luck Wedding Cake is still mentioned in the local newspaper at least once a month. Customers at my candy shop regularly ask not which chocolate tastes the best, but which one will bring them the most good luck."

"So why do you think someone put a curse on your necklace?"

"Not the necklace. My family." After a moment's hesitation, she sighed and said, "We were told it's an ancient curse upon our family that dooms us to be unlucky in love."

She gave him a brief synopsis of the McBride sisters' visit to Hell's Half Acre before Emma's wedding. "Kat found the idea terribly romantic, and from that moment on, she eyed all her beaus as potential heroes to partner with her in ending the Curse of Clan McBride."

"Rory Callahan is nobody's hero."

Mari considered his assertion. Rory was Luke's

brother. He should know the man. Yet something else nagged at her, a thought just beyond reach. "Emma already had found her love in Casey, and Kat used to spend hours on end imagining what task the newlyweds would need to accomplish in order to fulfill their portion of ending the curse. Casey's death made it impossible for Emma to accomplish any sort of task, so that ended any possibility that my sisters and I could end the so-called curse."

"Why's that?"

"Casey was Emma's true love." Mari gave a small, red rock at her feet a little kick. But what if…maybe she and Kat would still have their turn. What if the curse wasn't nonsense? What if it was real?

What if Kat was working on her task?

Mari glanced up at Luke. "Maybe this wasn't a selfish elopement, after all. Maybe your brother *is* Katrina's true love, and the two of them are pursuing her task, and it has somehow prevented her from contacting us. Maybe by the time we find them, they will have fulfilled the first of the conditions for lifting the curse."

Luke tossed a dried mesquite twig into the campfire. The wood ignited, hissed and spit. "Look, Mari. I'm not denying that your family has had a run of romantic bad luck, and I'm not saying this clan curse isn't for real. One thing I can say for certain, however, is that Rory Callahan simply isn't your sister's true love."

"How can you be so sure?"

Luke opened his mouth to speak, then hesitated.

"Well?" Mari prodded.

"Just trust me."

"You're an outlaw," she grumbled. "You rob innocent people of their hard-earned money. How can I possibly trust you?"

He gave her a wink and a grin. "You know, honey, I've been asking myself that question ever since you sashayed into my saloon daring me not to come along on this adventure."

She wrinkled her nose and growled at him. Luke laughed, and Mari answered with a reluctant smile. A moment later, she sighed heavily, then spoke from her heart. "I'm so angry at her, Luke. Look at what almost happened to me today. This day has been one of the most frightening of my life. I could deal with it better if I thought there was a reason—a good reason—it all happened."

"I understand. However, you're not gonna find the answers here beside the Perdenales, so let it go for now." He put his hands on her shoulders and massaged her muscles. "Try to relax, sugar. You're all wound up."

It took only seconds for all thought of curses and Kat and a rogue named Callahan to evaporate from Mari's mind. His hands felt like heaven. Strong fingers kneaded the tense cords beneath her skin, moving just where she wanted them in response to her silent request as she arched her neck first one way, and then the other. The jittery feeling inside her gradually subsided and Mari began to calm.

Began to melt against him.

"There, does that feel better?" Luke asked, his voice husky and low, his warm breath feathering against her neck.

Mari purred in response. His hands slid over her shoulders, and he squeezed them, then started to step back. "No," she protested. "Don't stop."

After a moment's hesitation, his hands continued their ministrations, his thumbs working their way down her spine. He massaged her back until she arched like a cat and let out a throaty moan.

"Dammit, Maribeth. You're playing with fire."

Mari knew it, and she couldn't explain it. Not three hours ago, she'd come close to being brutally violated. By rights, she shouldn't want to be near a man, much less in his arms. Why, after Emma's friend Sue-Ellen Johnson was grabbed and forcibly kissed by a drunken friend of her brother's, she flinched every time a man came within a dozen feet of her for at least a month. And Sue-Ellen hadn't had to look at her assaulter naked!

Now, the idea of looking at Luke Garrett naked sounded rather intriguing.

Good gracious, Mari. Maybe you really have lost your mind.

The massage softened to a caress as Luke's hands drifted lower, until they settled on her hips. Tension and a keen sense of anticipation hummed in the air. Finally, as soft as a whisper, he bent his head and brushed his lips against her neck.

Yes. That jumpy, edgy, needy feeling returned fully, and Mari realized the driving force behind it. She wanted him to kiss her. She wanted him to turn her around and wrap her in his arms like he had on the train. She wanted to lose herself in the shelter of his arms and the pleasure of his kiss and the delight of his caress. The promise of his desire. Never mind that he was a thief, a scoundrel, an outlaw. She *did* trust him. She wanted to enjoy him, to indulge herself. She wanted to live, even if it meant living dangerously.

That is such a McBride Menace thing to do.

The thought was almost enough to give her pause. Almost.

Today, she'd almost died. What a shame it would have been to have died a virgin. In the wake of her broken engagement and the mortifying gossip Alex had spread around town about her, she didn't anticipate getting married anytime soon. The men in town would either allow nonsense like Alex spouted to scare them off, or they would view her as a challenge to conquer.

Well, if any conquering was to be done, then she wanted to be the one to do it, not some villain intent upon wickedness. Not some lily-livered Lothario pretender who blamed others for his own failings. Mari wanted to be the one in control. She wanted to conquer Luke Garrett.

What would it hurt? No one would know. The two of them were all alone out here in the middle of nowhere. And despite the fact that Luke was an outlaw and a truly horrible bodyguard, she liked him. She liked his wit and his grin and the twinkle in his eyes and the dimple in his cheek. His sheer masculinity made her knees go weak.

Mari's heart pounded. Her fingers itched to touch him. Summoning her courage, boldly, she turned to him. "No."

His hands dropped away from her. "No?"

"Earlier, you asked if I wanted to be safe with you and I said yes. I've changed my mind, Luke." Reaching out, she hooked a finger around his belt loop and pulled him toward her. Going up onto her tiptoes, she used her free hand to bring his head down toward hers. Then, just before their lips met, she added, "Go ahead and burn me."

CHAPTER TEN

BURN HER, HELL. Luke was the one going up in flames.

Her lips were soft and hot as they molded themselves against his. His will to resist lasted less than a second, and when her tongue slid past his lips to tangle with his, heat shot straight to his groin.

His hands gripped her hipbones as he took control of the kiss. His tongue plunged and plundered the sweet hot wetness of her mouth. He took her mouth with a fierceness that fanned the wildfire raging between them, until she moaned and met his passion with a hunger equal to his. At that point, the kiss took on a life of its own, and Luke went along for the ride.

Mari pressed closer against him and her soft curves flattened against his solid form. He threaded his fingers through her hair, the silky strands sliding across his skin soft as a sunset.

It lasted for minutes or maybe a month until, finally, they both came up for air. When she took a step back, he let her go without protest, his hands dropping to his sides, curling into fists with the effort not to reach for her again. He watched the pulse throb at the base of neck and resisted the temptation to lick it.

Slowly, her hand lifted to the yellow satin bow at the center of her bodice. Grasping the trailing ribbon, she gave it a tug. The bow slipped free.

"This is a mistake," Luke said, his tone hoarse.

"Why?"

"You don't want this."

"Yes, I do." Her finger twirled the dangling ribbon. "I told you I changed my mind."

"More likely you've just lost it."

"I considered that myself, but rejected the idea." She laughed softly, seductively, and the sound sent a shudder skating up his skin. "I know what I'm doing."

"Do you?" Needing to touch her, he traced the curve of her cheek with the pad of his thumb. "*Are* you a virgin, Maribeth?"

She nodded.

He muttered a hard word beneath his breath even as he slid his thumb down her neck and along her collarbone, pausing to stroke back and forth across the hollow at the base of her neck. "I live my life like an outlaw without honor. You'd be well served to remember that when you start teasing me."

"I'm not teasing."

"Well, you're damn sure not thinking straight," he said, his thumb dipping lower, skimming across her skin just above the neckline of her dress. Just above the loosened ribbon.

Mari's breasts swelled toward him as she leaned forward into his touch. "Maybe not, but maybe it's time for me to think a little crooked. For years now I've tried hard to live down my reputation and what did that get me? I think I'll probably always be a McBride Menace in the eyes of Fort Worth, only now, thanks to my former fiancé, I'm the frigid McBride Menace. Do you have a clue how humiliating that is?"

"Sugar, Alexander Simpson doesn't have the sense

God gave a goat. Don't let him play with your brain that way."

"I want you to play with my body, Luke."

Her comment shocked him. Come to think of it, this entire exchange shocked him. While he had little experience with virgins—*no* experience with virgins, actually—he couldn't imagine many of them acted so forward. "You're a bold bit of baggage."

His hand cupped the plump fullness of her breast. "You're reacting to the danger you faced today, Maribeth. You'd regret this tomorrow. You'd give me hell for it."

"Does the idea frighten you?"

"*You* frighten me."

Again, she gave that alluring little laugh, then her tongue came out to wet her lips. "You're a big bad gunslinger and you're frightened of the likes of me?"

"Mari, you gelded a man with a cactus. Any fella with a lick of sense is gonna be wary of you." He thumbed the hardened peak of her nipple and she purred.

"Hell," he muttered, then gave it one more try. "Be sure, Mari McBride. Once you've given your virginity, you can't get it back."

"*Given* is the salient word, here." Her smile was sultry as she swayed toward him and pressed her soft curves up against him. "It's my choice. My decision. Have you made yours?"

Luke stared down into her beautiful face, saw desire and need and a hint of vulnerability in her eyes, and he knew what he had to do. Speaking from the heart, Luke said, "You are a tantalizing woman, Mari McBride. I wanted you the moment I first laid eyes on you, and I want you so much right now it's like to make me crazy. But…"

Her long, curling lashes fluttered down once, twice. "You're turning me down?"

"Hell no. I may be crazy, but I'm not an idiot. I'm just trying to figure out the logistics. Your first time should be in a soft feather bed, but all I have to offer you is a bedroll shared with a snake."

Mari gave her head a little shake. "Let's leave Finn Murphy out of this."

"Fine by me, but I'm not talking about Murphy. I'm talking about that. See?" He pointed toward the grassy area that stretched beyond the bedroll spread beside the campfire.

Mari followed the direction he gestured. "See what?"

"There. In the grass. I figure it for a three footer, maybe three and a half. Just a bull snake, though. Nothing poisonous like that rattler you tangled with yesterday. However, I don't expect you'll be anxious to lie down with a snake—of the cold-blooded variety. I'm arguably a snake, but I'm definitely hot-blooded. Now…" He made a show of looking around even as he felt her going stiff in his arms. "Where's a good spot I can move the bedroll so you won't need to worry about—"

"No!" Mari scrambled away from him, turning in a circle, scanning the ground with a wild look in her eyes. "I'm sorry, Luke. I can't. That's just one too many reptiles today."

In a lucky coincidence of timing, something rustled in the nearby bushes. Mari screamed and scrambled atop a nearby rock.

Watching her, Luke knew a real sense of regret. She truly was tantalizing, and he honestly did want her more than he'd ever wanted another woman.

Some days it was damned hard for a man to be a hero.

AFTER A NIGHT spent precariously balanced in a hammock fashioned from Finn Murphy's bedroll and a rope, suspended between a cottonwood and a live oak, Mari awoke the following morning surprisingly rested and hideously embarrassed. It was bad enough that she'd acted the empty-headed fool and refused to sleep on the ground last night, but her conduct before that, the way she'd thrown herself at Luke, then changed her mind like a wishy-washy tease left her mortified.

It was just the sort of behavior that Alexander Simpson had accused her of.

In her defense, it wasn't frigidity on her part that put a stop to events. She'd quite simply gone batty for a bit at the notion of tangling once again with a snake. Considering the day she'd had, a temporary lapse was understandable. Embarrassing, but understandable.

The problem was that now she didn't know how to act toward Luke. It was, in a rather unusual sense of the term, an awkward morning after.

Gathering her courage, Mari opened her eyes, checked the ground below for slithery things, then swung to her feet. Luke lay atop bare dirt, propped against a saddle, his hat pulled over his eyes. His chest rose and fell with a steady rhythm. He appeared to be fast asleep.

Mari seized the opportunity to escape down to the river to wash. Just as she left the campsite, Luke let out a snore that had her jerking her head around, eyeing him suspiciously.

His lips twitched. The villain *was* awake and pretending otherwise. In that instant of recognition, pique overrode Mari's embarrassment. She wrinkled her nose and stuck out her tongue at him. His laughter rang in the air and followed her down toward the water.

When she returned to the campsite, washed and prepared to take him on, she found both horses saddled and Luke ready to ride. He handed her a kerchief filled with blackberries saying, "This will have to do for breakfast, I'm afraid. If I remember right, we should run across a stand of peach trees not too far along the trail back to town."

That, apparently, was that. No recriminations, no sly remarks, not even any teasing. And he had taken care of breakfast. Mari could have kissed him for making it easy for her. But then, kissing was what got her into trouble in the first place, wasn't it?

Luke set a hard pace, and they made good time, stopping once for peaches, then periodically to rest the horses. They didn't converse during the ride, and he limited talk to neutral topics during the breaks. Mari was glad of it. She told herself so, anyway.

She didn't know what she'd say if he asked if she wanted to take up where they'd left off last night before the snake sighting.

She pondered the question at length during the journey, giving the matter serious thought. Pros and cons showered through her mind like a springtime rain. So intent was she upon exploring the possibilities that she didn't immediately notice when Luke abruptly reined his horse to a halt and pinned her with a glare. "Would you quit staring at my butt?"

Mari felt the heat of a blush crawl up her face. "I didn't…I'm not…I…uh…I apologize."

"You know, Mari, I've tried to be a gentleman about this, but I've about run out of patience. I'm trying to get us to the Trickling Springs Hotel just as fast as I can."

"You are?"

"I am."

"So, are we going to…?"

"That's up to you. I thought about it all night long. I figure I'll get you within tossin' distance of a bed, and then it's up to you. You've had time to sleep on the notion now, so that lets me off the hook as far as taking advantage of you goes."

Mari scowled at him. "Why in the world are you worrying about that? You're an outlaw. You make a living from taking advantage of people."

He scowled right back at her. "Not virgins."

"You don't steal from virgins?"

"Their money, maybe. Not their virtue."

Mari lifted her chin. "Well," she drawled, "aren't you Mr. Ethics."

"Actually what I am is hot and hungry and hard as a petrified fence post, and that makes for a damned uncomfortable ride. So keep your eyes on the trail, sugar, and give me a chance here. I'm doing the best I—" He broke off abruptly and went completely still.

"What is it?" Mari asked.

He put a finger to his mouth. Listened hard. "Riders," he said flatly. "Coming fast."

He looked around, pointed toward an outcropping of rock off to the right. "There. Get behind those rocks until I can figure out if they're friend or foe." When Mari hesitated, he said, "Go!"

"But what about you?"

"I'm the bodyguard, remember? Don't you think it's time I do my job? Besides," he added, flashing her a quick, sharp grin. "I'm hoping to talk 'em into sharing their lunch."

Mari kicked her horse and rode for the shelter of the rocks. She wasn't about to hang around and risk another encounter with the likes of Finn Murphy. Luke was right. He was the bodyguard. She needed to let him do his job.

As she drew near her target, she realized the space wasn't big enough for her and her horse. Glancing around, she spied a stand of cedar trees not far from the rocks. She veered in that direction, guided her mount deeply into the trees, then slid from the saddle and secured the reins. Safely hidden now, Mari moved to a spot where she could watch what transpired on the trail.

While she sought cover, Luke had moved to higher ground. Whatever he saw must have reassured him, because after a moment's study, he once again descended to the trail. Mari considered following, but he looked in her general direction and waved her off.

Impatient, she waited. Moments later, she spied three riders approaching. They were a rough-looking group. All lean and hard. Two wore brown felt hats, the third black straw. Each of them was armed with pistols and rifles and bowie knives.

Mari shifted farther back into the trees. Tense, she watched the men approach her bodyguard. She was too far away to read their expressions, but Luke appeared loose and relaxed rather than on guard. Of course, considering his lack of success as a bodyguard, no telling what she should expect.

Then the black-hatted man reached into his saddlebags and Mari held her breath. The rider drew out...

"Lunch?" Mari watched in surprise as Luke took a bite of what appeared to be jerky. Be hanged if the man didn't get lunch, after all.

The men dismounted and Luke started talking. Mari watched while he finished his jerky and started on a piece of bread, gesturing with it while he spoke. Minutes later, the four men broke into laughter. Well, didn't the four of them just look all cozy and friendly? Obviously, these folk were not foe.

Mari retrieved her horse and headed back to the trail. As she approached, the men fell silent. The three newcomers watched her warily. One of them took a step backward. Luke smirked and said, "Show 'em your hands, Maribeth, so they know you're not carrying." After a significant pause, he added, "A cactus."

Embarrassment caused Mari's cheeks to flush with heat as the men shared grins of amusement. She'd make Luke pay for that once they were alone again.

Mari dismounted and offered the group a polite smile, waiting for Luke to perform introductions. Instead, he addressed the man in the straw hat saying, "I think I've told you everything. Y'all can head on out. Happy hunting."

"We'll get the job done," Straw Hat said. "You know you can count on us, boss."

One of the other men handed Mari a neckerchief with its ends tied together. Peeking inside, she spied two biscuits and three strips of jerky. "Thank you, Mr...?"

He tipped his hat but didn't reply. Taciturn fellows, she thought as the riders mounted their horses. With an arch of her brow and a pointed look, she demanded an explanation from Luke.

"They're going after Murphy," he told her as he sent the men off with a salute.

"Oh?" Mari settled an even more interested stare upon the departing riders. "Who are they? How did they happen to be here?"

"I sent for them yesterday. We've been looking for that son of a bitch for a long time."

"Who is 'we'?"

"*We'd* better get going. Still a ways to ride into town. You gonna eat both those biscuits? I'll take one if you're not."

"Luke!" she said in a warning tone. "Who were those men?"

"Friends of mine. Don't ask any more, Mari. I don't want to lie to you."

She thought about that a moment. "Are they members of your gang?"

"Damn, but you're a hardheaded woman." He exhaled a frustrated sigh. "All right, they were members of my gang. Those men were Texas Rangers. They're hunting down Finn Murphy and the Brazos Valley gang to capture them and bring them to justice. I sent 'em a telegram, and they dropped what they were doing and came here straight away."

Mari narrowed her eyes. "Fine. Just be that way. I guess it doesn't matter who they were as long as they shared their biscuits."

"That's right," he shot back. "Now you get it. So, are you ready to ride?"

"Definitely. The sooner we get there, the better." She climbed back onto her horse.

"That's what I say." He swung up into the saddle.

"Good."

"Fine."

They rode for almost half an hour without exchanging another word. Finally, Luke yanked back hard on his reins and said, "It was the truth, Mari."

"What was the truth?"

"Those men. They really are Texas Rangers."

She reined her horse to a halt. "Right. You made your point, Luke. If you want to keep their identities secret, that's your business. However, I'd prefer you simply say it straight out. I abhor liars."

"Dammit, I'm not lying."

"They called you 'boss.'"

"Well, I am their boss."

Mari sniffed with disdain. "That's ridiculous. I might have believed you corrupted one Texas Ranger into joining your outlaw gang, but three?"

"I didn't corrupt anyone into doing anything. Mari, I'm a Texas Ranger, too."

Luke, a Texas Ranger. Right. Sister Gonzaga might have bought that lie, but Mari knew better.

"I'm captain of a special company appointed by the governor to conduct a secret investigation of suspected collusion between law enforcement and outlaw gangs operating in the Fort Worth to San Antonio corridor."

Mari looked at him, took his measure. "Sure you are, Mr. Garrett. And I'm the Tooth Fairy."

LUKE BROODED the rest of the way to Trickling Springs. He stewed off and on all night in his hotel room—his own, personal, separate, lonely hotel room—and by dawn, he'd worked himself into a smoldering temper.

She didn't believe him. *He* couldn't damn well believe *that*. For the first time ever, he cared that someone knew he wasn't an outlaw and what happened? She thought he was a liar. It really chapped his butt.

For some reason, he wanted her respect. Her admiration. He wanted her to know the real Luke Garrett.

To hell with that.

Rain had moved in overnight and dim, gray light provided only minimal illumination for Luke as he picked the lock on Mari's hotel room door and slipped inside. He took a moment to appreciate the picture she made, lying in bed like a fairy-tale princess, her golden hair fanned across her pillow, a touch of rose in her flawless, sun-kissed complexion. A hint of a smile in her lush, pink lips. She wore the crisp linen sleeveless nightgown she'd purchased at the general store yesterday upon their return to town. It buttoned up the front and delicate lace trimmed the modest neckline. The top two buttons were undone, revealing a tantalizing amount of skin. In an effort to be a gentleman, Luke did his best not to look as he sat at the end of her bed, reached out and gave her shoulder a shake. "Wake up."

Mari's eyes flew open. She blinked twice, a startled look in those gorgeous sapphire eyes. Then the light in her eyes changed, turned fearful. "What's wrong? Murphy?"

Luke scowled. He hadn't intended to frighten her, but dammit, he wanted this settled. "This has nothing to do with Murphy. I want you to ask me questions about my job."

Again, she blinked twice. Then, abruptly, she sat up and clutched the sheet to her chest. "Are you crazy?"

"That's not the sort of question I want you to ask."

"What time is it?"

"Sun's up. That's not the right kind of question, either. Ask me about the Texas Rangers, Mari."

For a long moment, she simply looked at him, stared at him as if he were a bug. Then she folded her arms. "Are the Texas Rangers downstairs ready to arrest you?"

Exasperated, Luke sighed. "You're determined to be difficult about this, aren't you?"

"Excuse me? I'm the one asleep in bed. You're the one breaking into my hotel room. I should think the difficult label belongs to you."

"All right. I'll start." He looked away from her, toward the soft rain falling outside her window, and collected his thoughts. "I was already well connected with a number of unsavory characters in Texas when I did my first job for the Rangers back in eighty-three. Because we figured those connections might be useful, when I officially joined the force a year later, we kept the fact quiet. Until yesterday, the only people who knew the truth were the five men in my company and the governor himself."

"How convenient," Mari observed.

He wanted to snarl at her snotty tone, but he refrained. "Like I said yesterday, most of my work involves gathering information about the outlaw gangs who operate out of Fort Worth. Train robbers. Bank robbers. Cattle rustlers, too, although they're not as high a priority. Twice now I've been 'convicted' of a crime and sent to Huntsville in order to infiltrate a gang."

"Uh-huh."

This time he did show her his teeth. "My special interest is recovering stolen items of historical interest. In fact, I was involved in just such a duty the night of the Spring Palace fire—until the McBride family interfered with my plans. Ask me questions, Mari. Ask me whatever it will take to prove to you that I'm telling the truth."

Mari leaned back against the headboard. She drummed her fingers against her arm. For the first time since she'd opened her eyes, Luke sensed she just might be ready to listen.

He expected her to ask him something about the governor or the clandestine nature of his activities. Instead, she surprised him. "If your position is so secret that only six people know the 'truth,' then why in the world would you tell me about it? Isn't that compromising your job?"

"Not unless you decide to sashay on down to the telegraph office and send out a statewide bulletin. Do I need to fret over that?"

She wrinkled her nose and sniffed. "No one would believe it, even if I did."

"But you won't do it."

"No, I won't."

"I knew that. You are a trustworthy woman, Mari McBride, and I can only think of one other woman I would say that about."

"Oh?" Curiosity gleamed in her eyes.

"My sister, Janna," he responded, answering her unspoken question. "She moved to Galveston awhile back, lives there with her two little girls. Although they're not so little anymore, I reckon. Young ladies, now."

Mari fluffed her pillow, then settled back against it. "So, let me get this straight. You think I'm trustworthy, so you broke, what was it, seven years' worth of silence to fill me in on your deepest secret? What would your men think of you putting them at risk that way?"

Actually, he had another secret she'd probably consider to be his deepest, but he knew better than to address that particular bucket of worms anytime soon. Luke rubbed the back of his neck. "I'm not putting my men at risk, Mari. Their identities are not secret like mine. I didn't introduce y'all yesterday because that was before I decided to tell you the truth."

Noting the skepticism in her expression, he continued, "It's more than that. You wouldn't have tangled with Murphy, you wouldn't have gone through hell, if not for my job. I put your life in danger, and for that, the least I owe you is some honesty."

The look in her eyes softened, though the doubt didn't totally disappear. He was making some progress. "What else can I tell you, Mari?"

After a moment's consideration, she said, "Murphy. Let's talk about him for a minute. There's more to that story than what you've told me, isn't there? Something personal?"

Luke grimaced. The woman was too intelligent for his own good. "You would have to pick my least favorite topic, wouldn't you."

The smile that played at the corners of her mouth encouraged him, and made the idea of revealing his connection to Murphy a little easier to stomach. "That Irish blackguard and I go way back. It's not a pretty story. If I tell it to you, are you gonna make it worth my while? Are you gonna believe what I say?"

"That depends. If you tell me you met him while the two of you were in seminary studying to be priests, I rather doubt I'll buy that tale."

"Actually my stepfather brought him home because we were a family of thieves, and he thought Murphy would fit right in."

"Now that I find totally believable," Mari said, nodding. "So, you grew up doing what? Rustling cattle? Robbing stages?"

"Nothing so plebeian." Luke sat on the side of the bed and reached down to tug off his boots. "Brian Callahan was a gentleman thief."

"What are you doing?" Mari asked, as he stripped off his socks.

"I told you it's a long story. I'm gettin' comfortable."

As he settled back beside her on the bed, Mari

clutched the sheet tighter to her breasts. "You behave yourself."

"Do you want to hear this story or not?" Because he was still annoyed at her attitude, Luke indulged in a minor bit of retaliation by draping his arm around her shoulder and pulling her against him. She stiffened but didn't protest. Obviously, her curiosity was stronger than her desire to act snitty.

"A truly charming man, Brian performed as a magician at society functions in New York City. It was a perfect cover for his true vocation, stealing, and for years he went about his business undetected. That ended the night he cracked the safe of Bernard J. Kimball."

"The railroad baron?"

"Railroads, steel, shipping. That's him. He caught Brian with his hand literally in the safe. What people don't know about ol' Barney is that in addition to being an industrialist, he was also an avid collector of historical treasures. He wasn't always particular about the legality of his acquisitions."

"Let me guess," Mari said. "He hired your stepfather to steal for him."

"Bernard called him an acquisition specialist. See, back after the War Between the States, Kimball developed a special interest in documents and artifacts relating to Texas history, and he sent Brian to Texas to oversee search and procurement efforts. Brian was happy to make the move because he'd run afoul of the local constables."

"Ah. Another of our infamous G.T.T. rascals," Mari observed. So many men from other states had fled their homes in avoidance of the law that "Gone To Texas" had become a common expression.

"Exactly. Brian didn't enjoy leaving New York the way he did, so for a while after his arrival in Texas, he actually tried to stay on the right side of the law. It was during that period that he first called upon my widowed mother."

Luke played with a lock of Mari's hair, enjoying the soft sensation of silk sliding over his fingers. The scent of rose water clung to her, teased his senses, and for a moment, he lost his train of thought.

"So your mother married him and they had Rory," Mari said, drawing the logical conclusion. "How did Murphy enter the picture?"

Luke didn't want to talk about Murphy. He'd much rather play with her hair. Nuzzle her neck. Trace her collarbone with his tongue. Release those buttons at her bodice and—

Mari jabbed him with her elbow.

Luke sighed. "Brian played cards with him one night in East Texas and was impressed by Murphy's skills at sleight-of-hand."

"He was a cardsharp?"

"The best for his age that Brian had ever seen. He brought him home to teach me. By that time, Brian had abandoned his attempt to stay straight."

"Really? What did your mother say about that?"

Luke's lips twisted in a sad smile. "My mother died in childbirth with Rory. I was nine, Janna, fourteen. We figured Brian would run off, but he stuck. Janna mothered Rory and tried to manage me. Brian taught us magic tricks, and he had a grand scheme going for taking our show on the road."

Luke paused, absently stroking Mari's shoulder as he thought back to those days, his mood wistful. All in all, life had been good back then. Brian had been a good man, big and bold and boisterous. He'd truly cared about his family. He simply had a different set of values when it came to matters involving money.

"My hands were the problem. They were too big. Too slow." He flexed his fingers in front of her. "I had a devil of a time learning to pick pockets."

He had learned, though. Eventually. Even all these years later, he still had the talent. A touch light enough to slip a row of bodice buttons with nary a notice. "Murphy taught me. He had the hands of a phantom, and, to my everlasting regret, the charm of the devil. Janna fell for him like a flour sack off the back of a wagon."

"He took advantage of your sister?"

"Worse than that. He married her."

Mari sat up straight. The front placket of her gown gaped open, giving Luke a tantalizing view of her breasts. "Wait a minute. Are you telling me that Finn Murphy is your brother-in-law?"

"'Fraid so," he replied, distracted. Her nipples were the size of quarters, a sweet, rosy pink.

"Finn Murphy is your brother-in-law and Rory Callahan is your brother."

"Uh huh." Luke's fingers itched to touch her. His mouth craved her taste.

"And I thought the McBride family had its share of black sheep. Y'all are an entire herd. So, are there any more surprises I need to know about? Any other family skeletons I might wander into on the trail?"

Oh, yeah. Definitely. Without a doubt.

But damned if he'd answer that question. Not now. Luke was tired of talking about his family. He was tired of talking, period. He sat up, turned toward her and licked his dry lips.

He had something much more enticing in mind.

CHAPTER ELEVEN

"WELL?" MARI PRESSED as she watched Luke's eyes narrow.

"Well what?" he asked, his voice low and thick like hot caramel atop cold ice cream.

Unease shimmered up Mari's spine. He was in a strange mood this morning, one she couldn't quite read. She didn't know what to think of him. She couldn't decide how much of his story she believed. "Do you have any more unpleasant surprises for me, Luke? Any more skeletons in the closet?"

"I have surprises. Oh, yeah. Not unpleasant, though. Never that. I'm better than that." His gaze drifted over her sheet-clad body. "Maribeth?"

She cleared her throat. "Yes?"

He looked up, stared into her eyes. "Did you have a good night's sleep?"

"Yes. Until I was rudely awakened." What did the way she slept have to do with anything, anyhow? They were talking about his family. A family where nobody had the same last name. A family of sinners with one saint. *If* she believed Luke's story, that is. Did she believe him?

He traced his index finger across the knuckles of her fist.

"You're right. I was rude. Let's do it over, shall we?"

"Do what…" Mari's words trailed off as Luke reached up and gently shut her eyes.

"Go to sleep, sugar, and let's do it right."

Sleep? She couldn't go to sleep now. She was wide-awake. He was drawing spirals on her shoulder and every nerve in her body had bristled to attention.

Then, she felt it. His breath danced over her skin. His lips, as soft as a butterfly's wings, made a gentle, lazy journey across her face. He kissed her closed eyelids, her temples, her cheekbones. "Sleeping beauty," he murmured. "Wake up, beautiful."

Heart hammering, her lashes fluttered open. His dark eyes stared into her very soul and turned her bones to butter. "What are you doing?"

His slow, knowing smile exposed his roguish dimple. "Saying good-morning."

Then he slowly, deliberately, brought his mouth back to hers.

Mari's lips parted at his first touch. His gentleness lulled her, his tenderness seduced her. As he increased the pressure against her mouth, bit by delicious bit, her hands reached up to grip his arms.

Her head started to spin.

Luke's tongue teased her lips, seeking entrance. Exhaling a breathy sigh, Mari went pliant and allowed him in. He played with her, darting, licking, exploring. He captured her upper lip, then her lower. With lazy seduction, he made love to her mouth. Outside, raindrops thudded against the roof, providing music for lyrics of sighs and gasps and soft, silken moans.

This was more than a simple good morning, and part of Mari, her self-protective side, tried to assert some control.

Luke Garrett might be a Texas Ranger, but he is definitely no saint.

Then his fingers slipped buttons free, pushed the nightgown from her shoulders and grazed the swell of her naked breasts. Undeniable desire overtook reason, and she banished the last fragment of doubt. Mari arched her body toward him.

She wanted this. She wanted him. She'd been good for so long, and she'd be good again. But right now, here in the middle of nowhere, where nobody knew her to judge her or to damage her reputation, she wanted to be bad.

She wanted her former fiancé's ugly accusation put to bed, so to speak, once and for all, if only for herself. No woman who willingly gave her virginity to an outlaw could possibly be labeled frigid!

Besides, Luke Garrett was an adventure she simply didn't want to miss.

Mari tangled her fingers in his thick, silken hair, subtly yielding, silently urging him on.

Luke was quick to take her hint. He deepened the kiss, the thrusts of his tongue growing demanding. His hand cupped the fullness of her breast, caressing, fondling. "Mmm…" he said, flicking his thumb across her rigid nipple. Arousal zinged straight to her core, and she let out a little groan.

"Like that, hmm?" he asked. His teeth scraped against her neck as his hand continued to move, caressing each breast in turn.

"Yes…" she breathed.

Wickedness danced in his eyes as he glanced at her and declared. "Then you're gonna love this."

He dipped his head and took her nipple into his mouth.

Mari's arms fell to her sides, her hands flexing and gripping the sheet as sensation flooded her. His hot breath fanned her skin as he laved the sensitive peak with his tongue. He teased and nibbled, using the tip of his tongue to torture the tight bud. When he settled down to suckle, she surrendered to his need for fulfillment. "Luke. Oh, Luke."

Writhing upward, she held his dark head in her arms while her body pulsed with delicious sensation. He tormented, teased, tasted. She begged, cried, prayed. It went on for minutes—or maybe days—and left her weak and trembling. Aching. Hot.

She let out a sigh of loss when he released her, rolled back on his knees. Breathing hard, his eyes dark with need, Luke stripped off his shirt. Mari's gaze trailed over his muscular, masculine beauty and a hollow, achy yearning filled her. This man. This moment. She'd remember it all her life. She licked her lips and said, "I want to touch you."

Wordlessly, he lifted her hand to his chest.

Mari trailed her fingertips across the dusting of dark hair, the intriguing ripple of muscle. When she scraped a nail across his nipple, he sucked in an audible breath. Encouraged, she stroked the hard, rippled muscles of his stomach until she reached the sprinkling of hair dusting his navel.

With a pained, ragged groan, Luke grasped her hand into his. "If you want to stop this, Maribeth, you need to do it now."

"I don't want to stop."

His hot, molten eyes captured hers. "You sure?"

She nodded.

"Thank God."

He climbed from the bed and slipped off his trousers. At the first sight of his jutting erection, Mari recalled the previous day's events and experienced a quick flash of panic.

Firmly, she willed it away, determined to forget yesterday's trauma. She trusted Luke. Being with him was good. It was right. This was what she wanted. He was who she wanted.

Her throat worked convulsively and, noting it, Luke paused. He gently stroked her cheek with the pad of his thumb. "It's all right, sugar. I promise."

"I trust you, Luke."

"I know, and I won't betray that trust."

"Remember, it's my first time."

"I remember." Satisfaction gleamed in his warm brown eyes. "I'm honored by your gift, Mari, and I'll treat it with the respect it deserves. I want to make it good for you. I won't hurt you."

No. No, he wouldn't. He wasn't anything like Finn Murphy. Looking at that man had made her want to run screaming. Looking at Luke made her want to…touch.

So she did.

Heedless of the nightgown that pooled at her waist, Mari sat up and reached for him. Velvet steel, she thought as she trailed a trembling fingertip along his rigid length. His body twitched at her untutored exploration, until she reached the satin tip of him. With a low, growling noise from deep in his throat, Luke thrust against her hand and shuddered. "Jesus, Maribeth."

As he shifted her hand away, she felt a warm glow of feminine triumph at the glazed, desperate look in his eyes. *She'd* done that to him. Her. Mari McBride, frigid virgin. *Ha!*

The mattress sagged beneath his weight as he settled beside her. "Lookin' mighty pleased with yourself, there, sugar."

"I made you twitch."

He let out a strangled laugh. "Honey, you've been making me twitch for months, since the first time I laid eyes on you."

"Really?"

"You looked at me all sassy and proud, challenging me to resist your—" he grabbed hold of the nightgown pillowed at her hips and with one great yank, tugged it loose "—kisses."

His lips returned to hers and his tongue plunged inside her, taking and tasting and savoring. Then he drew back. "Temptations," he breathed, his smoldering gaze slowly scorching a trail across her naked skin, her breasts, her navel, her womanhood.

Mari shuddered with need.

Then he reached out and touched her, his practiced hands skimming lightly over her sensitive skin, stroking and teasing and exploring. Luke stared deeply into her eyes, into her soul, and whispered, "Sinfuls."

Mari gasped as he slipped a finger inside her, stretching her, sending her mindlessly into a storm of sensation.

His fingers conjured a magic from deep within her. The air seemed too thick to breathe. She writhed beneath his touch, her hands gripping the bedsheet. His hands, his mouth were everywhere, pushing her forward, driving her up, until she felt as if she teetered on a high, narrow ledge. "Luke," she groaned, thrashing upon the bed, pleading for relief.

His cheek, bristly with a day's growth of whiskers, scraped against the sensitive skin of her belly as he kissed his way toward the juncture of her thighs. His hands gripped her hips, stimulating, steadying. Anticipation sharpened to anxiety as his goal became clear, and she attempted to pull away. "No."

Luke lifted his head, his eyes hot with passion. "Don't be afraid, Mari."

"It's too…too—" she all but sobbed the last word "—much."

"Shush, Mari-mine," he soothed. "All right. I'll wait. We'll save it for next time." He braced himself above her, kissed her lips, stroked her hair, her cheek, her breasts until she lost herself in the maelstrom once again.

His hand skimmed down her stomach, leaving shudders of pleasure in its wake before delving into the folds of her womanhood with slow, gentle strokes. "So hot. So wet. So beautiful."

She tried to think, tried to find words to describe the sensations swirling inside her. Physical and emotional reactions gave rise to feelings Mari had never experienced before, feelings she'd never known were even possible. "Luke, I…"

Then two of his fingers rubbed a slow, sensual circle around the bead of nerves at the apex of her sex. Ribbons of pleasure fluttered outward from the spot, and instinctively, Mari rose against his hand. "Luke!"

"That's my girl," he urged, his voice a low, coaxing rumble. "Go up. I want to watch you go over."

Mari's tension spiraled higher as he worked his magic between her legs. She was back on that ledge again, swaying once more on the edge. She fought for breath, tried to find her balance. It was too much. *He* was too much.

"Don't fight it. Let it happen."

As if sensing her need, he slipped one, then unbearably a second, finger into her slick wet sheath and pressed the pad of his thumb against her core. She climbed higher, tighter, tenser. Reaching toward…

"Go," Luke said against her lips. "Let go, Mari."

He kissed her as she climaxed, as she tumbled off the ledge into a free fall of sensation. She grabbed his shoulders, holding on for dear life, flying through a world of bold and brilliant pleasure.

Then, before her feet touched the ground, he rose above her. Need tightened his expression into sharp angles and hard planes. His breathing was harsh, his voice raspy with desire as his hands skimmed her thighs, lifting her, spreading her open. "Again, Maribeth." His hot, hard length probed at her entrance. "This time, with me."

With one hard thrust, he took her. The pain was brief and minimal, all but overlooked by Mari in the wonder of the moment. He filled her. Completed her. It was…amazing.

Luke looked down at her, his expression achingly tender. Slowly, he smiled. Gently, he kissed her. Sweetly, he murmured her name. *Mari-mine.*

Then he started to move. He drew out, then thrust in, his strokes painstakingly slow and sweet. His mouth brushed hers in sweet challenge, provoking her to respond. Taking his face in her hands, Mari kissed him fully, exploring his mouth with utter abandon. She wanted more than sweet. She wanted raw. She wanted *him.*

Lifting her hips, she met his next languid thrust and caught his surprised moan. Riding the surge of feminine power once again, she daringly slid one foot up the back of his thigh.

Luke's mouth crushed down on hers as his pace

quickened. His hands supported his weight above her as his hips pumped harder, taking her in primitive impatient drives that made Mari whimper against his plundering mouth.

She scaled the wondrous height once more. Flesh slapped against flesh as instinct took control. The earthy sounds of their lovemaking blended with the rhythm of the rain. Wrapping her arms and legs around him, Mari climbed the last few steps to bliss. Their skin grew slick, their bodies melted into one. They rolled on the bed, thrashed across the sheets. Her nails pressed into his bare back and he shuddered, driving harder. He nipped her neck and angled his hips to spread her further. It wasn't gentle anymore, but hard and greedy and ruthless. Primal. Male and female.

"Look at me," he demanded.

Her eyes fluttered open, focused. His skin was flushed, his jaw hard. His eyes hot, burning, branding her as his. Her outlaw. Her bodyguard. Her lover. She whispered his name. "Luke."

Without taking his eyes from hers, Luke reached down and stroked her where their bodies were joined.

The second climax hit Mari without warning and she cried out. Luke grasped her hips and plunged once, twice, three more times, then he stiffened, groaned, and Mari welcomed the hot wet gush of his seed.

Her outlaw. Her bodyguard.

Her first true love.

LUKE HAD ALWAYS been good at morning-afters. He knew just the right note to strike to charm his women, soothe any insecurities, and make them feel special while avoiding any noose they might be dragging.

With Mari, his tongue knotted up like a bowline. He

didn't know what to say or how to say it, or why his heart continued to pound like a smithy's hammer even after he summoned the strength to scoot out of bed and climb into his britches. He couldn't believe he had trouble meeting her eyes or shaping his mouth into a smile that wouldn't come across as fake. Lovemaking with Mari had left Luke as confused as a woodpecker in a petrified forest. Mari, on the other hand, didn't appear to be suffering in any way at all.

For a recently deflowered virgin, the woman was way too perky. She sat up, clutched the sheet to her naked breasts and chattered on about women and men and her preconceived notions about sex. She confessed to allowing minor liberties with a few of her previous beaux. When she got to the part where she praised Luke's talents, he tuned in a little closer.

"…from the time I learned who you were," Mari was saying. "I guess there is something about wickedness in a man that appeals to a woman. At least, for purposes of a dalliance."

Dalliance? Is that what this was? Luke considered it, then decided he didn't like the term. And what was this business about wickedness? Luke didn't much like that, either. "Hold on just one minute. Are you trying to say that I'm wicked, Maribeth?"

She gave him a look both patient and pitying. "You're an outlaw, Luke. By definition, outlaws are wicked."

"Outlaw! Excuse me, but I thought we settled this. You know I'm a Texas Ranger."

Her expression turned indulgent. "Whatever you say, Luke."

Luke's jaw gaped, then hardened. "You *still* don't believe me?" When she smiled and shrugged, his world went red. "I poured my guts out to you, gave you all the gory details about my relations, and you don't believe a word I said?"

"Look," she said in a placating tone, "let's not bother with all that right now."

"No." He braced his hands on his hips. "I say let's do."

"But there's really no need. What does it matter what I believe?"

"I don't know. It just does."

Mari sighed, then propped her pillow against the iron headboard and leaned back against it. "Look. Maybe I'm not sure what I believe. I haven't exactly had time to think it all through. Besides, you gave me a lot of information, Luke, but certainly not the whole story."

"I told you what's important."

"And I'm supposed to just take you at your word?"

"Yes!"

Annoyance flashed in her eyes. "So you think that just because you kissed me senseless, I'm now stupid? For instance, I'm not supposed to notice that you never explained how you went from being a pickpocket to a member of the most respected law enforcement agency in Texas. That's an awful big stretch for anyone with a brain to make without some sort of explanation."

He wanted to bare his teeth and snarl at her. He truly did. "So, you think I've lied about everything, but you gave me your virginity anyway?"

Mari bristled with indignation. "No, I don't believe that's what I said."

"Well, that's the way it sounds to me, and it's damned insulting, Maribeth McBride. I can't believe it. I'm good enough to bed if I rob trains, but if I'm the guy trying to catch the train robbers, I'm a boring milquetoast."

"I did *not* say that!"

Luke knew that. He understood he wasn't thinking or acting quite rationally at the moment, but it seemed better to escape into illogic than to ponder why he felt so completely out of rhythm. "You were a virgin!"

"Yes."

"You gave that treasure to me thinking I was the kind of man who'd take it. A man like Murphy."

"That's not true. You're nothing like Murphy. That's something I'm certain of. You're a good man, Luke."

He scoffed. "For an outlaw, you mean?"

Mari rolled her eyes and sighed. "Fine, then. Finish the story. Tell me how you came to be a Texas Ranger."

Oh. Hell. He was right back to where he'd started when he decided to quit talkin' and begin kissin'. Why did he do this to himself?

At least she hadn't brought up family skeletons again. He'd rather talk about Harvey than confess any more of his brother's sins, and Luke hated talking about Harvey. He hated remembering that he was in large part responsible for the death of such a fine, brave man. "You gonna believe what I have to say?"

Mari tilted her head and studied him, just long enough to rile his temper before saying, "Probably."

And damned if she didn't let out a little giggle. Then, scooping her nightgown from the bottom of the bed, Mari slipped it on and settled back against her pillow. "Finish your story, Luke. Tell me how you came to be a Texas Ranger."

He tore his attention away from the way the soft cotton caressed her breast. Why hadn't he kept his mouth shut and his butt in bed? He blew out a harsh breath.

"I told you Murphy married my sister. Well, wasn't long before he got tired of Brian Callahan's small-potatoes thieving, and he took to robbing stages. Eventually, he talked Brian into going with him. They dragged me along a time or two."

Luke paused, his thoughts drifting back. He remembered Janna, so happy with her babies, so distressed over her men. "That sort of thieving wasn't for me. Brian, either, to be honest, but Murphy was calling the shots by then, and I was powerless to change it. So I left."

"How old were you?" Mari asked.

"Sixteen. Thought I was a man, but I was dumb as a snubbing post." His mouth slipped into a rueful smile. "Proved that the day I tried to steal a knife from a Texas Ranger."

"Ah, the connection."

"Harvey Rowan. The best man who ever walked the face of this earth." Luke moved to the window, where he pushed aside the curtain and stared out at the muddy street. "I supported myself by supplying Brian Callahan's New York collector with Texas artifacts. Harvey Rowan's pa was a close friend of Sam Houston's, and Harvey had a knife Houston had carried at the Battle of San Jacinto. He treasured the knife, didn't take kindly to my trying to lift it. He was hauling me into town to jail when we stumbled on a stage holdup in progress. I helped him, and I got shot in the process." Glancing over his shoulder, he added, "I thought I was dying, so I spilled my guts about my family. A deathbed confession of sorts."

Mari glanced at the scar high on his chest. "So Mr. Rowan saved your life?"

"First by digging the bullet out, then by taking a

chance on me. He gave me a way to redeem myself. I stopped taking artifacts for Kimball and began giving information to the Texas Rangers."

"You were a spy?"

"That has a nicer ring than informant, but yeah. Thanks to my brother-in-law, I had an established identity as an outlaw, so we used it. About that time, I stumbled into a card game with some investors from back East and ended up with part of a railroad in my pocket. Having money made the whole job easier. After a couple years, Harvey talked the governor into establishing a special force of Rangers to take on special tasks and they made me official. I've been a Texas Ranger for years, though like I said before, only a handful of people know it."

Turning to face her, he folded his arms. "That, Miss McBride, is God's honest truth."

Silence stretched like warm saltwater taffy as he waited for her to respond. He had a rock in his gut about it, and he didn't really know why. What did it matter if she believed him or not? Why did he care?

The answer waited just beyond reach, flirting with his consciousness, when Mari finally spoke.

"I believe you." Mari clutched the sheet up all the way to her neck as she quietly repeated. "I believe you."

Vindication was a sweet treat that turned sour when a blush stained her cheeks, she shut her eyes and dropped her head back against the pillow. "This is awful."

"Excuse me?"

Her cheeks flushed pink. "You're not an outlaw at all. You're *respectable*."

Luke unfolded his arms and braced his hands on his

hips. "I may be wrong here, but you're making it sound like that's a problem."

"It is a problem!" She sat up, the look in her eyes wild. "You were safe when you were an outlaw. Now you're not safe!"

"What?" Luke's brow wrinkled as he tried, unsuccessfully, to make sense of what she said.

She scrambled from the bed, taking the sheet with her, making sure to keep it wrapped around her tight as she dashed for the dressing screen in the corner. "I didn't want to believe you before, so I took the risk. Why did you have to tell me? Why am I now one of a handful? Haven't you ever heard that ignorance is bliss? It's one thing to be a Menace with somebody even worse than me, but you…you…" She poked her head out from behind the screen and glared at him. "You're a hero!"

She said it like an accusation and left him standing speechless, staring in bemusement at the dressing screen, listening to the sounds of her getting dressed. Then, because it seemed like the thing to do, he looked around for the rest of his own clothes.

Scooping up his shirt, Luke attempted to collect his thoughts. "I'm sorry, Maribeth. I'm having trouble following this conversation. Surely you're not saying what I'm thinking I'm hearing."

He shoved his arms in his shirtsleeves and began to work the buttons. He noticed the bed and the blood-stained bottom sheet. "This business about risk taking and being a menace. Are you possibly referring to what just took place on that mattress?"

He waited for a response, but all he heard was…sniffling. Ah, hell. Luke finished buttoning his shirt, then shoved his fingers through his hair. "Mari?"

He waited a full minute before she emerged from behind the screen. She'd donned a pretty blue cotton gown that matched her eyes. Her sapphire necklace, its chain repaired, hung around her neck. Color lingered on her cheeks. Her eyes were red and swollen. "I apologize, Luke. I'm afraid this has all been a bit…unsettling."

Yeah, well, he wouldn't argue with that. Luke sat on the bed and reached for his socks and boots. "Just clear one thing up for me. Why was I 'safer' as an outlaw than as a Texas Ranger?"

Her posture ramrod straight, she drew a deep breath, then confessed. "It's difficult to explain. You were safe because I knew we had no future. I knew not to even dream about it, not to invest my heart. It's humiliating to admit, but my fiancé hurt me badly. I needed to prove to myself that his assertions weren't true. You were my opportunity."

"Your opportunity," Luke repeated, offended. "You were using me."

"Well, yes."

Damned if it didn't make him feel cheap.

"It's the McBride Menace in me," Mari continued. "I've worked so hard to subdue that part of my nature, but it got the better of me. Please, accept my apology."

Well, now. This was just getting worse and worse. The woman had just apologized for having sex with him. Now, there was a first. Angrily, Luke tugged on his socks, shoved into his boots. Standing, he snapped, "So, then. It won't happen again?"

"Oh, no. I…oh, no. No."

Oh. Well, hell. Luke pretended not to see the tears she rapidly blinked away. "All right, fine. That's fine. Now we know. Right?"

"Yes. Right."

"All right. Good. You ready to go, then?"

"I don't know." He was ready to leave this room, that's for sure. "Breakfast. We need to go get some breakfast."

"Yes. Breakfast would be good. I'm sure I must be hungry."

"Yeah. Me, too." Luke watched as Mari glanced around the room, a slightly troubled expression upon her face, until she spotted the handbag lying on the floor between the bed and the nightstand. She went to pick it up and in a movement that betrayed her loss of composure, rather than making a ladylike dip and scoop, she bent at the waist and reached.

Her skirt molded to her derriere, and Luke's mouth went dry.

Without pausing to consider his words, Luke said, "Hey, Menace?"

"Hmm?"

"Since we're not gonna be doing this again, how about we have one for the road?"

CHAPTER TWELVE

"ONE FOR THE ROAD," Mari muttered beneath her breath, her face turned toward the window to catch the breeze rushing past as the train chugged southward in the hot summer sunshine. "Really."

On the seat beside her, Luke sat reading a copy of the *Trickling Springs Gazette*. Or pretending to read it, anyway. Mari had kept a close watch on him, and he didn't turn the pages with any regularity. What he was doing, she believed, was sitting there brooding.

The man's mood had deteriorated steadily since they left the hotel that morning. At first, Mari had felt bad because she knew she'd behaved poorly. Not during the, um, event. That had gone quite well. She had no doubts about that. But the aftermath had preyed upon her conscience. She'd been so mixed-up, so confused, she couldn't remember exactly what she'd said.

Love did strange things to a person.

Oh, it wasn't true love. Not the sort of love that her parents and Aunt Claire and Uncle Tye shared. Theirs was the kind of love that Roslin had talked about—love that was powerful, vigilant and true. The love that Mari felt for her outlaw bodyguard was wicked and exciting and stirring—undoubtedly the product of her own self-doubts, the forced intimacy of traveling alone together, and the fact that the man had a body that made her toes curl. This kind of love had turned her brain to mush.

As the day went on, with Luke growing grumpier by the minute, pique took the place of guilt in Mari's mind. She hadn't done anything to warrant a winter chill from Luke Garrett. Just because she'd dismissed his suggestion of one for the road didn't give him reason to act so sullen. Although, she didn't think that was the reason for his grumpiness. He'd laughed off her refusal. The cold front had come on gradually after that.

Mari couldn't figure it out. She couldn't figure *him* out. Maybe he was as confused as she.

Mari glanced at Luke. A muscle in his cheek twitched, and she quickly looked away. Could that be it? It must be difficult to live a lie. He was a hero at heart who walked in the boots of a villain. She could see how that could cause all kinds of inner conflicts in a person.

Maybe he was pulled in two different directions just like she was. Maybe they both had a Menace side that got the better of them sometimes.

The notion was intriguing.

More in charity with him now at that thought, she decided to strike up a conversation. "Where are we due to stop next?" she asked.

He answered without looking up. "Paradise Prairie."

"Paradise Prairie," she repeated. "What a lovely name. Is it as big a town as Trickling Springs?"

"No."

Mari waited for more, but apparently he wasn't in the mood for small talk. She tried again with a question that required more than a yes or no response. "What sort of facilities can I expect to find?"

He flicked her a sidelong, suspicious look. "What are you looking for?"

"Nothing in particular. Well, except for a church, of course. Even though I know my sister is alive, it would be nice to have physical confirmation to show my parents if we have trouble finding Kat and your brother."

Finally, Luke looked at her fully. "This is only a water stop. You might not have time for something like that."

"I'll hurry. I'll know exactly which date to check, so it won't take me long."

"I don't think it's a good idea. The last thing you want is to miss the train again."

Mari considered that for a moment. Luke was right. Aside from the fact that missing the train would once again delay her search for Kat, it would also mean another day without her luggage, which was hopefully awaiting her in San Antonio. Her new carpetbag filled with purchases had disappeared from the alley in the wake of Murphy's attack, and she'd replaced her wardrobe replacements with but a single change of clothing upon their return to Trickling Springs. While an excess of vanity wasn't ordinarily one of Mari's vices, she couldn't help but want to look her best, under the circumstances. "You could stay with the train and convince the engineer to wait for me if I was running a few minutes late."

"No. Absolutely not. I learned that lesson. As long as I'm your bodyguard, you're not leaving my sight."

He didn't have to sound so unhappy about it, Mari thought. Wrinkling her nose, she turned her head back toward the window and abandoned her attempts at conversation. Let him sit and stew if that's what he wanted. She didn't care. And she wouldn't indulge in the childish temptation to stick her tongue out at him, either.

The remainder of the ride to Paradise Prairie passed

in silence. Mari did a bit of stewing herself and decided she darn sure would check church records at their next stop, whether *he* thought it was a good idea or not. She had a feeling about that town. The moment she heard the name, it registered with her. It made her neck niggle. Besides, she knew her sister. She'd love the idea of getting married in a town named Paradise Prairie. It would suit her sense of drama just perfectly.

Any lingering doubts Mari entertained evaporated as the train pulled into Paradise Prairie, and the steeple on the north end of town caught her attention. This was exactly the type of church that would appeal to Kat.

It was a small building, its architecture a traditional rectangle with a gabled roof and steeple at the front. Painted a pristine white, its clear glass windows sparkled in the sunlight. What made it so picturesque, so perfectly suited for Kat McBride's wedding, were the brilliant yellow roses that encircled the church. "That's it, Luke. That's where they got married. I don't care if it means I miss the train, I'm going to take a look at those church records."

Paper rattled as he slammed his newspaper shut. "You know, Maribeth, if your head had a point it could etch glass. Fine. We'll trot off to the church, but if the train leaves without us, I don't want to hear a single word of complaint escape those luscious lips of yours."

Since Mari didn't know whether to feel insulted or complimented, she responded with only a smile.

When the train rolled to a stop moments later, Mari was the first person off. According to the conductor, she had twenty minutes. Since the church was barely a five-minute walk away, she should have plenty of time.

She walked briskly. Luke ambled behind her, stopping once at the train station to buy another newspaper from a boy, and a second time in front of the general store where he purchased a dill pickle, Mari having declined his offer of one for herself. Despite the delays, he managed to keep up with her. Mari heard him grumble something about stubbornness a time or two, but for the most part, she ignored him. Her thoughts were on her sister and the proof she hoped to find in the charming church's registry.

The scent of roses perfumed the air as she hurried up the walkway leading to the large oak doors. "I hope someone is here this time of day," she observed, as much to herself as to Luke.

"We don't have time to go chasing all over town for the preacher," he warned, then took a bite of his pickle.

"I wish you'd stop being so pessimistic." Mari lifted a hand toward the church door.

Luke reached around her and tugged the door open. "Not pessimistic, realistic."

Mari stepped inside, spied a man wearing a minister's collar flipping through sheet music stored in a piano bench, then shot a quick, triumphant glance over her shoulder before starting up the aisle. "Excuse me, sir," she called, her voice a hollow echo in the high-ceilinged building. "Are you the pastor here?"

"I am." He was an older gentleman with salt-and-pepper hair and a round, kind face. "Reverend Barlow Hart. May I be of service to you?"

"I do hope so. My name is Maribeth McBride. This is Mr. Garrett. I'm afraid we're in a bit of a hurry because we need to be back on board the train when it pulls out, so I won't go into a long explanation other than to say that we're looking for our siblings, who we believe eloped back in May. I'm hoping you can tell me whether or not you might have married them? Katrina

McBride and Rory Kelly, although, he might have been using the surname Callahan."

"Hmm…" The reverend scratched his chin. "What part of May?"

"The very end. It would have been May thirty-first, in fact."

"That's why I can't recall. The wife and I took a holiday, then. Went to visit our grandbabies down in Houston."

As Mari's stomach sank with disappointment, Luke rested a comforting hand on her shoulder. Then the reverend continued, "Seems to me I recall something about a wedding during those two weeks, hmm…"

Mari's hopes rose as his brows knit in thought. Then abruptly, he snapped his fingers. "Judge Parkin. I remember now. When Mrs. Hart and I returned from Houston, Judge Parkin told me about a little spitfire who wouldn't settle for being married in his courtroom. Had to be done in the church."

Mari reached up and grabbed Luke's hand. "That's Kat. I know it is."

"Mari, you thought the same thing at two different churches in Trickling Springs."

Ignoring Luke, she addressed the minister, she said, "Would the judge have listed the marriage in the church records?"

"I do believe he did." The minister held up two fingers and gestured for them to follow. "Let's go see, shall we?"

Reverend Hart led them to a small antechamber to the right of the altar. From a shelf next to a desk, he removed a large book. "May thirty-first, you say?"

"Yes, sir." Mari had a lump the size of a Parker County peach in her throat.

Paper crackled as he flipped the pages forward, then backward, then forward, once. Twice. Mari swallowed hard as he slid his index finger down the page. "Hmm…Margaret Thurman's funeral on the twentieth. We baptized the Hawkins boy on the twenty-second. Here. Judge Parkin's handwriting." Clearing his throat, the minister read, "'United in marriage. Miss Katrina Julianna McBride and Mr. Rory Wilcox Callahan, May the thirty-first of this year.'"

As a smile burst across Mari's face, the pickle slipped from Luke's grip and fell splat against the floor. "So help me God," he said, "I'm gonna kill that boy."

LUKE WENT TEARING OUT of the church as if the devil were at his heels. Halfway down the walkway, the red haze of his anger cleared long enough for him to recall his duty. He pivoted and returned to the church where he grabbed Mari's arm and began pulling her toward the door.

"What are you doing?" she protested, attempting without success to dig in her heels.

"We need to get back on the train."

Abandoning her resistance, Mari called her thanks back over her shoulder to the reverend. Luke slammed the church door behind them with a bang.

"What's wrong with you?" Mari asked. "I don't understand, Luke. We've proved they survived the fire. You should be happy. Thrilled. Your brother's alive!"

"Not for long."

Mari grabbed the rolled-up newspaper from his back pocket and hit him with it. "Why are you so angry? You're frightening me."

Luke didn't answer her question. He couldn't. After everything that had happened, all his no-good, sorry family had put hers through, he couldn't get his tongue to wrap around the facts. Not without thinking it through, anyway.

Maybe there was a way to fix this. He simply needed to calm down and concentrate. He'd find a way. Hadn't he been cleaning up after his family in one way or another for a good part of his life?

"Luke?" She slapped him again with the newspaper.

He let out a growl and yanked it out of her hands. "Would you stop that?"

"Would you talk to me?"

"Aargh!" he growled. He stopped, shoved the newspaper back in his pocket, then took a deep breath and exhaled in a rush. "Fine. You're right. I'm sorry if I scared you. Let's just get back on the train, and we can talk about it there."

She tapped her foot against the pathway, considering him, then said, "You promise me you'll talk to me? No more of the icehouse attitude?"

"What icehouse attitude?" he responded belligerently before turning to head back to the train station. Though he knew what she meant. When a man felt off balance with a woman, he tended to guard his tongue. And now this. He couldn't believe Rory had up and married Kat McBride. Other than wringing his brother's neck, maybe punching his face a time or twelve, Luke didn't know what he wanted to do about it.

The train whistle blew as they approached the station. Mari increased her pace. "Do I have time to send a telegram? Emma will be so thrilled to hear this bit of good news."

"The train is fixing to leave, Mari. Your telegram will have to wait until the next stop."

"Where is the next stop?"

"San Antone. Should be there in about three hours."

Mari nodded. "I'll need to send Emma word of our arrival, anyway. Who knows? Maybe we'll find them the minute we get to town. Wouldn't that be wonderful?"

"It'd be something, all right," Luke drawled, picturing how he'd react to the first sight of his brother.

Mari shot him a narrow-eyed look as they passed through the station. Upon reaching the platform, she said, "I am anxious to hear what has you in such a tizzy."

Luke took her elbow, steadying her as she stepped up onto the train. "I'm a Texas Ranger," he growled softly into her ear. "We don't have tizzies."

Mari snorted, then held her tongue as they returned to their seats. From the look in her eyes, Luke could tell that particular blessing wouldn't last long. In self-defense, because he still wasn't certain just what information he wanted to share, he pulled the newspaper from his back pocket and opened it to an inside page. It was a regional newspaper with news from surrounding towns. Almost immediately, he caught a headline that read Magnifico! Magician Puts On Dazzling Show In Parsonsville.

Quickly, he scanned the article. *Masked magician...beautiful assistant...* Luke checked the date on the paper. Yesterday. The performance was night before last. "Son of a bitch," he muttered beneath his breath.

Newsprint crackled as Mari pushed the paper away from his face. "Don't try hiding, Luke. It's time for you to—" She broke off, apparently seeing something in his expression that alarmed her. "What is it? What did you read?" She gasped and clutched his arm. "Is it Murphy?

Is there something in there about him? Did he escape the Rangers?"

Hell, that'd be all he'd need, Luke thought. "Not Murphy. Magnifico."

"Who?"

Luke wasn't paying attention to Mari. Even as the train whistle blew and the wheels began to roll, his mind raced toward a decision. The article didn't say where the act was headed next. Parsonsville sat at the intersection of two of the major roads through the Texas Hill Country. Stagecoaches ran through it, but it wasn't on a rail line. It was a half day's ride from Paradise Prairie. They could remain on the train and send telegrams upon reaching San Antonio, or…

"Come on," he said, standing. He threw his saddle-bags over his shoulder, then took her arm. "Hurry. We're getting off."

"What!"

He pulled her to her feet and out of her seat. "Faster, Mari. It's a lot easier to do this when the train is going slow than after it picks up steam."

"We're jumping off the train?" she said as he pushed her up the aisle toward the door. *"Again?*

"But…wait a minute." She planted her feet. "What about my clothes? I don't want to do this again. My bag is in San Antonio!"

Luke reached around her to open the door leading to the landing. "Your clothes are in San Antonio, but night before last, your sister was in Parsonsville."

Mari's head twisted around, her eyes bright with hope. "How do you…she was in the newspaper?"

"Go, Maribeth." He put a hand to her back and propelled her out onto the landing. "This train gets to going any faster and you'll fall when you land, maybe rip your dress. I don't want to hear any whining about it because you won't have anything else to wear." He unhooked the safety chain. "Now, go!"

Mari jumped, hit the ground feetfirst, then promptly lost her balance and fell on her knees. Luke made the jump upright. He helped Mari to her feet and winced when he saw the tear in the fabric of the blue dress. Rather than complain, she brushed the dirt off her skirt, then offered him a brilliant smile. "We found them?"

"I think so." He gave her a quick synopsis of the article, and explained why he believed the pair were Rory and Kat. "Magnifico was my character, mask and everything, but I never used it in public. It's too much a coincidence to think that somebody else would come up with something that close. Not when we know Rory's been in this general area within the past three months."

"I think you're right. Kat has always liked the name, and she's such an actress. She'd make a great magician's assistant. Oh, Luke." She threw her arms around him. "This is wonderful, wonderful news."

Luke winced as her words raised little welts of guilt on his conscience. She wouldn't be nearly so happy if she knew what he knew. Damn, but his secrets were becoming burdensome. They'd never bothered him before, but this time...

"Thank you thank you thank you thank you!"

He didn't know what to do about his secrets, but when she punctuated her thanks with a sisterly peck on the cheek, for the first time since leaving her bed that morning, Luke knew exactly what to do with Mari McBride.

He put his hand beneath her chin, tilted her face up to his, and captured her mouth in a long, thorough kiss.

MARI APPROACHED Parsonsville tired and sore and swearing that once this trip was over, it'd be a cold day in August before she climbed on the back of a horse again. Yet, at the same time, she was more excited, more filled with joy and thankfulness than she'd been in…well…her entire life. Chances were good that before this day was done, she'd see her sister again.

She'd spent much of the four-hour ride imagining the reunion. Probably, the moment she laid eyes on Kat, Mari would squeal with delight and throw her arms around her sister for a good long hug. She'd likely cry and kiss her cheeks, then, once that first rush of relief and good feeling was done, she'd either shake her silly or give her a roundhouse to the jaw.

Beneath her gratitude lay a cold and bitter fury. How dare Kat McBride Callahan have done this to their family! Her sister had much to answer for.

Yet underneath her anger lay a seed of doubt. Up until this incident, selfishness wasn't part of Kat's nature. Yes, she loved melodrama and being the star of attention, but the sister Mari knew and loved would never have knowingly caused her family this sort of overwhelming grief.

"Time will tell the story," Mari said to herself as they rode past the first houses at the edge of town. She might just need to save one of her punches for Luke's younger brother.

Mari kicked her horse and rode up beside Luke. "Where should we look for them first? The hotel?"

"Yeah. Even if they're not staying there, it's where they held the magic show, according to the newspaper."

Scanning Main Street, Mari spied the hotel in the middle of the block on the right. "There it is. Thank goodness."

Luke's mouth quirked in a grin. "You just want off that horse."

"As soon as possible," she replied with a sigh. Something cool to drink didn't sound all that bad, either. A bath. Clean clothes. But first, Kat and Rory.

They dismounted in front of the Red Hawk Hotel and secured their horses to a hitching post. As they climbed the steps to the front door, Mari blamed the weakness in her knees on the hours in the saddle. Truth be told, her nerves were a wreck. Luke must have sensed her tension, because he caught her hand and gave it a comforting squeeze.

The lobby of the Red Hawk Hotel boasted a carved oak bar that doubled as a registration desk. Luke escorted Mari to a bar stool and ordered them both lemonade.

Mari wanted to barge ahead with questions, but she took her cues from Luke. He was, after all, the professional. Still, she all but squirmed in her seat as he sipped his lemonade and observed a card game taking place at a round table in front of the fireplace.

Finally, just when Mari's patience was about to run out, he spoke to the man behind the bar. "This lemonade sure does hit the spot. It's a hot one today."

"That's a fact." The bartender eyed a thermometer on the wall. "Makes it eight days in a row we've hit a hundred degrees."

The weather small talk continued until Mari got hot. She nudged Luke with her elbow, then shot him a demanding look.

"Hold your horses, sugar," he chided in a patronizing tone. "Let me finish my lemonade first, then I'll see about getting us a room."

To the bartender, he said, "We're newly wed. I love

the little filly, but she's got to learn who controls the reins. Know what I mean?"

While Mari seriously considered kicking Luke's shin, the bartender nodded. "You're a smart man to start out on the right foot."

"Oh, for crying out loud." Mari drummed her fingers against the bar. "Sir, I read a newspaper article regarding a magic show your hotel recently hosted. Is the show still playing?"

"See what I mean?" Luke set down his glass. "Impatient."

She gave in and kicked him, then stared hard at the bartender. "Sir?"

He cleared his throat. "No. No. The magician performed here for three nights. Last show was day before yesterday."

"That's too bad," Luke observed. "I saw that same fellow perform a few months ago in Fort Worth. I told the missus here about his show and she got all excited to see it. Does he still do that trick where he turns a chicken into a dove?"

"He does." The bartender shook his head. "That magician fella is something, that's for sure. Y'all missed a mighty fine show."

Luke sighed and patted Mari's hand. "That's too bad. I know you're sorely disappointed over that bit of news, sweetheart." This time, he was the one who gave her a kick.

What was he doing? Why the roundabout questioning? Why didn't he come right out and ask where the heck his brother was? Glaring at him, Mari snapped. "I am."

"You know I want to make you happy, Earldean. Tell you what. If the magician is still in town, I'll see if I can engage him to give a private performance. Would you like that?"

Earldean? Mari blinked twice. "Yes."

They both looked to the bartender, who shrugged. "I believe they left town yesterday. She did, anyway. Never saw him except during the performances."

Mari's stomach sank from disappointment at the same time curiosity prodded her to ask, "Oh? That's strange."

"I thought so. They checked into the hotel about a week before the first show. She's the one who talked the hotel owner into hosting the event. She's a go-getter, that one. Pretty thing. Made herself well-known around town, but kept him all mysterious-like. I figured they did it to build interest in their show, but then I got to wondering if he didn't have reason to keep a low profile. Like maybe he was hiding from somebody. Never did see the man without the mask. Shoot." He gestured toward Luke. "For all I know, you could be him."

"Nah." Luke flashed a wicked grin. "I only work my magic behind closed doors. Right, sugar?"

"So you keep telling me."

Luke slapped a hand to his heart. "Oh, I'm wounded. You've a serpent's tongue, Earldean." He put his arm around her waist and pulled her against him. "I guess you'll just have to take my word for it since it looks like mine's the only magic you're gonna get to see. Unless…" He glanced back at the bartender and casually asked, "Do you know where Magnifico and his assistant were taking their show next?"

He shook his head. "I don't, but Tom Phillips over at the newspaper office might. He's the one who interviewed the little lady for the story he printed."

"We'll talk to Mr. Phillips, then, but in the meantime, we need to get a room." He leaned over, nuzzled Mari's neck. "My magic hands are starting to tingle."

She slapped him away, Luke and the bartender both laughed, then Luke signed the guest register as Mr. and Mrs. Homer Percy. *Earldean Percy*, Mari thought. The man's sense of humor was awful.

But he did make her smile.

She waited until they were in their room with the door shut behind them to demand an explanation for his approach. "You gotta understand where you are, Mari. A lot of men come to this part of Texas to hide. As a result, other men come here looking for the first group. If we go in and start asking questions right off, folks tend to clam up."

All right. That made sense. She sat on the edge of the bed and reviewed what they'd learned. Most important, they were a day behind her sister. "If they took the train after leaving here yesterday, they could be anywhere by now."

"True, but not likely." Luke sat down beside her and started pulling off his boots. "I suspect they'll stay away from the rail lines."

"Why?"

One boot hit the ground with a thud. "Sounds like they have trouble on their tails."

Mari frowned as the second boot followed the first. Luke rotated his ankles, stretching his feet, dividing Mari's attention between her sister's circumstance and the puzzle of her companion's more immediate intentions. "Explain it to me."

Luke rose and crossed the room to where a pitcher and bowl sat atop a small wooden chest. He poured water from the pitcher into the bowl, then splashed it onto his face. As he wiped his face dry with a hand towel hanging from a nearby rack, he said, "Rory's hiding. Wearing the mask, then making himself scarce—that's not part of the act or my brother's natural behavior. He's an actor. He thrives on recognition and accolades. If he's avoiding it, he's got a reason."

"Oh, wonderful. That's just lovely news."

Luke's hands went to the placket of his shirt and he started to slip the buttons free. "It might explain why they allowed us all to think that they were dead."

Her attention on the vee of bare skin expanding with every button released, Mari nodded. "She obviously loves him. She'd do whatever was necessary to protect him. I guess I could even see her justifying what she's done to our family if she thought her husband's need was greater than ours."

"Yeah, well. Rory can make anybody believe just about anything." Luke shrugged out of his shirt, and Mari's mouth went dry. "I think they're on the run and layin' low, except when they need money. Whether we find them easily or not depends on how much they took in. My guess is that they'll do a quick series of shows in this part of the state, then pull up stakes and head elsewhere until their money runs out."

His hands moved to his belt buckle, and Mari forgot all about Kat. "What do you think you're doing?"

"I'm hot and I'm dirty and I'm tired. I'm going to wash up, cool off and take advantage of this bed, since we have it and sleep for a bit. You're welcome to join me, or not."

Mari couldn't quite get her tongue to work or her focus to shift away as he shucked out of his pants. With his back to her, he dipped a washcloth in the water and methodically dragged it over his skin, washing away the day's grime. He's so beautiful, Mari thought. Lean and hard, like the marble statues she'd seen in the museums in Europe.

When he finished washing, tossing aside the washcloth and approaching the bed, she noted that a mere fig leaf wouldn't do the job for a marble sculpture of Luke Garrett. She scrambled off the bed when he reached to pull off the quilt.

"I left half a pitcher of clean water if you want some," he told her, stretching out on his stomach against the bleached white sheet.

Moments later, while Mari stood in the center of the small room reeling from this turn of events, Luke dropped off to sleep. No tossing, no turning. Just shut eyes and a snore.

She didn't know whether to be relieved or insulted. All she was certain of was that she felt rather…let down.

How could he sleep at a time like this? They needed to talk to the newspaperman and pick up Kat's trail once again. This was no time to delay. No time to sleep. Naked. Against cool sheets. Beneath the relaxing stir of a ceiling fan.

"Maybe I'll at least wash up," she murmured softly. What would that hurt?

She poured the dirty water into the flowerpot on the windowsill, then emptied the pitcher into the bowl. Darting a glance over her shoulder, she verified he still slept, then unfastened the buttons at her bodice.

The water felt like heaven against her skin. Maybe Luke had a point. After all, they needed to spend some time up here after he'd made such a point to the bartender about showing her his "magic." Also, even if they did speak to the newspaperman and find out where Kat and Rory went, they wouldn't strike out after them in the hottest part of the day. Not when her hind end still ached from four hours in the saddle.

Despite her good intentions, Mari's gaze drifted back to Luke. She wondered if *his* posterior hurt. It certainly didn't look injured. It looked…tight. Touchable. She could picture her hands on it, skimming over the his skin, massaging….

Maribeth McBride!

She whirled around and finished her ablutions. I'll sit in that ladder-back chair beside the bed and rest, she told herself. That'll be fine.

It wasn't. The wooden seat was as hard as brick and a trial against her aching backside. She sat primly, hands folded on her lap, uncomfortable as could be, trying not to stare at the plump, inviting mattress.

She toed off her shoes and thought about her sister. Where was Kat? What was she doing this hot afternoon? Was she ensconced in a hotel room, lying beside her husband, taking an afternoon nap? Or was she otherwise occupied?

Was her sister somewhere making love with Callahan? What would Kat say if she knew that just that morning, Mari had done the same thing with Rory's brother?

Mari shifted in her seat. Well, it didn't matter what Kat thought, or anybody else, for that matter. It was nobody's business what did or did not occur between Mari and Luke Garrett. The only person Mari had to answer to was herself.

"Herself" was quite the sympathetic person at the moment.

"One for the road," she whispered. Maybe she shouldn't have been so quick to dismiss him. After all, just because he was a Ranger instead of an outlaw didn't make him safe. He still lived his life on the shady side of the law. He'd given no indication of considering a possible change in the status quo, and she simply couldn't live her life that way.

No. She'd be a fool to think she might have a matrimonial future with him. They had no future. They only had now.

Now.

She dropped her head forward, staring down at her folded hands, knuckles white with the force of her grip. She felt wicked and wanton. She felt hot and achy and needy. She felt like a McBride Menace all grown-up.

Mari took a deep breath, then looked up. Luke was awake, lying on his side, staring at her. His body was blatantly aroused.

"Maribeth?" he said, his voice husky.

Heat washed through her. She shuddered and swayed in her chair. "Yes?"

"Come here."

CHAPTER THIRTEEN

LUKE HAD SLEPT just long enough to dream of her, so he was already floating in a haze of arousal when he awoke. He opened his eyes to see her watching him, recognized the sultry look and responded.

She actually did as he commanded, rising from her seat, moving toward him. Even as the heady sense of power, of anticipation, washed through him, Luke recognized that Mari McBride obeyed him only because she wanted to. She wanted him, and the knowledge made his blood ignite and his pulse pound.

She halted beside the bed and Luke reached out and took her hand, then pressed a kiss to the center of her palm. She visibly shuddered.

"You are so beautiful," he said huskily. He wanted to give her pleasure. He wanted to make her burn.

Gently, he nipped at the pad of her thumb. Her swift intake of breath went through him like lightning. She was close enough to him that he felt the heat of her body and inhaled the seductive scent of her arousal.

Next, he wanted to taste it. To taste her. He began with her fingers, kissing them, nipping them, licking them one by one, watching her eyes burn with suppressed desire. Her lids grew heavy, and almost imperceptibly she swayed toward him. He drew her little finger deeply into his mouth, bathed it with his tongue,

holding her there with a gentle suction that brought a
quiver to her skin. When, finally, he allowed her to
slide free, she spoke in a husky voice. "Oh, Luke."

The sound of his name on her lips struck a chord
deep inside him, and in its echo, Luke detected an undeniable truth. This was not a simple, lazy summer afternoon tussle with a transient woman. This was something more. Something special.

Mari McBride was someone special.

That thought alone should have made him flee the
bed, flee the room. Yet, even as he considered it, she
took the final step and sat upon the mattress, looking
at him in a way different from anything he'd ever seen
in a woman's eyes. Mari looked at him as if he were
the center of her world.

Her expression humbled him and an unfamiliar
tightness in his chest stole his breath. Luke Garrett
knew, sure as he was lying naked in this bed, that he
didn't deserve Mari McBride. Didn't deserve her sitting there next to him all soft and warm and willing.
And he damn sure didn't deserve the trust gleaming in
her eyes.

He *was* an outlaw, he thought. He might bear the title
of Texas Ranger, carry all the rights and privileges of
a true lawman, but in this bed, he was nothing more
than a goddamn thief. The first time he made love to
Mari, he'd stolen her innocence. Taken something that
could never be restored. And here he was again, ready
to take something that didn't belong to him. Something he didn't deserve. If he were Trace McBride...

Luke grimaced. McBride had a father's right to
shoot him right between the eyes. *After* he castrated
him.

"Luke?"

As if sensing that he needed her touch, she reached over and stroked his cheek. "Is something wrong?"

Wrong? Hell no, nothing's wrong. I'm naked, hard and about to have the only woman who ever tied me up in knots, and all I can think about is facing her father's wrath. Dammit, Mari, I never cared about that before. I never cared about a woman's parents, her family, her reputation. I never cared about a woman before.

Until you.

"No," he said, his voice cracking. "Nothing's wrong, sugar." Clearing his throat, he shook his head and smiled as a shudder of longing shot through him. "I just wanted to look at you."

She tentatively ran a finger across his lips and gave him a sultry grin. "I like looking at you, too. But not as much as I enjoy touching you." Mari then slid her finger into his mouth and mimicked his earlier movements. In and out, she teased him, quickening her rhythm. His hips thrust forward on their own accord.

Well, hell. So much for the momentary attack of conscience. Morals, ethics, right, wrong, good and bad disappeared as Luke breathed in her lemonade-and-sunshine scent and almost drowned in a wave of lust. With a thick sound of pleasure, he pulled her down against him and took her mouth in a hard, deep kiss as his hands went to work ridding her of her clothing until she lay beside him, as naked and hot as he.

He caressed her breasts and tugged at her nipples until she whimpered and moved hungrily against him. She returned his kiss, her tongue tangling with his own. Her whimpers intensified, the sounds greedy and demanding. The musky scent of her arousal seduced him, made him want more. Made him want to taste.

He released her mouth and trailed his lips along the

soft, sweet length of her neck. He kissed first the upper
swell of her breasts, then the heavy underside, before
settling down to feast at her nipples. His tongue laved
one, then the other, suckling until he knew she was
peaked and tender. Helplessly, she arched against him,
her head thrashing back and forth upon the bed, and her
responsiveness added fuel to the fire of Luke's own
arousal. He kissed her flat stomach, dipping the tip of
his tongue into her navel and delighting in her surprised squeal.

He drew back, gritting his teeth against a groan of
need as he straddled her, drank in the naked beauty of
her, rosy and dewy with desire. "Mari," he said, somewhere between a plea and a prayer.

Her eyes flickered open, their gazes met and held.
Her eyes were blue jewels afire that scorched him with
sensual heat and demanded more. So Luke abided.

Deliberately, he kneed her legs apart, reached between them and found her moist center. He played with
her a moment, stroking and exploring, until the urgent
movement of her hips signaled her wishes.

She cried out when Luke penetrated her with his finger, probing into the tight, slick sheath. She was soft
and supple, yet strong. Strong enough to take him, to
hold him, to stroke him with her inner muscles until she
drove him out of his mind. He eased his finger higher
and added pressure and heard the hitch in her breathing. Knowing she was right at the brink, he pressed
down on her swollen flesh and reveled in her euphoric
shout.

Silky heat spilled into his hand, and Luke fought for
self-control. He could have her right now. He could
bury himself in her hot, welcoming body and end this
sweet agony in moments, but that would be too easy,

too quick. A hot, slow, summer afternoon called for hot, slow sex.

Except he needed her now. Wanted her now. He had to have her now.

So he chose a delicious compromise.

Luke withdrew his finger, cupped the soft, round globes of her buttocks, and tilted her upward as he lowered his mouth to taste her. At the first rasp of his tongue against her petal-soft skin, Mari gasped. "Oh. Oh! Luke, what…oh…oh…ahh."

Luke smiled against her. Even if she'd wanted to argue further, he'd stolen her thunder with a kiss unlike any other. He savored her sweet elixir, steeped himself in the pleasure of sharing with her the ultimate intimate kiss. He lingered in the sensitive places, those mysterious, hidden places, moving his tongue in, out and around. And as his mouth tasted, his hands continued to caress, to flow over silky skin, delighting them both.

She began to whimper, little murmurs of pleasure-pain, and she grabbed his shoulders, her nails digging deep. She was close, he knew. Taut and tense, she unconsciously urged him on with the flex of her fingers, the rock of her pelvis, and those achy desperate sounds escaping her throat. "Oh, please, please…"

"Mari-mine," he whispered, covering her with his full mouth, then sucking gently, tenderly, gave her a climax that arched her entire body.

Luke felt as if he owned the world.

Before she'd quite come back to earth, he moved above her, sank into her. Her legs wrapped around his hips, her body warm and wet. Accepting. Nothing in his life had ever felt so good. Ignoring the demands of his body, Luke summoned the last vestiges of self-control and held himself still, steeping himself in the moment, reluctant for it to end.

This dangerously beautiful woman lying beneath him was everything a man could ever want. All he could ever need. He needed her mussed hair, her lips swollen from his kisses, her soft body curved around his own.

He needed her saucy mouth, her spunk and determination, her loyalty. He needed her trust. He needed her to need him.

That stopped him cold. He'd never wanted a woman to need him before. That signified ties he'd always refused. First it was morals, now this? Had he lost his mind?

Unwilling to dwell on his confusion any longer, he leaned down and kissed her gently. His name was a sigh on her lips when she moved, arching her hips, drawing him deeper until Luke surrendered to the pulsing, desperate need for completion.

He thrust high and hard, losing himself within her. He moved slowly at first, taking easy strokes, wishing to prolong their encounter until he was blind with need. But she was so wet, so willing. So perfect. He couldn't resist taking everything she offered.

Bracing his arms on either side of her, Luke leaned down and kissed her again, harder this time, demanding she respond to his passion. His thrusts increased in tempo, became stronger, harder. Her fingers dug into his shoulders as Mari's desperate moans shattered the stillness of the room. Unable to resist her demand for more, he buried his face into her neck and pounded into her, giving all he had. Her hips arched upward and her knees rose, sending Luke tumbling over the edge.

They cried out together, and Luke spent himself

completely. Then, when he had nothing else to give, when continuing to breathe took a conscious effort, he collapsed atop her, heavy and sated.

Long minutes passed before he found the energy to move, and even then, he took care not to slip from her as he rolled onto his side. He gathered her close and held her against him. For a moment, neither spoke, the sounds of their breathing a tranquil melody. Finally, Mari sighed with contented pleasure and trailed her finger lazily across his back.

"What are you thinking?" he asked, when her smile turned rueful.

She lifted her eyes. "I'm afraid that, despite all my efforts, I may never leave my Menacehood behind."

He lowered his head, and locked his lips with hers. It was a long, sweet kiss that touched Luke's soul.

"That's all right, sugar. You can menace me anytime."

WHEN LUKE AND Mari rode into Sawhorse Mill four days after leaving Parsonsville, the first thing Luke saw was a handwritten broadside nailed to the side of a building advertising Magnifico the Magnificent's magic show. First performance tonight, the sign read. Seven o'clock. Luke checked his pocket watch. Ten after seven.

Looks like the coin flip at that last crossroads had been a lucky one. They'd finally tracked them down.

Luke glanced over at Mari to see if she'd noticed the advertisement, but she was busy fiddling with the hat he'd bought her in Parsonsville. It was a man's cowboy hat and just a shade too big for her head, but she loved it. He discovered he loved putting a smile on her face.

She'd done a lot of smiling in the past four days, even though they'd remained a step behind their siblings. Something had changed for Mari in that hotel room. It was as if she'd given herself permission to quit worrying about anything more serious than the fit of her hat on her head.

Not that Luke was complaining. After all, hadn't he reaped the benefits of her newfound independence every night and at least once each day?

And yet, while she'd apparently quit worrying, it hadn't quite worked that way for him. Something had nagged at his consciousness ever since the morning he took her virginity, something of import about Mari McBride that remained just beyond his grasp. He'd missed a clue, he suspected. It wasn't like him. Of course, neither was bedding a virtuous young woman of good family, if not good sense.

Not that he was showing much good sense, himself. Hell, when you stripped bark down to the wood, his actions weren't much better than Rory's. It was a sobering fact.

At least he'd done his best to be responsible in his irresponsibility. Since the first time—well, the first couple times—he'd done his best to prevent any unintended consequences. Bedding her was dishonorable enough; getting her with child would be…damn, bet she'd be a beauty when ripe with child. With his child.

The thought nearly knocked him off his horse. Better keep his mind on matters at hand.

"Mari?" he called. When she gave him her attention, he gestured toward the sign. "Looks like we found them."

She immediately quit fiddling with her hat and noticed the flyer. She went still, her eyes wide and rounded as she read the notice. "They're here? Really?"

"Magnifico and his assistant are here, and I'll eat your hat if they're not Rory and Kat."

Absently, she moved her hands to her hat, then said, "Don't you touch."

"I won't have to." He expected her to kick her horse and go galloping into town to find the Prairie Star Saloon where the show was being performed.

Instead, she licked her lips. "I'm scared, Luke."

"This isn't a trail of fairy dust we've been chasing, sugar. You were right all along. Your sister is alive. You've found her."

Slowly, Mari nodded. "Maybe. I hope so. Truly, I do. But...then what?"

To Luke's surprise and dismay, a pair of big fat tears spilled from her eyes and slid slowly down her cheek.

Mari swiped the wetness away with the back of her hand. "What explanation will she give me? What if it's something selfish and unforgivable? What will I do then? Or what if she refuses to come home? He *is* her husband now. If she wants to stay with him, if she doesn't think she needs her family anymore, I can't make her do anything."

"Why don't you ford that river when you reach it," Luke advised. "No sense worrying yourself sick over something that probably won't happen."

"But I need to be prepared." Mari closed her eyes and visibly shuddered. "If this elopement of hers was nothing more than a dramatic frolic, if she's put my family through hell for no good reason, then I'm going to regret ever coming after her."

What he should have done was remind her that they believed Rory was trying to hide from someone, and that Kat's silence to her family might be an effort to protect them. Instead, the question was on his lips and out of his mouth before Luke had the sense to stop it. "Will you regret me, Maribeth?"

"What?"

It was a straightforward query. What didn't she understand? Luke's chest suddenly felt tight, and his muscles tensed as he repeated his question. The answer, he realized, mattered.

"Regret you?" She gave her head a little shake as if to clear it. Then she looked him straight in the eyes, her honesty and sincerity shining like a beacon, as she declared, "I'll never regret you, Luke Garrett. Never. No matter what happens. My grandmother Monique always taught us that a woman should never regret her first love."

First love. It was a bullet between the eyes. *That* was the elusive truth that had ghosted through his mind for days now. It was a warmth to fill the cold void inside him, the essence of a bone-deep yearning he'd refused to recognize. It was a dream he'd long denied. Somehow, it had sneaked up and taken hold of him.

Luke Garrett, outlaw, spy and erstwhile bodyguard, had gone and fallen in love with Maribeth McBride.

And she thinks she's scared?

AS SHE STOOD poised on the steps outside the Prairie Star Saloon, a disturbing mix of anticipation and trepidation churned in Mari's stomach. Her breaths came in shallow pants and her heartbeat fluttered like a hummingbird's wings. What if Luke was wrong? What if it wasn't her sister? What if—

"Oh, stop it," she murmured before taking a deep, calming breath. Whatever happened, she'd deal with it. She was strong.

As Luke stepped up beside her, she grabbed hold of his hand and gripped it hard. "You ready?" she asked.

Inside the saloon, applause broke out. Mari took another deep breath, then moved toward the door.

A ticket taker stopped them before she could push past the swinging saloon doors. Restlessly, Mari waited for Luke to dig out the required coin. When laughter erupted from the saloon, she abandoned what little patience she had left and darted around both men. The wooden door felt cool against her palm as she pushed it open. The scent of sulphur teased her nostrils as she stepped into the building, but it was a particular sound that grabbed her attention.

Feminine laughter. Rippling, joyous, irresistible feminine laughter. Familiar feminine laughter.

Mari turned her head toward the sound, and her knees turned to water. "Kat."

The trembling came from out of nowhere, and it rippled through her body like a fever. She swayed on her feet and might have melted to the floor had Luke not offered her a supporting hand.

"Kat," she murmured again, drinking in the sight of her sister.

Kat stood elevated on a temporary stage at the far corner of the room. She looked thinner, Mari thought. Thin and tanned and beautiful. She wore a rather shocking costume, a shoulder-baring toga of emerald silk the color of her eyes—and the pendant hanging around her neck. So, Rory hadn't sold the piece after all. Thank goodness. Mari's hand lifted to clutch at her own pendant. She'd had it repaired in Trickling Springs and worn it ever since. Mari blinked back tears and watched her sister assist her masked companion in a trick that turned an audience member's six-shooter into a snow-white dove.

It was when the audience applauded and Rory and Kat clasped hands to take a bow that Kat appeared to sense something had changed. In the midst of dipping her head toward the floor, the magician's assistant froze. Her head snapped up. Her gaze panned the room.

Mari took half a step forward.

Kat saw her and gasped. She dropped her partner's hand and brought both of hers up to her mouth. Mari could see her lips move, but it wasn't until the applause died that she was able to hear Kat say "Maribeth?" Then, louder, "Maribeth?" After that, a squeal. "Maribeth!"

Kat leaped off the makeshift stage and rushed toward Mari, who darted forward to meet her sister in the middle. Both women had tears streaming down their faces by the time they wrapped their arms around each other. Mari clutched her sister against her, breathed in her familiar cinnamon-and-sunshine scent, and sent up a quick, heartfelt prayer of thanksgiving. She was only vaguely aware of Luke as he brushed past her, headed for the stage.

"I can't believe you're here," Kat said. "Why are you here? How did you find us? Or is this just a wonderful coincidence? And what in the world are you doing with Luke Garrett?"

Mari glanced around. The audience's attention was divided equally between her and Kat, and the stage where Luke was holding a quiet discussion with Magnifico the Magnificent. "Let's go somewhere private to talk."

"All right. In a few minutes, though. I need to finish the show." But as she turned around, the masked man on the stage spoke in a heavily Spanish-accented voice.

"Ladies and gentlemen," Rory Callahan said with a flourish. "This man, this infidel, has dared to question

Magnifico's magic. Watch now as I demonstrate to him the true extent of my powers."

Kat took a step toward the stage, saying, "What in the world?"

Luke made a show of scoffing. "Powers? Ha. This 'magic' of yours is nothing more than cow patties. Just a bunch of smoke and mirrors hoo-ha."

A crusty old cowboy in the audience stood up and said, "Yeah!"

A chorus of others joined in. On stage, Luke folded his arms. Magnifico flourished his cape, then smiled magnificently at the crowd. "My friends, prepare to be amazed."

"What is he doing?" Kat murmured.

Shaking his head, Luke turned his back on Rory and began to leave the stage. A puff of smoke exploded at his feet. He stopped, his eyes going round with shock, then narrowing with disdain. "Smoke and mirrors," he repeated.

The masked magician held out his hands, an offer of innocence, and Luke gave him a dismissive wave, then took another step. Smoke puffed from the floor at his feet. He shot the magician a suspicious look but took another step. More smoke. Now alone on stage, Rory folded his arms. Puffs of smoke followed Luke all the way down the aisle as he moved toward Mari and Kat.

"My," Kat breathed. "I've never seen him do something like that. How is he doing it?"

"He's not," Mari said flatly, quietly. The audience's attention was back on the stage. "Luke is. Come on, let's go."

"Luke? How does he—"

"Hush, Kat." Mari grabbed hold of her sister's arm and tugged her toward the door.

Kat dragged her feet. "But…the show…"

"Luke will finish it. He's giving us the chance to talk. Let's take advantage of it."

"Luke Garrett? What does he know about magic?"

Mari thought about that morning on the trail, when she'd awoken to the dance of his fingers across the bare expanse of her flesh. "You'd be surprised, sister."

Outside on the street, Mari looked around for a place for them to talk. She wanted privacy. Now that the first exultant rush of joy was fading, the anger she'd nursed for so long had begun nipping at the edges of her consciousness. If their discussion took a turn toward the ugly, she'd just as soon it not happen out on the street. "Do you have a hotel room?"

"Well, sort of."

"Let's go there to talk. Which way is it?"

"I'm not sure that's such a good idea," Kat said, grimacing. "It's…um…upstairs."

Upstairs? Above the saloon? "You're sleeping in a whorehouse?"

Her sister shrugged and smiled sheepishly. "It's cheap."

Another woman might have been horrified, but not Mari. The McBride sisters weren't strangers to such places, although it wasn't their practice to spend the night in one. At least, not ordinarily. "Remember that time we sneaked into Rachel's Social Emporium and spent the night?"

"Just barely," Kat replied with a smile. "That was before Papa married Jenny, right? I was awfully young. I didn't have a clue what all that giggling and groping was about."

That wasn't the case anymore, for either of them.

Kat was a married woman. Mari had learned plenty about giggling and groping during the past few days. "It's early yet. It shouldn't be too busy, especially with the show still going on. Is there an outside staircase?"

"Around back."

Mari gestured for Kat to lead the way. Kat slipped her arm through Mari's as they walked, and Mari expected her to ask about their family. Instead, she said, "I wish it would rain tonight. Those clouds building off to the west look promising, don't you think?"

The weather? She wanted to talk about the weather? Well, she probably preferred privacy herself for the upcoming conversation. Still, it depressed Mari a bit to think that she and her younger sister had come to filling conversational gaps with talk about the summer drought. How times had changed. Offering a weak smile, Mari agreed, "Rain would be nice."

The back staircase led to a narrow, second-story hallway lined on each side by a half-dozen closed doors. Kat led the way to the last door on the left. Inside was a bed and nothing else. Maybe this wasn't a good place to talk, after all.

Before Mari could broach the subject, Kat climbed onto the bed and sat cross-legged. "Sit down, Mari. I'm dying to hear all the news from home."

Funny she should use that particular turn of phrase. Mari walked to the dirt-fogged window that overlooked Main Street and pushed aside a threadbare curtain. Where to start? Staring down into the near-empty street, she said, "I think it's safe to say that home is pretty anxious for news from you, too."

A long moment ticked by in silence. Finally, with a hitch in her voice, Kat asked, "Are they?"

Mari glanced over her shoulder. Her brows winged up at the earnest expression on her sister's face.

"Be honest, Mari." Kat plucked at a loose thread on the bedspread. "I'm prepared. I know they probably hate me. I know what I did was awful."

"Yes, it was," Mari shot back, surprised herself at the amount of venom in her tone. "How could you, Kat? How could you do that us? To me and Emma, Billy and the boys and to Mama. And Papa. God, Kat. How could you have done that to Papa?"

Tears welled, spilled from Kat's eyes. "I don't know. I didn't set out to elope that night. I was mad at Papa because he'd forbidden me to see Rory again. It got all over me, Mari. All over me!"

Mari was surprised to feel tears swelling in her eyes. The emotion of that awful night had come rushing back, and she now had a cold stone of pain lodged within her chest, weighing her down.

"I was angry with Papa, and in love with Rory, so I acted irresponsibly," Kat continued. "I'm so sorry, Mari. Not for loving Rory, mind you, but for acting indiscreetly that night. And for our argument. It haunted me that the last words we exchanged were so harsh."

"Haunted you!" Mari snapped, whirling around. "For three months, I had to live with the fact of those words." *Dead cold ashes.* She shuddered at the memory. "I thought I'd had a premonition, and that by ignoring it, I sent you to your fate. That's what I've been living with, Katrina. While you've been gallivanting around Texas with your new husband, that's what I've had to deal with. Not to mention the family's grief. That's a whole other subject."

Now, a hint of mulishness joined the heartbreak in Kat's expression. "I won't apologize for marrying the man I love. The family could have accepted that, accepted him. You ask how I could have done this to y'all. Well, I ask how y'all could have done this to me? Was eloping with the man I love such an unforgivable thing? How could you cut me out of your lives this way?"

"You were *dead* to us, Kat."

"That was cruel!"

"Yes, it was!"

Seated on the bed, Kat clenched her fists. At the window, Mari wrapped her arms around herself. So much anger, hurt, and pain swirled in the room that it seemed as if a third person had joined them.

Finally, Kat sighed. "I knew Papa would be mad, but I never thought he'd totally turn against me. And Mama...I know they always try to present a united front to the children, but I honestly can't believe she went along with him. They ripped my heart out, Mari. The day I got that telegram was the absolute worst day of my life."

Mari waited a beat, tried to think it through and make sense of what Kat had said. She couldn't. "What telegram?"

"Papa's telegram. The one he sent in answer to mine."

Mari went totally still. "You sent Papa a telegram? When?"

"Right after Rory and I got married. I wish you could have been there, Mari. We found the prettiest little church in Paradise Prairie. It had a brand-new coat of white paint with yellow rosebushes in bloom all around it." She smiled wistfully, then sighed. "The preacher was out of town, but we got a judge to do the honors. It was the happiest day of my life, but also the saddest. I was marrying the man of my dreams, but my family wasn't there."

Mari's heartbeat thumped in her chest. "And you telegraphed Papa with your news?"

"Yes, that, and I asked if the family was all right, because I heard about the Texas Spring Palace fire."

"And he responded."

Kat nodded, her tears welling anew. "He said everyone was fine, but that he was ashamed of me and disowning me, and for me to never contact the family again."

"What?" Mari screeched.

Kat frowned, blinked twice. "You didn't know?"

"It didn't happen!"

"Yes, it did. It really did. Papa said those things to me. I couldn't believe it. I cried for a week afterward. I even sent two more telegrams, one to Mama and one to Emma, but I guess he wouldn't let them reply."

"No!" Mari paced the small space between bed and window, and waved her arms as she spoke. "You don't understand. It-did-not-happen. Papa never got a telegram from you. When I said you were dead to us, I meant d-e-a-d. We thought you died in the fire, Kat. We thought we'd lost you forever!"

Kat's mouth dropped open. "Dead?"

Mari nodded.

Color leached from Kat's face. "You thought I was *dead?*"

"Yes!"

She ducked her head, thought for a moment, then looked at her sister and asked, "Not you're-not-family-anymore-and-I-won't-think-about-you dead, but dearly-departed dead?"

"Cold corpse in a coffin in a Pioneer's Rest Cemetery plot dead."

"I always liked Pioneer's Rest Cemetery," Kat absently observed before the confusion in her expression cleared and she demanded, "Why? How could you think such a thing?"

The words tumbled from Mari's mouth. "Billy was watching when you knocked over the candle, then went back behind the curtain. He saved Luke, but by then the fire was too hot, and he couldn't get to you. They told us there was no other way out."

Speechless, Kat simply stared at Mari, shaking her head. "I didn't…we left right away…I never even knew about the fire until the next…oh, wait. Wait! You said I knocked over a candle?"

Reluctantly, Mari nodded. It was a sign of Mari's distress that she'd mentioned the candle in the first place since she'd never intended to share that particular detail with her sister.

Kat's eyes rounded in horror. "Oh, my God. Mari, did *I* start the Spring Palace fire?"

"They never determined exactly how it started."

"But I knocked over a candle. Oh, Mari, people died in that fire! Because of me." She wrapped her arms around herself and rocked back and forth. "I killed them. I killed them!"

"No, honey." Mari rushed to sit beside her sister and take her in her arms. "No, it was an accident. Just an accident."

"People died because of me," Kat murmured before burying her head against her sister's bosom and sobbing.

Mari held on, stroking Kat's hair, quietly shushing her, offering soft words of comfort until the storm ended. When Kat finally dried her eyes, Mari returned to the subject of the telegrams. "Honey, who sent the telegrams?"

Sniff. Sniff. "Rory."

"Hmm…"

"What do you mean, hmm…?"

"Obviously, something isn't right about all this. Papa never received a telegraph from you, Kat."

"Maybe he did. Maybe he hates me for starting the fire and running away. Maybe he just let the rest of you think I was…I was…"

"No. You know better than that, Kat. Your father loves you. He *loves* you."

"But—"

"No! Stop that right now. You're being foolish. Think about it. Even if the world turned on its axis, and he decided he didn't love you anymore, he still wouldn't have lied to the rest of us. Kat, this nearly killed Mama. And Billy? Oh, Kat, you wouldn't recognize him, he's changed so much—and not for the better. He carries the weight of your 'death' on his shoulders like a yoke. In fact, Papa and Mama were so worried about him that they took the boys to Britain to visit the Rosses. That's why, when I learned you might still be alive, *I* came looking for you, not Papa."

Mari told Kat about the letter from their friend, and the mention of the necklace. Holding her emerald pendant in her fist, she asked, "But if Papa didn't send that reply, who did?"

"It had to be Rory. He must have lied to you."

"No!" Kat pushed off the bed, backed away from her sister. "No, Rory wouldn't do that to me. Why would he? He loves me."

"Why does he stay masked? Why are you the person out on the streets soliciting an audience for your magic shows? Is he running from someone, Kat? Hiding from someone?"

"Well, yes. Yes, we have a bit of a problem. There are these men…but no. No. Rory sent my telegrams. I was with him when he sent the third one."

"He must have bribed the telegraph operator, then."

"No! No. I won't believe it."

"Won't believe what, darlin?" Rory said from the doorway.

Neither Mari nor Kat had noticed the men's arrival, but now both women turned. "Why did you pretend to send my family Kat's telegrams?" Mari demanded. "Why did you lie about my father's response?"

Guilt flashed in his eyes and Kat gasped. "Rory!"

"Ah, darlin'." The Irish brogue came on thick. "Don't be a-lashin' me with yer tongue. I have an explanation."

"I'll just bet you do," Luke observed from behind his brother. "You always have an explanation."

Kat turned white. "They thought I was dead! They *mourned* me."

Her husband attempted a smile. "Won't they be happy to learn they were mistaken?"

"Why, Rory?" Kat asked, advancing on him. "Why did you lie about the telegrams?"

"I didn't exactly lie," Rory said, his brogue disappearing.

"Rory," Kat warned even as she swiped furiously at the tears spilling from her eyes.

"All right. All right." Shedding his attempts at charm, he tugged impatiently at his black cape's string tie around his neck. "It's all connected to the Dickerson brothers."

Kat folded her arms. "Why am I not surprised?"

"Who are the Dickerson brothers?" Mari asked.

"We've been running from them since we left Fort

Worth, although I don't know why, since Rory gave him all our money on our way out of town."

Luke muttered an invective. "I wondered why you were selling magic-show tickets with ten thousand dollars in your pocket."

Mari and Kat looked at each other, then at Luke.

"Ten thousand dollars?" Mari repeated.

"And I'm bunking in a whorehouse?" Kat asked.

"Care to explain that one, brother?" Luke said to Rory.

"Brother!" Kat exclaimed.

"Half brothers, actually," Mari clarified.

Kat lifted her fingers to her head and began massaging her temples. "Just what is going on here? Obviously, there is much about this situation that I don't understand."

Rory tossed his black cape onto the bed, then raked his fingers through his hair. In the action, Mari for the first time saw a familial resemblance between the two men. "You remember Tom and Joe Dickerson, don't you, Luke?"

"Those redheaded boys? The ones you and Murphy used to go fishing with?"

Murphy, Mari thought. Wonderful. She was liking this less and less.

"I ran into them last time I was in Galveston, and we got into a bit of a scrape. It was bad business, Luke. More than I had bargained for. The long and the short of it is, I left town with something they think is theirs. They're looking for it, and I don't want 'em to have it."

"That was an eventful trip to Galveston," Luke drawled. "You may have taken something with you, but need I remind you that you left something else behind?"

Mari glanced at Luke. Though she found herself quite curious about this "something" Rory referred to, a note in Luke's voice, along with the hard look in his eyes, told her to pay close attention to what he'd said.

Something left behind?

Rory rubbed the back of his neck. "I remember. Maybe we could talk about it another time?"

"Soon," Luke snapped. "So, let me see if I follow this. You gave those redheaded Dickerson boys the ten thousand dollars you stole from your sister, the only support money she's ever received from her children's father, but that wasn't enough to get 'em off your tail?"

"I didn't exactly steal Janna's money. I borrowed it. I have every intention of paying it back. I only had about eight of it left when I turned it over to the Dickersons. I think it would have been enough, but they talked to Murphy and told him what I had. Murphy wants it, of course, so I knew they wouldn't stop coming after me." Glancing at Kat, he added, "Not unless they thought I was dead."

Mari put the clues together. "You read the obituaries in the newspaper, didn't you? You knew we thought you'd died. That's why you didn't send the telegram."

Still looking at Kat, he nodded. "I thought it was the best way to protect your sister."

"Not to mention yourself," Luke observed with a snort.

Her expression wounded, Kat said, "You lied to me. All this time, you've been lying to me. How could you? I'm your wife!"

Below his breath, but loud enough that Mari heard it, Luke muttered, "Where have I heard that before?"

The comment frightened Mari. What secrets were they keeping? Instinctively, she shifted closer to Kat.

"Murphy's not a problem any longer," Luke said.

"He's in jail. What the hell do you have, Rory, that's worth all this trouble?"

Rory hesitated. He scowled and hemmed and hawed, then sighed. "Pirate treasure."

"What?"

Tossing her husband a scornful glance, Kat elaborated. "He and the Dickersons fished with an old man who lived on the south end of Galveston Island. When they were all drunk one night, the fisherman confessed to having found part of Jean Laffite's treasure. Rory talked the poor man into showing them, and when he did, the Dickersons murdered him."

Luke closed his eyes and grimaced. "Murder. Dammit, Rory!"

"Hey. I didn't know they were gonna up and do something like that," he defended. "I felt real guilty about it."

"Not so guilty that you didn't take your share of the bounty, though, right? Not so guilty that you turned yourself into the law."

Rory snorted. "Sure. Right. That sounds funny coming from your mouth, jailbird."

Now Mari shifted a step back toward Luke. He shot her a quick, curious look before addressing his brother. "So, what are they after, Rory, other than your hide?"

"An altar cross," Kat offered dully.

"Pa used to talk about it, remember, Luke?" Rory said. "It's the lost Sacred Heart Cross. The one Spain was sending to the church in the New World when Laffite took the ship. Folks always thought it might turn up in Texas. It's beautiful. Solid gold and encrusted with jewels—the heart-shaped ruby in the center is as big as a hen's egg."

Kat wrapped her arms around herself. "He said he was going to give it back to the church."

"Sure," Luke snidely observed. "Right after he magically turns himself into a dove of peace." He frowned at his brother, and scratched the back of his neck. "You have managed to land yourself in a world of trouble, haven't you? Where is the cross? Do you have it with you?"

"No. It's hidden."

"He didn't think we should travel with it," Kat added. "He told me he was protecting me."

Sarcasm all but dripped from Luke's tongue as he drawled, "Isn't that just like good ol' Rory, protecting his womenfolk."

Mari decided she'd had enough. "What is it with you? What do you know about Rory that you're not telling us?"

The two brothers shared a look. Luke said, "Maybe you should go ahead and tell her. Just get it all out in the open now. She's gonna have to know."

"Know what?" Kat demanded.

Watching the men, witnessing the silent communication between them, Mari had a thought. An ugly, awful, horrible thought. She recalled Luke's unshakable belief that his brother would not marry her sister. She remembered his shock and his heated reaction to the news at the church in Paradise Prairie. Why would he react that way? Why would he make such cutting remarks to Rory about "leaving something behind" and "protecting his womenfolk"?

Unless the something he left behind was a woman. Was a wife.

Oh, dear Lord, no. Surely not.

"It's really not necessary." Rory said to Luke, "There are better ways to do this."

Damn you, Luke, for not telling me.

"To do what?" Kat demanded. "What is this all about? What else are you keeping from me?"

Mari knew her sister. Better for Kat to rip a scab off a wound all at once than to pick at it little by little. "Answer her, Rory."

Pleading now, Rory said, "Kat's a sweet, sensitive girl."

Luke gave Mari a quick, apologetic glance, then looked sadly at Kat as he said, "So is Melissa."

That's it, Mari thought. I was right. She reached out and took her sister's hand.

Luke continued, "She gave birth to a son on February tenth, Rory. She named him Brian, after your father."

With that, understanding dawned in Kat's expression. She gripped Mari's hand hard. "You deserted a pregnant mistress, Rory?"

"I…uh…no. I…uh…oh, hell." He sank down on the bed and buried his face in his hands.

Her heart breaking for her younger sister, Mari reached up with her free hand and cupped Kat's cheek. "I don't think he means his mistress, Katie-cat. I'm afraid he means his wife. I'm afraid the bastard you married is a bigamist."

"A bigamist?" Kat shot a disbelieving look at Rory. He didn't respond. Didn't even look up. "No…"

Kat's eyes rolled back and she swooned. Unprepared for that reaction—she'd never known Kat to faint—Mari was slow to react. Thankfully, Luke didn't hesitate. He caught her before she hit the hardwood floor.

Rory scrambled off the bed, making room for Luke to lay her gently on the mattress. Mari stroked her sister's hair saying, "Kat? Kat, are you all right?"

Rory Callahan cleared his throat. "Um…Maribeth?

Don't worry. She saw a doctor a couple weeks ago, and he told us it's not unusual for a woman to faint when she's pregnant."

CHAPTER FOURTEEN

ANGER SAT in Luke's stomach like a cold, hard stone as he took control of what had become an ugly scene. Kat, having revived from her swoon, lay sobbing into a pillow. Mari sat beside her sister, a mama grizzly protecting her cub, literally baring her teeth to either man who attempted to speak. Rory wore the shifty expression that usually meant he was about to flee. Better make his brother his first priority.

Luke grabbed Rory by the arm and pulled him to his feet. "C'mon. She's obviously not of a mind to talk to you right now."

His brother was only too happy to quit the room. His outlook changed, however, when Luke escorted him to the Parsonsville jail, identified himself as a Texas Ranger, then asked the local sheriff to lock up his prisoner until Luke made preparations to take him back to Fort Worth. "What? You a Texas Ranger?" Rory scoffed with derision. "That's as big a lie as anything I ever told Kat."

"Shut up." Luke removed his Warrant of Authority from a hidden pocket inside his gun belt and proved to the sheriff that Rory's angry protestations were simply the ravings of a guilty man. A short time later he exited the jailhouse, leaving Rory safely behind bars.

Talking with Mari occupied the next spot on his list

of priorities. He wanted privacy for this conversation—chances were it wouldn't be pretty—and damned if he'd hold it in a whorehouse.

He stopped two women exiting the general store, explained that he needed a nice spot to watch the sunset with his sweetheart. They told him of a bluff called Inspiration Point on the Colorado River within walking distance of town. With giggles and good luck wishes, the ladies sent him on his way. He hoped they didn't take note of his destination.

Back at the saloon, he stopped for a quick shot of Dutch courage, exchanged a few words with one of the working girls, then headed up the inside stairs. The women hadn't moved, though instead of crying, Kat lay sleeping, with Mari seated on the mattress beside her staring out into space. She looked sad and heartsick and defeated, and seeing her that way broke Luke's heart. "Mari, we need to talk. Will you come with me?"

"I can't leave Kat."

"Just for a little while. I've arranged for a woman to stay with her."

"Where is your brother?"

"In jail. Sheriff locked him up for me. I didn't want him running off."

"Jail." She nodded. "Good. That's where he belongs."

"Come with me, Maribeth." When she didn't respond, he added, "Surely you have a thing or two or twelve you'd like to say to me."

Then he saw it, a brief flash of fire in her eyes, and it made him feel marginally better. Mari might be down, but she wasn't out. Not by a long shot.

She stroked her sister's hair, then looked at him and nodded.

A purple dusk drifted across the land a short time later as Luke escorted her along a well-worn path leading out of town. They didn't speak, only the birds in the trees and the scuttle of gravel beneath their feet breaking the heavy silence between them.

The path sloped gently upward, and before long, they stood atop weathered stone. Beneath them, the deep green river drifted in peaceful solitude on its long and winding path toward the Gulf of Mexico. The hill country gradually gave way to the lowlands rolling east and south, allowing Luke to trace miles of the river's course as it meandered over sand, slower and flattened between tall, bright cottonwoods and oak and pecans. Though it couldn't compare with the true mountain vistas he'd seen while tracking the Harmon Gang through Colorado and Wyoming last year, the view was enough to make a man stop and recall his unimportance in the grand scheme of life.

Yet when he looked at his companion, saw her standing tall and strong and proud against the majestic crimson-and-gold backdrop of an early fall sunset, he sensed that he'd lived his entire life for this moment.

He drew a deep breath, collected his thoughts, then confessed the one thing that mattered the most. "I love you."

Never before had he spoken those three words to a woman.

They were absolutely the wrong words to say.

She whirled on him like a storm, thunder in her expression, lightning flashing in her eyes. Her words pummeled him like hailstones. "How dare you. How dare you say that to me now, under circumstances like these! Haven't you spoken enough lies already?"

"I'm not lying about this," Luke declared.

"Oh? And I'm supposed to know that how? Because you've always been truthful with me? Because every word out of your mouth is gospel? Because honor and honesty are your watchwords?"

Luke grimaced, heaved a sigh, jammed his hands into his pockets and looked away. He guessed he had that coming to him, that and more. But damn, the first time ever that he had bared his heart, she used it for target practice. That was hard on a man.

He attempted to speak calmly, convincingly. "Believe what you will, Mari, but that's the God's honest truth. This whole thing with Rory and your Kat, it's a damned bad deal. I handled it the best way I knew how."

She braced her hands on her hips. "Oh? And you think neglecting to mention the fact that your brother was a bigamist constituted handling it well?"

"What good would it have done for me to tell you?" he said in a halfhearted effort to defend himself. "You would have spent every minute of every day since we left that rose-covered church fretting yourself half to death over this situation."

"Not to mention being distracted from the other activity that kept *me* busy and *you* smiling like a cat in cream for the past four days," she responded with a disdainful sniff.

Luke's temper flared. "Now wait just one minute."

"I asked you point-blank if you had any other surprises, any other family skeletons, and you avoided the question. You *made love* to me in order to distract me!"

"That's not why I—"

"By the way," she continued, as though he hadn't spoken, "considering what I've learned regarding the your family, I probably should ask. Do you, too, have a wife and child stuck away somewhere you haven't bothered to mention?"

It was a slap to the face and Luke sucked in a breath. The sick feeling in his stomach intensified. Quietly, he asked, "Do you think so little of me, Maribeth? Do you truly believe I have so little honor?"

Seconds stretched like hours as he waited for her answer. He was losing her. Right here, right now. He could sense the situation spiraling out of control.

"I don't know," she finally replied, each word chipping away at Luke's heart. "I don't know you, Luke Garrett. I thought I did. I believed in you. I *trusted* you. But you've harbored too many secrets. Told me too many lies. I don't know who or what to believe anymore."

Luke's pulse pounded. His chest ached. A lump of emotion lodged in his throat. *Goddammit, Mari!*

Desperate now, he reacted like a man, not with words, but with action. He grabbed her, yanked her against him. He cupped her cheek in his hand and demanded, "Believe this."

He captured her mouth with his, pouring all the frustration, pain and heartache churning inside him into his kiss. Silently, he implored her to open her mind and her heart. Wordlessly, he demanded that she believe him, believe *in* him.

With a sob, she tore herself away.

"That's the truth, Mari," he said, breathing heavily, his heart wrenching at the sight of the tears now streaking down her cheeks. Tears he had caused. Not her sister, not Rory. Him. "That's the God's honest, barenaked truth. As plain as I can say it. Maybe I should have told you Rory already had a wife. Maybe I should have sacrificed these last few days when things have been so perfect between us."

Mari wrapped her arms around herself and rocked slowly side to side.

Luke fished in his pocket for his handkerchief, then held it out to her. When, finally, she took it and wiped the wetness from her cheeks, he cleared his throat. "But you know what? I was selfish. I didn't want to bring all that up. I didn't want family sins and obligations to come between us. I've spent a good portion of my life cleaning up after my family, and this time, for these few short days, I wanted some time for myself. I wanted this time with you."

He took a step toward her and spoke from the bottom of his heart. "I love you, Maribeth McBride. I'm *in love* with you."

"Oh, Luke."

"And you know what else? I think you're in love with me, too." He paused, waited for her to respond with more than his name, only Mari remained silent.

"Dammit, Maribeth." He reached for her again.

"No!" She pushed him away, turned away from him. She paced back and forth across a plot of land no bigger than a grave. "It's over. All of it. Kat has been found. My goal is accomplished. My sister and I will leave for Fort Worth first thing tomorrow morning. We'll work out a story on the way home. Emma will have told everyone that Kat eloped, so we'll just tell them she's now a widow. Her husband had an accident. A tragic accident. He's been hit by a train. Maybe gored by a bull. Something really awful."

Everything inside Luke went cold. He wanted to grab her, to physically stop her. *You're not leaving me!* He managed to keep his fists clenched at his sides as he flatly said, "No. You're not traveling alone."

"I won't be alone. Kat will be with me. We'll be

fine." Mari gave a harsh little laugh. "The only time
we've been in trouble is when we tangled with members of your family. Rory and Murphy are both in jail,
so they're no threat. Do you have any other brothers I
should know about?"

"Stop it!" Luke braced his hands on his hips. "Just
stop it."

"It's an honest question. After all, Luke—you, Murphy, Rory…your family hasn't exactly been good news
for mine."

"Don't lump me in with them," he snapped, temper
and nausea rolling in his gut. "I'm not my brother, and
I'm certainly not Finn Murphy. I'm happy to own up
to my own sins, Mari, but I'll be damned if I'll pay for
theirs."

The deepening dusk cast shadows across her face as
the gentle evening breeze gusted, lifting errant strands
of long golden hair to dance around her. Impatiently,
she pushed them behind her ear. "I don't want you to
pay for anything, Luke. I just want you and your
brother and your brother-in-law to leave me and my
family alone. This is a big state. All I ask is that you
stay away from Fort Worth. Keep your murders and
robberies and spying and lying away from us and our
home, for your own sake, if not for mine. If you or any
of your kin are within spitting distance when my father
learns this story, he'll kill you. Frankly, I don't want
that on my conscience."

"So that's it?" Luke drew back his leg and viciously
kicked a loose stone, sent it flying over the side of the
bluff. "I'm supposed to just walk away from you? From
us?"

"There is no us!" she cried. "There can't be. Your
family…my family…" She shook her head.

"Dammit, Mari." He took her shoulders in both his hands, barely restrained himself from shaking her. "This isn't about our families. This is about you and me!"

She wrenched away from him, raised both hands to her head, shut her eyes and shouted, "No! You don't understand."

"Then tell me," he implored, shaken by the misery in her countenance, a misery reflected in his heart. "Explain it. Make me understand. You love me, don't you?"

"Yes!" The word ripped from her soul. "I love you! But it can't matter, not now." She opened her eyes, and her beautiful damp blue eyes begged him to hear her. She fisted her right hand, thumped it against her chest. "It *is* about family, Luke. That's who I am, who we are. It's who we've always been. We're the *McBrides*. Kat is my sister, and she needs me now, like never before. Right now, she has to come first."

A lump of emotion had lodged in his throat. She had told him she loved him but that it didn't matter? Well, it goddamned mattered to him. "You've been a McBride, but you're grown now. You're a woman. It's time you let go."

"Luke, please."

"I want you to be a Garrett, Maribeth." He took a step toward her, reached for her. "I want you to be my family. I want you to marry me."

Mari flinched away from him. She sank to her knees, her answer a wounded mewl, the sound of an animal caught in a trap. Hearing it, Luke knew he'd lost. His arms fell to his sides. His heart shattered at her feet.

"She's pregnant," Mari said, her expression stricken, her voice breaking. "Alone. You're the brother of the man who's responsible."

Silence settled between them like death. Luke wanted to rage and roar and lash out against something, anything. Instead, he turned and walked a few steps away. Though he stared at the glorious vista before him, he saw only the dust of dreams destroyed.

After a long moment, Luke closed his eyes, swallowed his pain and locked it away. Then, his emotions numb and under his control, he turned toward Mari.

She sat with her face buried in her hands, quietly weeping. Luke approached her and gently helped her to her feet. He took her in his arms and held her. "All right, sugar. Don't worry. I understand. I'll leave it alone. I'll leave you alone. Everything's all right."

"I'm...I'm sorry," she said, her voice a broken whisper.

"Me, too, Maribeth." He pressed a kiss against her hair. "Me, too."

To Mari's dismay, Luke insisted on escorting them back to Fort Worth. No matter how much she objected, protested and complained, he remained determined to see his job of bodyguard through to the end. Mari might not have resisted him so vigorously had he not insisted on bringing that low-down, scalawag of a brother along with him. She didn't care that he couldn't leave Rory behind for fear that he'd disappear again. So what if the sheriff of Parsonsville refused Luke's request to lock Rory up until Luke could return for him? Why should she and Kat be subjected to the adulterer's presence?

Luke promised to make certain his half brother left the McBride women alone, and for the most part, he kept his word. Twice Rory Callahan attempted to talk to Kat, who then curled into herself and wept. Both times Luke hauled the scoundrel away before Mari herself was forced to get physical.

Nevertheless, the two-day trip home to Fort Worth proved difficult. Though Luke maintained a respectful distance, just knowing he was there kept Mari's heart squeezed in a vise. She couldn't help but recall his scent, the feel of his hard body against her softness, the husky rumble of his voice as he murmured earthy words in her ear when they made love.

Mari gave herself a little shake. They couldn't get home fast enough. The sooner he was gone, the sooner she could start getting over him. Mari suspected the task might take an exceptionally long time.

Two days after leaving Parsonsville, Mari watched through the train's passenger-car window as the Fort Worth skyline came into view. "Almost home, Kat," she said.

"Thank goodness."

When Kat lifted her head from Mari's lap, Mari was heartened to see that the green tint to her sister's complexion had faded somewhat. The railroad car's sway had played havoc on her constitution, and she'd spent the hours of travel in pure misery.

"Instead of hiring a driver, would you mind walking from the station to Willow Hill?" Kat asked. "Once my feet hit the ground, I want them to stay there."

"A walk sounds good," Mari agreed.

Kat smoothed her skirt, then added, "They won't be there when I meet the family, will they?"

Mari instinctively checked over her shoulder toward the back of the passenger car where Luke sat beside his brother. Luke caught her look and nodded. She jerked her head around and faced forward.

"They absolutely will not come with us to Willow

Hill. I couldn't stop him from following us from Parsonsville, but Willow Hill is private property."

"Mr. Garrett obviously takes his bodyguard duties seriously." When Mari limited her reply to a shrug, Kat added, "Are you ever going to tell me about him?"

"What do you mean?"

"The tension between you two is thicker than cold grits. Something happened between you two, didn't it?"

Mari didn't know how to respond. She didn't want to lie to Kat, but neither did she wish to relay the whole distressing story. She knew Kat would feel responsible for Mari's decision to end her relationship with Luke, and she didn't need that burden on top of everything else.

Mari was worried about her sister. More than just the stomach sickness, Kat displayed a sickness of spirit. She seemed fragile, as if a wrong word or harsh look might cause her to shatter into a million pieces. Seeing her this way made Mari angry enough to take a knife to Rory Callahan's two-timing heart.

"Now is not right for that," Mari finally said, dodging the question about Luke. "Let's think about home. Emma will be waiting. The McBride Menaces will be together again. What a glorious reunion that will be."

"I'm almost glad Papa and Mama are away," Kat told her. "It will be so hard to face them. They deserve better than to have me return from the dead a fallen woman."

"Don't," Mari snapped. "Stop that right now. You are no fallen woman." *That would be me.* "We've been through this before, Katrina. You believed yourself married. The shame isn't yours, it is his."

"I wish I could believe that," her sister murmured.

"I was such a fool. I should have suspected something was wrong. Sometimes things he said just didn't add up. But he dazzled me."

Mari knew about being dazzled.

Conversation waned as the train whistle blew, the brakes squealed, and the McBride sisters returned to Fort Worth. They gathered their belongings and waited their turn to disembark. Mari couldn't help but glance to the back of the car where Luke waited with Rory. For once, Luke wasn't staring at her, but looking through the window, his attention focused on the platform.

He was the first person off the train, dragging his brother with him. Mari was taken aback by his quick departure, and to her dismay, tears stung her eyes. *I thought he'd at least say goodbye. Don't I at least deserve that?*

They moved toward the door, then abruptly, Kat stopped. "What if somebody recognizes me? Oh, Mari, I don't think I want to walk after all. In fact, I don't think I want to get off this train. Let's just ride on to Dallas, shall we? We can visit our grandmother. Monique would like that."

"Calm down, honey. Everything will be all right. I promise."

"I'm scared."

"Don't be." Mari waited a moment. "You're alive, Kat. That's the best news our family could ever receive. Do you honestly think a little scandal could dampen it?"

Her sister smiled wanly, then nodded. "Still, let's go home the fastest way."

"I'll hire the fastest driver in town."

A few minutes later, among the last people to exit the train, she discovered that Luke had already accomplished the task for her.

He waited for Kat and Mari on the platform. Rory was nowhere in sight. "I have a wagon waiting to take you to Willow Hill. Not much of one, I'm afraid. The train from Dallas arrived a quarter hour before us and somebody else had already hired most of the drivers."

Mari drew a deep breath. "Thank you, Luke." She held out her hand for him to shake. "It's been a pleasure to—"

He mouthed a curse and glared at her. "I will see you to your front door."

"But—"

"I'd wired ahead, and one of my men took Rory into custody. It's just me, Mari, but I will see you home."

He escorted the women to a waiting wagon. Before leaving the train, Kat had pulled on a wide-brimmed, face-concealing bonnet, and now she walked with her head down. An acquaintance attempted to waylay Mari, but she simply waved and kept on moving. The ride to Willow Hill took just over ten minutes.

"Home," Kat said, as they drove up the hill toward the house their father had designed and built when she was a child. "It feels like forever since I've been here. I've missed it."

"Willow Hill has missed you, too. It was a sad, empty place this summer, Kat, but I suspect that's about to change. As soon as the family gets home from Europe, it'll be like Christmas in October."

"You think they'll be home that soon?"

"Definitely. Emma will have sent word. I have no doubt they'll be home as fast as physically possible."

The wagon turned into the circular driveway at the top of the hill and rolled to a stop near the base of the steps leading up to the broad front porch. Luke paid the driver and sent him on his way. At Mari's curious look, he said, "I'll walk back. Need to stretch my legs."

He assisted first Kat, then Mari to the ground. Kat stood beside the wagon and silently faced the house. Mari had a lump the size of a walnut in her throat when she turned to Luke.

This time, he headed her off. "Don't argue," he said, his jaw set. "I'm delivering you to your door, by God."

He was a dog with a bone, and Mari knew that the quickest way to see this painful moment finished was to let him have his way. She nodded, and when he offered her his arm, took it.

It was the first time she'd touched him since their return from Inspiration Point. His muscles were tense, his manner grim. The sandalwood scent of his shaving lotion teased Mari's nostrils.

As the three of them climbed the steps, Kat asked, "How late does Emma stay at the Harrisons'? Will she be home, do you think?"

"I suspect she will. It's after three, and she's usually home by then."

"Good." Kat drew a deep breath, pulled the strings on her bonnet and slipped it off, then opened the front door. Mari braced herself to say goodbye to Luke, but then a sound coming from inside the house captured her attention.

"Mama!" came the sound of a young boy's voice. "Tommy won't give me my slingshot!"

Mari's brows winged up in surprise. Kat gave a little gasp. Footsteps emerged from the kitchen, and Mari heard Jenny McBride say, "Ten minutes. We haven't been home ten minutes. What is it with those bo—"

Her eyes lit on the arrivals, and the glass water pitcher she carried slipped from her hand and crashed to the tile floor. Shock stole her breath, and she swayed on her feet amidst a sea of shattered glass. Luke started forward to help just as Trace McBride hurried out of the kitchen saying, "Treasure, are you all—oh God!"

Kat stepped forward and offered her parents a watery smile. "Hello, Mama. Hello, Papa. I'm home."

CHAPTER FIFTEEN

LUKE KNEW he should probably slip on out the door and leave the McBride family to their reunion, but he stayed right where he was. He'd been present at Kat's "death," so it felt somehow proper that he witness her resurrection.

Besides, he'd known all along that Trace McBride would demand an accounting of him eventually. Might as well get it over with at once.

Understandably, Jenny and Trace McBride had been shocked silent at the first sight of Kat, but when the prodigal daughter stepped forward and declared herself home, euphoric chaos erupted. Jenny let out a squeal and rushed toward Kat, catching her in a hard hug. Big, tall, stoic Trace had tears streaming down his face as he wrapped both women in his arms, then buried his face in his daughter's strawberry-golden hair.

Mari watched it all with teary eyes, her smile as wide as Texas. Compelling as the scene was between parents and daughter, Luke couldn't tear his gaze away from Mari. She'd given her all to make this moment happen. Kat had returned to Willow Hill because of Mari. Family was everything to Mari, and she'd just given them the greatest gift imaginable. How wonderful that must make her feel.

Two pairs of footsteps pounded on the staircase. "What's going on?" the shorter, towheaded boy asked.

The McBride parents released Kat long enough for her to lift her face toward her brothers.

"Holy shit!" the taller boy exclaimed, dashing downstairs.

Despite the excitement of the moment, Jenny McBride retained enough maternal presence to scold. "Thomas Trace McBride. Your language!"

The younger boy held back. In a trembling voice, he asked, "Are you a ghost?"

"No, squirt. C'mere so I can pull your ear."

"Kat!" he hollered, then joined his family in their celebration, the tears now turning to laughter.

"Where have you been, Kat?" the older boy asked, his question unleashing a torrent of others. Kat glanced to Mari for help. She stepped forward, linked her arm through her mother's, and said, "It's a long story. I think Kat might want to rest a little bit before she gets into the whole thing."

Luke didn't miss Mari's quick, significant glance toward her father or the little squeeze she gave her mother's arm. Her parents shared a glance, then for the first time, Trace met Luke's eyes and acknowledged his presence with a nod. He guided the group toward the parlor off the entry hall saying, "Why don't we—"

"Papa! Mama!" A long-legged whirlwind burst into the house yelling, "Emma says she's got spectacular news. We're supposed to…" Billy McBride came to an abrupt halt at the entry to the parlor, and his voice trailed off as he caught sight of Katrina. He blinked twice, then all the color left his skin. He wobbled a moment, then slowly sank to his knees. "You're alive. Oh, God. Thank you, God. I thought…I thought I killed you, Kat."

Kat knelt beside her brother, hugging him hard.

Emotion clogged her voice as she said, "I'm fine, Billy. Just fine. Don't worry. I'm so sorry you've felt responsible all this time. Mari told me all about it, and you didn't do anything wrong. All of this was my fault. I'm so, so sorry."

The boy started crying, hard, deep, from-his-gut sobs, and his family rallied around him. His brothers patted his back. The women hugged and cuddled and coddled; his father clapped him on the shoulder and made a couple of jokes that brought a fleeting smile to the boy's face. Moments later, Emma arrived at Willow Hill, squealed with delight upon seeing her family, and a new round of hugging and embracing commenced.

Luke took a step back, mentally and physically, and studied the scene before him. This was the McBride family, complete and whole. It wasn't simply a collection of eight individuals, but a single entity, strong and invincible. This was the reality Mari had tried to explain to him. The reality he'd not truly understood. Until now.

In his defense, how could he have? If he'd enjoyed this kind of unity within his family once upon a time, back before his father died and his mother married Brian, he couldn't recall it. He and Janna loved each other, and he adored her children, but time and divisive forces—primarily Janna's husband—had weakened the bond between them.

No, Luke's family life hadn't prepared him for dealing with Mari's, and from the outside looking in, Luke couldn't help but feel a twinge of envy.

Mari was lucky. Damned lucky. No wonder she'd refused him. Witnessing this outpouring of emotion today, seeing firsthand the deep, unifying love and loyalty this family enjoyed, Luke could finally comprehend the sacrifice he'd asked her to make.

Mari loved him. Luke believed that. She wouldn't have given herself to him otherwise. Yet, her love for her family was as much a part of her as the color of her hair or the blue of her eyes, and by asking her to marry him now, with family matters standing the way they currently did, he'd put her heart at odds with her soul.

However, this wasn't a case of Montagues versus Capulets. He sure as hell wasn't any Romeo. In this love story—and it was, by God, a love story—the heroine stood solidly with her family and a true hero would expect nothing less.

That didn't mean the hero had to give up, however. The hero had to figure a way to make it work.

Winning Mari's heart wasn't enough. Luke would have to win her family, too.

Talk about a tough row to hoe. Trace McBride hadn't liked him sniffing about his daughter months ago. Now he'd done a helluva lot more than sniff. Add that to the baggage he'd be forced to tote because of Rory's and Murphy's sins against Kat and Mari—hell, he'd be lucky if McBride didn't take his head off.

It didn't matter, though. Luke might be going away, but he wasn't going anywhere, so to speak. He'd found the woman he wanted for his own, the woman he'd waited for all his life. He wouldn't let a little thing like family stand in the way.

He'd win them over. One way or another, he'd rally them to his cause. Luke knew how to turn on the charm when he wanted.

Besides, he had a secret weapon, one that even an overprotective father could not defeat. Luke loved Mari, truly, deeply and completely, and she returned that love. And because the McBrides loved her, too, eventually, once they could see past their anger into his heart, they would give Mari and Luke their blessing. It was only a matter of time…and proper planning.

Luke gave the family one last look, then edged nearer the door. He wouldn't say goodbye, after all. He'd be back, sooner rather than later. It shouldn't take too long to get Rory's situation settled. If luck and train schedules were on his side, he'd return to Fort Worth within a week.

THE McBRIDE MENACES had been sent to their rooms.

They chose to congregate in Emma's bedroom. Kat lay upon her sister's bed, exhausted. Emma sat beside her youngest sister, gently stroking her hair. Mari stood at the window overlooking the backyard and watched her father swing his ax, splitting enough firewood to last them through two winters. "He'll be so sore tomorrow he won't be able to lift his coffee cup," she mused.

Emma looked at Mari. "I've never seen him in such a temper."

"He hates me," Kat declared, her voice thin and weak.

"No." Mari shook her head. "He hates what happened. You can't fault him for that."

"Did either of you notice how he kept clenching his fist, over and over, while you were telling your stories?" Emma asked. "It was the only part of him that moved."

"I wanted to die when he left the room without speaking, but Mama said he's furious at the situation and at Rory, not at me." Kat reached for her handkerchief and blew her nose. "That was the hardest thing I've ever gone through."

Emma and Mari shared a look. As uncomfortable as

the tale-telling had been, it had been a walk in the park compared to other family events in recent months—the gathering on the front porch the night of the fire and Kat's memorial service, to name two.

Once the initial excitement of Kat's return waned, their mother had correctly read Mari's hesitation to provide any explanations in front of her younger siblings. Jenny sent the boys on a series of errands, and together, Mari and Kat had relayed the story to their parents.

Part of the story, anyway. Mari did her best to brush over the time line of her part of the tale. Nor did she mention her brush with evil à la Finn Murphy. She certainly didn't let on that she'd given both her heart and her virginity to Luke Garrett while on the trail. That was nobody's business but hers. And Luke's.

Luke. Thinking about him, Mari's heart caught. He'd slipped away when she wasn't looking. He'd not given her a chance to say goodbye. Mari shifted her focus from her father to the horizon. Was he gone? She'd heard the evening train whistle blow a short time ago. Had Luke been aboard when the iron horse pulled from the station?

She expected so. Better for them all that he got Rory Callahan out of town before Trace decided to go hunting for him. The last thing this family needed was for her father to commit murder.

Below her, he swung his ax hard, and an oak stump split in two.

Mari's heart felt something like that stump. One half held her love for Luke; the other, her love for her family. Was she being strong or weak to put her family's needs before her own? Just what did she owe the McBrides? What did she owe Luke? What did she owe herself?

She was so confused.

Maybe eventually she'd see her way clear of the muddle. Right now, she'd continue to take one step, one crisis at a time.

"I'm tired of crying," Kat said, sighing heavily as she sat up. "It's all I've been doing for the past two days. I need to stop."

Mari offered her a reassuring smile, sat beside her, and gave her a hug. "You will. Mama and Papa know the story now. The hardest part is over."

Kat placed a protective hand on her stomach. Her sisters observed the movement. No one spoke the obvious thought, that the most difficult time for Kat lay ahead.

"How can everything change so fast?" Kat mused. "I was worried about the Dickersons, but still, I was happy. He was so sweet to me. Kind and gentle and loving. How could he fool me so completely?"

Emma took a seat on her other side. Solemnly, she said, "I think, Kat, that men like Rory Callahan— charming liars—are not all that uncommon."

A note in her voice gave Mari pause. "Why do you say that, Emma?"

She shrugged.

"Evil, wicked men aren't that uncommon, either," Kat observed. "Mari, why didn't you tell Mama and Papa about getting kidnapped?"

"Kidnapped!" Emma exclaimed.

Kat nodded. "By Rory's brother-in-law. She got away by whacking him with a cactus. In the privates."

Emma gawked at Mari, who rose from the bed and began to pace the room as she answered. "Thanks, Kat. Did it ever occur to you that if I'd wanted anyone to know about that particular adventure, I'd have mentioned it? How did you find out anyway?"

"Remember that first day when Luke put Rory in jail, and I took to my bed? I woke up thinking—hoping—that maybe it was all a mistake. You were asleep in your room, so I went looking for Rory. Luke was in the jailhouse shouting at him, telling him all the awful things he was responsible for, and that's when I heard about Finn Murphy. I can't believe there's still another black-sheep brother in that family. Was it awful, Mari? Were you frightened to death?"

"Wait just one minute." Emma rose from the bed, folded her arms, and gave Mari her severe schoolteacher frown. "You will tell me the entire story. Begin at the beginning."

Mari truly didn't want to revisit the incident, but since Kat had opened her big mouth, she didn't see a way to avoid it. Besides, a little sharing on her part might goad Emma into explaining her remark about charming, lying men. "All right. Promise you won't say anything to Papa?"

"Fairy's promise," Emma agreed, using the vow of their childhood.

Mari gave her sisters a full account of the incident with Finn Murphy, up to the point where Luke rendezvoused with the Texas Rangers. Though she'd trust her sisters with her own life, Luke's true vocation was his secret to tell.

"Thank goodness this man's been arrested," Emma said. "I'd worry about you, otherwise. I fear he'd come looking for revenge."

"I think there's cause to worry," Kat said, "except the one to keep an eye on is Luke. He watches you, Mari."

She tried to act surprised. "What?"

"He's attracted to you. Every time I turned around he was staring at you. Surely you noticed."

"Well…"

"A couple of times you looked back," Kat accused. To Emma, she said, "I was a little worried. It's Mari's turn, I'm afraid."

"My turn for what?"

Kat lifted her hand to the emerald pendant she wore around her neck. "I realized it yesterday. First Emma lost dear Casey, then I tangled with the likes of Rory Callahan. Mari is probably next. Heaven knows if she fell for an outlaw like Luke Garrett, it couldn't help but be a disaster. It's our destiny."

"What are you talking about?" Mari demanded, annoyed and maybe just a little afraid.

Kat held up her hand, palm out. "It's our Bad Luck Love Lines. Judging on what's happened up until now, that Roslin woman was right. We're destined to be unlucky in love."

The three sisters sighed together, then shared a moment of silence until Emma pinned Mari with a pointed look and said, "What? No disparaging comment? No protest that the Curse of Clan McBride is all hogwash? No declaration that Roslin of Strathardle was nothing more than a charlatan?"

"No. No protest." Mari's stomach did a flip as the shadowy idea that had been flitting through her mind in recent days finally took form. "But sisters, I've been thinking. What if I *was* wrong? What if the curse is real?"

Kat rolled her eyes. "Isn't that what I've been saying all along? And just how stupid does that make me? I went and fell in love when I should have known the relationship was doomed from the start. But no, I thought the love Rory and I shared was like Papa and Mama's, like Uncle Tye and Aunt Claire's. I thought that our elopement and the Dickerson problem would be the bad luck struggles we'd have to overcome to be happy." Tearing up, she laughed with a sob in her voice. "How silly was that?"

"Not silly," Emma told her. "I believe in the curse, but I also believe in the examples Papa and Uncle Tye have set for us. Just because Casey's death means the three of us can't end the curse forever, I don't see a reason to think that true love is beyond reach for us."

"What if," Mari said in a tentative voice. "What if ending the curse is still possible?"

Emma frowned. "My husband will not rise from the dead like Kat, Maribeth. He died in my arms."

"I know, Em. But what if…well…remember what the Scotswoman said? 'When, in any one generation of McBrides, three sisters, three daughters marked with the sign of Ariel, find love to prove the claim of Ariel and accomplish their assigned task, the curse will be broken for all time.' Now, the claim of Ariel was that the love she and her McBride shared was powerful, vigilant and true, and that no trial or challenge would change it. Well, it doesn't say anything about it being a first love or an only love."

Mari waited a moment to let her point sink in. Emma shook her head. "I'll never love another man."

"Never say never, Em," Kat said. "I never thought I'd end up in my current predicament." Addressing Mari, she asked, "So you think we get second chances?"

"Well…" She lifted her shoulders. "I don't know. It's just an idea, and it only has merit if she wasn't a fake, and then a person has to believe in that sort of thing. I'm not sure I do."

"I do," Kat declared. "The McBride family history is filled with instances of bad luck in love."

Emma wrinkled her nose. "Casey Tate was the love of my life."

Mari offered Emma an encouraging smile. "He was the love of your *youth*. You've still a lot of life to live, Em. Maybe you'll meet someone somewhere down the road who will offer another chance to break the curse. Maybe we all will."

Maybe I already have.

"Not me," Kat said. "I'm done with men."

"You're not even twenty yet, Kat. You're the one who just said never say never."

"And for once in our lives, you're the one being dreamy instead of realistic. Think about it, Mari. Not long after Christmas, I'll have a child to care for. A child I'll be responsible for. All by myself. Even if I wanted a man in my life—which I don't and won't—what man would want me?"

"A smart one," Emma said. "And you won't be alone. You'll have your family with you every step of the way."

Mari blinked, then silently repeated her sister's words. *You won't be alone. You'll have your family.*

It's true. She'd have *all* her family. Not just Mari and Emma.

She'll still need me, but not quite as much. Not quite as much.

Again, conversation waned as the three sisters privately considered their own thoughts. Emma crossed to the bedroom window and watched her father swing his ax. Kat absently rubbed her hand over her stomach, then stretched out on the bed once again. Mari sat in the rocker beside the fireplace, then put forth the rest of her idea. "It's the necklaces. If there is anything to this curse at all, then I think our necklaces are the key."

"She told us to wear them all the time," Emma said, still facing the window. "May I point out, Mari, that you seldom wear yours?"

"I've changed. Remember about the task we're supposed to accomplish? I think our necklaces will have something to do with that, and it's possible the task might connect us with the men we're supposed to love."

Emma glanced back over her shoulder, then slowly turned all the way around. "You think Kat's…um…adventure was somehow related to her task?"

Kat propped herself up on her elbow. "Mari. Surely you don't still think Rory is the man for me."

"No." Mari drew a deep breath and blew it out slowly. "I didn't think about this before, but I wonder…well…what if the task was mine. What if my task was to find you?"

Kat pursed her lips. Emma's expression was thoughtful.

Mari continued. "Maybe I'm supposed to be the one who finds the love that is powerful, vigilant and true in all of this. Maybe instead of me being the last to find the love that will help break the curse, I'm the first."

Her sisters considered the idea a moment, then shared a look of alarm. Kat shot up straight. "Oh, my God. What a disaster. You went and fell in love with Luke Garrett, didn't you, Maribeth?"

CHAPTER SIXTEEN

LUKE'S TRIP to Galveston began on a sour note. Though he was able to place a pair of Rangers on the Dickersons' trail with relative ease, arranging private security for Mari and Kat proved more difficult than he expected. Plenty of men wanted to act as bodyguards for the McBride women. It took Luke longer than anticipated to find a couple of men he trusted not to take advantage of the situation. As a result, he and Rory damned near missed the train.

Then, at the first stop in Dallas, Rory created a diversion and attempted to run off. Luke grabbed him just before he disappeared into the crowd milling about the station. Rory spent the time until the second stop arguing the case that it'd be a bad idea for him to return to Galveston, and when Luke wasn't convinced, Rory attempted to jump from the train as it pulled away from the platform. Luke lost what was left of his patience. He kept his brother handcuffed the rest of the trip.

They arrived in Galveston at the end of a long, uncomfortable night. As the train pulled into the station, Luke was greeted with the promise of a pink dawn in the east, where a sliver of sun peeked above the gray waters of the Gulf of Mexico. He nudged his brother awake. "We're here."

Rory stretched and groaned. "What time is it?"

"Early." Too early, Luke thought, to go knocking on Melissa Callahan's door. Maybe they'd stop at a restaurant and get breakfast first. His brother would be glad for the reprieve.

Rory was in no hurry to return to his wife. That didn't surprise Luke, although Rory's ambivalence regarding his new son left Luke mystified. If he were ever blessed with children, he wanted to be in on all the action.

It wasn't hard to picture himself in a well-appointed parlor, pacing the floor, staring anxiously toward the staircase that led to the bedroom where Mari lay giving birth. Her mother would come to the landing and call his name. He'd look up to see the blanket-wrapped bundle in her arms. A little girl, the image of her mama, maybe with his brown eyes. He'd dash up the stairs, meet his daughter, then greet his wife, looking tired but beautiful, glowing with joy in their bed.

On second thought, maybe it wasn't too early to go by Melissa's. The sooner his business here started, the sooner it'd be done. The sooner he could get back to Fort Worth and the woman he wanted for his own.

Luke unlocked Rory's handcuffs but kept him close as they traversed city streets already bustling with activity despite the early hour. The aroma of baking bread floated on air heavy with the scent of salt, and sparked the brothers' hunger. Wagons clattered over brick-lined streets, and voices called hellos and questioned weather predictions for the day. Hot with no rain appeared to be the consensus. No surprise there, Luke thought. Fall weather wouldn't reach this far south for another six weeks.

The streets grew quiet as Rory and Luke left the business district behind and walked through a residential neighborhood toward their sister's home. Janna supported herself and her two children by serving as governess to shipping magnate Horace P. Wentworth's three children, and she lived with her two daughters in a carriage house on her employer's estate.

Luke was gratified to find a light shining in the window of the apartment. Janna was awake. His boots thumped against the wooden steps as he climbed the outdoor staircase. Rory followed but hung back, waiting halfway down the stairs as Luke rapped on the solid oak door. To his surprise and consternation, a man in shirtsleeves answered the door. It was just after six o'clock. Had Janna moved? "I'm looking for Janna Murphy?"

The stranger widened his stance and folded his arms. "And just who are you?"

Luke didn't like the fellow's tone or his body language. "Look, mister, let's not—"

"Jared? Did you say…" Janna Murphy walked up behind the stranger, holding a baby in her arms. "Luke? Luke, is it really you?"

The stranger stepped back, smoothly accepting the child Janna handed his way before throwing herself, laughing, into her brother's arms. "Luke!"

They hugged tightly, then Luke took a step back and looked at his sister. She looked different. Her hair was still brown and curly, her eyes still the color of melted caramel. The difference, he detected, shone in her eyes. Janna Murphy looked happy.

Luke gave the stranger a second look, then the baby. *Well, now. What's going on here?* "Hello, sunshine."

"Oh, Luke! This is such a wonderful surprise. It's so good to see you. It's been too long."

"That it has, Janna. That it has." Luke felt a wave of affection rise within him as he again hugged his sister, and he couldn't help but think of the McBride reunion he'd witnessed the day before. That family would never let a year go by without getting together. "It's wrong of us to let it stretch this long between visits."

She squeezed him hard. "Come inside. You must have arrived on the morning train. Bet you can use some coffee."

"Definitely. But first…" He nodded toward the stairs. "I didn't come alone."

He crooked a finger toward Rory who climbed the remaining stairs like a prisoner approaching the gallows. Poking his head into the doorway, Rory waved. "Hello, Janna."

Her chin dropped. "Oh, my heavens."

"Jan?" the stranger asked, stepping forward, concern in his tone.

"Rory." She jerked her head around and spoke to the stranger. "It's *Rory.*"

The stranger muttered a curse, then moved away from the door. "Let your brothers in, honey. I'll put the baby down and join you."

Luke stepped into the apartment, which consisted of two bedrooms off a central room that served as a combined kitchen, living and dining area. He noted new curtains on the windows. New rugs on the floor. The oak dining table that had graced their mother's kitchen was set for two. An iron skillet sat on the stove, eggs and sausage laid out on a cutting board ready to cook. He had a dozen questions, but he started with an easy one. "Girls not home?"

"They're staying over at a friend's house. It'll break their hearts that they weren't here when you arrived. You are staying in town, though, aren't you? You're not leaving right away?"

Luke glanced from her to the stranger who had emerged from the girls' bedroom with empty arms. Might as well cut to the chase. "Actually, I'd hoped to stay here."

The stranger crossed the room to stand beside Janna. He rested his hand possessively at her waist. "That makes sense, honey. You and the girls and the baby can move on up to the house. It'll make everything easier."

"I think an introduction's in order, don't you, Luke?" Rory piped up.

Janna's smile flickered, then when the man gave her a comforting squeeze, went tender and sweet. "Yes. Definitely. Luke. Rory. I'd like you to meet Jared Harper, my fiancé. We're to be married in two weeks."

"Your fiancé?" Rory's brows winged up and he glanced at Luke. "I thought you said Murphy was in jail. Did those friends of yours kill him, after all?"

"His trial is set for next month," Luke said, raking Jared Harper with suspicious eyes.

Rory pursed his lips. "So that means...hell, Janna. You wouldn't make the mistake I did. You finally worked up the nerve to divorce Finn?"

Janna's chin came up. Temper snapped in her big brown eyes. "Yes."

"I'm surprised." Rory scratched the back of his head. "I didn't think you believed in divorce."

"I changed my mind."

"Because of him, right?" Rory gestured toward Jared Harper. "Guess you're human after all. Funny how fast our convictions can change when faced with something we want really bad."

Luke watched his sister's eyes narrow and her mouth stretch into a grim line. He knew that look. He'd grown up seeing that look. Rory was fixing to get it.

"Actually, *brother,*" she drawled. "I changed my mind because I saw how good divorce has been for a dear, dear friend of mine. A sister of mine, one might say. Divorce has been a wonderful thing for her, so I thought I'd give it a try."

Oh. Puzzle pieces fell into place. Luke pursed his lips and blew out a silent whistle as he anticipated what was coming.

Janna continued, "Her husband deserted her, and she divorced him and her friends have been supportive. It wasn't near the scandal I expected. Now she's remarried and on her honeymoon with a dear, wonderful, *dependable* man. In fact, I'm babysitting for her now. They chose not to leave town, of course, since the baby is still nursing, but they have a private room in a lovely home, and she is blissfully happy."

Harper squared his shoulders and added, "We're prepared to do whatever it takes to ensure she stays that way."

Rory's baffled expression told Luke he didn't get it. "Rory, she's talking about Melissa."

"Melissa? What does she…? Whoa. She divorced me?"

Janna lifted her chin even higher. "Yes, she did."

"Oh. Well." Rory walked over to the dining table, pulled out a chair and sat. He pursed his lips, drummed his fingers on the table and thought for a full minute. His tone held a note of accusation when he finally said, "I didn't sign anything."

"It wasn't required. You deserted her."

"Yes, well…" He continued drumming his fingers. "Divorce. That's a fine thing for a fellow to hear out of the blue."

Janna folded her arms and her toe went to tapping.

"Well, what did you expect? You seduce her away from her longtime beau, stay long enough to get her with child, then disappear without a word. No goodbye, no financial support. Not even a letter asking if she'd yet given birth to your baby!"

"Luke said she had a boy. Brian. He's…wait… you're babysitting for Melissa? Is that kid you were holding mine?"

"Finally," Luke muttered beneath his breath.

"Only by accident." Janna gave her head a toss. "George is the boy's father in every way that matters."

"George Honeycutt?" Now Rory was the one whose chin dropped. "She went back to him?"

"He never stopped loving her. Once she came to her senses about you, he forgave her and took her back. He loves Brian, too."

Again, Rory fell silent. His fingers continued to drum. Eventually, he nodded. "Well, I guess that's good. Honeycutt was always a steady sort. Say, when did this divorce take place?" Glancing at Luke, he said, "Maybe I am married to Kat after all. Wouldn't that be great?"

Great wasn't the word Luke would choose. The question had occurred to him right off, as had the potential consequences. Pregnancy notwithstanding, Kat McBride was better off without the likes of Rory Callahan in her life. Not to mention that his own plans for Mari didn't need the complication.

"Melissa was granted the divorce two weeks ago," Janna's fiancé responded, just as Janna asked, "Who is Kat?"

Weariness melted over Luke. "It's a long and not-so-pretty story better saved for another time. Janna, I'd love that cup of coffee you mentioned."

Serious conversation halted while Janna added two cups and saucers to the pair already on the table and filled all four with coffee. Luke took a seat, then sipped the strong black coffee, groaning with pleasure.

Janna took the opportunity to tell her brothers more about her fiancé. Harper owned the house next door, and he'd become acquainted with Janna during a dispute over a barking dog. Like his neighbor, Horace Wentworth, Jared Harper owned a shipping company.

"I love your sister. And her girls," he reassured Luke. "It took work to win her, but I was a determined man. I intend to spend the rest of my life making her happy."

Well, how could a loving brother argue with that?

Luke took another sip of coffee. "I've wanted her to kick Finn Murphy out of her life for going on a decade. The man is poison."

"He's evil," Jared Harper said flatly. "I met him just last week."

Luke's cup banged against the table. "You met him? Tell me you visited him in jail."

"Yes. The Texas Rangers notified Janna that he'd been arrested. She wanted to be certain he'd been notified about the divorce. It was important to her symbolically." Harper took a sip of his coffee, then casually observed, "He had a message for you should we meet."

Just as casually, Luke remarked, "Oh?"

"He said to tell you he knows your weakness, and that he intended to say hello the next time he visited Fort Worth."

Mari. Hell. Luke shrugged, and tried to tell himself not to worry. His friends were keeping an eye on the McBride sisters. "Murphy undoubtedly has a date with a hangman. Won't live to see Thanksgiving this year."

The conversation was interrupted by an infant cry

and a coo. Belatedly, Rory expressed interest in his son. Luke and Jared Harper cooked breakfast while Janna oversaw the introduction of little Brian to his father.

In the hours that followed, Luke had little time to dwell on Finn Murphy and his threats. He had a decision to make. His main reason for dragging Rory back to Galveston no longer applied. Rory didn't need to take responsibility for Melissa and her son. George Honeycutt had done that. Luke could wash his hands of his brother, leave him to fight his own legal battles, and return immediately to Fort Worth and Mari.

It was a tantalizing idea, and he might have done just that had Janna not asked him to give her away at her wedding in two weeks. Luke decided to use the time looking into Rory's legal troubles and seeing if he couldn't save him from hanging. As a Texas Ranger, Luke couldn't ignore his brother's crimes. As a brother, he had to do whatever possible to help.

His first discovery surprised him and Rory, both.

"The fisherman is alive," he told his brother, returning to Janna's home after having confirmed the fact. "Apparently, he recovered from the beating and gunshot wound the Dickersons gave him and returned to his daily routine."

"So I'm not a murderer!" Rory exclaimed, heaving a sigh of relief. "What did he tell you? Did he say anything about me?"

"I didn't speak with him. Unfortunately, he sailed south a week ago to do some fishing off the Yucatán Peninsula. You're not off the hook, Rory. The sheriff has issued a warrant for your arrest."

"A warrant? For what?"

"Theft."

"Hell. I could still hang!"

Luke nodded. "You need a lawyer. I'll talk to Janna's beau, get the name of someone from him."

Jared Harper's attorney told Luke that the ownership of pirate booty was a gray area to begin with, and that he felt confident he could get the charges dismissed by Janna's wedding. Hearing that, Luke planned to catch the first train out of town following the ceremony.

Four days before the wedding, the lawyer brought the good news that Rory was officially a free man. That same afternoon, Luke received a telegram from Fort Worth.

"A sheriff nabbed the Dickerson brothers during a bank robbery attempt in Palo Pinto County," Luke told Rory. "They're in jail."

Rory let out a whoop of joy, then rushed out of Janna's home where he'd been hiding. He spent the rest of the day carousing and raising hell all over Galveston. That was the last Luke saw of him before the wedding.

Rory was his old charming self at the reception at the Wentworth mansion, and when Luke realized he'd danced three straight dances with a pretty young woman, he dragged him away from the ballroom at the Wentworth mansion. Outside in the rose garden, Luke unloaded on his brother. "What's the matter with you?" he demanded. "If you just have to have a woman, visit a brothel! Don't prey on another poor virgin. Don't leave yet another bastard baby in your wake."

"Hey, wait one minute. Melissa's boy isn't a bastard and Kat's won't be, either. I intend to marry her. Again. Give her baby a name. I'm not totally without honor."

"No, you're just totally without heart." Luke scooped a handful of pebbles off the dirt path and tossed them one by one toward a cottonwood tree he'd chosen as a target. "What makes you think Kat McBride will even speak with you again, much less marry you?"

"She'll forgive me," Rory said with a casual shrug. "They always do."

Sadly, Luke couldn't argue with that. Ever since Rory was a baby, all he'd had to do was smile at a female and she was his.

Luke gazed up into the inky black sky and shoved his hands in the pockets of the new suit he'd purchased to wear when he gave the bride away. He honestly didn't know what was best. Would Kat and her child be better off if she married Rory? Or, would it be kinder in the long run if she never saw or heard from his brother again? Without a doubt, having Rory Callahan for a husband would be a bad bet for any woman. Was giving Kat's child legitimacy enough to offset what was bound to be a lifetime of disappointment and pain as Mrs. Rory Callahan?

No, not in Luke's opinion, it wasn't. This was Texas—The Land of Beginning Again. Hell, half the people populating this state were bastards, if not by birth, then by act.

Of course, Luke wasn't a woman, and they tended to have different viewpoints about such things. Still, Kat had to know that Rory Callahan wouldn't change. Any woman who thought he might was betting awfully long odds.

But in the end, Luke's opinion didn't matter. This was Kat's decision to make.

Luke dragged his attention away from the sky and pinned his brother with a look. "So, are you determined to return to Fort Worth?"

"I am."

"For Kat, or the pirate's treasure?"

"For the sake of my child," Rory declared, though his eyes shifted as he said it.

Dammit, I called that one. "A warning, Rory. If you cause Kat or any member of her family one more minute's worth of pain or trial or trouble, I'll take it out of your hide. You understand?"

"Yeah."

"All right, then." Luke threw the last of his pebbles, then faced his brother. "I'm leaving on the morning train. If you want to come with me, I won't stop you."

CHAPTER SEVENTEEN

A HUSH HUNG in the sultry evening air as Mari sat alone on the back porch swing at Willow Hill, watching a pair of squirrels play on the branches of the towering bur oak that shaded the gazebo. The house was quiet, her parents and the boys away for a meeting at school. Kat rested in her room and Emma had holed up in Papa's library, polishing her knowledge of the Revolutionary War in preparation for a lecture the following day.

Mari toed the ground and set the swing moving, glad for the peace at the end of a busy day. The past two weeks had been both the happiest and most miserable weeks of her life. The McBride family as a whole was ecstatic. Individual members had had their ups and downs.

A screen door squeaked and Emma approached, carrying two glasses of lemonade. Mari scooted over on the swing to make room for her sister. "So, do you now know everything there is to know about the American Revolution?"

"No, but I am more knowledgeable about muskets. That's what's important to nine-year-old boys."

The two women sipped their drinks in companionable silence and watched the scampering squirrels. "The way they chase each other reminds me of Tommy and Bobby," Emma observed.

Mari laughed. "Or Billy and Kat years ago. Remember how he'd pull her pigtails, then run, and she'd chase him and yank his ears?"

"I saw Kat pull Billy's ear in the kitchen before supper. I thought that was a good sign."

"Her color is better, too."

Guilt and remorse had sapped Kat's strength in the days following her return to Fort Worth. Twice she'd experienced cramping that sent her to bed, and the doctor had advised Jenny that her daughter must come to terms with the turmoil in her life or the safety of her babe would be threatened. After that, their mother and Aunt Claire shut themselves in Kat's room and the three women developed a plan to smooth Kat's reentry into Fort Worth society.

Papa hadn't liked it at all.

"Do you think they did the right thing, Mari?" Emma asked. "Mama's plan?"

Mari gave the swing another push. "I worried about Kat confessing to the fire marshal that she'd accidentally started the Spring Palace fire. I understood that she felt she needed to take responsibility, but I was afraid of what the authorities might do."

"Just between us, I think Papa had already talked to Captain Reese."

"Really?"

"Remember those weeks after the fire? Papa tried to learn every bit of information he could about what happened. I'll bet the fire department already knew everything Kat and Billy told them yesterday."

"Hmm," Mari mused. "You may be right. So do you think Captain Reese told the truth when he told Kat that his investigation failed to pinpoint a definitive ignition point, and that they'd had two other reports of carelessness with fire that night? That boys playing with matches in the agriculture hall could have just as easily caused the conflagration as Kat's knocked-over candle?"

Emma shrugged. "I don't know. I don't think it matters as long as the Spring Palace fire was an accident. Accidents happen. If telling her story helped Kat feel better, then I'm glad she did it. I'm even more glad that Captain Reese told her they hadn't publicized the matches incident, and that they wouldn't be publicizing her confession, either."

"Me, too. Hopefully, having this burden off her back will ease her burden."

Emma sipped her lemonade and waited a full minute before saying, "Yes. Maybe then she'll act a little nicer to you."

The swing creaked as Mari rose and walked to the porch rail, and tossed the ice from her glass into the rose bed below. "She's upset with me because of my feelings for Luke. I hate that. I knew she'd react this way."

"She told me she wouldn't object if Luke Garrett came courting."

"Yeah, she told me the same thing. Joan of Arc never looked any more the martyr."

Emma smiled. "She's not lost all her talent for the dramatic, has she? You realize she's feeling jealous, don't you? She lost her love, even though it wasn't real, and you found yours. What's more, you found true love."

"Did I?" Mari gave her sister a wistful smile. "He left me. I may never hear from Luke Garrett again."

"Now who's being the dramatic one?" Emma rose and linked arms with Mari. "Believe me, you'll hear from Luke Garrett again. Sooner rather than later, if I have my guess. The man cares for you. He arranged bodyguards for you and Kat before he left town, for goodness' sake. Even Papa was impressed by that."

"Yes, well, I'm glad the Dickersons are in jail and those men are off the job. I'll never again take for granted the pleasure of privacy. It was unnerving to walk out here and know someone was watching, even if I couldn't see them."

"I know." Emma tossed her ice after her sister's. "I'm hoping that now, life around Willow Hill will return to normal."

"Normal ear pulling, frogs in our beds, Papa snatching kisses from Mama in the mudroom…"

Emma laughed. "It sounds heavenly. Speaking of frogs in our beds, I think I'll go upstairs and give my own a thorough search. I saw Tommy with a cup of worms earlier. Are you coming in?"

"Later. Looks like there's a storm brewing. I think I'll watch for a while."

Emma took Mari's empty glass and headed inside. At the door, she paused. "Mari?"

"Yes?"

"I've been thinking. I hope you're right about the necklaces and the tasks we're supposed to accomplish. It's nice to think I might have something to look forward to."

As Emma disappeared into the house, a flash of light drew Mari's attention skyward. To the northwest, an arched crescent of gunbarrel-blue cloud rolled high and fast toward the city. While Mari watched a trident of lightning claw across the dark churning cloud, her mind lingered on the change in her elder sister.

Emma was healing, finally, and it filled Mari's heart

with gladness. Wouldn't it be wonderful if her theory regarding the necklaces someday proved true? Emma should have a new man in her life, someone to fulfill her dreams of happiness and love. Someone who would give her a family of her own. She was a good woman. She deserved happiness. It brought Mari such pleasure to see her sister looking forward again, rather than living in the past.

With a sweep of leaves and sand, a slam of cold air hit. Mari placed both hands on the porch rail and leaned forward, lifting her face into the wind, experiencing an uplift of spirit. She'd think positively from now on. For Emma, for Kat. For herself.

"Come back to me, Luke," she said into the chilling breeze. "Come give me another chance."

The land fell into shadow as cloud consumed the last flame-edged tints of sunset. Lightning forked across the sky. Thunder cracked and boomed while fat drops of rain spatted down through the violent air.

Mari welcomed the bluster and wondered if this would prove to be the first norther of the season. She hoped so. It was time for a change. Time for something new.

A flurry of lightning turned the darkened sky a flickering white, illuminating the black-clad figure half-hidden by weeping branches of the willow nearest the house. Beneath the wide brim of a hat pulled low, eyes gleamed like a cat's, and Mari gasped. Yet, even as fear flared within her, she recognized the man and love warmed the chill in her blood. "Luke."

Was she imagining the moment? Had the yearning in her heart conjured up a phantom the likes of which to make Roslin of Strathardle proud?

The wind whipped the hem of his long, black duster

as he stepped forward into the rain. No phantom, this, but a man. Her man.

Mari felt the wildness of the storm sizzle through her. Her man, her bodyguard, her lover had come back to her. Cold rain pelted her skin as she dashed off the porch to meet him halfway. With a strangled cry, she leaped into his outstretched arms.

His mouth descended upon hers in an instant, pulling a desperate whimper from her throat. They kissed as if the surrounding storm had unleashed within them. Violent. Endless. Beautiful.

"Mari," he murmured against her lips. Dragging her back into the shelter of the gazebo, he kissed her again. Then again. His mouth moved across her skin, nibbling on her chin, her throat, her earlobe. "Mari. God, how I've missed you."

"You came back."

"Of course I came back."

"But I sent you away." A sob tore itself from Mari's throat. "I told you I wouldn't marry you."

Luke drew away just far enough to stare down into her face. He tenderly drew his thumb across her cheek. "Sugar," he chided. "Why would you think I'd give up after the first try? I love you, Maribeth. Now and always."

She collapsed against Luke's chest. Incredible joy dissolved her into a mixture of tears and laughter. He loved her. He still loved her. He'd come back for her.

He cupped her chin in his hand and lifted her gaze to his. Even in the shadowy moonlight, Mari could still see the fiery emotion brimming in caramel eyes. With a tentative smile, he asked, "So, then. I'm guessing you still love me, too?"

Though he tried to hide it, Mari knew Luke sought reassurance. Like her, he needed to know her true heart.

Needed to hear her say the words. The hopeful note in his voice touched her heart and brought fresh tears to her eyes. "Of course I do, you confounded man. Just don't ever leave me again."

His smile widened. Kissing her forehead, he brushed aside her tears with his thumb. "Never again. I promise." He sought her mouth again, and their kisses melted into a frenzy of urgent desire.

Luke drew her against him, his arms holding her captive in his embrace. "Tell me again," he whispered against her lips. "Please, honey."

"I love you." Moving in a slow circle, they danced to the rain's gentle music as the storm thickened then slacked around them.

"Again, Maribeth. I'll never get tired of hearing it."

Sweet, needful yearning filled her. She wanted him. Wanted nothing more than to sink onto the soft grass of the gazebo floor and yield her body and soul to the man who'd already snared her heart.

"I love you, Luke Garrett." Affirming her words with her hands, her mouth and the insistent press of her body, Mari knew he'd be powerless to resist. She wanted him, and she wanted him now.

"Ah, hell, sugar," he said as his hands worked free the buttons on her bodice. "Tell me your daddy isn't standing with shotgun ready at the kitchen window."

She tugged his raincoat off. "Only my sisters are home."

"How's their aim?" Cool air caressed her heated skin as his hand cupped her breast. Luke nipped her skin at the base of her throat, his tongue swirling circles upon her skin. He stroked her nipples gently, rolling them between thumb and forefinger. Bending to take one in his lips, he gave it a strong, demanding suckle.

Mari's head lolled back. "Emma is an even better shot than Papa," she managed to say. "Oh, yes, there, right there." She reveled in pleasure as he feasted. Her voice hitched higher, "If Em wanted to kill you, you'd already be dead. Kat, on the other hand, can't hit the broad side of a barn." She yanked his shirt free from his pants, tore at the buttons.

"So I have a chance of getting out of here alive?" He mumbled against one breast while his hand toyed with the other. "I'd be damn sorry not to finish this." Recapturing her nipple, he drew it into his mouth with a sigh.

Mari laughed as her hands explored the bare skin of his chest. "Don't worry, Ranger. You'll live to see morning. I'll see to that."

Luke hissed when she dragged a fingernail across his nipples. "Good. That's good. Ah, God, honey, you're killing me."

Again he took her mouth with a vengeance. Fierce, hard. The rain fell around the gazebo in sheets, the sound blending with their whispered moans and murmured promises.

Mari's body ached for him, needles of pleasure reaching every muscle, every bone. She wound her arms around Luke's neck and kissed him ravenously, with as much demand as he kissed her.

He coaxed her to the grass, his lips never leaving hers. His body enveloped hers in another embrace. The heat and power of his erection pressed against her belly and Mari lost herself in the moment.

"Luke," she whispered, pleading. "Luke, I need… please, can you…"

"Hush, now. I'll take care of you." He raised her skirts and his hand froze against her bare hip. "Damn, Maribeth. Where the hell are your drawers?"

She laughed. "I was getting ready for bed. I decided to get some air." She nuzzled his neck, breathing in his scent. "Of course, I didn't expect to be ravished in Mama's gazebo by my former bodyguard."

He placed his hand boldly between her legs, wringing a surprised cry of pleasure from her. Stroking her most intimate place, he informed her, "I'm still your bodyguard. I will be until the day I die."

He bent and kissed her mouth, her jawline and her eyelids while his hand worked magic against her tender skin. "Mari, honey?" he breathed. "I don't think this is gonna happen slowly."

"No," she told him. "It won't." Mari couldn't resist touching him. He was here, and he was hers. Fast, slow, it didn't matter. Nothing mattered, except that they loved each other. The rest could take care of itself.

Running her fingers through his hair, she nuzzled his neck, his shoulders, his chest as he pushed down his open trousers and kicked them away. When she reached down and closed her hand around his length, Luke cried out hoarsely and thrust into her palm.

Mari stroked him, feeling a woman's triumph over her man. His velvet body responded, swelling in her hand. When she daringly leaned down and touched her tongue to the tip, his control snapped. With a thump, Mari landed on her back in the grass. She stared up into Luke's slightly shocked and feverish face.

"That would finish things for us both, little lady."

"But I want to."

"Hell, I want you to, too." Luke strangled out a laugh. "Just not tonight. And not in the shadow of your father's house, that's for damn sure."

Taking his revenge, Luke returned his hand to her wet heat. He explored her, teased her, made her mindless. Mari bucked toward his touch, tossing against the damp grass, pleading senselessly, calling his name and God's in one agitated breath. Finally, with one long, satisfying thrust, he claimed her.

Mari almost cried in relief as joy and fulfillment raced to every last nerve ending in a perfect blend of bliss. For a few exquisitely beautiful moments they lay connected, body and soul. Their lips brushed, sweetly at first, then built a momentum that their bodies soon followed.

He took her quickly, finding the easy rhythm that true lovers share. He withdrew and delved again. She met him, urged him. No words were spoken, the language of their loving enough. The pace became more desperate, seeking what they both needed from each other. Rapture. Release. Renewal. They were together again. Nothing on earth would keep them apart.

Luke's breathing grew ragged against her neck, as his strokes became short, rapid. Her fingers threaded his hair and traveled down to his shoulders where the muscles rippled and tensed. Sensing he was close, too, Mari tilted her hips and angled her thighs to spread further, allowing him greater access. The slight movement was enough to drive him deeper, provoking her release. She cried out as the first tremors ripped through her.

"That's it, Mari, come with me," he coaxed in a raspy whisper.

The storm inside the gazebo broke as Mari shattered completely in Luke's arms, surrendering to his seductive plea. Her body arched, her spirit soared, her soul sang. It was magic, pure and simple. As the rain continued to fall, Luke followed her over the edge with a guttural cry. He swelled and stiffened, then poured himself into her keeping. With a sated sigh he collapsed atop her, his head pillowed between her neck and shoulder.

When their breathing slowed and their heartbeats returned to normal, Mari reached up and brushed a lock of damp hair from Luke's brow. This was the best part of making love, she decided, the quiet time afterward. The precious lull that followed the exhilaration when a woman doesn't know where she ends and her man begins. When she cannot fathom his heartbeat from hers. When she wants nothing more than to fall asleep in his arms so she can wake to be loved again.

He was still inside her, holding her close when she smoothed his hair again. Kissing his temple, she closed her eyes and pressed her cheek against his. She'd found a love to last a lifetime, and in that, Mari knew, she'd finally found a part of herself.

"I love you," he told her, his voice a low rumble like faraway thunder. "I don't deserve you, but I don't care. I'm not letting you go, Mari-mine."

"I love you, too. And you deserve me. We deserve each other. We should be happy."

"I'm happy," Luke said with a satisfied yawn, as he slipped from her, rolling onto his side. "They say that love makes a man insane, and now I'm inclined to believe it. For I'm nearly naked, loving you in the rain, half-expecting a bullet to graze my bare ass, but I'm happier than I've been in all my sorry life. If that isn't crazy in love, I sure as hell don't know what is."

"Truly?" she asked, encouraged.

"Truly."

Crazy in love, was he? Mari waited a defining moment, drew a deep breath, then asked, "In that case, Luke Garrett, will you marry me?"

His head shot up. "What did you say?"

"I love you, too, Luke Garrett. Will you marry me?"

He sat all the way up, totally silent, completely still, staring at her. Nervousness had Mari reaching for her soaking wet dress. She slipped it over her head and tugged it into position, then busied herself by fastening her buttons.

When he still didn't speak, Mari filled the yawning silence with babble. "I figured it's my turn to ask. I mean, it's only fair. I had it all planned out. I intended to make you a special piece of chocolate and I thought I'd bring it and a nosegay of flowers—although, come to think of it, I changed my mind about the flowers. I decided on brandy instead of flowers. And here we are and I don't have either chocolate or brandy…shoot…I don't even have flowers. But it seemed like the right time. Was I wrong?"

Standing, he cleared his throat as he reached for his pants. "No."

"All right. Well…" She paused, chilled by both her dripping dress and the delay in his response, and watched him pull on his britches. "Was that a 'no' to the first question or to the second one?"

"Oh." He picked up his shirt. "The second one. Definitely the second."

"Good, then." On the verge of wringing her hands, she laced her fingers and rested her hands in her lap. "Yes, well…?"

"Wait a minute. I'm confused here." Luke shrugged into his shirt. "I wasn't sure you'd even open the door to me when I called at Willow Hill. I certainly never anticipated, um—" he gestured around the gazebo, smiled slightly "—this. And I'd have bet my life that you would not have asked the question you just asked."

"If I was wrong?"

"No, the other one."

"You mean the one you haven't answered yet."

"Yes."

"All right. Yes, to which?"

His lips twitched with a smile. He extended his hands toward her. When Mari took them, he pulled her to her feet. Without releasing her, he said, "Both."

"Oh." Then, she smiled back at him. *"Oh!"*

"That's what I say." Luke lifted her hands to his mouth and kissed the center of first one palm, then the other. "I'll be proud to marry you, Mari McBride. It's why I came back to Fort Worth. I was…I am…determined to make you mine. I, too, had a plan."

"You did?"

"Uh-huh. I intended to prove to you and your family that I am dependable, trustworthy, and totally in love with you. I wasn't going to rush it. I wouldn't lose my patience. And I swore that I absolutely, positively wouldn't attempt to seduce you back into my bed—no matter how badly I wanted you there."

"I like my plan better," she said, her lips lifting in a wicked grin.

"It definitely has some stellar points. Although, something tells me we'll need to keep those particular points private if I stand any chance of romancing your family. I still will need to win them over, right? The McBrides don't want an outlaw for an in-law, correct?"

Mari smiled. "That hasn't changed."

"So what did change, Maribeth? Why did you do me the honor of proposing marriage to me?"

Straining to see him clearly in the deepening shadows, Mari spoke in a solemn tone. "My family didn't change, Luke. I changed. I realized the truth in what you tried to tell me that day at Inspiration Point. I am a woman grown. It is time for me to make a woman's choice, to make a family of my own. If I must choose between you and the McBrides, then I choose you."

"I don't want it to come to that," Luke said. "It won't. I'll win them over, Mari. Believe me. Believe in me."

"I do." Love filled her heart, and with it, confidence. How could anyone not see the goodness in this man? "I think you will win them over, most of them, anyway. The boys won't be a problem—you've a notorious reputation, and they'll love that. Mama and Emma understand love, so I imagine they'll come around in a short amount of time. And Kat, well, it's going to be hard for her, but I think she'll try. She may need to do a bit more growing up, but I have faith in her—and in you. Papa, however, is another nut to crack. I don't know that he realizes it, but you are so much like him. I worry that it will take a very long time for him to accept you."

"And you're all right with that?"

"Oh, I'll never stop trying to change his mind. We'll see which of us is more stubborn in the end." She touched his face. "I love you, Luke Garrett. I want to make a family with you. I want you to be my future."

He kissed her then, and it was a kiss like no other they'd shared before, a heady combination of promise and passion. When finally they broke apart, Luke tenderly brushed a finger down her cheek. "I'd better go. I left Rory at the Blue Goose and I'm afraid he'll—"

"Rory?" Mari's voice went shrill. "Rory's back in town, too?"

Luke winced. "Hell, I forgot. I took one look at you, Maribeth, and forgot one of the reasons I came by here tonight. Yes, Rory's back, and he's no longer married. Kat has a decision to make."

Mari thought a moment, then blew out a heavy sigh. "You'd better come inside."

CHAPTER EIGHTEEN

TEN MINUTES LATER, Luke sat at the kitchen table eating a piece of Mari's pecan pie. Though he'd refused a loan of her father's clothing, he'd made good work of a towel. Mari had changed her dress and, while upstairs, convinced her sisters to come say hello to their guest.

If Luke had to guess, judging by Emma's tense smile, the pained expression in Mari's eyes and the hot glare of accusation Kat fired his way, either Mari had shared news of their engagement or someone had noticed his and Mari's gazebo frolic and expressed her displeasure. Either way, the visit was awkward from the outset.

Luke preferred to ease into the subject of Rory, so he attempted to make small talk with the McBride sisters. His efforts fell flat as a flour tortilla. Mari tried to encourage conversation and act as if everything was normal, but she couldn't quite rinse the starch from her speech. Emma kept her comments short, and Kat did nothing but glower.

Luke finished his pie, then decided he might as well be blunt. He set down his fork, leaned back in his chair, looked Kat straight in the eyes and said, "It occurs to me that you're bound to have a truly beautiful baby. You're pretty as a field of bluebonnets, Katrina, and no one can deny that Rory has a fine-looking face of his own."

Kat fumbled her fork, and it clattered to the floor. Emma's mouth gaped in surprise. Mari eyed her younger sister warily.

Luke pressed on. "That's been part of his problem from the get-go. He was such a good-lookin' cuss, even from the day he was born, that folks just naturally favored him, let him get away with nonsense all his life. I wish Rory could have known our mother. She'd have kept him on the straight and narrow. She was a good mother to me and my sister. I'm sure you'll be the same way, Kat. You have fine family upbringing that will stand you in good stead. Your baby is a lucky one in that respect. So, are you hoping for a boy or a girl?"

Kat's dumbfounded expression, along with Emma's look of alarm, suggested to Luke that Kat's loved ones tended to tiptoe around the subject of her child. Maybe he'd taken the wrong approach, but hell, Luke couldn't tiptoe worth a damn.

"A girl," Kat said after a long moment's pause. "I think illegitimacy might be an easier burden for a girl to bear."

"Hmm." Luke rubbed the back of his neck. "About that. I couldn't in good conscience recommend that any woman tie herself to my brother. The fact is, Rory is a sorry individual and I honestly don't think that'll ever change. However, I think you have a right to know what we found in Galveston, and if you decide you want to do something about it, you have my word that I'll see that it happens."

"See that what happens?" Kat asked.

Emma reached across the table and held her sister's hand in a silent offer of comfort and support. Uncer-

tain whether he'd be considered the bearer of bad news
or the messenger of glad tidings, Luke briefly met Mari's
encouraging expression, then matter-of-factly stated.
"Rory is no longer married. His wife divorced him. Kat,
if you want to marry him to give your baby his name,
then I'll see that he says his 'I do's.' Personally, I'm not
certain that marrying Rory is in your best interests.
However, that's your decision to make."

Kat slumped back in her chair, obviously stunned by
the news. Emma shut her eyes and rubbed her temples.
Mari chewed on her bottom lip, her gaze flitting from
one sister to the other.

"One other thing, Katrina," Luke added in complete
sincerity. "No matter what you decide about Rory, I'll
always be your child's uncle. I am not my brother. I take
family seriously. If you ever need my help for anything,
it's yours. You can count on that."

Tears welled in Kat's eyes. Blinking rapidly, she offered Luke a shaky smile. "Thank you. I appreciate
that. As far as the other goes…" She turned beseech-
ingly toward her sisters. "Emma? Mari? What do I
do?"

"Nothing right now," Mari advised. "You have
plenty of time to think about it. Right, Luke? Nothing
must be decided immediately."

Luke nodded, then judged the time had come to
lighten the mood. "Actually, one very important decision must be made immediately. I know it's rude of me
to ask, but may I have seconds on the pie?"

"Of course you may," boomed a masculine voice
from behind him.

Trace McBride. Luke couldn't help but wince. Half
an hour ago, he'd been rolling in the grass with the
man's beloved daughter. McBride would surely pick up

on it, note the telltale redness of the skin on Mari's neck, the dampness of her hair, the sated glow of a well-loved woman.

"In fact," Trace continued, his tone sharp as a bowie knife, "we'll both have some pie while we talk. Jenny, my love, would you please bring a couple slices to my study?"

Luke noted the concern on each of the McBride women's faces. *Well, hell. I'll be lucky to get out of here alive.*

THE HIDDEN STAIRWAYS inside Willow Hill had been a gift from a doting architect father to his three lovable Menaces. Patterned after the home Trace had grown up in, the Willow Hill "secret passages" had provided countless opportunities for mischief over the years involving all six members of the McBride brood.

As part of her effort to put her Menacing days behind her, Mari hadn't entered the passages in years. Seldom did she think about them. But the minute her father closed the study door, closeting himself inside with Luke Garrett after denying her entrance, she made a beeline upstairs to the parlor that offered access to a hidden staircase. From there, she quietly made her way downstairs until she reached the peephole she and her sisters had drilled into Papa's study years ago.

She put her eye to the pencil-width hole. Trace was seated behind his desk, Luke in one of two leather chairs opposite her father. Well, she didn't see any blood. She put her ear to the hole and strained to hear.

"...in a quandary," her father was saying. "Without your help, it's doubtful Kat would be home with us today. For that, I owe you my undying gratitude. Yet, it's clear you've taken advantage of Mari."

"Mr. McBride," Luke began. "I—"

"For that," Trace continued as if Luke hadn't spoken, "I'd like to kick your ass from here to the Great Wall of China."

Wisely, Mari thought, Luke refrained from comment.

"Now, most men in my position would gather up a shotgun and host a wedding, two of them, if what I heard you telling Katrina is true. However, the thought of you and your no-good sewer rat of a brother becoming permanent members of my family curdles my stomach. You know, Garrett, Mari's been subtly singing your praises for the past two weeks, so I knew I'd be well served by learning something about you."

Mari took a second to look through the spy hole. Her father wore his brow-lowered, eyes-narrowed, I'm-mean-so-you-should-fear-me expression and drummed his fingers on his desk. Luke met him straight on—calm, confident and fearless.

The unstoppable force meets the immovable object, Mari thought with a silent groan. This was not what she'd wanted in a conversation between her father and her lover. Her stomach churning, she put her ear to the wall.

"…not now and never have been on any Texas Ranger roster."

Mari waited for Luke to defend himself, to explain how he led a special force that reported directly to the governor. He remained distressingly silent.

"You're a liar, a convicted thief, a con man. While I owe you for one daughter, I will not pay you with another. After the fire, you told me you owed my family a debt. I'm calling it due. I want you to leave Willow Hill and never contact my daughter again."

Papa, how dare you! You can't do that. Mari wanted to bang on the wall and shout it, but not as much as she wanted to hear Luke's reply.

Finally, he spoke. "Mr. McBride. I appreciate your position. It cannot be easy for a father to see another man supplant him in the affections of his little girl."

Not a good choice, Luke. Not a good choice at all.

"Listen, you piece of—"

This time Luke was the one to continue as if the other hadn't spoken. "I love your daughter. I could sit here and attempt to defend myself, to convince you I am deserving of the gift of her love in return, but we both know that is a lie."

What?

"No man will ever be good enough for Maribeth. Period. However, I can promise you that no man will ever love her more than I will. No other man will honor her, cherish her, respect her like I will. No other man will better support her dreams or comfort her disappointments. I will provide for her financially, physically and emotionally. Your daughter will want for nothing married to me, except, perhaps, for acceptance from her father. That, I'm afraid only you can give her."

Mari took a fast look into the study. Luke stood facing her father, straight and tall and proud. Papa's complexion had blanched white.

"But you're a goddamned thief!"

"I stole her heart, perhaps. It is my most prized possession and I will not give it back. You know, Mr. McBride, at risk of making things worse, may I offer you a bit of advice? Respect Mari's intelligence. She knows what and who is right for her. Now, if you'll excuse me, I have a family commitment I must honor."

Mari heard footsteps walking away, the click of a turning doorknob, then her father's voice. "You'll marry her?"

"As soon as she wishes."

"You don't have another wife squirreled away?"

For the first time in the conversation, Mari heard an edge in Luke's voice. "I am not my brother, Mr. McBride. I'll thank you not to charge me with his character failings."

"What about him?" Trace asked belligerently. "Aren't you going to tell me that I can't stop him from marrying my Katie-cat, either?"

Mari darted a look. Luke stood in the doorway, looking down at his feet. "Honestly, Mr. McBride," he said. "If I were you, I'd utilize that boot-in-the-ass you mentioned earlier. Knowing Rory, that's all it would take to chase him off."

When Luke exited her father's study, Mari lifted her ear from the peephole and prepared to dash upstairs to the exit. She wanted to catch Luke before he left Willow Hill. A *pound, pound, pound* on the wall by the spy hole stopped her in her tracks. "Come to my study, Maribeth. Now."

Suddenly, she was an eight-year-old mischief maker about to be called up on the carpet once again. *How did he know?*

Oh, for crying out loud, Mari, her eight-year-old self replied. *Papa always knows everything. Eventually.*

She grimaced and dropped her chin to her chest, then dragged her feet and made her way toward her father's study. Luke was gone by the time she arrived.

Trace stood facing the family portrait hanging on the wall. Without taking his eyes off the painting, he said, "Talk to me, Maribeth."

Her stomach dipped. Her heart ached. He looked so miserable.

What she was fixing to say would only make it worse.

"I love him, Papa."

He winced. "He's not good enough for you."

"He's perfect for me. Papa, Luke is strong and he's steady and he's dependable. He makes me laugh. I trust him."

"Oh, Mari. That shows such poor judgment. It's something a McBride Menace might do. I thought you'd outgrown that foolishness. You might as well be a little girl again."

His words hurt, but Mari knew that fear and concern for her put the words in her father's mouth. *Something a McBride Menace would do.* It occurred to Mari that maybe being a Menace wasn't such a bad thing. "Papa, Luke has proved his strength of character time and again. He's a good man."

"He's an outlaw!"

"No, he's not. He told you the truth, Papa. He really is a ranger. He has a Warrant of Authority. I've seen it."

"Probably forged," Trace muttered. "He's lying to you, just like that weasel brother of his lied to Katrina."

Stubborn as an old mule, her father. "Luke didn't lie about this, Papa. But if you need proof, look no farther than the Fort Worth jail. Finn Murphy was arrested because Luke summoned the Texas Rangers."

As she expected, Trace had no reply to that. "Papa, I love him. I want to marry him. I want him to be the father of my children."

Trace grimaced. "Please, Mari. Don't talk about such things. I don't like to think about you…"

"Growing up?"

He shoved his hands into his pockets and shrugged, reminding her of Tommy. Reminding her of…that's when it hit her. "They say women pick out men like their fathers. Well, Papa, in many ways, Luke is a lot like you. He can be stubborn. He always thinks he's right, at least until I show him otherwise. He gets the same look in his eyes when he looks at me that you get when you look at Mama, and he would, he *has,* protected me with his life. He's my hero, Papa. Just like you are my hero, too. Give him a chance. You'll see. If you're open-minded and fair, you'll see. He'll prove himself to you. Please, Papa?"

From behind her came the sound of her mother's voice. "Well, now. That seems like a fair enough request. Don't you think, Trace?"

He scowled blackly. Mari flashed her mother a grateful smile. Jenny McBride continued, "In your father's defense, Maribeth, this comes as quite a surprise. You need to give him some time to grow accustomed to the idea and to get to know your young man. You're not planning on eloping, are you?"

"Oh, no. I want a big church wedding, Mama. I want to wear the Good Luck Wedding Dress, and I want Aunt Claire to bake us a magical wedding cake."

Jenny crossed the room and slipped her arm around her husband's waist, giving him a reassuring squeeze. "So we can anticipate a long engagement?"

"That sounds good," Trace piped up. "Five years." When his wife sniffed and rolled her eyes, he amended it. "All right, I'll go as low as three."

Mari met her stepmother's gaze. "Not an inordinately long engagement, no, Mama. Just long enough to plan a wedding, I should think." She chastised her father with a frown and added, "Certainly not three years."

"Well, you can't fault a fellow for trying," he muttered.

"One thing concerns me," said Jenny. "It's probably not fair to you, Mari, but we dare not ignore the issue. Luke Garrett is Rory Callahan's brother. Bringing that connection into our family will be difficult for Kat."

"I know, Mama. Believe me, I know. Before Kat and I came home, I told Luke we didn't have a future together because of Kat."

"She gave you her blessing?" Jenny asked, her brows arching in surprise.

"Not exactly." Mari gave her father a significant look as she added, "Despite the fact that Luke is a blood relative of the man who so viciously betrayed her, Kat is trying to be open-minded about him."

Jenny's lips twisted as she tried, and failed, to stifle a smile. Trace folded his arms and shook his head. "Cheeky little thing. Your daddy obviously didn't swat you often enough when you were little, Maribeth McBride."

"My daddy hardly ever swatted me," she responded, her grin going wide. "He loves me, you know. He only wants me to be happy."

Trace's sigh was long and heartfelt. "That he does, Meri-berry. That he does."

ANOTHER WAVE of thunderstorms blew in just as Luke departed Willow Hill, so he took refuge beneath the spreading, leafy boughs of a cottonwood tree and waited out the worst of the storm. It had been an interesting evening, to say the least. He shoved his hands into the pockets of his duster and leaned against the tree trunk, whistling.

She'd asked *him* to marry *her.* Didn't that beat all?

He was a little worried about her at the moment. Luke wondered if Trace McBride intended to have it out with Mari tonight or wait until morning. Luke had wanted to see her before he left, but her mama had shuffled him right out the front door following his little chat with her daddy, Jenny's excuse being that her daughter had retired for the evening.

As if Luke believed that. More likely she'd hid in the bushes beneath the study window, hoping to hear just what was being said inside.

All in all, the evening had gone much better than anticipated. Infinitely better. He'd half expected to be met by the business end of a Remington. Instead, he'd left with the promise of a future.

This line of thunderstorms moved fast, blowing out of town as quickly as it had swept in, and soon Luke continued his way down the hill. In the wake of the storm, a three-quarter moon and a myriad of stars illuminated Luke's path and revealed a shadowed figure coming toward him. Luke recognized the man's walk and let out a string of curses blue enough to make a whore blush. "Rory Callahan, tell me you're looking for me and not headed up to Willow Hill."

"Hey, Luke. What are you doing here?"

Well, that answered his question. "It's after ten, Rory. You can't go calling on a family at this time of night."

"I'm not calling on the family. I need to see Kat."

Tonight? Over my dead body. "Have you been drinking, brother?"

"Hell, no. I've been digging. In a graveyard no less. Have to tell you, Luke, it's creepy to get caught in a graveyard during a thunderstorm."

Luke wondered why he was surprised at Rory's first action upon his return to town. First things first, after all. "So, you retrieved your pirate treasure."

"No, I didn't. That's why I have to speak to Kat right away. It's gone. She must have taken it."

"Why would Kat have taken the cross?"

"To sell it. It's worth a lot of money, and she's gonna need cash, what with the baby and all."

A baby and no husband, Luke thought. He grabbed his brother's arm. "Look, you're not going up to that house tonight."

"Yeah, I am. I need to see my wife."

"She is *not* your wife."

Rory waved Luke's objection away. "A technicality. That's all."

"Listen, Rory, I left there right as this latest storm blew through. Now is not a good time for you to go to Willow Hill."

"Why?"

Because I don't want you interfering with my plans. Luke sighed heavily. "It's late. I'm sure they've all gone to bed by now."

"Good. I don't want to see any family other than Kat. Our conversation needs to be private."

Luke shut his eyes and shook his head. Hell, maybe it would be best to get this over with before the hour grew any later. Luke knew his younger brother. The only way he'd stop him from pestering poor Kat this evening would be to knock him out and tie him up. Frankly, Luke was too tired to fight that particular battle.

"All right. But I'm going with you."

Minutes later, the two men stood beneath Kat McBride's bedroom window. Rory scooped up a handful of pebbles and began pegging them toward her window. Both his arm and his aim were poor. Finally, Luke grabbed the small stones and got the job done.

Kat's window opened, and she leaned her head out. "Who's there?"

"It's me, honey-dove. Your Rory."

The window slammed shut.

"Again," Rory said, motioning toward the remaining stones.

Luke rolled his eyes but did as his brother asked. It took three full minutes of steady rock throwing to get Kat to appear at the window again. "Would you go away! My father will kill you."

"Not until you talk to me."

"I do believe we've said all there is to say to one another."

"Kat, please. It'll just take a minute. Come downstairs. Look, what I have to say affects the baby."

She hesitated, but Luke could tell Rory had chosen the right string to pull. Moments later, she nodded and closed the window. When she exited the house, Rory said, "You can excuse us, Luke."

"No, I don't think so."

He considered Kat his sister-in-law, one way or another, and he decided he should stay around in case she needed protection.

She gave Luke an appreciative look, then turned to Rory. "If you're looking for some frolic in the gazebo like your brother enjoyed, you are totally out of luck."

"Frolic?" Rory asked.

"Never mind." Kat folded her arms. "What do you want, Rory?"

If Mari had asked him that question, Luke would have responded, *You.* Rory, being Rory, said, "I went to the graveyard tonight. The cross is gone. What did you do with it, Kat?"

For a minute, Luke expected Kat to draw back and wallop Rory. Instead, her voice grew even chillier. "Let me see if I have this right. You show up on my doorstep uninvited. You don't bother to ask me how I'm doing, or how *your baby* is doing. Instead, you ask me if I stole the stolen altar cross from you. Is that what you're saying?"

Dumb, brother. Dumb.

"Well, it's not where I hid it, and it is worth a lot of money. You have the baby coming and all, so..."

"So, of course, I took it." She braced her hands on her hips. "You really take the cake, Rory Callahan. It's missing, so I took it. Like I haven't had more important things to take care of during the past two weeks. Admitting to the Spring Palace fire. Explaining to every person I meet where I've been for the past four months. Trying not to see the disappointment painted on my parents' faces over the fact that in a few months I'll be giving birth to their first grandchild, a grandchild born out of wedlock."

"Hey, about that. I have good news. I'm not married after all, so we can tie the knot."

Kat shook her head in wonder. "Have you always been this senseless, and I simply didn't see it? Was I that dazzled by your charm?"

Rory winked nervously at Luke. "Did you hear that? She thinks I'm charming."

"Actually, I heard her say you're downright stupid, and I quite agree."

Kat laughed without amusement. "Listen to your brother, Rory. He's smart. He also knows how to treat a woman. There was quite a difference between the way he greeted my sister tonight and the way you greeted me." She sighed then, long and sadly. "I didn't take your silly stolen cross, Rory. Either you told someone else what you did with it, or somebody else stumbled across it. Now, you'll have to excuse me. I'm tired and my doctor has advised me to get lots of rest. Stress-free rest. Good night."

Luke watched Rory's face as she turned to leave. "Somebody else," his brother murmured. "The letter. But he's so far away…."

At the doorway, Kat paused, moonlight painting her complexion ghostly pale. "By the way. About your oh-so-romantic proposal? I intend to think about it. I know how I want to respond, but I need to make certain it's the best thing for my child."

When Willow Hill's back door shut behind her, Rory turned to Luke and gave a smug smile. "See? I told you she'll forgive me. They always do."

Luke shook his head sadly and headed back down the hill. "Maybe so, brother. However, I suspect that one of these days, you won't be able to forgive yourself."

CHURCH BELLS TOLLED eight o'clock as Mari turned onto Main Street and made her way toward Indulgences. She noted a stir among the women congregated in front of the dress shop that had advertised a sale beginning that morning. One lady carried a newspaper and two others peered over her shoulders, avidly reading. Wilhemina's column, no doubt. "Kat, I hope you're ready for this."

Yesterday, three weeks after Luke and his brother returned to Fort Worth, that lying snake Rory held an interview with notorious gossip Wilhemina Peters for her newspaper column, *Talk About Town.* In an effort to force Kat's hand in marriage, Rory had told the story of their elopement with a dramatic flair that had little to do with the truth.

The front-page scandal proved good for Mari's business. When she opened the shop at nine, a half-dozen people were lined up outside the door. By noon, she'd sold a record number of chocolates and answered more questions than a kindergarten teacher. She hung the Closed sign on the doorknob, locked the door for her lunch break, and drew the window blinds with relief.

No sooner had she taken a seat at one of the shop's tables and unwrapped her sandwich than she heard a rap on the back door. "I'm not expecting any deliveries," she mused aloud.

Mari attempted to ignore the summons, but the knocking continued, grew louder and more insistent. "Grr..." Mari murmured.

She rose and peeked through the blinds. "Kat?"

She unlocked the door and her sister slipped inside.

Kat looked harried, her expression tired and drawn. Concerned, Mari slipped her arm around Kat's waist and led her toward a chair. "Honey, are you all right?"

"Yes. I'm just...I decided to face the gossip head-on. I went to the general store and to Aunt Claire's bakery and I even stopped by the Ladies' Benevolent Society meeting. I have to tell you, Mari, Genevieve Broussard's oatmeal cookies taste awful."

"Are you sick to your stomach, then?"

"Yes, but not because of what I ate. Oh, Mari." Kat sank into her chair and dropped her chin to her chest. "It's just so hard. I could kill Rory Callahan!"

"I know, honey."

"Did you read this morning's paper?"

"I did, I'm afraid."

"What a liar he is! 'A minor legal technicality voided my marriage to Kat McBride and now she refuses to make an honest man out of me.' Can you believe that drivel? A wife and son are a minor technicality?"

"I hate to say I'm not surprised by anything Rory does," Mari replied.

"The swine. Have you noticed that every time Luke gives you a gift, Rory sends one to me? Luke brings you flowers, I get a bouquet. Luke writes you a love letter, Rory recites a love poem beneath my bedroom window. He's not doing it because he wants me, you understand. It's a contest. He doesn't want Luke to win. That, and he thinks I have the blasted altar cross."

"Honey, you need to calm down. This isn't doing the baby any good."

"I can't calm down. He's taken our private business public. To the cruel, awful public. Mari, when I left Willow Hill this morning, I knew to expect the stares and the catty remarks and the questions and suggestions, but I didn't anticipate they'd bring up every mistake I've ever made. For the first time in my life, I understand your aversion to being called a McBride Menace."

"Oh, Kat. I'm sorry." Mari walked to the counter behind her display cases and poured her sister a glass of lemonade, then placed a selection of her best chocolates onto a plate. Carrying both to the table, she set them in front of Kat. "It was brave of you to face them."

Kat sipped her lemonade. "I wanted to get it over with. I thought facing the worst of the gossip all at once would do the trick. I wanted to fight back, to give them my side of the story. As much of my side as I could bear and still live in Fort Worth, anyway. But when they bring up that prank the three of us played on the Butler boys when I was only six years old, it makes me realize that I'll never live anything down, not in this town. Not even when I'm old and gray. Whether I bow to pressure and marry that charming, low-down snake or not, I'll be hearing about this for the next fifty years."

Mari helped Kat the only way she knew how. She pushed the plate toward her sister, saying, "Here, have a chocolate."

Katrina chose two. "Luella Renfro was the worst. Can you believe she had the nerve to tell me to my face that my situation was all my fault because I pushed Rory Callahan into marriage? Like he wasn't the one who asked me to elope? Like he wasn't the one who conveniently forgot to mention that he already had a wife? A pregnant wife?"

"Luella Renfro is not a nice person."

"No, she certainly is not. She turned her poisoned tongue on you and Emma, too. Can you believe that?"

"Emma! Emma hasn't done anything worthy of ugly gossip."

"That didn't stop Luella. She said Emma has over-stepped her authority with the Harrison children. She said she's trying to usurp their mother's role."

"Oh, that's ridiculous."

"That's what I said. And when she started yammering on about your wedding, I told her to hush her mouth."

"My wedding? Just what pearl of wisdom did she have to say about my wedding?"

Kat wrinkled her nose. "She said you shouldn't wear Mama's dress, that since Emma wore it and Casey died, the good luck has rubbed off. She said people in town are back to calling it The Bad Luck Wedding Dress, and they say if you wear it to marry Luke the marriage is headed for a bad end."

"Why, that pinched-face, snot-nosed witch! Of all the…oh, wait. Wait one minute. The last thing I need is for Papa to hear about this."

Kat winced. "It's not going any better with him?"

"He's being stubborn, Kat. Luke is bending over backward to win his good graces, but Papa is acting hardheaded as a stump. The wedding is two weeks away, and Papa is still grumbling about it. He claims he wants me to be happy, but he looks like he's sucking a sour ball whenever Luke's name comes up."

Now it was Kat's turn to offer comfort. "He'll come around. You know he will, Mari."

Mari wasn't so certain. "I realize Papa won't love Luke like he loved Casey when he gave Emma away at the altar, but I'd at least like to walk up the aisle without worrying that my father might decide to punch my groom in the stomach."

"He'll kick him in the privates if he catches the two of you in a tête-à-tête the likes of which he almost walked in on last night."

"We weren't doing anything."

Kat snorted. "You were doing everything *but* anything, and it was darn sure on the menu. You better thank your lucky stars that Tommy threw up and we had to leave Uncle Tye's house when we did. If we'd stayed for dessert and then come home, it would have been ugly. I have to say, though," Kat added, her eyes twinkling, "Mama, Emma, and I thought those broad bare shoulders of his were mighty fine looking."

"You saw!"

"Through the parlor window. Why do you think we

made so much noise coming in the front? Be glad Papa couldn't see for carrying Bobby. Come on, Mari. For everyone's sake. Can't you wait until the wedding?"

Mari leaned over and banged her head against the table. Kat laughed. "You know why Papa is so persnickety about Luke, don't you? The two of them are so much alike it's frightening. Do you know how lucky you are, Mari? Luke has substance. Why does his brother have to be so different?"

"Have you decided what you're going to do, Kat?"

She let out a long, sad sigh. "Yes, I think so. I think, for the baby's sake, I'll have to marry him. I'll marry him, then I'll hold out hope that you are right about our accomplishing tasks and finding love that is true. Maybe I'll get lucky and end up a widow like Emma."

"Why, Katrina Julianne!" Mari exclaimed, a shiver running down her spine. "That's a terrible thing to say."

"Yes, well, I'm feeling terrible. Actually, that's the truth. I think I should go straight home and rest. I have one more stop on my list, but would you mind doing it for me, Mari?"

"Sure, honey. What is it?"

"Emma broke the chain on her necklace this morning, and she asked me to drop it by Haltom Jewelry to be repaired. He's closed for lunch, too."

"I'll take it. I need to go by there anyway. I had Luke's wedding ring engraved with our initials and our wedding date and it's supposed to be ready today."

"Thank you." Kat finished her lemonade, popped another chocolate into her mouth, then stood. Deciding she looked a little wobbly, Mari suggested, "Why don't I flag down a driver, Kat? It's a long walk home."

She shook her head. "Thanks, but I saw Uncle Tye at the bakery. He had the baby with him. She's such a doll—so tiny and pink and pretty. Anyway, he has the carriage and he said he'd take me home when I was ready to go. I'll head over there now."

"All right. Tell him I said hello and give the baby a kiss for me."

After Kat's departure, Mari ate her sandwich and tidied her shop in preparation for the afternoon rush. In the back room, she'd just removed a bowl of mint-chocolate filling from the icebox when she heard the another rap on the door. Thinking it was Kat, she opened it without looking. "Did you forget something?"

"I surely did." Luke sauntered into the shop, his hot caramel eyes glowing with a devilish promise. He walked up beside her, dipped his finger into the cream, then slowly licked it clean. "Mmm…I forgot to finish what we started last night, and you know me well enough to know I hate leaving a job half-done. Grab that bowl and c'mere, woman."

Mari was a full hour late reopening her shop after lunch, but she felt too good to regret it. No sooner had she turned the lock on the front door than she noticed a streak of mint-chocolate filling dipping down into her bodice. Now, how had he missed that? She hurried into the back room to wash just as the front door bell jangled. *Well, shoot. Customers already.*

She made quick work of the mess on her skin, then pasted a friendly smile on her face and carried a pan of chocolates into the front of the shop. "Good afternoon. May I help—"

She gasped and the chocolates hit the floor with a bang.

CHAPTER NINETEEN

LUKE SAT in his attorney's office, reading over the bill of sale for the Blue Goose Saloon and his other Hell's Half Acre properties. This was it. After almost two hours of meetings, discussions, negotiations and proposals, his signature at the bottom of this page would conclude the divestiture of assets and appointments connected to his clandestine life.

He'd resigned his position with the Texas Rangers and following the wedding, he'd begin his new job as, of all things, city sheriff, the vacancy created just last week when the previous sheriff ran afoul of a shotgun down in the Acre. It was an interim position for Luke. If he wanted to keep the job he'd have to stand for election next April, but it would give him something to do until he and Mari decided if a continued career in law enforcement was right for their family.

He felt good, he thought as he scrawled his name on the document transferring the properties to their new owner. He felt clean, clean and renewed, and ready to meet his future with the woman he loved by his side.

Or on top of him, as the case may be. With mint-chocolate-cream filling drizzling from a spoon. His lips twitched with a grin. The things that woman could do with dessert.

"So, will there be anything else?" the lawyer asked, jerking Luke from his most delicious memory.

"Actually, yes." Luke stood and stretched. "The lot directly behind mine on Summit Avenue has been offered for sale. I've made arrangements with the owner to buy it. I need you to see to the paperwork for me."

"Certainly, Mr. Garrett."

They discussed Luke's wishes regarding financial terms for the purchase, then Luke took his leave. Standing on Main Street across from the Tarrant County courthouse, he checked his pocket watch. Twenty minutes before his next appointment. Good. That gave him just time enough to breeze by his lodging and retrieve his wish list for the house he wanted to build for Mari. Undoubtedly his architect, her father, had plenty of ideas about what would best suit his second-born daughter.

"Like separate his-and-her bedrooms, built at opposite ends of the house," Luke grumbled as he glanced toward the throng of men milling around the jailhouse. Trace McBride thawed about as fast as a glacier. If he had his way, instead of being two weeks off, Luke's wedding day would be set for the turn of the century, if that.

An angry shout from the crowd down the block snagged his attention, and Luke decided to take the long way home, detouring by the jailhouse to see what was causing the ruckus. What he discovered turned his blood cold.

"Jailbreak?" he repeated to a bystander, dread pooling in his gut.

"Yep. They're saying it must have been the Brazos Valley gang. Shot two men dead, wounded three others.

Did their evil right in the big middle of the day. Do those fellas fear no one?"

Luke ignored the question; he already knew the answer. His feet were already making an about-face to find Mari.

"You joining the posse, mister?" the stranger asked. "They'll be leaving in minutes. Goin' north. That's the direction the outlaws headed. The marshal hopes to catch up with 'em before they reach Grapevine."

Luke shook his head, his mind on the message sent to him via Jared Harper. Cold fingers of fear crawled up his spine. *I know your weakness.*

Mari. He had to get to Mari.

"It's stupid to worry," he told himself as he broke into a run. Murphy wouldn't have had his gang break him out of jail just so he could hang around town and wreak his revenge on Luke and Mari. The man would have to be crazy to do that.

But Finn Murphy *was* crazy. Luke increased his pace. Within minutes, he rounded a corner and Indulgences came into view. Luke's mouth was dry. His heart pounded as if he'd run eight miles instead of eight blocks. *She's there. She's inside. She's safe and sound.*

The sign in the window read Closed.

Luke's heart skipped a beat. He muttered a foul curse and put on a burst of speed that carried him to the chocolate shop's front door. He twisted the doorknob and pushed. Nothing. Locked up tight. Drawing his gun, he kicked the door in and stepped into the candy shop. "Maribeth?"

Evil tainted the air. He could feel it on the back of his neck, smell the stench of it all around him. His finger twitched on the trigger as he moved on silent feet to the front of the shop.

The sight that met his eyes took his breath away. Mari's necklace dangled from a blade of the slowly turning ceiling fan.

I know your weakness.

Luke closed his eyes and staggered beneath the weight of the fear that turned his boots to lead. For a long moment, he couldn't think. Couldn't react. Bone-deep terror unlike any he'd known before gripped him.

A violent pounding sounded on the back door, yanking him back to reality. "Maribeth?" Trace McBride called. "Are you in there?" *Pound, pound, pound.* "Open the door, sweetheart."

Luke flipped the lock and tugged the door open.

Relief in his tone, Trace said, "Thank God. I was worried. Did you hear that Finn—"

"He's got her," Luke said, his voice rusty. He pointed toward the necklace. "He's got her and this time, he won't let her take him by surprise."

"Oh, God." Trace, reacting much like Luke had, stood frozen in horror.

"We need to find her, McBride. Right away. We need to organize…" Luke's voice trailed off as he noted something out of place in Mari's candy kitchen. Why was a bowie knife sitting next to Mari's sugar canister? A knife that looked hauntingly familiar?

Rory, what the hell have you done?

The knife lay atop a page torn from a recipe book. Scratched across the page in pencil in his brother's handwriting were the words *Finn took Mari hostage. I'll lay a trail. Hurry!*

"Goddammit, Rory, you stupid son of a bitch," Luke muttered as he handed the note to Trace. His brother was no match for the likes of Finn Murphy.

"This is from your brother?" Trace asked. "What is

he doing with Finn Murphy? Was he part of this? Did he help break that bastard out of jail?"

"No," Luke said, hoping, praying that was true. "Rory wouldn't do that. He and Finn had a falling-out months ago. He'd have no reason to pull a stunt like that."

Not unless Rory's precious altar cross was somehow involved.

MARI CAME TO slowly. Her mind was mushy and it took her a moment to recall what had happened. She'd made a chocolate bar out of Luke, then...what?

Memory returned like a nightmare. *The tray of chocolates falling. Finn Murphy's mouth stretched into an evil smile as he pointed a revolver at her head. "Hello, darlin'. I'm here for somethin' sweet."*

She'd expected to feel a bullet, but instead, he'd raised the gun and brought the butt down upon her head. She remembered nothing more after that.

So where am I now? She knew she was alive. Her head hurt too bad for her to be dead. She lay stretched out on her back, and she couldn't move her arms or her legs. Something gagged her mouth. A cloth. It tasted of sweat. She opened her eyes, but she couldn't see. Something lay atop her body. Something scratchy that smelled like...was it onions? Yes. Onions. Onion sacks. She was hidden beneath burlap onion sacks.

I'm in a wagon and my ankles and wrists are tied with rope.

She'd been abducted by Finn Murphy. Again.

Fear washed over her like a cold winter rain. *This time, he'll kill me.*

She couldn't tell how long she'd been out. Hours, perhaps. Had night fallen? She sensed no sunshine beaming down upon her, and she heard the drone of cicadas all around her. No sounds of town. They were out in the country traveling a bumpy, rutted road.

Then, to Mari's shock, she heard a familiar voice. I'm telling you, Finn," said Rory Callahan. "Taking a hostage was a mistake. Especially this particular hostage. It's bad enough you're gonna have every lawman in the state after your hide, now we're gonna have Luke on our ass."

"I owe him."

"This wasn't part of our deal. I wasn't counting on crossing my brother again. I'm not sure getting my hands on that treasure is worth it. What good will it do me if I'm dead?"

"Just shut up and drive the wagon. I'm not comfortable out here in the open. Somebody might see us."

"We've already been seen and the disguise worked like a charm. Nobody's gonna recognize you. Who'd ever connect Finn Murphy with a priest?"

"Shut up!"

Rory took the hint. Mari's mind spun. What deal? Had Rory helped Murphy escape from jail? He must have. Murphy must have promised him he'd help recover the treasure. That stupid pirate treasure. Look at how much trouble it had caused, to so many different people. Better for everyone if it had just stayed buried.

Fear nibbled at the edge of Mari's thoughts as she tried to plan a way to save herself. Was this a flatbed wagon? Could she roll herself off the back without being noticed? Or should she look for a way to loosen her ropes? Take the men by surprise when they came to do whatever nefarious deed they had planned.

Mari feared she knew what that plan might be. After all, last time, Finn Murphy intended rape.

I won't let it happen, she told herself. She'd stopped him once before, hadn't she? She could do it again. She would stop him again. Or die trying.

Except she didn't want to die. She had too much to live for now.

Mari gathered her thoughts. Had he searched her pockets? Maybe the two on the outside of her skirt, but not the hidden one in the seam, she'd bet. What was in there? Anything to use as a weapon? A handkerchief. A stubby pencil. Emma's necklace.

Emma's necklace! She'd never made it to the jewelry store, so she still had Emma's necklace.

In that fact, Mari found comfort. The necklaces were special, magical. The necklaces were good luck. Somehow, having it would help her. She knew it in her heart.

Moving as quietly as possible, making the best of her limited mobility, Mari searched the wagon bed for a sharp edge, anything she could use to cut the rope binding her hands. Nothing. Desperate, she did manage to work free one of the ever-present safety pins fastened to her hem. With the pin in hand, she continued to search, her concentration so focused on her task that at first she didn't notice the slowing of the wagon.

"Here it is," Rory said, blowing a relieved sigh. "The turnoff to the old place. I haven't been out here for years. I was half afraid I wouldn't remember the way. Sure hope your men found their way here all right. If our getaway horses aren't here, we'll be up the creek."

"They'll be here," Murphy said.

"Look, Finn. There's that big old flat rock Janna liked to picnic on. That's a good place to leave Mari. Since we got clean away, we don't need a hostage anymore."

"Just drive on to the old place, Rory."

"But—"

"Drive."

The menace in his voice caused Mari's pulse to race. Whatever he had planned for her, it would happen at the old place. No way would she work free of her bindings before they arrived. All she had for a weapon was her mind and a safety pin. Not much better than last time. But she'd survived then. She'd survive now.

Less than five minutes later, Rory hollered, "Whoa, there, fellas. Whoa."

The wagon rolled to a stop and Mari braced herself.

"You want to check on the horses?" Rory asked. "I'll see to Maribeth."

"I don't think so." Evil glee hung in the outlaw's voice. "The little lady is all mine."

Mari went stiff when Finn Murphy grabbed her feet and pulled her out from beneath the burlap bags covering her face and body to the end of the wagon. For just a second, Mari saw the beauty of a multitude of stars against an inky sky, then he hoisted her over his shoulder and she saw nothing but shadows on the ground.

Rory exclaimed, "Wait a minute, Finn! What do you think you're doing?"

"Oh, Miss McBride knows what I'm doing. Don't ya, darlin'?" He swatted her hard on the rear. "We have old business to finish."

Mari struggled. With her hands secured, the pin was of little help. When she realized Murphy was enjoying her wiggling, she went still as a possum.

"I've been looking forward to this," Murphy said. "Before I'm done, you're gonna wish you'd died out there by the pond that day."

He stepped across a threshold of some sort. Mari

heard a match flare and lantern glass rattle. A wick caught and a soft yellow glow illuminated the room. "I had my men lay in a few supplies. They outta be around here somewhere. Yep, there it is. That's the important one." He tossed her onto a bed and laughed maniacally. "It's the cactus I ordered."

Inside, Mari trembled, but she was determined not to show fear.

Murphy rubbed his crotch. Again and again. Then he frowned and stroked it harder. "Goddamned bitch. You're gonna pay for what you did to me. I'm taking my manhood back, right here, right now!"

"No!" Rory Callahan stood in the doorway, a Colt revolver aimed at Murphy. The hand holding the gun visibly trembled, but his eyes glowed with angry determination. "This wasn't the deal, Finn. You're not gonna hurt her."

"Put the gun down, kid. You're not gonna shoot me."

"I don't want to shoot you. Finn, you're my brother. You're family, but I can't let you do this. She's Kat's sister. I won't allow you to hurt her."

Finn Murphy slowly looked around. "Do you honestly think you can stop me? You? Jesus, Rory. You're dumber than dirt. Always have been."

Moving like lightning, Murphy drew his gun and shot Rory Callahan low in the torso.

Mari gasped in horror as Rory clutched his belly and dropped to his knees. Murphy advanced on him, snarling. "I used you to get out of jail, you stupid shit. Not to hunt down Kimball and find some goddamned pirate treasure." He turned his head and spit on the floor.

"You've killed me," Rory said, disbelief in both tone and expression, even as he fell the rest of the way to the floor. "Finn, we're *family*."

Murphy glared down at Rory in disgust. "You brought it on yourself, Rory. You brought it on your-self." He turned his back on the man he had shot, and focused his attention once again on Mari. "Well, shit. Now it stinks like death in here. I don't like that smell. I'm not gonna be able…shit."

Murphy shoved his gun back into his holster. "Not what I had planned," he grumbled. "Not what I had planned at all."

His own family. He murdered a member of his own family. He's mad. True terror, sharp as a razor, sliced through Mari.

The villain stood for a moment, thinking. Tears spilled from Mari's eyes at Rory's final words. "Tell Kat…I'm sorry," he said. "Tell her the…the…trea-sure…baby…find Kimball. He has the cross."

Murphy muttered a curse, then once again hoisted Mari over his shoulder. He stepped over Rory's prone body and stomped away from the dilapidated house. Gagged and unable to speak, Mari lifted her head and locked her gaze on Rory's. *God's peace be with you,* she silently said.

Lying in the doorway bleeding to death, Luke's half brother smiled.

Murphy toted her into the trees, out of sight of the house, mumbling as he went. "Goddamned fool. Why'd he make me do that? Stupid shit. Ruined my fun with you. Ruined my revenge. Pecker damned well better work next time I try to use it, or I swear I'll dig him up and shoot him again."

He carried her for what seemed like hours but what was probably less than ten minutes. She still had the safety pin clutched in her fist. She hoped she had the chance to use it against him somehow.

"At least I'll have my revenge on Luke," Murphy grumbled. "He'll never find your body, and it'll plague him the rest of his life. That's a lot better than killing you outright for him to find. I'm gonna enjoy thinkin' about it when I'm living down there in Bolivia. I'll get me some tequila and a good cigar and one of them Spanish gals. That'll heal me. It doesn't have to be you."

Abruptly, Murphy stopped. "Here we are. Down you go, bitch."

As he bent forward to shift her weight over his head, Mari made her move. She twisted her body violently, throwing him off balance. She gouged him with the sharp pin and he screamed. She'd gotten his eye.

"Aargh!" he hollered, grabbing at her. His hand ripped her dress. She felt the seam tear and the necklace spill from the hidden pocket. Then he was pushing her, shoving her forward. "Die, bitch. Fall down that hole and die. Hope you take good and long to do it, too. No one's ever gonna find you."

The solid ground beneath her feet gave way and Mari fell down, down, down into pitch-black darkness. She hit hard and once more, the world went black.

LUKE'S HEART LEAPED when he spied the lantern light burning at the old homestead. Had he guessed right? Please, God. Let him have guessed right. He'd lost the trail with the sunlight and had gambled on where they might have gone. It made a crazy sort of sense for Murphy to bring Mari here to Luke's childhood home to perpetrate his undoubtedly evil attentions on her. It was scene-setting that would appeal to a man like Finn Murphy.

McBride had agreed with the idea to press on to the homestead, and he rode with Luke, silent, his visage grim.

"I think that's the house," Luke told him. "See the light?"

"Off to the north? Four, five hundred yards?"

"Yeah. My sister still owns the land. Shouldn't be anyone there unless squatters have set up house."

"How do you want to play it? Shall we go in afoot? Ride right in? What do you think is best?"

Luke reviewed what he knew about Finn Murphy. Considered the surprise Rory had thrown him today. "I don't think we have a minute to lose, but if we can surprise them, Mari is bound to be better off."

"Afoot, then."

A hundred yards out, Luke lifted his hand, signaling Trace to stop. They tethered their horses to an oak tree, then each man grabbed a rifle from his saddle. Luke strapped a bowie knife around his thigh. Luke wore a pair of revolvers on his gun belt. Trace had a pistol strapped on his right hip.

Luke looked at Trace and nodded once. Silently and steadily, they moved toward the light. *Hold on, Mari. We're almost there. Hold on.*

As the reached the top of a rise overlooking the cabin below, Luke dropped low and gestured for Trace to do the same. They crab-walked the last few feet, then just as Luke lifted his face to peer down upon the cabin, a gunshot split the night.

A man screamed.

Luke leaped to his feet and started running, Trace following right behind him. He spied Finn Murphy lying facedown on the ground, but he didn't so much as pause.

Rory sat propped in the doorway, a bloodstain the size of a dinner plate on his shirt. Smoke rose from the barrel of the gun beside him. Moonlight and blood loss had turned his complexion an unearthly white. *Rory!*

Luke's heart thundered as he looked past his brother into the house. The empty house. "Mari. Where's Mari, Rory?"

A single tear spilled from Rory's eye and trailed down his cheek. "He got me good. Sorry, Luke. Sorry about Mari. Sorry I couldn't save her."

Luke grabbed him by each shoulder, supported him, willed his own vitality and strength into his brother's body. Grief and panic had a stranglehold around his neck and he worked to force the words, "Where is she, Rory! Where is she?"

But it was too late. His brother couldn't answer. Rory Callahan had died.

TWO FULL DAYS following the jailbreak, the citizens of Fort Worth couldn't stop talking about the McBride family's bad luck. In the *Daily Democrat*, the story of the jailbreak and the principal players' connections to the McBrides ran beneath the headline The Bad Luck Brides. What stirred the gossips the most, however, wasn't the elements of scandal, sex or even pirate treasure. What kept the people of Fort Worth shaking their heads in disbelief was the way the family reacted to Maribeth's tragic demise.

They continued to plan the wedding.

It boggled the mind. Wilhemina Peters claimed that collectively, the family had finally had one too many crosses to bear. The butter had done slipped off their noodles.

While the McBride men searched the old Garrett homestead for Maribeth, or, as most everyone agreed, Maribeth's body, the McBride women flitted around town finalizing wedding arrangements. Really, did Jenny McBride honestly believe that she'd need a pair of white turtledoves come a week from Saturday? Did Emma seriously think it mattered whether the special order white kid leather slippers to match the bridesmaids' gowns arrived on time? And the food—what in the world would they do with barbecue for four hundred?

The townspeople talked about Luke, too. Volunteers from town who helped in the search returned at the end of a long, fruitless day speaking of Luke Garrett's fierce determination to find the woman he loved. They said he seldom rested, barely slept, and grew vicious when anyone dared to suggest that Mari McBride might not be found alive. He was a wounded animal, one man said. Frantic. Ferocious. Grieving.

When the searchers awoke to a hard, cleansing rain on the third day, Luke went a little crazy. He disappeared inside the old homestead cabin and quickly fired off five shots of his gun. Trace gave him a few minutes, then opened the cabin door.

"Garrett?"

Luke stood staring at an old iron stove and the tin coffee pot atop it now plugged full of holes. "Murphy had a real taste for a good cup of coffee."

"We'll find her, Garrett."

"Yeah." Luke waited a beat, then said, "My men say I could can track a minnow through a swamp. I lost his trail in the rocks, McBride. Most important search of my life, and I might as well be sorting sewing thread spools in a general store. Now the rain…" His voice cracked. "What the hell kind of bodyguard am I?"

"Goddammit, Garrett. Don't you dare give up!"

Taken aback by the other man's vehemence, Luke's eyes widened.

"You want to waste more time cursing, crying and

shooting stoves, go right ahead. But remember this much, boyo. Mari didn't give up on Kat. If this situation were reversed, Mari wouldn't give up on you, either. Now, you've had your little pity party, so go find my daughter!"

Fury erupted inside Luke like a volcano and spewed out into his words. "You hardheaded old coyote. I haven't given up on anything and damn you for suggesting I have. I love her, and by God, I'll find her!"

"Good. Then go do it!"

"I will! I'm going!" Luke shoved his gun back into its holster and glared at Trace McBride.

Trace shoved his hands into his pockets and glared right back at Luke. Seconds later, when they'd both calmed down, he said,

"We should look at the rain as a good thing. I've been fretting she might not have water, and now that worry is done. She's a strong girl. A smart girl. She'll figure a way to keep alive until we find her. I know it in my bones. Now, let's get after it."

Luke nodded, then followed Trace McBride from the cabin, his determination renewed. Before they split up, each to return to his assigned section of the search grid they'd established, Trace paused. "You really love my girl, don't you, Garrett?"

"Yes, sir. She's my heart."

Trace rubbed his hand over his three-day beard. "I understand, son. I understand. You know, you'll never be good enough for her."

"I know."

"But I'm thinking, just maybe, you're as close as anyone could get."

The morning's search proved no more fruitful than the previous day's, and by the time the rain ended just around noon, nerves had rubbed a bit raw. The older

McBride boy sniped with anyone who dared speak to him. Trace and his brother Tye snapped and snarled with each other and everyone else. Luke just wanted to get away.

Taking a break from his assigned search grid, he turned his face into the wind and began to walk. He paid little attention to where he was going. He simply followed an unfamiliar birdsong and an intriguing flash of sapphire blue flitting from tree to tree. He'd never before seen such a brilliantly blue bird in the Lone Star State. He'd give anything if Mari were here to see it. The bird was the same color as that necklace of hers. She'd get a real kick out it.

Watching the bird, Luke's eyes burned. He blinked away the sting, clenched his teeth. *You'll see it, sugar. I swear, I'll find you.*

With the necklace so recently in his thoughts, when Luke first saw the pendant dangling over the side of a rock halfway up a small hill to his right, he thought he'd suffered a hallucination. He took a second look, then rubbed his eyes. It *was* a necklace. Not Mari's blue pendant, but the red one. Emma's necklace. How the hell did Emma's McBride's necklace get here?"

Luke froze, almost afraid to hope. "Mari?" he said. He cleared his throat and tried again, louder. "Maribeth?"

He listened hard. Nothing. Keeping his eye on the necklace, he climbed the hill. The necklace lay just beyond his reach. He went down on his knees. Reached for the necklace. "Mari, sugar? Can you hear me?"

His fingers brushed the chain. He went down on his belly, stretched as far as he could reach. Hope, fear and dread swirled inside him like a dervish.

"Maribeth McBride? I want to hear you call my

name." He snagged the chain, dragged the necklace across the rocks toward him. He clutched the pendant in his hand, searching for sight of her or a hiding place or any sign that she might be near. "Mari!"

"Here, Luke. I'm here. I knew you'd find me."

His voice broke. "Mari?"

"Look below you. There's a shaft. It's the entrance to an underground cavern. Luke, I'm really ready to get out of here."

Luke spied the black slit in rocks and sweet blessed relief washed over him. He clambered over the rocks to the cavern's entrance. Lying on his stomach, he stretched out over the hole. "Mari?"

He heard a shuffling sound, then a figure moved into the thin beam of light piercing the darkness of the shaft. She looked dirty and torn and tattered. He'd never seen such a beautiful sight.

"Please hurry, Luke. I have so much to do. We're getting married in little more than a week. I think I've lost a little weight, so Mama might need to alter the dress again. Plus, we still need to find turtledoves, and I have to tell Aunt Claire that I've changed my mind about the cake topper. I want fresh flowers. Yellow roses. Is that all right with you?"

With his mouth stretched in a smile as big as the Texas sky, Luke sighed long and hard. "Maribeth McBride? I do love you, but you are such a Menace."

EPILOGUE

MARI'S WEDDING DAY dawned bright and beautiful, the autumn air crisp, the sky cloudless and a beautiful azure blue. It was a perfect day for a wedding.

On the lawn at Willow Hill sat rows of tables decorated in the bride's colors of sapphire-blue and lemon. The last of the briskets cheerfully furnished for the event by little Billy Waddell's forever-grateful father smoked in two iron barbecue pits. The meat had perfumed the air for two days in preparation for the guests who would attend the barbecue at the bride's home following the ceremony at First Methodist Church.

Collectively, the citizens of Fort Worth held their breath, wondering what mischief to expect at today's ceremony. The McBrides were well-known for having calamitous weddings. Hadn't the bride herself helped turn loose cats, dogs and mice at her own parents' wedding? Hadn't the family pet fish swum in the holy water font at her aunt and uncle's nuptials? Then there were the bigger animals the McBride boys released at Emma's wedding, along with the disappearance of a wedding guest, the complete story of that mystery something the people of Fort Worth had yet to be told.

No, something was bound to happen today, which was why an invitation to the afternoon event was the hottest ticket in town. Everyone wanted to see firsthand what disaster was bound to occur when the Bad Luck Wedding Dress was worn by a Bad Luck Bride.

The morning of Luke's wedding day, Janna and her new husband pitched in to help him spruce up the Rankin Building apartment where he and Mari would live until the completion of their house on Summit Avenue. The previous day they'd held a small, private funeral service for Rory. It had been a hard day for Luke, his sister, and especially Kat McBride, but they'd made it through. They'd all taken comfort in the fact that Rory had died trying to do the right thing.

By noon, Luke and his family had the apartment cleaned, polished and prepared to be a perfect wedding night bower. Considering all the travel the bride and groom had done of late, Luke and Mari were content to delay a honeymoon until the spring, after Kat's baby was born. Luke made certain the apartment was stocked with supplies to last a full two weeks. He and his bride didn't plan on leaving the apartment for at least that long.

Mari slept late the morning of her wedding and awoke with a smile on her face. She luxuriated in the pampering overseen by her grandmother, Monique Day, and when the females in her family removed to First Methodist Church at noon, two hours before the wedding was scheduled to begin, she all but floated above the streets in a haze of happiness.

The church looked beautiful, the flowers and decorations perfect, just the way she'd dreamed. The women fussed with some last-minute ribbon tying, then repaired to the vestry to dress. Jenny's mother-of-the-bride dress was a stylish design of yellow silk shot with threads of sapphire. Mari thought her mother had never looked more beautiful. As her attendants, Emma and Kat were dressed alike, the shimmering sapphire of their high-waisted gowns a triumph of fabric and design.

"Oh, Mama," Mari said when her sisters finished dressing. "You have outdone yourself with these gowns. I don't think I've ever seen anything quite so beautiful. You are the most talented dressmaker in the entire world!"

"I'm glad you like them, honey. I wanted this day to be everything you've dreamed of."

"It will be. It is." Tears pooled in her eyes as Mari smiled at her mother, Emma and Kat in turn. "I'm marrying the man I love, and all of my family is here to share this day with me."

"Sans the family pets, I trust," Emma said. "The boys swore on their favorite slingshots that they'd leave the wildlife at home this time."

At that, Mari tried to remain nonchalant. Only yesterday, she and Luke had been walking in the gardens at Willow Hill and stumbled upon a meeting between her younger brothers. The despondent boys were bemoaning the fact that due to the no-animals promise they'd been forced to give, Mari's wedding was bound to be dull, boring, and missing an important family tradition. So convinced were they that the wedding was doomed to be a letdown of enormous proportions for guests who had come to expect excitement at a McBride wedding, that Mari and Luke reconsidered.

Janna's daughters would do the honors. Halfway into the ceremony, a dozen ducks were scheduled to be released onto the floor of the First Methodist Church of Fort Worth.

Mari couldn't help but grin in anticipation.

"What?" Emma asked, her eyes narrowing suspiciously.

Mari was saved from responding when Jenny looked at her watch and declared it was time for Mari to dress. The women then helped her don the wedding gown that Jenny wore when she wed Trace, the same gown Aunt Claire wore when she married Uncle Tye, the dress Emma wore when she married her beloved Casey. Some people in town called it the Bad Luck Wedding Dress, but the McBride women knew better. Even Emma, who had lost her dear Casey after such a short time, recognized the magic in the gown. It wasn't luck, good or bad, that gave the gown its power. What made the gown special was the love that filled the hearts of the brides who wore it, the love that would bless the brides' marriages, be those marriages long or painfully short.

"Oh, my goodness," Kat breathed when the buttons were all fastened, the train attached, and Mari's sapphire necklace in place around her neck. "Look at you. You are breathtaking, Mari. Simply breathtaking. Luke Garrett is gonna take one look at you and swallow his tongue."

A knock sounded on the vestry door and Trace McBride called, "Hello? Are y'all ready in there? It's about time to start."

Jenny opened the door, then went up on her tiptoes and pressed a kiss against her husband's cheek. "You might want to shield your eyes when you come in, sir. The bride's beauty is blinding."

Trace took one look at his daughter and went speechless. Jenny listened to him clear his throat, blink back tears, and took pity on him, ushering the others outside, leaving father and daughter alone.

"Oh, Mari-berry. You are as pretty as a ripe summer peach."

"You're pretty handsome yourself, Papa, all dressed up in your new suit."

Trace ran a finger along his shirt collar and mumbled something about it being too tight. "Maribeth, I have to ask. Are you absolutely certain you want to go through with this? You know, all you have to do is say the word, and I'll take care of everything. You'd never have to see that bounder again if you don't want to."

"I love him, Papa."

"Yeah, well. So what?"

"You like him too, now, don't you? You can admit it, you know."

"Yeah, well. So what?"

Mari laughed and father and daughter embraced. Hugging her tight, Trace said into her ear, "I love you, baby. I always will. Be happy."

"I love you, too, Papa. You'll always be the first man I loved, and I will love you until the day I die."

"If he doesn't treat you right, you tell me. I'll take care of him quick as a minute."

"Oh, Papa." Laughing, Mari kissed his cheek, then they joined the rest of the family in the vestibule of First Methodist Church. Moment's later, the organist sounded the cue for the mother of the bride, and Jenny gave Mari another quick hug and kiss before Billy escorted her down the aisle. Kat waited for her cue, then glanced back at Mari and said, "I'm glad you brought me home, Mari."

Emma hugged Mari, whispered in her ear, "The love you've found with Luke is powerful, vigilant and true, Mari. You've given me hope."

When her sisters reached the front of the church, Mari and Trace took their places at the end of the center aisle. The first notes of Mendelssohn rang out and the congregation rose to their feet.

Luke waited for her at the altar, standing tall and proud and certain. He wore a charcoal-gray suit with a matching vest over a pristine white shirt, and he was so handsome he stole her breath away.

On their way up the aisle, Trace murmured, "You can still change your mind."

Mari giggled and patted her father's arm. At the altar, Trace paused before handing her over to Luke. "You treat her right, son."

"I'll guard her with my life, sir," Luke told him, then he turned toward his bride. "My God, woman. Look at you." Warm admiration gleamed in his eyes. "So beautiful. I've got to be the luckiest man on earth."

Luck. Good luck. A lifetime of good luck. Laughter bubbled up inside Mari. "I'm feeling rather lucky, myself. You're looking mighty fine, yourself, Mr. Garrett. May I mention that the duck feather in your boutonniere is quite the touch?"

A wicked glint entered his eyes and Luke fingered the item. "I thought you'd like it."

Excuse me?" interrupted the minister. "Would the two of you mind if we got on with the ceremony?"

"Sure, Reverend," Luke said. "Just one…"

He swept Mari into his arms and kissed her thoroughly. She was only vaguely aware of the scandalized buzz coming from the congregation and the insistent clearing of the minister's throat. Her body hummed with desire when he finally stepped away.

Luke turned to the now red-faced minister and grinned. "Now we're ready."

Mari couldn't stop smiling. Joy filled her heart. When she heard the first quack, she let out a laugh.

"Oh dear," murmured the minister.

Luke winked at Mari. "*Now* this is shaping up to be a McBride Menace wedding."

"Yes, isn't it?" Mari replied as one of the guests let out a screech. She laughed softly, and Luke lifted her hand to his mouth for a kiss. Right on her Bad Luck Love Line.

His eyes glowed with tender pride. "Have I told you how proud I am to be marrying a McBride Menace?"

"You are?"

"Without a doubt. Menaces are strong, they're loyal, they're courageous, and when they love, they love with every fiber of their being."

Tears stung Mari's eyes. "You see those things in me?"

"Damn straight, I do."

"Please, sir," interrupted the minister. "You're in church!"

"I never saw it." Determined not to cry, Mari blinked away the wetness. "I only saw the mischief, the troublemaking. The bad reputation."

Quack. Quack. Quack. Quack.

"Oh, for crying out loud!" Trace McBride exclaimed. "Tommy, keep that mallard out of the gardenias, would you please?"

Luke tucked an errant strand of hair behind Mari's ear. "You just had to find yourself, sugar. That's a difficult task for all of us."

A difficult task. Find yourself. Mari's eyes widened as she heard the echo of Roslin of Strathardle's words. *At the proper time, your task will be revealed.*

Had that been her task? Not to find her sister, but to find herself?

Luke fished in his pocket and withdrew a ring, a beautiful square-cut sapphire in a setting designed to complement her necklace. He slid it onto her finger, then took both her hands in his. "I love you, Maribeth McBride, Menace extraordinaire. With you at my side, I feel like the luckiest man alive. I vow I will guard your luscious body and protect your tender heart all the days of my life."

"Oh, Luke. I love you, too, and *I'm* the one who's lucky. Because of you, my family is whole, with brand-new hopes and dreams of the future. Because of you, my heart is mended, my spirit is found and my soul is complete. I vow I will cherish your love and honor it as long as we both shall live."

He kissed her again, long, and deep, and oh-so-sweet. When it was over, he looked up at the minister and asked, "Are we done here?"

"This is quite irregular," muttered the reverend.

Quack. Quack. Quack.

"Actually, this is exactly what Fort Worth has come to expect from a McBride family wedding." Wilhemina Peters sniffed with disdain as she rose from her seat in the pew just behind the giggling McBride boys. "Pronounce them, Reverend, so I can make my deadline. I had the story already written, you see. All I need to do now is fill in the type of animal."

"I put twenty dollars down on rabbits," Trace McBride observed, his gaze on a downy white duck quacking its way up the aisle.

"I had twenty-five on turkeys," Jenny McBride added.

"Turkeys!" Emma turned and scowled at her mother. "Please. I knew Mari would pick something more re-fined than turkeys." She smiled at her sister. "I put my money on kittens."

Kat let out a chortle. "You're all a bunch of losers. I had fifty on ducks at ten-to-one odds."

The minister hung his head. "I now pronounce you man and wife. Mr. Garrett, you may now kiss your bride. Um, again."

Quack. Quack. Squawk! Luke had leaned in to kiss his wife for the very first time when Billy shouted, "Uh-oh! Watch out. Everybody, duck!"

As the angry, feathered fowl launched toward Mari, Luke reacted instinctively to guard her body. He swept her into his arms and lowered her gently to the floor, then covered her body with his own. The orange bill nipped at his shoulder, but Luke firmly shoved it away. His hot, hungry gaze remained locked on Mari, who didn't stop giggling until his mouth captured hers.

The newspaper headline read McBride Menace Gets Lucky In Church.

* * * * *

Turn the page for a look at the next
BAD LUCK BRIDES *story*
HER SCOUNDREL
Coming from HQN Books
December 2005

CHAPTER ONE

Galveston Island, Texas, 1890

HE STOOD HIP-DEEP in water, shirtless, broad of shoulder and corded with muscle, his deeply tanned skin glistening beneath the warm winter sunshine. His dark hair was long, sun bleached and shaggy, and it hung over his face as he gazed down at the object he washed in seawater.

"Is that him?" Kat McBride tapped her brother-in-law, Luke Garrett, on the shoulder. "Is that Jake Kimball?"

"I think so." Luke reined in the horses, and their carriage rolled to a stop on the hard-packed sand. "Most of our dealings were with his father. I only met Jake once at the Adolphus Hotel in Dallas, and about all I remember is that he was knee-deep in women and drowning in alcohol at the time." Scowling, Luke added, "At least he had his clothes on then."

"In that case, it's our lucky day." Seated beside Luke, Kat's flamboyant grandmother and renowned sculptress Monique Day winked over her shoulder at Kat and her sister Mari. "I must say I've never seen the Galveston scenery looking so good."

Kat didn't care about the scenery. She didn't care if the man was naked or dressed or wearing a dress, she intended to have a chat with Mr. Jake Kimball. The newspaper might call him an adventurer, a treasure hunter and an explorer, but she knew better. Jake Kimball was a scalawag and a thief.

But he was also the man who would make things right for the fatherless child she carried in her womb.

Kat climbed down from the carriage and stepped to the edge of the grass-covered dune. The man looked up, and she caught her breath. Kimball hadn't shaved in days, but his scruffy beard didn't hide his rugged, masculine beauty. He had a sharp jaw, thin straight nose, and eyes as blue and hard as the sapphire necklace hanging around Kat's sister's neck. Something stirred inside of Kat when his eyes met hers, and she felt a flutter of awareness unlike any she'd known before. Different, even, from anything she'd felt with Rory when he'd drawn her under his spell.

"Well, now." Monique clucked her tongue as she linked her arm with Luke's. "Isn't he a fine specimen? Reminds me of the model I used for the bronze Apollo Mrs. Astor bought for her Manhattan home."

Kat thought he looked more like a pirate than a Greek god, especially with a gold hoop earring dangling from one ear and a jeweled knife in his hand. She cleared her voice and said, "Mr. Kimball?" she called. "Mr. Jake Kimball?"

"Yeah?" His mouth lifted in a slow smile as he studied her face. "I'm Kimball."

Then his attention slipped lower, locked on Kat's belly. He frowned and his eyes widened with alarm as he examined her features again. The alarm faded.

No, I am not a ruined lover come to seek the father of my babe.

"What can I do for you?" he asked as Luke stepped up beside her.

The question reminded Kat of the purpose of her visit, and her mouth flattened. She had no business noticing the man's attractive physique. Jake Kimball was a means to an end for her, that's all. Period. She'd had her fill of scoundrels.

Kat placed a protective hand upon her burgeoning stomach as Luke shot her a quick, curious glance, then took the lead. "I'm Luke Garrett, Kimball. My stepfather, Brian Callahan, worked for your father. You and I met once in Dallas. May my family and I have a few moments of your time?"

Kimball nodded and sloshed toward them, and despite her best intentions, Kat couldn't drag her gaze away from the slow revelation of tanned, toned skin rising from the water. The man obviously spent a good deal of time outdoors without his shirt. The wet, dark hair on his chest clung to his skin and arrowed down his flat stomach to his navel and...

Kat gave herself a mental shake. Her mother had warned her that a pregnant woman's emotions ran the gamut, but Kat *never* expected to find herself staring at a man's washboard stomach and wondering how it might feel beneath her fingertips. *This isn't good.*

Luke stepped in front of Kat, blocking her view. "Perhaps you could join us at our buggy once you're, uh, decent?"

"He looks pretty decent to me," Monique observed, she and Mari having joined Luke and Kat on the dune.

Luke muttered beneath his breath as he herded the women back to the carriage. Kat picked up words like "scoundrel" and "thieving bounder" and "home knitting booties." At the last, Mari glanced at Kat and rolled her eyes. "Baby booties" had become a rallying cry for the men in their family ever since Kat first proposed this trip to Galveston three days ago. After reading an article in the Fort Worth *Daily Democrat* about Jake Kimball and his discovery of a cache of treasures attributed to the pirate Jean Laffite, she decided she had to contact the man. The girls' father, Trace McBride, had suggested she stay home and knit baby booties instead. Then he compounded the mistake by suggesting the rest of the females in the family join her.

Needless to say, the suggestion didn't go over well with the McBride women, especially once Luke and the older McBride sons adopted Trace's suggestion as their own. While they understood that Trace equated knitting with safety, Kat, her sisters, her mother and grandmother dealt with the issue by wrinkling their noses and going about their business.

In Kat's case, her business was planning the trip to Galveston to confront Jake Kimball. Her father had argued against her going, but she promoted her point just as strongly. Then, because Trace McBride had been unable to refuse her anything since she'd returned to a family who had mistakenly believed her dead, he'd given in.

"So here we are," Kat said softly as the babe in her womb gave her a kick. Kat didn't care that the newspapers called Jake Kimball a courageous explorer, a brave adventurer. To her, he was nothing more than a criminal.

A criminal who even now climbed the sand dune while buttoning a blue cotton shirt. Kat's eyes widened at the sight of his dripping denim pants, cut off above the knees and plastered to his skin. He was barefoot.

"Luke Garrett." Kimball's mouth quirked in a crooked smile. "I wondered if I might run across you or your brothers during my time here in Texas. How are Rory and Finn?"

"Dead."

Kat didn't believe Kimball's expression of surprise, and she stepped into the fray by stating a truth in spirit if not in fact. "I married Rory Callahan, Mr. Kimball."

The pirate arched a brow.

"You've made quite a discovery here on Glaveston Island, sir, and I believe it's fair to say that wouldn't have happened if not for Rory."

Kimball's eyes swept her from head to toe, pausing again briefly upon the bulge of her seven-month-gone belly. Sympathy colored his tone as he said, "I employ many individuals in the course of my pursuits, Mrs. Callahan. I pay them well for their assistance, extremely well, whether their help results in a find or not. I do not offer shares in the discovery, ma'am, so if that is what you seek, I am afraid—"

"I want the cross."

His focus shifted from her, to Luke, then back to her. The slight narrowing of his eyes told her he knew very well what she meant. "The cross?"

Kat lifted her chin. "The Sacred Heart Cross that was lost almost a hundred years ago when pirates attacked the Spanish ship bringing it to America. It is solid gold and encrusted with jewels, including a heart-shaped ruby at its center. You stole if from Rory Callahan. I want it back."

He studied her, taking her measure. His attention once again slid to her swollen womb and pity softened his eyes. "I'm sorry, ma'am, but I did not steal the cross from your husband. Rory sold the piece to me for a substantial amount of money."

No. Kat's stomach did a slow somersault. Had Rory lied about that, too? Lied as he lay dying? As Mari reached over and took her hand, Kat went hard and

brittle inside. Had the man been totally without re-
demption?

No. No. No. He'd saved Mari, hadn't he? In the end,
he'd done what was right. In the end, he'd tried to provide for Kat and their child.

"I don't believe you." When Kimball simply
shrugged, Kat continued, "He told my sister that the Sacred Heart Cross was our child's inheritance. He said it
on his deathbed. Not even Rory would lie at a time like
that."

"Maybe he referred to the money I paid him," Kimball suggested. "The account is in a New York bank. As
his widow have you seen records of it? Perhaps the
money is still there."

"I'm not." Kat looked away. "I'm not his widow, that
is. It turned out our marriage wasn't legal."

"Oh, I see."

Kat closed her eyes against the pity she'd surely
see. She'd witnessed too much of that from her family
in the months since returning to Fort Worth. It made her
feel like a fool.

Of course, that's exactly what she was. A fool. She'd
married the King of Liars, hadn't she? A man already
married, already a father. If he'd lied about that, why
wouldn't he lie about the cross?

Luke placed his hand on her shoulder. "If the money
is there, Katrina, we'll get it for you. Rory would want
your child to have it."

Shaking her head, Kat said, "No. No, I don't want
money."

She wanted the cross. She had to have the cross. It
was the answer, the key to everything. It would fix the
trouble she'd caused, help wipe away the shame.

Kat straightened and her chin came up. "Very well,

sir. I will buy it back from you. I trust we can reach a fair price. I won't begrudge you a profit over what you paid Rory."

"I'm sorry, but the cross is not for sale."

Frustration rolled through her like a storm. "Everything is for sale, Mr. Kimball."

"Not the Sacred Heart Cross."

Beneath her skirt, Kat's toes took to tapping. "Mr. Kimball, I come from a family of business people so I appreciate the fine art of negotiation. However, at this particular moment I have neither the time nor the inclination to dicker. Please, sir, name your price."

He folded his arms and shook his head. "Listen to me, lady. The cross is not for sale, not under any circumstances, at any price."

"Why not? I don't understand."

Kimball looked toward Luke. "Your father worked for mine for many years. Surely you recall my father's passion for his quests?"

"Brian was my stepfather," Luke was quick to correct.

Even in her agitation, Kat noted how he always made the distinction that her family hardly ever made with Jenny. That illustrated one of her great worries for her child. Her baby should have a stepfather who was simply a papa, just like Jenny was a mama to the McBride girls.

That's one reason why it was so important for Kat to succeed in securing the Sacred Heart Cross. She needed it for her child, for the reward its restoration to its rightful place would bring.

Kimball continued, "My father collected art, coins, toys, and even butterflies, but his special interest was artifacts related to Texas. With you family's help, he amassed quite a collection of Texana before he died. While he continually added and deleted items from his other collections, he never surrendered a single piece of Texana. That is the way of collectors."

Impatient, Kat interrupted. "What does your father's Texana collection have to do with my cross?"

Jake's expression hardened. "First off, ma'am, the cross isn't yours. Secondly, the Sacred Heart Cross was the last gift I gave my father before he died. It was the crowning piece to his Texana collection. That collection is his legacy and I'll not break it up."

He sounded frustratingly sincere, and Kat sensed she'd need to use her strongest arguments to sway him. "How did your father die, Mr. Kimball?"

Curiosity at her question registered in his eyes. "He was playing golf and a thunderstorm blew in. My father was struck by lightning."

Kat nodded, totally unsurprised. "It's Bad Luck. I knew it. Rory died because if it. That altar cross has brought bad luck to everyone who's come in contact with it."

Kat's grandmother leaned toward Mari and murmured, "The Bad Luck Altar Cross? I'll go along with Bad Luck Dresses and Bad Luck Cakes, and even Bad Luck Brides. But religious icons? That's taking this family trend a bit overboard, wouldn't you say?"

"Kat," Mari added in a chiding tone.

Kat turned toward her sister. "It's true, Mari. I know it. The cross is cursed, and it's all part of the Curse of Clan McBride, don't you see?"

"Oh, honey." Mari glanced at the gaping men. "Excuse us a moment, please?"

She led Kat away from the buggy, then lowered her voice and said, "Kat, what's going on here? I thought you wanted the cross because Rory left it to you and the baby. I thought you wanted the money it would bring so you wouldn't be dependent on Papa. You never said anything about the curse. Please, tell me you don't truly believe that the altar cross is bad luck."

"Stop it!" Irrational fury surged like fire through Kat's veins. "How can you do this? How can you revert to your old, skeptical self? You believe in the McBride Bad Luck and in the curse and the cure, Maribeth. Don't try to tell me you don't."

"I believe," Mari snapped back. "But Kat, this makes no sense. Why would you think that Rory's lost cross has anything to do with breaking the curse? It hasn't a fig to do with anyone named McBride!"

"But it does. This is *my* task, Mari. It's been revealed to me, just like Roslin of Strathardle said would happen!"

Two years ago, prior to their elder sister Emma's wedding, the three sisters visited a gypsy fortune-teller in Fort Worth's Hell's Half Acre. Instead of Madame Valentina, they encountered an ethereal Scotswoman who gave them each a beautiful necklace and told them a fantastical story about a family curse—the Curse of Clan McBride. She imparted the news that the three sisters, the McBride Menaces, had the chance to end the curse for all time. All they needed to do was find a love that was "powerful, vigilant and true" and complete a task of great personal import—one that would be revealed at the proper time.

Mari had thought the woman a charlatan and dismissed her claims until earlier this year, when she found her true love, Luke Garrett. Now, Kat believed, her turn had come. She grasped the emerald necklace hanging around her neck with her left hand while placing her right hand over the child in her womb. "You figured out your task, and now I've figured out mine. I must return the cross to its rightful place. That's my task, Mari. Once I do that, then *I'll* find a love that is powerful, vigilant and true. I'll find a father, not a stepfather, for my baby so she can grow up safe and happy and secure!"

"Oh, Kat." Mari hugged her sister, then took a step back. "I understand now. I do. You've had us all fooled, you know. The family thought you were taking this pregnancy so well, that you were feeling positive about the future. You must be so frightened."

Tears stung Kat's eyes, but she furiously batted them back. "I'm not frightened," she declared. "I'll be fine and my baby will be fine. I don't need to worry about being a scandal or having to live off Mama and Papa the rest of my life. I know that we'll be all right, that we'll have a man in our lives to support us and comfort us and love us. There is a great love waiting for me out there somewhere, a man who will love my baby as his own. The first step in finding that love is to get that cross from Jake Kimball and put it where it belongs!"

"All right," Mari soothed. "Settle down, now. Don't get yourself all worked up. It can't be good for the baby."

Kat glanced over to the buggy where Monique sat regaling the men with one of her never-ending stories, attempting, Kat realized to distract them from the scene the sisters were making.

"What do I do, Mari? He doesn't seem to want to cooperate."

"No, he doesn't, does he?" Mari glanced at Jake Kimball, then clucked her tongue. "Monique was right, wasn't she? He is a fine specimen of manhood."

"Mari Garrett! What a thing for a newlywed to say."

"I'm married, but I'm not blind, Kat." She let out a sigh. "Well, if you're certain this is your task, then I'll do everything I can to help you." She paused a moment, then asked, "Do you really think the cross is bad luck?"

"Taking its history just from the time of its discovery…" She ticked off on her fingers. "The poor man who dug it up was almost killed, the men who took it from him are in jail, Rory took it from them and he's dead. Kimball's father was struck by lightning, for pity's sake. Mr. Kimball, here, is an accident waiting to occur."

Mari grimaced. "I believe in the Curse of Clan McBride, but it goes against my nature to accept that an altar cross, of all things, is bad luck. However, since you're sure, then we need to come up with a plan for you to get it."

Kat smiled wistfully. "I love it when you sound like your old Menace self."

"It's who I am," Mari said, shrugging. "I've accepted it. In fact, since we're talking about the curse and the cure, you should know that I've come to believe that the task I needed to complete was not to find you and bring you home, but to find myself."

Kat wrinkled her nose. "So finding me was just what? An afterthought?"

"Finding you was the best day of my life."

"Even counting your wedding day?"

A man's voice answered, "Even that." Luke stepped up beside them and said, "We love you, Kat. We want you safe and happy. The sun's going down now and the air is beginning to cool. Why don't we go back to my sister's house and have a cup of tea?"

Kat glanced back toward Kimball, who was bent

over double laughing at something Monique had said. "But what about him?"

"I think we should take our time with Mr. Jake Kimball. He's obviously no pushover. We need to get Emma in on this, too, and develop a plan fit for a McBride Menace."

A smile played on Kat's lips. "He won't stand a chance."

"No, he won't."

Amusement glinted in Luke's gaze as he looked from one woman to the other. "I pity the man. I probably ought to warn him about tangling with the likes of the McBride Menaces, but I think I'll stay on the sideline this time out."

"Good decision, dear." Mari patted his arm.

"Are you ready to leave, then, Kat?" Luke asked.

"I am. Let me have a minute to visit alone with Mr. Kimball. I want to try one more time. It's only right that he be warned that he's risking a run of bad luck by keeping the cross. I won't have his death on my conscience."

Kimball continued to laugh with the girls' grandmother as Luke escorted Kat and Mari back to the buggy. Kat imagined that Monique had relayed one of her more colorful tales, because the man now had a wicked glint in his eyes and a mischievous slant to his smile.

Mari leaned toward Kat and whispered, "Now that's one pirate most damsels wouldn't mind boarding their boats."

Kat elbowed her sister in the side. "Hush. You're terrible. It's obvious you've been spending far too much time with our grandmother."

"Girls!" that same grandmother said as they approached. "Guess what? Jake and I have mutual friends in London. Isn't it a small world?"

"It's not the world that's small, Monique," Kat said, her smile indulgent, "but your circle of friends that's so large. The only reason you don't have friends on the moon is that you haven't found a way to visit the place."

"Give me time, Katrina. Give me time."

It was as good a segue as Kat could hope for.

"Time does change things." She met Jake Kimball's eyes. "Sir, may I speak with you alone for a moment?"

Kat walked far enough away not to be heard by inquisitive relatives, Kimball falling in beside her. Though she didn't look, she felt the weight of his attention upon her.

Out of the blue, he stated, "You have beautiful hair. The color reminds me of…" He reached into his pocket and pulled out a coin, a Spanish doubloon. Handing it to her, he finished, "…old gold that's been rescued from the sea."

The coin was fascinating, Kimball's comparison to her hair disconcerting. Kat tried to hand the coin back to him, but he wouldn't take it. "For the child."

Her child. Yes. Kat could not, would not, forget about her child. "Have you had enough time to reconsider? Will you sell me the cross?"

"Sorry, but no."

Kat lifted her shoulders in a casual shrug that belied the intensity of the emotions churning within her. "You're making a mistake. Just remember, Mr. Kimball, when bad luck begins to haunt your door, I know a way to turn the tide. I'll stay in touch, Mr. Kimball. Believe me, there will come a time when you're only too happy to be rid of the Sacred Heart Cross."

"That sounds like a threat, You know—" the scoundrel winked at her "—if you weren't so gorgeous, with all this talk about bad luck and curses, I'd worry I'd stumbled across a witch."

Cocky pirate. Kat brazenly reached up and patted his cheek. "I'm no witch, Kimball. But you should still beware. I'm a McBride Menace."

"A Menace, huh? Interesting." He grinned, reached out and touched her old-gold hair. "Sounds like a witch to me. Have you cast a spell on me? Will you turn me into a toad? Somehow I can't see a woman like you chanting incantations over a cauldron."

A part of Kat marveled that the man was such a scoundrel as to flirt with a woman seven months gone with another man's child while her family stood within shouting distance. Yet, another part of her, the feminine side of her, drank in the attentions of this alluring man.

She leaned toward him and slowly smiled. "You'd be surprised at what a woman like me might do."

His smile flashed wicked. He touched her hair again, gently tugged a strand from her braid and let it slide across the skin of his fingers. "Oh, yeah?"

"McBride Menaces don't rely on spells to get what we want, Mr. Kimball. Our methods are far more creative."

"Is that a fact?" His gaze focused on her mouth.

"Oh, no." Kat licked her lips, swayed toward her. His eyes narrowed, blazed heat, and power washed through Kat like an ocean wave. *Typical man. Typical scoundrel.*

"No, Mr. Kimball," she repeated, stepping away and grinning. "It's a promise."